Waves in the Wind

Wade J. McMahan

Untreed
Reads

Waves in the Wind
By Wade J. McMahan

Copyright 2014 Wade J. McMahan
Cover Design by J.D.Netto, JD Netto Designs

ISBN-13: 978-1-61187-723-6

Also available in ebook format.

Published by Untreed Reads, LLC
506 Kansas Street, San Francisco, CA 94107
www.untreedreads.com

Printed in the United States of America.

Publisher's Note

Dedication

In memory of that gentle Irishman,
Michael D. Mitchell of Belfast, who provided
much of the inspiration for this novel.

"I am convinced that the terrestrial paradise is in the Island of Saint Brendan, which none can reach save by the Will of God." Christopher Columbus

CONTENTS

Acknowledgment

Our thanks to Beatrix Färber, Project Manager for CELT (Corpus of Electronic Texts), University College Cork, Ireland, for generously granting use of a reference from the mysterious, ancient Irish manuscript, "Annals of the Four Masters."

Book One

Chapter 1
Eire. 516 A.D.

The Morrigan came to me today, an old gray crow squatting in the field of stones outside my cave mouth. Behind her, the vast emptiness of the wave-tossed western sea swept the horizon.

"Ossian," she croaked. "What a poor thing you are, a king of stones and rotting fish.

Your wounds are healed, your father will not rise from the dead, nor will your sisters. Your gods are fading, Ossian, old gods fall before the new, as I will. But not yet, though the followers of the Risen One grow stronger every day."

Now, it is a poor thing to be mocked by your gods when you have tried to keep faith with them. Where was she when the Corcu Duibne came, my family slaughtered and our village put to fire? I had only the chance to strike one blow before a rider knocked me senseless and left me in the fields for dead. A simple kirtle to cover my nakedness and the serpent ring but all I carried here—here in my solitude these many months by the western sea.

Firelight danced upon the cave walls as I rose to face her. "Why do you come here to scoff at me now, My Queen? I have nothing, nothing! Why do you come to me now when there is naught more I can do for you?"

"Naught more?" she cackled. "Naught more you can do for me? I expect nothing and need less from you, Ossian, for you not only have nothing, you have become nothing. We had great hopes for you during the short years you stood beside us, but no more. Now you choose to cower within this lowly cave where you endure hunger and shiver from the cold. What a miserable being you've become, little man."

"My Queen, I..."

"Silence!" she shrieked. "You will soon die here in this wretchedness of your own choosing. Oh yes, you will die unless once again you desire to wear the mantle of a man." Her hoary wings spread wide. "The choice is yours, though the Lordly Ones care little either way."

Her wings flapped once as she took flight into the murky, midday sky, and she was soon gone from view. The Lordly Ones little cared whether I lived or died, she had said. In that, they shared my own view of myself.

I threw myself upon my simple bracken bed as thoughts battled within my head. A thousand times I had prayed to the Lordly Ones that they might direct me from what I had been toward what I might become. A thousand times they ignored my pleas. Now, they sent their goddess, the Morrigan, but to what purpose? To warn me that I faced death? Yes, I might very well die here, and with no thanks due any of the gods for their beneficence.

It had not always been so for me. Was I not of the Eoghanachts of the Cork region, son of Ciann Mehigan, son of Gicrode? Was I not highly educated and trained in the ways of the Druids?

Augh! Of what measure were such thoughts, such remembrances when they offered no consolation and merely compounded my torment? Perhaps they weren't even true. Perhaps an evil fairy planted false memories in my mind as a means to taunt me. Even so, the past came flooding back from a time before the skies grew dark...

* * *

My father sat upon a stone in the Sacred Grove. His face revealed no emotion as he spoke. "Ossian, I received word today through a messenger that my petition to have you placed in the school at Dún Ailinne has been accepted."

Boyish excitement flooded through me, though I stood silent, respectful before him. I knew Dún Ailinne well. Had I not accompanied my father there more than once for the annual Beltane celebration?

High above us, interlacing gnarled branches of towering oaks created a magical bower of dark green foliage. Dappled sunlight illuminated my father as he sat there, an image I had seen countless times.

The hood of his immaculate white robe framed his face, a sharp contrast against his shoulder-length red hair and carefully groomed beard. He continued. "You have reached twelve years; it is time for your formal education to begin. We may only pray the many lessons I have taught you here within this Sacred Grove will serve you well. Now, I place you in the hands of the Master at Dún Ailinne, who shall further your education that many years from today you may carry the sacred staff of the Druids as I do, and as did my father before me."

Gentleness flowed from his blue eyes as was often the case when he spoke with me. It was a characteristic he held closely within him, one he rarely, if ever, displayed beyond the intimacy of our immediate family. I knew what he was seeing as I stood there, a boyish image of himself, a rather tall boy, skinny in the way of many lads at that age, my red hair flaming in the sun.

He nodded. "Now, you may speak."

In my young eyes, my father was the wisest of all men, for he was Druid and chief advisor to King Domhnall. A proper response was expected. It was with the thought of pleasing him that I chose my words. "Thank you, father. I shall endeavor with all my heart and mind to honor you, our family, and our King. If it is the will of the gods, I shall succeed."

"Hmm. Yes, I see the truth in it, Ossian, though it is not your heart that I entrust to the Master, only your mind. I know you will do your best, but do not place over much reliance in the Lordly Ones; they can be a capricious lot. Always remember, to be accorded the order of Druid is not a birthright, nor is it founded upon prominence or political favor. You must follow a long, difficult path to wisdom, to at last be measured on your merits alone."

He rose, gestured for me to follow and we walked from the Grove to our village, Rath Raithleann, a thatch-roofed community of nine hundred souls. Already, news of my selection for the school at Dún Ailinne had swept through the folk there. The men were working their fields, but the women and children greeted my father with great reverence, and to me they offered encouraging smiles and words.

That night following our evening meal within my father's spacious roundhouse, my sisters Ceara and Aine badgered me with questions. Ceara was two years my elder, with dark hair and eyes. Within a year or two she would catch the eye of her future husband. Where Ceara was dark, Aine, at eight years, was sparkle and light with flashing blue eyes and long auburn hair.

"Oh Ossian!" Aine chattered. "You are going away to school at Dún Ailinne? Oh how glorious that will be. How I wish I were a boy and could go to school too."

"No," I smiled to her, "you must stay here and learn the ways of women from Fainche. Your fingers are still far too clumsy for the weaving of linen."

"Humph, that is not true! Well, not very true anyway. Fainche says I am learning quickly. Tell me, when you come home from school, will you teach me the powers of necromancy?"

"Of course I shall do no such thing! You must learn to mind your tongue girl, for you might be overheard. It is dangerous to speak of the dead. Now, be away with you. I have much thinking to do before I leave."

I could never be angry with Aine. Was she to blame that her birth was ill omened? Our mother died during Aine's birthing, a family tragedy preordained by the gods. Soon afterwards, our father found Fainche, an older, generously proportioned widow who came to help with our raising. She was a kind woman who saw to our needs with caring hands.

Later, I lay in my bed, my mind busy with thoughts of the school at Dún Ailinne. At some point I drifted off to sleep, and for the first time in many years my mother entered my dreams, her shrouded face a gray shadow against a dark sky. She turned and gestured behind her. In the far distance, spanning the black horizon, the world was on fire…

Chapter 2
Dún Ailinne

I waited in the stone-paved compound of the school at Dún Ailinne feeling very small, and, for the first time in my young life, all alone. It was the silence I noticed most. Breathless quiet altogether unlike the busy bustle and chatter I had grown up with in my home village.

A few students clad in the brown robes of acolytes strode among glistening white wattle and daub buildings serving as dormitories, classrooms and a dining hall. The students pursued missions I could only imagine.

Sweat trickled down my face as I stood fidgeting under the hot morning sun. My new rough woolen robe itched, and chafed my skin. In time, my name would be called to climb the tall, grass covered hill before me, the sacred Knockaulin, and at last stand before the Master.

When the sun reached its peak, my turn came and I began the long walk up the earthen pathway to the crest. My head swiveled 'round as goose bumps ran down my body. During past visits I overheard whisperings that in olden times human sacrifice was practiced here. What boy wouldn't fear the presence of ghosts, the angry shades of the dead ones sacrificed by ancient Druids in foolish rituals?

At the mid-way point I rested and gazed down on the compound surrounded by the thatched roofs of the school. Beyond a wooded grove, and further on, partially screened by the trees, lay the small village of Kilcullen. Why did the old priest Patrick choose the village so near our sacred Dún Ailinne to build a Christian monastery?

Solitude ruled the shrine at the summit, and I recognized the grand design of it, one that reminded me of ripples created by dropping a pebble into a quiet pool—an outer, perfectly circular earthen wall and within it two deep inner trenches. Blackbirds fluttered, cackled and roosted among numerous heavy wooden posts forming the innermost circle.

I hesitated, a lump in my throat. The Master dwelt within his small stone sanctuary at the center of the shrine's universe.

My future would begin here. Upon hearing of my acceptance at the school, King Domhnall had declared a feast of celebration, and my name was raised within all the homes throughout my village. Again, I bowed under the burden of it as I stood there, and again I felt the weight of the gold paid by my father that I might follow in his footsteps.

The polished oak door of the sanctuary loomed before me and I rapped upon it with my knuckles. There was no response. Uncertain of what do, I considered tapping again when a deep voice bade me enter. Upon opening the door, a musty aroma of ancient dust mingled with incense assaulted my nose. My eyes grew accustomed to the candle-lit dimness as I shambled forward, my new soft sandals making swishing sounds as I crossed the stone floor.

Before me a mighty, fearsome image, the Master posed in an ornate high-backed chair behind a table piled with manuscripts. A full gray beard framing his round face cascaded from his chin to spread across a considerable paunch concealed beneath a Druid's black and white striped robe.

Here sat Tóla, his stern, gray eyes holding me in their grasp as he leaned forward to inspect me. "And so, Ossian, your father prepared you well for our school here?"

My teeth gripped my quivering tongue as I bowed and forced myself to murmur, "My father sends his reverent greetings, Master Tóla, and asks you be the judge of it."

"Humph, yes, of course. Your father was one of my best students, who has since matured into a fine advisor to the King at Rath Raithleann and priest to your people. As for you, we shall measure the scion against the tree."

My heart skipped at hearing his words. I feared I would look foolish indeed in the eyes of the Master if he were to compare my poor skills against the great knowledge and boundless wisdom of my father.

He leaned back in his chair, and cocked a bushy gray eyebrow. "So tell me. The history of our land is closely held within our oral traditions. As a Druid who merits the right to be called Wise One, you shall be expected to recite Eire's history from the time of the Great Deluge forward, year by year. Do you know why that is important?"

"My father says what has been will be again. The past offers a window into the future."

Gray eyes seemed to bore through me as he leaned forward. "Your father says? What say you?"

It took a moment to swallow a pesky lump forming in my throat before replying. "I say my father is most wise."

"Hmm. Yes," he muttered, clasping his hands atop the table.

The annoying lump returned as he continued. "We still don't know about your wisdom, do we? Complete this quotation for me if you can. It was the Age of the World, 3303..."

So, the testing of my preparation was to begin immediately. An anxious chill ran through me beneath the fullness of my robe. In the manner learned through my years spent in the Sacred Grove, I closed my eyes and calmed my mind so that a correct response might form.

It was a straightforward question, for 3303 might well be the most important year in Druidic Irish history. I began, "For thirty-seven years the Firbolgs ruled Eire. It was in this year the Tuatha De Danann arrived and gave battle to them in Connaught. During the battle King Eochaidh of the Firbolgs was slain by the sons of Neimhidh of the Tuatha De Dannans, and the Firbolgs were vanquished and slaughtered."

"Stop!" The Master held up his hand. "It seems you have a quick mind and gifted memory. However, remember this, for it is very important. When you tell the history of this land, do not simply recite it. Your stories must bring mood and motion to the peoples of the distant past, give your listeners a sense of actually being there."

"I begin to understand, Master, and shall strive to improve."

"No, Ossian, you must improve."

Remaining rigidly erect, I nodded my understanding. Sweat trickled down my spine beneath my robe.

His questioning resumed. "We realize humans descended from trees. Our Tree Calendar speaks to the thirteen phases of the moon. Tell me, what is the significance of the seventh month?"

There was much that could be said in response to his question, but what did he truly wish to know? The wisest course seemed to remain wary, so I offered the only liturgy I knew. "The seventh month is that within which the royal tree, the Oak, rules under the hand of the god, Duir. It is said that its midsummer blooms speak to endurance, strength and triumph. It is further said that it was on the 24th day of the month the Oak-king was sacrificed by fire. The final seven days of the month, which are also the first seven days of the second half of the year, are dedicated to his remembrance, and each year includes a great feast in his honor. There is—"

"Enough!" The Master peered at me, eyes squinting. "You have arrived at Dún Ailinne, but I wonder if you recall the story about the girl for whom this place is named?"

"Yes, Master Tóla, I think so." I blessed my father's foresight to prepare me for this question. Again I closed my eyes, thought back and quoted,

Across the snow the wolfpack raced,
Wolves or men still all the same,
Within the rath the he-bear slept,
He lost his cub to the wolves that night.

In Leinster the black shroud unfurled,
Grief unchecked the kingdom wept,
King Lugaid called his voice unheard,
By one, his one and only one.

Ailinne the fair, cheeks roses kissed,
Hair the sun, her eyes the sea,
By love betrothed to Conchobhar,
Noble prince of the Dal Cormaic.

Chaste maiden amid the beasts,
Powerless, most cruelly used,
Faded away and died of shame,
Through her grave an apple tree grew.

Word spread throughout the Leinster realm,
Lugaid, mindless rent his hair,
And wailed throughout the lonely nights,
The last to hear was Conchobhar.

Anguish unquenched the stately prince,
Chose to accept the dagger's thrust,
And from the ground an apple tree grew,
Through the grave of Conchobhar.

Among the Chieftains the Apple proffered,
Life eternal for prince and maid,
United as one, Conchobhar and Ailinne,
Forever young at Tír na nÓg.

Tóla's eyes twinkled as he leaned back with a sigh. "Your father prepared you for that question, did he not?"

At my nod he continued. "Of course. Your father was always the clever one. But yes, that is one version of the story, and the one I

13

prefer. It is the cruelest fate for a young girl to be captured and ravaged by brutal men, don't you think?"

"Yes, Master," I replied, although the girl's fate of which he spoke was held within an old story. I had little interest in it.

"I asked you three questions. In each case your delivery was hesitant, awkward and you omitted many important details. I shall demand much improvement."

"Of course, Master Tóla," I replied, greatly relieved that at least for a while his questioning had ended.

"You are one of twenty students desiring to become Druids who were admitted to our school this year. Provided you have the intellect and necessary qualities to be retained, you will be with us for twelve years. Are you prepared to make such a commitment?"

Long I had looked forward to this moment, this very question, and I responded with soft assurance, "Yes, Master."

"Good. Here, you will learn mathematics, astrology, medicine, ceremonial doctrine, alchemy, philosophy, culture, arts, nature, divination, the art of war and many more of the scholarly arts. You will learn to read and write in Greek as well as our own Irish Ogham alphabet. Beware, Ossian, few students may enter here, and fewer still succeed to at last stand alongside learned men."

* * *

The years passed swiftly, and it was during my fourth year at Dún Ailinne, I attended a class meant for bards. The room was crowded. Learning old songs and poetry was important, for they told the rich history of our people. Still, I thought it unjust that the poor performance of those of us studying the art of Druidry was judged equally alongside talented musicians.

I knew none of the bards, for they tended to remain together and not talk with the rest of us. Unlike those of us clad in our acolyte robes, they wore whatever clothing they chose and cavorted among us like an unruly flock of colorful birds fluttering within a drab, brown sky.

A lecture on the structure of ballads was underway when Master Tóla strode through the door. He muttered to the lecturer, a noted bard himself.

The Master then turned his frowning face to the class. "Among the one hundred and four students at our school, a dozen of you study to be bards. Important business with one of you brings me here." He pointed to a student. "Laoidheach. Come forward."

A youthful bard wearing a radiant yellow tunic and fawn leggings rose and proceeded forward to stand, head bowed, before Master Tóla. He had been at the school only a short while, but appeared to be about my own age of sixteen years. Like me, he was tall and thin, though his shoulder-length hair was golden his features fine, almost feminine.

The Master rested a hand on the bard's shoulder. "Young man, you have been here but a few months, and already this is the second time I must reprimand you. The first time I did so privately, but since that did you no good perhaps it will go better if I do so in front of your fellow students. You know this matter of which I speak?"

Laoidheach slumped even lower, and nodded.

"You remind me of another lad known for causing trouble who, as a prank, attempted to steal the harp of the goddess, Aibell. Surely you recall her magical harp, for any human overhearing its music will soon die. The goddess was so infuriated she transformed the troublesome youth into a toad and he was forced to survive upon flies. Fortunately, after a while he came to enjoy the flavor of flies. Do you like flies too, Laoidheach?"

Several class members laughed aloud and I hid a smile behind my hand, as Laoidheach mumbled, "No, Master...um...that is...um...I think not."

"No?" the Master mused, as he stepped back and eyed the young man up and down. "Hmm. Perhaps another punishment is in order." He snapped his fingers. "I have it! Beginning tonight, you alone will wash every dish and pot at the dining hall, and you will continue doing so every night for a month. If I encounter more trouble with you, I shall make the assignment permanent. Then again, who knows, Laoidheach? Perhaps you will come to enjoy washing dishes and pots."

Laughter filled the room, including my own, as a shame-faced Laoidheach returned to his seat. Master Tóla mumbled his apologies to the instructor for disturbing the class, and strode through the door, leaving us laughing.

When the class was dismissed I was in no hurry, and by the time I reached the center of the compound, Laoidheach sat alone under a tree like a lump. The troublesome bard interested me, so I walked over to join him.

"Laoidheach, I am Ossian. May I speak with you?"

He looked up at me from where he was sitting, and shrugged. "Why not? I know you, Ossian, everyone does."

I settled upon the ground beside him. "You know me?"

"I know who you are. Everyone here speaks of you as though you are the son of the Dagda himself."

"What manner of foolish talk have you heard? I am a simple student, the same as you."

"Not the same, I think. Not so simple either and certainly not the troublemaker I am said to be."

I grinned. "Said to be, Laoidheach? Was the Master wrong then?"

"No, he was not wrong…oh I don't know, somehow it seems I attract trouble. This time it was a girl, don't you see. She must have said something."

"A girl? There are no girls here."

He rolled his eyes and shook his head. "Of course not here." His hand gestured toward the grove of trees, indicating the village of Kilcullen beyond. "She lives there. Someone learned of our meeting and spoke to the Master."

"Your meeting? I suspect it was more than that."

"Of course it was more than that, but I was not the cause of it. I walked through the village, don't you see, minding my own affairs when the girl stepped into the doorway of a small shed. She is a lovely thing and gave me a glorious smile…well, when I receive an invitation I know it."

He was a bold one. "Yes, I see. Then you were not the troublemaker, but merely an innocent victim?"

"That's right, I am a victim, and there you have the truth of it," he replied, but I could see the laughter in his eyes.

"Hmm, but the Master said this was your second bit of trouble since you arrived here. Was a girl also involved in your first problem?"

"Ahem, well yes, you see—"

"Stop right there, for yes, I do see. I see a pattern where girls are usually involved in your problems. Am I right?"

A wink accompanied his wicked grin. "You can rely upon it."

I rolled onto my back and laughed loud. Finally, I regained my breath, sat up and sputtered, "Then I foresee a lifetime of trouble for you. Tell me, Laoidheach, why are you here at Dún Ailinne?"

He remained quiet for a moment. "My father is a harpist in our village; my mother was a simple peasant girl. Her family was shunned in the village she came from because it was rumored that her mother was a changeling child and daughter of Belimawr."

What an amazing thing if it was true! To have an actual god in one's lineage was a virtually unheard of wonder, though ancient legends spoke of such occurrences. "Your grandmother was a changeling, half human-half goddess, and daughter of Belimawr, the fire god himself? Are you sure of it?"

"Sure of it? Now, how can I be certain of such a magical thing though I believe it to be true? It is still often spoken of by those who knew her."

What manner of lad was he? If what he said was true, how much of the changeling had he inherited from his mother's line?

His voice was soft, low and wistful. "My mother, Una of the Bright Hair, they called her, died while I was very young, and I have little memory of her."

"In that, Laoidheach, we share a common sorrow, for I lost my mother as well."

"You say so? Hmm, yes, it is a sad thing. Children should learn from the loving sides of their mothers, don't you think?" He pondered for a moment, and nodded. "Yes, I think children could learn much from their mothers. Oh well, my father is a good man and fine musician. He trained me well, and my songs pleased our local king. So much so, he petitioned the Master here that I might further myself as a bard."

It was no small thing that he attended the school at the aegis of his king; it spoke well of his talent. And it was no small thing to be pronounced a bard, a man who would be welcomed into any village, a man widely acclaimed for his poetry, songs and music.

The day slipped away. "Laoidheach, I'm sorry, but I must hurry to prepare for another lecture. Can we meet later?"

"Yes...but, wait. Of course! Ossian, I'm meeting two girls tonight. Why don't you come with me?"

"Oh, no! When you meet girls, you get into trouble. Thank you, but leave me out of it for I have no interest in washing dishes."

"There will be no trouble. I've, uh, that is, they are delightful, agreeable creatures. A flagon of ale waits in the bushes within yon grove of trees, and beyond, a short walk to the village and barn where we'll meet the girls. Everything is prepared and you can't say no to it."

He was right. Then again, what eager lad of sixteen years could say no to it?

Chapter 3
An Acolyte's Quest

I woke to the sound of a soft morning rain pattering on the thatched roof of the dormitory. It was there I slept alongside two dozen other students.

A gray dawn illuminated the windows, and I rose from my blankets. During fair weather, we received lectures under the trees in a manner reminiscent of the days I had spent in the Sacred Grove with my father. But today it was raining and there was little to like at the thought of it.

"Ossian?" a sleep-laden voice rasped beside me. "Is it rain I hear?"

"Of course it's rain, Cass, and what else would it be?"

Cass was one of only four students remaining out of the twenty who entered the school with me only four years earlier. He sat up, stretched and spat on the earthen floor. "So then, you'll not be lighting your first sacred fire today."

I grunted my disgust and walked to the open doorway. A tendril of smoke lifted from the chimney of one of the three other longhouses circling the compound. A student dashed toward the privy hut, his acolyte's robe flapping in the wind. It was a visit I must soon make as well. Aside from the obvious reason, I would freshen myself in a water basin, and the thick plaited braid falling down my back like a red banner required attention.

Cass was correct; today I was to build my first sacred fire. It was a day decreed by Master Tóla, and an honor I had long looked forward to...but now? I had lain awake late into the night before, thinking through each step of the long, difficult ceremony. Perhaps the rain would end, but there was no sign of it.

19

Cass walked over to stand beside me and stretched a hand outward to catch the rain. "Bah! The Master called upon the goddess Cally Berry to predict the weather for today, and she claimed there would be no rain. I say it is a bad omen. This was to be a special day for you, but now...?" He shook the moisture from his hand as evidence of his thoughts.

"A bad omen? What you say may be true, for the Lordly Ones interfere in men's lives for their own mysterious purposes. As for Cally Berry, it is well known she often misleads us for her own amusement. Still, do you truly think the gods would bring rain upon this entire region to prevent a mere acolyte from building his first sacred fire? No, they brought it for a far more important purpose, one that will benefit the farmers hereabouts."

Cass stretched, scratched his belly. "As you say. I'll not argue it. No, it seems I'm bested every time I try to argue with you. You are overly clever and have a strong mind. Already you are more than a full year ahead in your studies. That is also why you were the first chosen from our remaining group to build his sacred fire."

The realm of learning captivated me from my very first day at Dún Ailinne, and I eagerly embraced each new opportunity to acquire knowledge. Therefore, it was true I was well ahead in my studies, but I found his comments overstated. "I have no special talents, nor is my mind stronger than yours. My father prepared me well for the school here and the gods have since smiled on me. That is all that separates us."

"Hah. You disregard your exceptional abilities, but have it your way."

There was no cause to discuss it more. Besides, the thought of warm barley cakes in the dining hall now captured my interest. A freshly oiled sealskin cape hung on a peg, so I took it, draped it over my head and scampered across the wet compound toward the privy.

I was almost there when I was stopped by a student of about twenty years named Earnán who I knew only slightly. He wore the red-striped robe of a First Order Druid and served as assistant to Master Tóla. "Ossian, the Master calls for you. He waits in his sanctuary, so you must hurry."

My stomach growled a disappointed response, but to keep the Master waiting was unthinkable. I hurried to the privy while wondering at the purpose behind the Master's message. Rain fell in sheets as I picked my way along the slippery, muddy path to the top of Knockaulin.

I rapped on the door of his sanctuary and entered at his beckoning response. Stooped over his table scanning a manuscript, he glanced up to growl, "You're late! And drop that old cape where you are before you drip water across my floor!"

I did as ordered and walked over to him. Of course, I wasn't late, but I bowed. "I beg your pardon, Master."

"Do you know what day this is?"

"Yes, it is the day I was to build my first sacred fire."

He cocked an eyebrow and growled again, "No! It is the day you shall build your fire."

Amazement swept through me as rain drummed overhead.

"Now," he continued, "you will travel a half-day's walk due south where you will find a grassy knoll. It is there you will build your fire. You remember the correct mantra?"

"Of course!" Immediately I regretted my mistake and cursed my stupidity at allowing myself to become disconcerted. I bowed low before him. "My apologies for my rudeness, Master Tóla. I intended to say, yes, I know the mantra."

His eyes blazed. "Is there something more you wish to say?"

"Again please excuse my disrespect, Master. Rain falls in torrents, there will be no dry fuel for a fire. Provided I could find dry wood, there will be no possible way to maintain a blaze on an open hilltop. Perhaps you will consider delaying my mission until a more suitable day?"

"Impossible. There can be no delay. This day was not chosen by me, but by the Lordly Ones. You must go today. Listen carefully; today you must create a fire that burns that which cannot burn."

His words passed me as my heart sank, knowing there could be no further appeal or expectation that I might be successful.

He continued, "You realize you will only succeed if a vision comes to you from the gods during the fire ceremony?"

I nodded though his question mattered little. There was no hope for a vision. Unless the rain stopped soon there was no hope of building the fire.

"Do not look so forlorn. Remember the words of Epicurus, 'The greater the difficulty, the greater the glory in surmounting it.' Besides, you should feel honored for the gods are testing you. Indeed, I cannot recall the gods challenging an acolyte with a more difficult trial. To succeed you must maintain confidence in yourself, keep your mind clear and apply the knowledge we instilled within you. Now, if there is nothing more you wish to say, it is time you begin."

* * *

The rain proved unrelenting. Large trees bent before the howling wind, their leaves flying through the air and skittering across the ground. My cape did little good as the driving downpour ran off it in rivulets, and soon I was thoroughly drenched.

I had begun my walk to the distant grassy mound with a leather bag and foul temper on my shoulder. The impossible task before me weighed heavily, though after a while the Master's words began to come back and buoyed my spirits a bit.

"To succeed," he had told me, "you must maintain confidence in yourself, keep your mind clear and apply the knowledge we instilled in you." And there was one thing more, a riddle of sorts with words so twisted that only the magical fairy folk could appreciate them. "You must create a fire that burns that which cannot burn."

Perhaps my trial was not impossible then. My reasoning continued, perhaps the rain itself was not the problem; perhaps it merely blinded my view of the solution.

I slowed down my mind as I walked along and called upon what I knew of alchemy. The world was made of four primary elements; air, earth, water and fire. Of fire I knew the least, but I understood that any fire required air, fuel and heat. Water was a fire killer for it suppressed the air around the flame and cooled the fuel. I sloshed on amid an abundance of water.

At last, I came to a tree-lined brook flowing full in the heavy rain. Beyond rose a grassy knoll that I knew for my destination. There was no help for it, so, disgusted, I waded the cold, thigh-deep water and began to cast about under the trees on the far bank for dry wood. I found nothing; even the partially rotten limbs that normally caught fire easily were saturated like a wet sponge.

I continued on to the crest of the hill where my view was obscured by a heavy curtain of gray rain. The wet grass underfoot would do me no good. Nearby were only large stones, a small flock of sheep huddled together in the rain. Again I searched for dry fuel, moss or lichens beneath the rocks that might be protected from the storm. Nothing was there, nothing of use.

I dropped my leather bag to the ground and plopped down beside it in defeat. Within the bag were an iron knife and piece of flint, useful for creating heat to start a fire...if I had dry fuel and could stop the torrential rain. A large clay pot contained magical herbs used in the sacred fire ceremony, now useless lacking a sacred fire. And of course there was no food, for it was dictated that the ceremony be a time of fasting...a silly thing it seemed now.

A sheep bleated, and my tired, drooping eyes were drawn to the small flock. "...burn that which cannot burn." Bah, as if I could burn a wet sheep. Yet, there was something tugging at my memory, something about the sheep. Sheep provided meat, milk, wool, lanolin...yes, of course, lanolin. Lanolin oil rendered from sheep's wool—oil that burnt with a bright, hot flame!

My mind went to work as I concentrated on the miserable beasts, and again past alchemy lectures proved helpful—"oil and water are enemies and will never come together." My hopes surged—lanolin burned in the presence of water! But the wool was on the sheep and the lanolin in the wool...augh!

I tugged the cape closer against the rain, my mind testing and rejecting idea after idea. After sitting for some time I jumped to my feet and roared aloud into the downpour at my own stupidity. It wasn't my mind that brought an answer, it was my nose! The old cape clasped about me all day was freshly saturated with lanolin oil.

It took time and work to complete the details, but I was there to conduct a sacred ceremony, not measure time. At last though a fire no larger than a sparrow burned within the clay pot beneath the protection of what remained of the cape after I had scraped the lanolin from it. The ritual must begin immediately, and I swallowed my boyish pride for having solved the Master's riddle. The sputtering flame would be a fleeting thing, so I sat cross-legged beside my fire and chanted aloud the ritual's opening mantra,

> O Gods of my fathers,
> O Mighty Lords of the Sidhe,
> Defenders of Ancient Mysteries,
> Purveyors of the Everlasting.

> See this poor mortal,
> See his unworthy fire of admiration,
> And take pity upon him,
> Hear his undeserving plea.

The ritual went on, time passed, darkness fell, and with it continuing rain. My tiny flame spit, sizzled and flickered but continued to burn valiantly, keeping the lengthy ceremony alive.

During the lateness of the night a vision came, a motionless painting in colorful, remarkable detail hovering in the air before me. There comes a point where weary eyes see though the mind refuses to serve its purpose. I forced myself to concentrate on the image, to press it within the folds of my memory for later study.

The ritual ended with the coming of the vision, and I muttered the prescribed closing, thanking the gods for it. Then, as though by magic, the rain stopped, the clouds cleared and stars bejeweled the night sky. I staggered to my feet and gathered my few belongings. Polaris sparkled high above to show me the way, and I began the long, mindless, muddy trek back to my bed at Dún Ailinne.

* * *

I awoke in my dormitory with sunlight streaming through the windows. Someone was shaking my foot. It was Earnán.

"Ossian, wake up. The Master calls for you."

A groan escaped me as I sat up, and he smiled as he handed me two barley cakes. "The kitchen is long closed for the morning. I thought you might like these before climbing the hill."

It was a kind act, and I thanked him for it before he left the empty dormitory. My robe was still damp and mud spattered. I donned it in disgust. The barley cakes were delicious, and I devoured them as I began a slow ascent up Knockaulin.

Upon my arrival, the Master was seated behind his table.

He cocked an eyebrow. "You built your fire?"

"Yes, Master Tóla. I burned that which cannot burn."

"And that was?"

"A wet sheep."

Humor glinted in his eyes, a currency he spent sparingly, as he nodded. "Lanolin. Yes, I hoped you would discover that solution. Now tell me, there was a vision?"

"Yes, Master, a vision came and I saw it clearly, but found no meaning in it. Within the vision were twin white sails upon a large curragh far at sea."

"Twin sails on one of our Irish boats, you say?" He frowned in thought, and shook his head, bewildered. "It seems a small thing."

"There was more. Centered on the sails was a large red cross, the cross of the Christians."

His questioning eyes stared into mine for a long moment before he asked, "Were you aboard the boat?"

"I don't know...that is, I'm not sure. The vision was so very plain, yet the gods' message behind it, if there was one, altogether obscure. Can you see the importance of it?"

He continued staring into my eyes; did I detect doubt or even accusation in his? If so, why? I saw no reason for it.

Finally, he shook his head. "No, but I am troubled by the symbolism. You have learned many Christian ways and beliefs in your religious studies. Perhaps that is all there is behind it." He sighed and relaxed in his chair. "One thing I promise you, Ossian. The vision sent you by the Lordly Ones, vague though it may be as to its true meaning, foretold a significant event. Someday, somewhere, you will see that boat again, and when you do you will face the greatest decision of your life."

Chapter 4
The Darkening

𝕷 aoidheach sat with his back against the bole of a tree idly strumming a lyre, his long legs stretched before him. A promising, straggling goatee sprouted from his chin.

I lazed in the grass nearby, my mind as idle as his fingers. I sat up, yawned, stretched and uttered an equally idle thought. "Are you aware we've known one another for four years?"

He didn't look up. "No."

"And do you realize we've wasted much of our time together on shameful adventures among the maidens in Kilcullen?"

His fingers strummed a peaceful chord. "Not so much, I'm thinking. Kilcullen is a small village."

My mind continued to wander. "Hmm. Eight years gone and now four more."

"What's that?"

"Nothing. I was merely reflecting on the years I've spent here and those that remain."

He finally glanced up. "I've been here four with two long years yet to go."

"Why 'long' years?"

"Alas, there are no more mysteries to solve in Kilcullen."

"Augh!"

He struck a discordant key, and grinned. "Now to more important things. There is to be a songfest tomorrow night, will you be coming?"

"Perhaps. The Master has acquired a new book at great cost. It's titled 'Elements,' and written by the famous old Greek mathematician, Euclid. We are studying his teachings on geometry. Learning his formulas is difficult and takes much time."

"Euclid? Geometry? I've never heard of them. Bards have no need to know such things."

Nothing my friend said surprised me anymore. "Geometry is an ancient mathematical form though Euclid extended its use. We are learning much more of it through his book. He was a great man, often cited by Archimedes himself."

"Archimedes? I've not heard of him either, but back to the songfest. You must come! Treasa, Dáirine and other girls will be there."

His mention of the girls raised my interest. "You will be singing, then?"

"Aye, I will be singing my new song, a ballad honoring the goddess Fachea the patron goddess of we bards. That is…ow!" He clasped a hand to his eye.

"What is it?"

"Some bloody tiny thing flew into my eye. It is nothing."

I happened to glance at the sleeve of my robe and saw it speckled with tiny gray dots. They disappeared when I rubbed them with my finger. "Ah, it's merely ash. The wind is blowing the cooking smoke toward us."

The sun dimmed overhead. Laoidheach glanced up and his mouth fell open as he gaped and pointed behind me. "Ossian! What is that?!"

I turned to look. Overhead, a thin haze shaded the sky light gray, but to the west lightning flashed across a towering, enormous black mass.

* * *

Master Tóla stood atop Knockaulin, his commanding gaze capturing the students grouped before him. Behind him a great sacral fire roared in the darkness, sending flaming brands skyward.

The Master uncrossed his arms, raised his hands palms outward and began. "Yesterday, a mysterious darkness fell across the land, and with it, darkness entered the hearts of men. Fear clutches the minds of all, as it does your own, for fear is the son of ignorance and ignorance the daughter of blindness. The immense fire behind me offers light in the darkness, not a light by which we might simply see but a light of knowledge, a light by which we might understand what lies behind the darkness itself. Now listen all, listen that you might learn, listen to the message brought by the great sacral fire, hear the words of the Dagda!"

A murmur swept the assembled group. The Dagda! Master Tóla had spoken with the High God of the Tuatha De Danann themselves, the Dagda, Lord of Perfect Knowledge.

Tóla's raised hands closed to form fists, and quieted the crowd. "Now hear you all and praise the song of the Dagda,"

> So, the earth revolves,
> and night turns to day.
> By the hand of Belenos, the sun gleams,
> and once again brings life to the Tree.
> The bole of the Tree stands steadfast,
> resisting all forces for all time.
> Branches spread outward from the Tree,
> from its branches all living things hold fast.
> Mother Earth shudders,
> the cauldron within her boils.
> A pustule forms and ruptures,
> cauldron smoke fills the skies.
> So, the earth revolves,
> but night remains night.
> The sun, at the hand of Belenos does not return,
> there is no life within the Tree.
> The bole of the Tree stands steadfast,
> resisting all forces for all time.
> Branches spread outward from the Tree,
> from its branches all living things fall.

Light within darkness,
from within the rath of the Sidhe.
Light where there is no light,
light where darkness prevails.
So, the earth revolves,
three times three darkness rules.
The sun, at the hand of Belenos returns,
bringing new life within the Tree.
The bole of the Tree stands steadfast,
resisting all forces for all time.
Fifth of seven chieftains,
from its branches all living things reborn.

* * *

A line of torches snaked down the side of Knockaulin as students returned to their dormitories. Someone jostled me in the darkness. It was Laoidheach.

"So Ossian," he whispered, "tell me. What was it the Master was saying?"

"He spoke of the darkness," I muttered, "and repeated the words of the Dagda. You heard him."

"Yes, I heard him, but what was he, or the Dagda, saying?"

"Don't you know?" My feet were feeling their way in the flickering torchlight, down the steep, narrow trail. "You are a bard and should understand such a song."

"Yes, I am a bard trained to sing such things. That doesn't mean I always understand them, for the gods often test us with their ridiculous riddles."

I almost laughed, but the solemn events on the hill dictated otherwise. "Very well then, the Dagda was saying the earth rotates, and the sun—"

"Yes, yes, I know. Without the sun everything dies. Go on."

"The Dagda further spoke of a Tree, meaning the Tree of Life where the bole is the never changing center of the universe."

"I knew that too."

"Somewhere Mother Earth has ruptured spewing smoke and ash into the sky. That is the cause of the darkness."

Laoidheach grunted. "Oh. I see. What was meant by the light in rath of the Sidhe, and something about three times three and the fifth chieftain?"

"The light from within the rath of the Sidhe represents the Light of All Knowledge, meaning the Lordly Ones understand everything. I confess three times three meant nothing to me until the mention of the fifth chieftain. You see, there are seven chieftain trees, ash being the fifth. So, the meaning is…"

"Nine months!" he gasped. "The Dagda was saying we face nine months of darkness!"

"Yes, I'm afraid so."

"May the gods have pity upon this land."

* * *

A fortnight passed, anxious days of unrelenting darkness. Word came that I had been called for an audience with Master Tóla, so I climbed the path up Knockaulin. The immense sacral fire now burned incessantly and cast an eerie glow to guide my way.

I rapped upon the door of the Master's sanctuary and entered upon hearing his muffled response. He was seated in his customary position though his eyes betrayed the weariness within him. That he spent his days in constant prayer and divination with the gods, we all knew, though I would not have the temerity to speak of it.

He nodded. "King Túathal Máelgarb has called a synod at Tara to discuss the darkness. He commands that leading Druids and Christian priests from across Eire attend. Your father and I will be among them. Each of us may bring one aide and Earnán will be siding me. Your father sent word and requested that you serve in that capacity alongside him."

I wanted to shout and leap into the air, but remained properly silent, my face calm. It was an amazing thing. Together with my father, I was going to Tara, the Royal seat of the High King of all Eire, Túathal Máelgarb himself.

The Master reached beside him and handed me a neatly folded red and white striped bundle. "You will wear this, the robe of a First Order Druid. Here, take it."

My hand trembled though I knew there must be a mistake as I accepted the robe. "But Master Tóla, I am merely an acolyte. At the very least it requires ten years of study to attain the First Order, while I have but eight."

A tired smile filled his eyes. "Not always. You are still a student here, but as of now no longer an acolyte. Yes, commonly the red robe requires ten years of study though it seems we have a special situation. It would be unseemly for your father, a Third Order Druid, to arrive at the synod with a simple acolyte as his aide. No, a man of his importance who himself shall in a few years be awarded the highest rank of Master Druid merits at least a First Order assistant."

I hugged the bundle to my chest, trying to grasp what was happening. "But…"

"Listen to me, Ossian. You are more than a year ahead in your studies here and show even greater promise. Yes, as Master of the school at Dún Ailinne, in my judgment you have rightly earned your new title in only eight years. I had already determined to bestow this honor upon you but the current circumstances require that I do so now in this ill-timed, informal manner. I have already signed the formal decree, and it will be sent to King mac Dúnlainge and sealed in the Royal Court records of Leinster."

For an acolyte of only twenty years of age to receive this high honor was unheard of, and I stood there like a statue, humbled, unable to form an appropriate response other than to whisper, "Thank you, Master Tóla."

"Humph, yes, of course. As you know, promotion to the First Order should be accompanied by a prescribed ritual in front of your peers followed by a festival and feast in your honor. Unfortunately, we leave in three days so your ceremony must be delayed until after we return from Tara. Meanwhile, wear this robe, Wise One. Upon this occasion and henceforth, conduct yourself as a Druid."

Chapter 5
Tara

"**O**ssian. You wear the First Order robe?" My father sat astride a tall horse in the center of the compound surrounded by a group of mounted, grim-faced warriors. Bronze armor glinted in the torchlight, every warrior heavily armed.

I hid my pleasure behind a humble shrug. "Yes. Master Tóla bestowed the honor upon me just three days past."

Pride flared in his eyes and he gave me a curt nod. "Come then, Druid. We must hurry! You are ready to leave?"

I walked closer. "Yes father, of course. I need only get my bag." I gestured toward the warriors. "You have need of this large escort?"

"These are dangerous times. People are terrified by this darkness and many aren't thinking clearly. Travelers are now at risk from far more than common bandits. King Domhnall insisted upon me traveling with these twenty men. Have you seen Master Tóla?"

"Yes. I'm sure he is aware of your arrival and will be here soon."

"Very good. Hurry now…get your bag that we might leave right away."

* * *

Midday torchlight flared and reflected off our warriors' armor as our calvacade rode through the gate of the wooden palisade surrounding the stone palace of the High King. Horses' hooves echoed as we crossed the cobblestone courtyard.

The four of us, Master Tóla and his aide Earnán as well as my father and I, dismounted and entered the foyer of the palace. Immediately we were met and ushered into the throneroom, where the four us knelt in a row before King Túathal Máelgarb, High King of Eire, descendent of Niall of the Nine Hostages.

Acrid smoke burned my eyes and nose, emanating from four flaming torches that lit the large, almost barren room. It is a sad day when you eagerly expect to find glitter only to discover dust instead. I sighed at the disappointment of it.

The King slouched in his heavy oak chair as we knelt before him on the cold stone floor. On his right stood an ancient bearded Druid, stooped and leaning on his staff, a Slatnan Druidheacht. A tonsured, stone-faced Christian priest stood on the King's left, garbed in what I knew to be a bishop's scarlet robe.

The King himself proved my second disappointment, a burly, most un-kingly, coarse-featured man. The broad golden band encircling his head spoke to his inheritance of power while his grease-streaked beard and dark, unkempt hair falling loosely to his shoulders questioned the purity of his royal bloodline. A common linen kirtle encasing his large girth ended at hairy knees; leather boots sheathed his feet and calves.

He stared at us through drooping eyelids as if with little interest. Finally, he acknowledged our presence. "So, Tóla, you bring news of the darkness?"

"Yes, Your Highness, that and a message from King Illan mac Dúnlainge of Leinster." Master Tóla removed a scroll from the loose-fitting sleeve of his robe and offered it to the King.

King Máelgarb leaned forward, took it from the Master's hand and passed it to the ancient Druid. He was not finished with the Master. "Tell me for truth, Tóla. Is it true King mac Dúnlainge has already sealed his borders?"

"I do not think so, Your Highness, for we met no guards along the trail on our travel here. With your permission, allow me to introduce Ciann Mehigan of Rath Raithleann, Druid to King Domnhall. Perhaps he can speak to your question."

The King's eyes turned to my father. "And so, Druid, I have heard your name though we have not met. What say you? Were you detained upon entering Leinster?"

My father bowed. "No, Your Highness. We encountered no men of Leinster on our journey to Dún Ailinne."

"The rumor is not true then." The King clapped his hands and smirked. "Of course…hah, I knew it for a dirty lie when first I heard it. King mac Dúnlainge is not a man who panics because of a little darkness."

King Máelgarb squirmed and settled back in his chair as his eyes swept us. "However, unrest already stirs among all the tribes. Without the sun crops will fail, people will face starvation and the resulting turmoil will inevitably spark war! A war over food! A war for survival! I look to you to put an end to the darkness before such terrible things occur." He turned and nodded to the Druid beside him.

The old man stepped forward. "The synod will not take place here, but upon the ancient sacred heights of Tlachtga, a short ride away. Go there, for preparations have already been made for your arrival. Two days hence we shall join together to offer prayers during a Great Fire Festival dedicated to Belenos and thereby assure that the power behind this darkness shall be overcome."

* * *

"Why was the Christian priest standing at the side of King Máelgarb?"

My father sat cross-legged on the ground beside me atop the hill named Tlachtga. Above us stretched a small, striped canopy. Nearby, other groups camped, while about us torches held back the darkness.

He waved his hands and wrinkled his nose. "Augh! Who is cooking that vile-smelling meal? By the priest you mean the bishop?"

At my nod, he continued. "The King sent us a message by the bishop's presence. He intended that we know his power extends beyond our faith and now encompasses that of the Christians as well."

"It's little I know of the Christians though I have a learned a bit about them in my religious studies."

My father glanced around, leaned closer to me and spoke quietly. "I do not want this overheard. Even Master Tóla has friends among the Christian priests. Kindly man that he is, he disagrees with my intolerance of them. You must always remember Christians arrived in Eire for the sole purpose of capturing the minds of all our people." He waved a dismissive hand. "Their priests are like lepers and spoil all they touch."

This was a side of my father I had not seen before, and his words washed over me like a cold rain. "Christians have been here but a short time. How is it they have gained such influence with the King?"

"Their priests speak loud and well. They gather about them the disgruntled, the disenfranchised, those who stand to gain the most by radical change. Regrettably, there are many such and the Christians have gained a large following. Most importantly, the Christians speak with the power of Rome at their backs. The King would be foolish to ignore them."

Despite eight years of confinement within an atmosphere solely dedicated to learning it came as a shock that I knew so little of Eire's political state. Still, I knew much of Rome and that its power was fading. "I see. Yes, but the Romans withdrew from Pictland more than one hundred years ago—"

"True, but Rome is still a power that must not be trifled with," he interrupted, "and their priests wield it to their advantage. Just think of it. Before his death their great priest, the one they reverently call Saint Patrick, had the audacity to banish all Druids from Eire. Though of course he had no authority to do so, consider the impertinence of even suggesting such an unheard of thing."

My father's critical views of the Christians differed from those I had studied and I was eager to hear his words. "I know little of Patrick. All their priests agree with his decree to cast us out of Eire?"

"Yes, though perhaps to a greater or lesser degree. Some revile us openly and claim our sacred symbol of the serpent represents evil spawned by a demonic spirit they call Satan who lives in the depths of the earth. As for those priests who remain silent on the matter, perhaps it is they who pose the greater threat to us, for silence can be mistaken for temperance and reason."

"But that makes no sense. They have their religion while we have ours. Why should they care about us?"

"By the teachings of their faith, Christians are obliged to bring all men to their one god. They will not have succeeded as long as one person, one soul still belongs to the Lordly Ones. Ridding Eire of all Druids simply makes their mission that much easier, don't you see?"

My stomach knotted as my father concluded, "My concern, and one I've shared with Master Tóla, is not knowing the lengths the Christians are willing to go to in order to be rid of us."

"They are our enemies, then?"

"They most certainly see us as theirs. So..." He stopped speaking as the Master himself stepped under the canopy to join us.

I sat quietly, uneasily reviewing my father's remarkable words as he and Master Tóla began to discuss the synod that was to begin the following morning.

* * *

O Heavenly Father,
O King of Kings,
O Lord of Hosts,
O Creator of All.
With upturned faces we look to You,

With lips of love we speak to You,
With eyes aglow, we worship You,
With ears attuned, we hear You.

We ask Your many blessings upon all assembled here,
We pray mercy for all who suffer within this darkness,

WAVES IN THE WIND

We pray for enlightenment for those who resist Your call,
We pray that they might see
through Your darkness and find You.

We pray all these things in Your Name,
O Lord of Mysteries,
We pray that you might consider them in Your Grace.
In the name of the Father, the Son and the Holy Ghost,

Amen

The Christian bishop, the same man who stood beside King Máelgarb's chair in his chambers, ended his prayer and stared at us, sixty-six unmoving and unmoved Druids from villages throughout all the territories of Eire. A nearby group of Christian priests and monks who honored his prayer raised their heads.

He ignored his fellow Christians. With his hands clasped behind his back, he began pacing back and forth beneath the great white canopy that covered us all. From time to time he cast glances in our direction as we sat cross-legged on the ground before him.

Off to one side the High King slouched in his chair, perhaps interested though unengaged in the proceedings. The bishop bowed toward him and then faced us. "King Túathal Máelgarb, may the Blood of Christ protect him, bade us arrive here to discuss and overcome the darkness that envelops this land. For two days I have heard the views of the learned Druids who spoke to us."

Eyes sad, his face long, he shook his head. "Yes, I heard their views though by God's Eternal Truth I must tell you that I do not hold with them. Now our King demands that I express my own beliefs, those of my church, and in my own poor way, relate to all the Word of God."

He stood erect, his flashing eyes sweeping us, his voice bold. "We seek the cause of this everlasting night and I say to you, for I know it to be true, there can be no cause other than it has befallen us by the Mighty Hand of God Himself!"

He paused to allow the import of his words to rest upon our minds, though the import, if such there was, had no effect on me. I already knew Mother Earth brought on the darkness, but was interested to see where the bishop would take his argument. He did not disappoint me for he began right away.

"Permit me to tell you a story." He reached to a large book lying upon a table and lifted it above his head for all to see. "It is a story written within this Holy Book of Scriptures, words written by God's Own Hand."

The bishop cleared his throat, placed the book back on the table and began pacing again. "I speak to you of an ancient time, the place...Egypt. There, Pharaoh, King of all Egypt, ruled with an iron fist. He held in bondage the Hebrew people, the people of the Book of Exodus. Among the Hebrews was a man named Moses, a prophet of the Almighty Himself. Moses came before Pharaoh, saying, 'Lest you set my people free, God's judgment will fall upon you and all Egypt.' Pharaoh refused and there ensued a series of ten deadly plagues, God's reprisal of which Moses foretold."

I listened intently for, of course, it is true that Druids loved a good story. No doubt, the bishop would link the story of Pharaoh to the darkness, and I was curious to see how he did so.

"God's vengeance," the bishop repeated it for emphasis, "God's vengeance descended upon Pharaoh and all his people."

He raised his hand, spread wide his fingers and counted, "In the first plague God turned the waters to blood, in the second He caused the sky to rain toads."

A chuckle ran through the massed Druids, and he scowled, his eyes fixed upon us. "Think not to laugh! For then came a plague of lice, and then flies, and then a disease among all the animals. Despite these trials, Pharaoh still refused to release the Hebrew people. Therefore, the plagues continued as next came a disease on people, boils that refused to heal. Then God brought thunder and hail against the land followed by swarms of locusts that devoured all the crops in the fields. Yet, still Pharaoh refused to yield.

41

Consequently, God brought darkness upon Egypt and finally death to all first-born children; death to all except the children of the Hebrews. It was only then that Pharaoh relented and set the Hebrews free.

"All these things and more God can do and has done against those who would defy him." He pointed outwards into the darkness beyond the canopy. "So how is it I know Eire's darkness fell by God's Hand? It is because He has done it before! Long ago He brought this very same darkness upon Egypt in retribution against Pharaoh's arrogance!"

His still-pointing finger turned towards us, accusing us. "By His Own words God said, 'Thou shalt not have any gods before Me!' Many years ago the Holy Saint Patrick, may God rest his immortal soul, decreed in God's name that you forsake your demons, your blasphemous idols and your pagan ways. And yet, like Pharaoh, you defied God, you refused to obey His command. Now look out there, see the darkness and see God's vengeance against you and this land for your insolence. Look not for the sun to reappear until each of you renounces your false gods, fall upon your knees, ask His forgiveness for your many sins and swear everlasting allegiance to Him and Him alone!"

Angry muttering swept through our assemblage of Druids but the bishop ignored it, turned his back upon us and began another prayer.

"O Heavenly Father..."

"One moment!" It was my father who spoke. He stood and bowed in the direction of King Máelgarb. "Please pardon my interruption Your Highness. However, with your gracious indulgence I would address this man."

The High King nodded and gestured that my father could continue. I suspected that while the King might be gracious with his indulgence, my father would not share the same with the bishop. He strode forward to confront the priest.

"Yesterday, Master Tóla, great Druid and wise advisor to us all that he is, sang for us the song of the Dagda. Within that song the source of the darkness was revealed, a natural occurrence within Mother Earth. Today you accuse us for causing it," his hand swept 'round to include the Druids, "through your story of Pharaoh, a fable speaking of vengeance by the hand of your god."

The bishop's neck grew red to match his robe as he blustered, "Fable, you say? Were you not listening when I told you the story of Moses is written in God's Holy Book? No, you ignored me just as you ignored the Truth proclaimed by Saint Patrick!"

"There is cause to ignore you for your intentions are as obvious as the flame of yon torch. Well I remember accounts of your priest called Patrick, and well I remember him being a man who sowed strife and turmoil among our people just as you would sow the same among those gathered here today."

Redness moved from the bishop's neck to his face as his arms crossed over his chest. "Today I spoke God's Truth. I promise you it would serve you well to hear me."

My father's hard eyes held the man and he waited for a count of ten before his quiet voice responded. "I heard you, priest. Now you hear me. Little it is I know of your god and little it is I wish to know, for I remain true to my own gods, the all-powerful Lords of the Sidhe. For thousands of years they have seen to the needs of Eire's people. Therefore, come not before me with your accusations and threats, for I care nothing for them."

"You think I speak idly, Druid? Continue then to defy Gods' Will, continue to worship your demons and feel the full measure of His punishment!"

The bishop turned and bowed to the King. "Your Highness, as you requested I have made my statement on behalf of the Ruler of the Universe, and see no point in arguing further with this...this man. In the end, by God's grace and through His divine guidance, only your wisdom and your words matter and will lead us from this darkness."

* * *

We stood beside our horses in a grove of trees. I was finally able to catch my father alone as we rested on our return journey to Dún Ailinne. "The bishop was intentionally rude and meant that his words would hang above us like an executioner's axe."

My father's weariness was voiced in his sigh. "Yes, he meant to intimidate us. I felt it was important to stand before him in the presence of King Máelgarb to make it known that his devices were not successful, that Druids do not cower before Christian priests or their god."

"Your words were well said, father." A warrior stepped up and took my reins to lead my horse to water in a stream. When the man was out of earshot, I continued. "Thanks to you the Christians will think twice before challenging us."

"The Christians will not stop defying us. They have long sought a means to undermine our hold on Eire. This darkness has given them a perfect opportunity. Laying the blame for a tragedy at the feet of your adversaries is an old ploy. Still, it can be effective when the same thing is said time and again before those who reach out for something or someone to blame for their fears."

"Then we must refute their god-cursed lies."

"Lies?" my father chuckled. "Is it a lie when you believe what you say to be true? Make no mistake. The bishop believed his own words. Henceforth, Christian priests will fervently preach loud and long to all who will listen that it is we Druids who are at fault for the darkness. Mark my words; many will believe them and go over to their faith."

"Perhaps, but most people will stand by us and the Lordly Ones when they hear the truth revealed by the Dagda."

"Common sense says you are right, but these are not sensible times. Families tremble beside their fires and call upon their gods, the old and new, for salvation and the restoration of order."

There was almost a tone of futility in my father's voice, but he was very tired. Perhaps that was all I heard. Still, I pressed him, for there was more I wished to know. "I must tell you the bishop's story of Pharaoh sickened my stomach. Do you think the Christian god can do all he claimed?"

"Perhaps, though we have seen no sign of it. The Christian god holds no sway here, the Lords of the Sidhe still rule Eire."

"Aye, but what manner of god do the Christians worship?"

My father yawned and briskly shook his head. "Pardon me. Now, how do you mean?"

"I think of the ten plagues the Christian god brought upon the people of Egypt because of Pharaoh's stubbornness. You recall the final plague?"

"No."

"All first-born children of Egypt died. Think of it—a god who killed an untold number of innocent children because of the actions of their king. What manner of god would do such a thing? And if he is a god who in his wrath kills children, what might he do to the people of Eire?"

"Your thoughts are well considered," he sighed. "Beyond that you speak to fundamental questions that must be asked of all faiths. I cannot answer your question, though I say again, the Christian god has little power here and I do not fear his wrath. However, the synod revealed the growing power of those who stand behind the god you described and I do fear we must prepare for their wrath."

Chapter 6
Flames of Rage

"Ossian, I have something for you." My father sat at the head table within the dining hall alongside the Master. He stood and removed a gold chain from around his throat that had been hidden beneath his robe.

I disengaged myself from a group of students, walked forward, bowed and accepted his gift from his hand. It was a spiritual thing of great significance, one that would reveal my Druid's status to all who saw it. A serpent ring; a solid gold body formed by three coiled bands joined as one, the crest a snake's head featuring bold emerald eyes glittering in the candlelight.

"It was your grandfather's," he explained as I slid it onto my finger. "I've worn his ring of the sacred serpent around my neck as a token of good fortune. Always it was with the thought I might present it to you as I do now during the celebration of your formal introduction as a Druid. May it always speak the truth of your dedication to the Lordly Ones and serve you well."

* * *

My duties changed immediately. Though I was still a student, as a First Order Druid I was assigned to teach the basics of alchemy to the youngest acolytes. Upon making this assignment Master Tóla's eyes gleamed as he told me, "Teach them to burn that which cannot burn."

I settled into my new standing and role while three months passed, each dark day much like the last. A day came, however, that while walking across the compound between afternoon lectures it seemed as though by accident a shadow moved among the nearby trees. I walked closer to investigate, and a short, cloaked man stepped into the fire-lit compound. Without comment he handed me a scroll.

I unrolled the vellum document and hurriedly scanned the Ogham figures on it. It was a message from my father. The mystery deepened when I raised my eyes to discover the messenger had disappeared. Puzzled, I concentrated on the scroll.

> Be warned, my son. Word has reached me of treachery at the highest levels in the halls at Tara. King Máelgarb publicly proclaims to remain true to the gods, but fears the growing strength of the Christians and has formed a secret alliance with them. Christian priests continue to lay the blame for the darkness at the feet of Druids. Their followers plan depredations against our most sacred places. The King cowers within his stronghold like an old woman and has agreed not to interfere. Remain vigilant and take whatever action you deem necessary, for the school and shrine at Dún Ailinne may be attacked without warning. Say nothing of this to anyone and share this message only with Master Tóla. Destroy this scroll so no others may read it.

The scroll in my hands trembled as the threat behind my father's words washed over me. Not only might I be in peril, but also the Master and my fellow students. He also insisted I say nothing to anyone other than Master Tóla. Why? Was it he suspected the High King had his own ears planted among us? Yes. I nodded to myself, yes, of course.

Master Tóla would be in his sanctuary. Since the onset of the darkness it was always there he spent his days. I hurried up Knockaulin with my heart on fire, rapped lightly on the door and entered upon hearing his quick summons.

He sat alone, cross-legged on floor. His sagging posture and bleary eyes revealed he had been in meditation, and he gestured for me to approach. His eyes sharpened but he remained motionless as he recognized the anxious expression on my face. I bowed before him, and he gave a questioning nod.

"Master Tóla," I forced myself to remain calm as I began. "I sincerely beg your pardon for disturbing you, but I have received an urgent message from my father. He instructed that I share it with you."

The Master took the scroll from my hand, read through it, scanned it again and then looked up to me. "And so?"

It was not the response I expected. "What should we... That is, what will you do?"

"Do? Of course, I shall do nothing."

"But Master, you've read my father's warning." My finger shook a bit as I shivered within the disagreeable dampness of the room and pointed to the scroll. "We face danger. Surely some action is needed."

He merely shrugged. "Your father's words are well intended, but I have come to know many Christian priests. We argue, yes, we disagree, yes, but the men I know do not sow violence among their followers. Believe me, there is no danger."

His conciliatory tone grated upon me as he ignored my father's warning. Much was at risk and I dared reveal my true feelings. "Christians, all of them, are a scourge upon Eire and cannot be trusted."

"Who taught you such a thing?" His eyes glinted. "Of course. You heard this from your father, for I know his strong feelings on it. You are wrong as is your father." He shook his head, somber reproach in his eyes, as he continued. "You must never condemn all based upon the actions of a few, or judge men solely upon their beliefs. Men may be guided by faith but you must look deeply into the heart and mind of every man, and measure him only upon what you find there."

"Of course, Master, I see the truth in it." I was almost dancing in frustration. "However, I think of one man, the Christian bishop at the synod. He deliberately threw his threats into our faces."

"Bah! I know the man. He blusters and postures to further his argument, but would never countenance actual violence." He re-rolled the scroll as he looked up at me. "Granted, we are a warlike people; kings, great and small, fight among themselves for land, wealth and power. Do not worry. Within the entire history of this land we've never once seen a war between religions."

The Master reached a hand upwards to me. "Give a man a hand, would you? I've sat here long enough and my old bones demand stretching."

I took his hand and heaved him to his feet. Upon becoming upright, the top of his head reached my chin and he glanced up.

"I hadn't actually noticed until now. You've grown tall in the ten years you've been here."

"Only eight," I reminded him.

"Oh yes, that's right, I forget. That makes you twenty years, am I right?"

"Yes, sir."

His hands gripped the edge of the table and he began a gentle knee-bending exercise. "Ah, that's much better."

I stood rigidly, trying to remain calm though I wanted to shout my frustration at his indifference to the rooftop. Finally, I blurted, "Christians are our natural enemies! Are they not dedicated to the destruction of our gods and Druidism itself?"

"Enemies?" He continued bobbing up and down as blood circulated through his legs. "We must not think of Christians as enemies, for within the meaning of the word there can be no mutual acceptance or respect. They are our adverseries, of course, and some will follow the standard raised by their fanatical priest Patrick who during his lifetime was relentless in trying to push us out."

He frowned, leaned across the table and brushed tiny speckles of ash from a manuscript. "That is unfortunate, for there is no place for unyielding intolerance among thinking men. Always remember, within our world there can be disagreement, but in the end there must be room to accept all manner of beliefs. We Druids must try to understand that, and while you might find a few rabble rousers among them, you will discover that most Christians believe it as well."

A lifetime of training held my emotions in check so my face remained calm while my stomach roiled. A disrespectful display of my growing sense of futility before the Master would never do. "You have also taught us that ignorance breeds intolerance and fear begets violence. This new darkness has sown ignorance and fear among all the people. My father's message speaks to those things and urgently warns that Christians plan violence against us."

The Master walked around the table, settled into his chair and sighed. "It is true your father speaks to those terrible things." His hands scoured his weary face. "Yet, his warning is weighted by his intolerance of Christians. I sense no urgency."

I stepped toward him, placed my hands on his table and leaned forward. "The message reveals my father's knowledge of pending danger, not his opinion."

"As a true son you support your father." A small smile flickered across his face. "Very well, I shall reply to his message and ask further clarification. Meanwhile, I see no reason to disrupt the harmony of the school or needlessly frighten the students. In the end, I am confident that even during these dark times reason will be the torch that leads us into the light of wisdom and peace."

Another chill ran down my spine, but at least he agreed to further investigate the warning. "It will soon be time, I think, for my afternoon alchemy lecture, and my students will be gathering. With your permission, Master Tóla, I must go prepare for it."

He nodded, and read the worry on my face as he handed the scroll back to me. "Yes, thank you for sharing your father's warning. Do not allow it to weigh on your heart. Though we must remain vigilant as he says, I doubt there will be serious trouble."

I bowed again. "As you say. Thank you, Master. May the Lordly Ones smile upon you."

"And you, Ossian. Indeed, may the gods smile upon us all."

I trudged down the hill, my thoughts in turmoil. My father's strong views and message haunted me, as did the defiant words of the Christian bishop, which, despite the Master's assurances, were sure to inflame his followers.

Foreboding stopped me, and I looked back up the hill. I must go back, urge the Master to write King mac Dúnlainge. Leinster warriors must secure the school and the sacred shrine of Knockaulin. In my frustration I kicked a stone to send it bounding down the hill, but yelped and hopped up and down on my uninjured foot when I simply managed to stub my toe. Augh, saying more to the Master now would do no good. I would merely look foolish in his eyes and he didn't expect that he must explain himself twice. Perhaps he would be more open to my suggestion at a later time.

* * *

Weeks passed, more weeks of unrelenting darkness. There had been no opportunity to again discuss my father's warning with the Master. Whether he wrote my father, I did not know. Therefore, as fears are wont to do lacking fresh fuel to feed their flames, mine dimly smoldered.

I sat on the ground in the night, my back against the outer wall of my dormitory. A single candle cast dim light upon the vellum codex open on my knees. My eyes quickly scanned across the Greek characters as I studied the principles of language. As was often the case, I marveled that the mind of one man could create such a remarkable thing as a book, and that others accurately transcribed each page time and again in breathtaking artistic detail.

"Psst! Ossian!"

He stood in darkness, but I knew the voice.

"Laoidheach, it is very late," I whispered. "Everyone is already abed. Why are you here?"

"Do you think you are alone in finding something of interest at a late hour? Put away your book and follow me, for I have a fresh flagon of ale under my arm and two willing women nearby."

I chortled, thinking of the single-minded purpose of Laoidheach's life. "Away with you, rogue! I have studying to do and an early morning lecture."

"Bah! Studying and lectures? What matter when women anxiously await your intimate attention? Come. Opportunity awaits!"

It was a rare occasion when I escaped the sensuous traps Laoidheach laid for me and this night was no exception. Within a short time we lay on the floor of a Kilcullen cottage in the arms of women who until that night I had never met. I winked to Laoidheach that he would know I approved his latest discovery.

The buxomly lass lying beside me trailed her finger across my bare chest and cooed, "So, Wise One, is it true that Druids have extraordinary powers?"

I drank from the flagon of ale, and whispered, "Yes, but they are at their best when demonstrated in privacy. The back room there, shall we enter it that I might show them to you?"

Much later I lay beside her, regaining my breath. I began to roll from her, but froze when I heard men's voices outside the cottage.

"What is it?" she murmured.

"Men are outside."

"Oh no! My husband!"

What was that? Her husband? I silently damned Laoidheach as I hurried into my robe and sandals. The voices outside continued and then I heard the clank of metal on metal. It was not one man or even a few. Many men were moving out there, stealing quietly through the night, skulking in the direction of the school.

I groped my way through the darkness into the front room, and in a quiet voice called Laoidheach. There was no response so I began to feel about on the floor in search of him.

At last I found a leg, a leg attached to a body. I nudged him with my toe and again called to him, my voice low. "Laoidheach! Laoidheach, wake up!"

Once more I nudged him and called his name, and received a muffled groan in response. Outside surrounding the cottage were footsteps, the sounds of large groups of men stumbling through the darkness.

Something was amiss. Something was happening out there and my mind reeled with sinister possibilities.

"Laoidheach!" I leaned down and shook his shoulder. "Wake up, damn you! We must get out of here!"

"Get out?" he mumbled. "Get out? Why?"

My thoughts leaped to the one thing that would start Laoidheach moving. "There are men outside. You must hurry. Perhaps these women's husbands are returning."

"Their husbands!" He leaped to his feet, scrambled into his clothes and whispered, "We mustn't use the door—the husbands may be waiting out there. Listen, there's an open window beside me. Come on, that's our way out."

We hastened through the window and stood in the dark, listening. The sounds of groups of men could still be heard but were growing faint as they neared the school.

Laoidheach was disgusted. "The women's husbands, eh? How many husbands do they have? There must be a hundred men out there."

"Their husbands is a matter I intend to discuss with you later. I had to get you out of there, don't you see? Those men are moving toward the school."

"And what of it? You scared five years off my life talking as you did, and a fine friend you are to do such a thing."

"Quiet!" There was no longer any indication of movement though I strained to hear it. "I think those men are Christians planning to attack the school."

"Attack the school, you say? And why would Christians do such criminal a thing?"

"The 'why' doesn't matter right now. Come on. Let's follow them. Perhaps we can find a way to stop them."

"Stop a hundred men who, if you're right, intend who knows what? Stop them how?"

I fumbled about in the dark, grasped his arm and tugged. "Come on."

We felt our way along narrow alleys, hopped fences and finally stopped within the stillness of the grove where we had a good view of the school. Almost immediately a torch flared, then another, and another...

A voice rang out in the darkness. "In the name of our Father! Death to all demon worshippers!"

Now a hundred torches were burning, possibly more, many of which were thrown through the air to land on the thatched roofs of the dormitories and nearby buildings. The roofs caught fire and we could then clearly see the throng of armed men encircling the compound.

Laoidheach's horrified voice trembled as he whispered, "They...they w-would kill us all?"

"So it seems." I stared at the flaming scene in disbelief. A student appeared in the doorway of my own dormitory. It was too dark...I was too far away to recognize him. He dashed towards safety, was intercepted by three men wielding swords and cut down. A second student ran from the building, followed by a third. Both shrieked as they died.

A dark robed figure carried a wooden cross to the center of the compound, a stark silhouette against the burning buildings. He raised the symbol of his god high as he exhorted the mob to greater acts of violence.

Panicked students erupted into the compound from all the blazing dormitories. They dashed through doors and leaped through windows. A slaughter ensued, the terrified screams of my friends and fellow students filled the night air as they were chased and ruthlessly hacked down one by one by the laughing, cheering multitude of Christian fanatics surrounding them.

"They have no chance," Laoidheach muttered, "no chance at all."

I turned away, sickened by the gruesome scene. The ale I so gaily consumed earlier that night spewed upon the ground.

"Ossian!" Laoidheach shook my shoulder. "The Master! Hurry, maybe we can reach him before those killers climb Knockaulin!"

Careful to remain in shadows, we raced around the flaming compound to the foot of the hill and began our ascent. We crossed the hill's face at an upward angle until we intersected the path, and continued climbing.

Master Tóla was coming down the hill toward us. Light from the fires below revealed that he held staffs in both hands, his Slatnan Druidheacht in one, the other bearing a gleaming white death's head pommel.

He stopped when he saw us looming in the darkness. "Who's there?"

"It's Ossian, Master. Laoidheach is with me. We came to warn you. Christians are attacking the school."

"Attacking the school?! I saw the fires and of course came to investigate, but I thought... Explain yourself!"

"A large group of Christians surround the school and have set fire to it. They are killing the students as they run from the flaming dormitories."

"They are killing my boys?" he gasped.

"Yes, Master. I'm afraid they intend to kill them all and there is no stopping them."

His voice trembled while dense smoke now swirled about him. "But no, that…that can't be possible. Why would they…why would Christians do such a horrible thing?"

"You recall my father's message?"

"Yes…yes, of course." He sighed aloud. "This is my fault. You and your father tried to warn me, and now the blame for this horrible tragedy rests with me."

I glanced down the hill as I spat, "The blame is upon the Christians!"

"Does it matter now, does it truly matter? What is done is done and that is the truth of it. I have failed my gods, my King and. most terribly, my students. It is they who now pay the horrible penalty for my lack of judgment."

"We must escape, Master. Follow us that we may flee this madness."

Master Tóla stood quietly as from below smoke and heat from the fiery buildings surged up the hill toward us along with the distant heart-wrenching din of victims' screams and assassins' cheers. "Flee?" his shoulders sagged. "No, Ossian, my place is down there with my boys."

Laoidheach coughed and wheezed in the smoke. "No Master! You mustn't go down there; those bastards will kill you for certain! Do something! Call upon the Dagda, call upon him to stop this thing; call for vengeance for our fallen, call upon him to strike every killer down."

The Master's voice came to us, a hollow resonance in the darkness. "Do you think the Lordly Ones are unaware of what happens here?" He shook his head in wonder. "You were right, Ossian, the Christians are our enemies and it was negligent of me not to see it, but…" His voice faded as though his own dream or nightmare swallowed him.

We remained silent, honoring his thoughts, patiently waiting for our beloved Master to continue. He cleared his throat, straightened his shoulders and said, "Now I call upon you, Ossian, and you,

Laoidheach, to protect our faith. We are in a war, a killing war between two beliefs. Tonight's attack was the first battle of that war and we have lost it. Spread the word among all tribes to take up arms against the Christians that we might never lose another. Tell the people what occurred here, tell them the gods demand blood for blood, bone for bone."

"Come with us, Master," I pleaded. My eyes watered in the smoke, or was it only the smoke? "Your word will carry weight where ours…"

"No. My time upon this earth has passed. The Lordly Ones have decreed that my proper place lies within the flaming furnace below us. My place has always been with my boys and so it shall be now. As for you, Druid," he handed the death's head staff to me, "the time for warfare has come. Take this staff that you may rally men to battle. You, Laoidheach, beat the drum of war; sing loud the songs that raise warriors' spirits."

I stood in awe, loving him, worshipping him. My breath caught in my throat and I dared not speak lest I disturb the spiritual peace I knew dwelt within him. Besides, there were no inspired words, nothing more that could add to his grandeur—Tóla the magnificent who would rise above death by becoming a martyr to his faith.

He hesitated only an instant more and then resumed walking past us down the path through the churning smoke, saying over his shoulder, "My reliance rests with you to speak for your gods and spread their words of vengeance. Remember—blood for blood, bone for bone!"

* * *

Laoidheach and I fled Dún Ailinne. From a distance I looked back one final time. Towering flames performed a macabre dance in the dark skies above the school while an enormous pyre now raged atop Knockaulin itself. It was a forgotten scene, one I scarcely remembered, an image revealed in a long-ago dream, a vision given me by my mother.

Chapter 7
Rath Raithleann

$\mathfrak{F}$or two days we traveled in darkness. Long it was we talked as we walked along, grim discussions about our past and what might lie ahead.

Vengeance was required. Laoidheach chose to follow me to my home at Rath Raithleann. From there we would launch our reprisals against Christians. How or where we would strike our first blow we did not know. Regardless, we would gather willing warriors about us and the time for revenge would come soon.

We stretched our legs on the third day as we followed a narrow lane, for day it was. A remarkable change occurred with the coming of morning. We could truly see, not in full daylight, more like the waning moments of twilight preceding full darkness.

The spring in Laoidheach's step reflected the lightening and for the first time since that fiery night on the side of Knockaulin his voice came to life. "So, think you the darkness may be ending?"

Our rapid pace proved tiring. Months of inactivity brought on by the darkness left me gulping for air. "We may only pray," I gasped, "the wound in Mother Earth is healing. Remember the Dagda's song, though." I gasped again. "We face nine months of darkness but only five have passed."

Laoidheach chuckled. "Maybe we... Look, someone comes."

Two men approached. My Druid's robe and death's head staff revealed my status so they stepped to the side, bowed and allowed me to pass. I slowed my pace and bowed in return, offering blessings upon them.

Perhaps it was the newness of the twilight setting, but many people traveled that day. In every case they stopped and bowed as I came to them. As a boy, I had seen my father treated with such deference, but this was a new experience for me. Each person we met greeted me as "Wise One," and I was amused to find myself discomfited in my new role. It would take time to feel at ease inside the skin of a Druid.

At last we neared my home. I gained a bounce in my stride as the country we passed through grew familiar. I visited my home only three times during my eight years at Dún Ailinne. Two years had passed since my prior trip. Despite the heaviness still weighing upon my heart, I anticipated the joy of seeing old friends and loved ones.

Three armored warriors rode toward us. As they drew near I recognized two faces from Rath Raithleann, men who accompanied my journey to Tara. We mounted horses to ride double behind two warriors while the third galloped ahead to the village to announce our arrival.

So it was that a short while later we rode into Rath Raithleann to find the people gathering to welcome us. Among the first I noticed was my elder sister, Ceara. I leaped from the rear of the horse and gave her a cautious hug, for she held a babe in her arms. Two small boys huddled within the folds in her skirt.

"Welcome home, brother." Her dark eyes glistened as she stood on tiptoes and kissed my cheek.

I hugged her again, knelt and was re-introduced to my nephews, who had grown a great deal since my last visit. Their large shy eyes peered at me from behind her skirt.

Laoidheach alit from his mount and stood beside me. I rose from where I was kneeling to find my father standing beside him, his hand rested upon Laoidheach's shoulder.

My father's eyes held a greeting, but something more—they demanded an explanation for our unexpected presence and the death's head staff in my hand.

I bowed. "May the gods' many blessings be upon you, father. I bring news of a great tragedy though I believe it would be best that we speak of it privately."

His raised hand swept 'round to indicate all those gathered about us. "You have returned to family and friends and are free to speak your news here."

Now hundreds of faces crowded around us as word of my arrival contined to spread throughout the village. They stood muttering questions among themselves at the import of the news I brought.

I held my staff above my head, calling for silence, and raised my voice so all could hear. "Three days past a large body of Christian zealots attacked and destroyed the school at Dún Ailinne and the holy shrine atop the hill of Knockaulin."

A gasp went up, and I gestured to Laoidheach before continuing. "My friend and I were fortunate to escape the school with our lives, for the Christians massacred all the others."

Again, a gasp rose among the crowd, and the beginning of angry whispering. I waved my staff again, begging silence, and a large lump grew in my throat. "Our leader, Master Druid Tóla, wise and holy man that he was, knowingly martyred himself by walking to his own death in defiance of the depraved murderers. By so doing he demonstrated for all time his undying reverence for his gods, the mighty Lords of the Sidhe."

Angry shouts came from the gathering, demanding vengeance.

"Strike them back!"

"Damn all Christians!"

"Revenge our martyrs!"

My left hand raised the staff, my right hand, a fist. "Yes! Master Tóla's last words to me spoke of vengeance, a war against all Christians. His death demands blood for blood, bone for bone!"

A roar erupted from men's throats while women's wild shrieks rent the air.

I glanced to my father, who bent down speaking into a man's ear. He gave the man a gentle shove, and he whisked away through the crowd.

"I sent the man to carry your news to King Domhnall," he murmered to me. Then, his hands were raised in the air to quieten the still rowdy crowd. His angry voice shouted, "Yes! Vengeance is demanded! Make ready your arms for war. If it is war the Christians want, we shall bring it to them!"

Again the gathering roared, and he waited 'til they quieted.

His voice softened as he continued. "This morning we gleefully offered our thanks to the gods that the darkness might be waning. But now?" He shook his head. "Now, our thoughts must turn to the lost ones, all those who died at Dún Ailinne. I ask that tonight every home offer prayers in their memory. I also ask that every home offer blessings upon Master Tóla, the martyr to our faith."

He waited a moment longer as his eyes swept the crowd. "This Druid and I must now take the tragic news to our king. I thank you all for gathering here to welcome my son to his home."

"You and Laoidheach follow me home," he muttered. "You must wash yourselves before you meet King Domhnall, and perhaps I have clothing to replace your soiled garments."

We no sooner entered the great-room of my father's home than a flashing blue swirl darted through the door behind us, leaped into the air and clasped slender arms around my neck. Aine! She squealed with delight as I twirled her about, her feet sweeping the air.

I relished the joy of holding her in my arms and reluctantly set my young sister on the floor. Extending her away at full arm's length, my hands held her shoulders while my eyes drank in her loveliness. At sixteen years, green eyes twinkled within her small, oval face, while silken auburn hair tumbled down her back to her waist. Never had I seen anyone or anything more beautiful.

"Oh Ossian, I've missed you so," she began and chattered on, though I confess I heard nothing more she said as I stood there enchanted by her gaiety.

The spell was broken by nearby coughing and loud throat clearing. It was Laoidheach, standing aside looking helpless and exceedingly jealous.

"Oh. Pardon me. Laoidheach, meet my sister, Aine." I gestured. "Aine, this is my friend Laoidheach. He will be staying with us for a while."

Aine dropped her head and gracefully curtsied before him. "It is my honor, sir."

His head bobbed, he swallowed hard and a harsh, meaningless screech escaped his lips, "Heeeek!"

Aine did not seem to notice his awkwardness, though a flush crept up her face as she flitted back to hold my hand.

My father cocked an eyebrow as his questioning eyes followed his daughter, but then he looked to me. "Come then. I shall see if I can find presentable clothing for the two of you."

He turned to leave the room, Laoidheach following, but I added, "Go on Father, you too Laoidheach. I'll be with you in a moment. First though I would speak with Aine."

My suspicions aroused, I waited until they left the room, crossed my arms over my chest and demanded, "Well?"

Aine was hanging her shawl on a wooden peg and turned to me. "Well, what?"

"The redness in your cheeks speak though you do not."

"The redness in my cheeks?" Her hands flew to her face. "That is nothing. I'm merely..." Her voice trailed away.

"Merely what? Thinking of Laoidheach?"

"Well what if I was?" Her hands moved to her hips and she glared back at me. "He is quite easily the handsomest man I've ever seen and he filled my eyes for a moment. That is all."

"All? Was it your eyes that were filled or your heart?"

Again she flushed. "My heart? What manner of foolish question is that? I do not even know the man!"

My friend devoured women like most folk would a tasty bowl of porridge, though I would not speak of it. "No, but I do and I know he will bear watching."

"Hah." Aine tossed her hair. "You make a big thing out of nothing. I doubt he scarce noticed me."

"Oh, I assure you he noticed you." I rocked back and forth from heels to toes, my arms still crossed, and smirked. "Laoidheach never missed noticing a pretty girl in his life. He's…well, never mind that, but good friend though he is, I'll thump him hard if he attempts to trifle with you."

She tilted her nose, wagged a finger at me and sassed, "It is you who should never mind, brother. If a man deserves thumping, I'll be doing it myself."

I groaned aloud. As if there wasn't trouble enough already, here was something new. If Laoidheach wasn't cautious, my father would take his head.

* * *

We ducked through the door of the King's longhouse and removed our shoes so as not to track dust across the reed mats carpeting the floor. Laoidheach and I stood by the door in our stocking feet. My father walked to the mid-point in the dimly lit room where King Domhnall and three landholders sat in chairs by the fireplace discussing the status of the kingdom's cattle herds.

Laoidheach muttered in my ear. "Is this a king's chambers or a hunting lodge?"

I leaned upon the death's head staff, shrugged at his question and smiled. Memories of past visits here filled my mind as I glanced at the many trophy heads of deer and boar hanging upon the walls alongside tapestries depicting hunting scenes.

My heart saddened to see the King's white hair and beard. The good man's lined face had aged greatly during the years I had been away to school. In short order he dismissed the landholders, who bowed to me on their way out the door.

Then we were sitting beside the King while I described the events at Dún Ailinne. My attention was captured by the flames within the fireplace as I spoke of the burning of the school, how my friends were slain and the martyrdom of Master Tóla.

"One question." My father relaxed beside me. "The attack occurred late at night. Why were you and Laoidheach not asleep within the dormitories along with the others?"

I cleared my throat, but Laoidheach spoke up. "We were visiting friends in Kilcullen that night. Ossian heard the movement of men in the darkness and insisted we investigate."

My father's hands remained folded in his lap as he cocked an eybrow. "I see. Thank you, Laoidheach. You were very fortunate. It seems little has changed since I was a student there." With a wink, he added, "I too occasionally visited friends in Kilcullen."

"The men who attacked Dún Ailinne, who were they?" The King's calm voice was little more than a whisper.

"I don't know, Your Majesty," I shrugged. "One hundred or more faceless men. In the night I could see no colors or banners to identify them or their tribes. Yet there was one man, their leader, wearing the unmistakable robe of a Christian monk or priest. Perhaps he was the only man among them who knew precisely why he was there—to rid the land of all who speak for the Lords of the Sidhe."

"You are certain they were Christians?"

"Yes, Your Majesty. I'm certain."

"Why do you say the leader's robe was unmistakable in the darkness?"

"I knew the robe by the cut of it and rope cincture about the waist. There became no doubt about what he was when I saw him as a silhouette in the fiery darkness as he raised the Christian cross."

"So now 'vengeance' is the word, eh?"

"Aye, Your Majesty. Laoidheach and I were charged by Master Tóla to collect warriors about us and bring retribution against the Christians. If the gods will it, so we shall."

The King looked to Laoidheach and pointed to a table across the room. "There is a bottle of wine and cups there. Pour some for us, will you? That's a good lad."

"It seems the High King gives us little option other than to raise warriors to defend ourselves and the gods," my father muttered. "Sire, a crime was committed at Dún Ailinne, a high crime against all who died there, against our faith, against humanity itself. Master Tóla, chief Druid to King mac Dúnlainge, and martyr that he now is, was murdered. Had King Túathal Máelgarb stood against the Christians such a tragedy would not have occurred."

"You are right, of course, Ciann," King Domhnall sighed. "Were it that simple, but it is not. King Máelgarb feels the primary thing he must do, always do, is retain power and by so doing secure the throne for his lineage. He will say the attack on the school is a matter between religions and beneath the notice of kings. You see, it only becomes a threat to his supremacy if he openly chooses sides and he will not jeopardize his position by doing so."

"Your Majesty—" I spun around at the crash of breaking crockery.

A shamefaced Laoidheach stood across the room, jagged pieces of a broken cup scattered about his feet. "I…I'm terribly sorry, Your Majesty. The silly thing slipped from my hand and…"

"No harm done," he chuckled. "It was merely a cup. Let us only hope you perform better as a bard than a servant."

Laoidheach, now on his knees scavenging for crockery shards, glanced up, his face crimson. "Yes, Sire, indeed I do…that is…yes, Sire."

King Domhnall looked to me. "You were saying?"

"Thank you, Your Majesty. I intended to ask how anyone could feel safe in a land where rulers refuse to rule. Are we now a land defined by chaos?"

"We are a land trapped within an incomprehensible, terrifying darkness. I'm afraid many of the rulers you speak of are lost within the darkness along with their people. Do not expect overly much of them," he shook his head, "no, not in these times, not now. The attack upon your school was not born of a war between kings or tribes. It speaks to a war among the people, between individuals holding opposing beliefs." He rose, stepped to the fireplace, held his hands to the fire and spoke over his shoulder. "If that is how you define chaos, I will not argue against it."

Laoidheach toddled back to us, cautiously balancing four cups of wine in his hands. King Domhnall took a cup and gave him an encouraging smile. My father and I took ours and the four of us remained quiet as we sipped the dark wine.

My father spoke, breaking the silence. "It is easy for a king to rule during good times. Never have the people needed their kings more than they do now. King Máelgarb has abdicated his authority over Eire. Now other kings such as our own Eoghanachts King, Eochaidh mac Óengusso, and Illan mac Dúnlainge, King of Leinster must step forward to maintain order in the face of Christian attacks."

Eyebrows knitted, King Domhmall asked, "Would you make the enemies of the Druids also the enemies of a king?"

"Kings rule at the benevolence of their gods."

Laoidheach interrupted. "Excuse me. My home is among the Ui Maine and I do not understand the hierarchal aristocracy of the Eoghanachts."

"My pardon, Laoidheach," my father replied. "Eochaidh mac Óengusso is King of Kings among the Eoghanachts and his realm encompasses seven houses. King Domhnall rules one of the houses here in Rath Raithleann."

"I thought it might be something like that. Thank you," Laoidheach nodded.

"Yes, Ciann," the King continued. "And do you forget that King mac Óengusso is a sworn Christian? He serves his god, not the Lordly Ones. Were it not for our King's tolerance he would force his beliefs upon us all."

"Of course I have not forgotten, Your Majesty. However, the unprovoked attack on Dún Ailinne revealed the Christians for who and what they truly are. Perhaps you and his other regional kings can now show King mac Óengusso the folly of supporting the Christians and their ways."

"He is a good, caring man and will be distressed by the atrocity at Dún Ailinne. Yet he is also an honorable man and will be reluctant to renounce his Christian god." The King paused to think before continuing. "Write a letter to him on my behalf, telling of Dún Ailinne. Write it in a subtle manner that speaks to my concern for the need to maintain order while protecting the security of all, including those who stand beside the Lordly Ones."

"Very well, Sire. I shall write the letter immediately."

"Immediately, yes. I would send it to King mac Óengusso by courier today." The King turned to me. "Now, Ossian. You and your friend would do battle against the Christians?"

"Yes, Sire. We will need warriors, and if the gods will it, we shall strike at those who would attack us."

He returned to his seat and leaned towards me, forearms on his knees. "You will find many men here who will wish to join you. That is all well and good but I must place a limit on the number who may go. I cannot permit Rath Raithleann to become unprotected. Choose no more than forty men to side you."

My heart was warmed by King Domhnall's support. "Thank you. You are very generous. With those men and others who will join us along the way we will become a formidable force."

He cocked his head and frowned. "Perhaps. You and your friend here will lead those men. What know you of war?"

"I studied the art of war during many lessons on it. I pray they will serve me well."

He watched my face closely as I spoke, but shook his head. "Studying war is not all the same as practicing it. You will need experienced help, for a battlefield is not a classroom. Bring to me the names of the warriors who volunteer to go with you. I will help you select those who will serve you best."

"Thank you, My Lord. It is comforting to know you are beside me when it seems many other kings will stand aside." Anger rose within me. "And, may they fall for turning their backs upon the Lordly Ones and may the carrion crows feast upon their rotting corpses!"

"Ossian!" My father shook his finger at me. "Remember King Domhnall's words. Many kings are lost within this darkness along with their people. Do not so quickly judge them. You are now a Druid. Act like one! Fight against them if necessary, but you must also search for ways to help those who are lost to find their way out of the darkness."

It was shamed I was, for of course he was right. "My apologies, Father." I turned to King Domhnall. "And to you, My Lord. Please excuse my stupidity and ill-chosen words." I paused for a moment to allow clarity to replace the anger clouding my mind. "Indeed, perhaps they are right to step away. If this be a war between religions and not kings, then so be it. Let it never be said that Druids turned away from a battle."

* * *

That night, following dinner, Ceara's family joined us at my father's home. I again met her husband, a serious-minded man of considerable wealth who owned much land and many cattle.

Laoidheach entertained us, sharing stories of our people and gods—Laegaire in Magh Mell, the wedding at Ceann Slieve, and the

House of the Quicken Trees. I watched Aine during the telling of them, and she laughed often, her eyes never leaving the bard's face.

He then recited an old ballad of Conn of the Hundred Battles, one of my father's favorites. However, his entertainment was not ended. From somewhere Laoidheach had borrowed a lyre and he strummed it while singing of young lovers whose passion was destined to remain unrequited due to the actions of a cruel king. Again I watched Aine, and once more she was captivated, her full attention on him as he sang the haunting melody.

Later as we lay on pallets in my old bedroom, Laoidheach whispered, "Why didn't you tell me you had a sister like Aine?"

There would be trouble. "Shut up and go to sleep."

Chapter 8
Spirits of Twilight

L aoidheach still slept when my father and I left the following morning. The new faint light returned and we walked to his fields where men anticipated the coming of sunlight and worked to prepare his ground for planting.

Afterwards we returned home to find Laoidheach slumped outside on a bench, elbows on his knees, chin in his hands.

I strolled over to stand beside him. "Why so glum?"

He straightened with a baleful expression on his face. "She won't speak to me."

"What's that?"

"Aine refused to speak to me."

My father snorted and strode into the house.

I knew my friend only too well and lowered my voice. "So, what suggestive thing did you say to her?"

"Suggestive? I only said 'good morning' and that's the truth of it." He shook his head in bewilderment. "I said good morning to her, but she turned up her nose at me," he flipped his hand outwardly, "and walked out the door without saying a word."

Two village women strolled past, stopped and bowed to me. I bowed in return, offering blessings. "May Brigid smile upon you and your homes. May she keep you and yours safe during these dark times."

They curtsied. "Thank you sir," one replied, while the other said, "And may the gods bless you as well," and they went on their way.

My thoughts returned to Laoidheach. Aine's behavior was baffling. She had been immediately attracted to him and only the night before clapped gaily during his entertainment. I stroked my chin as I thought it over. "You are certain there wasn't more to it?"

"That's all there was, and…" His eyes glinted as he pointed an accusing finger toward me. "Just a moment. What did you tell her about me?"

I grinned. "I told her I would give you a good thumping if you attempted to trifle with her."

"Trifle with her? Ossian, you know full well I would never…" He cleared his throat and squirmed on the bench. "Well yes, I suppose I have trifled with a few women now and again, but I would never consider such a thing with my future wife."

His words swirled through the air, entered my ears and my mouth fell open. "Your wife?! Are you daft? You only met Aine yesterday."

He rose from the bench, nose lifted, an indignant expression covering his face. "That makes no difference. If Aine will have me, she shall become my wife. Provided your father approves, of course."

I had seen Laoidheach animated over women many times but never had I seen him like this. He wished to marry Aine? Now I needed to sit on the bench so I elbowed him aside and plopped down.

"I realize she is sixteen years," he continued, "but many girls marry much younger. Besides, being four years her elder I will bring maturity and stability to our marriage, don't you see? So now, with your father's permission, there remains but one problem."

"That being?"

"She loathes me. Move aside."

I scooted to the end of the bench and he sat beside me. He then resumed his previous unhappy position, chin in hands.

My eyes reached out through the morning gloom. Nearby cottages appeared little more than vague shadows. Perhaps it was the grayness of the morning but my first thoughts of my friend and Aine marrying saddened me. It was an altogether selfish sentiment, for I realized that my relationship with them would forever change. Yet there was rightness about the feel of it I could not deny. A small smile crossed my lips; both were like a butterfly that alights upon your fingertip, an ethereal, innocent visitor that instills joy and beauty inside your heart. Perhaps the gods long ago destined they should meet and thereafter float within the world of butterflies side by side.

A dimly seen movement caught my attention. It was Aine flitting like an unswerving arrow towards our home. I rose and greeted her with a "Good morning," but she ignored me as she walked through the door and slammed it behind her.

Laoidheach groaned. "I told you."

* * *

Sparks swirled, darted and joined with the smoke rising above the fire blazing before the stone altar. It was here within the Sacred Grove, as a youth, I spent countless days with my father. This night it served my purposes as an open-air temple.

Four days had passed since my arrival at Rath Raithleann, during which time I had neglected my responsibilities toward my dead friends. My eyes closed as I stood before the fire; arms spread wide, palms upward, I intoned a prayer for the dead of Dún Ailinne.

> Within the still darkness,
> Spirits of the lost,
> Begging release,
> Seeking the eternal.

> O Aed, Lord of the Underworld,
> Souls of Dún Ailinne,
> Send them on their way,
> Free them for all time.

> By your gracious will,
> Paradise awaits them,
> Upon a distant shore,
> Beyond the western sea.

My prayer was just begun, though I intended it for others with no thought of becoming a part of it myself. The fire's smoke dissipated and the salty aroma of the sea filled my nostrils. I staggered to regain my balance as the ground beneath me shifted and sloped down to my right. Pitch-blackness prevailed while, again to my right, was the sound of waves washing upon an unknown shore.

It was a place I knew, a place told of in old stories, a place undefined by 'where,' but rather by 'when;' it was a place of waiting, a place of the dead. How or why I arrived there I could not imagine.

A shuddering moan broke the stillness and an ethereal green image shimmered before me only to whisk away and disappear into the distance. Spine-tingling shrieks, one atop the other, filled the air while I sensed more than saw spirit creatures churning within the darkness; indefinite forms not human, but which at one time might have been human. I cringed at the sights and sounds of those terrible dead things and trembled as unseen wings fluttered and swished overhead.

The ghastly essence within the distressful, lonely setting caused me to consider that perhaps I was merely the dupe of my own fantastic dream. I slapped my face hard, once—twice, but no. Conceivably I stood amid the reality of an implausible unreality, but it was no dream.

The haunting, dreadful sounds and motion ceased as unseen cymbals crashed, the reverberation emanating from I knew not where! Then ensued the deep throbbing of a drum—a double beat like the pounding of a man's heart, thrum-thrum, thrum-thrum...

My eyes were temporarily blinded as two torches flared on the beach a mere five paces before me. Now I could see that a single-masted ship lay there nosed against the sand, sail furled, a gangplank extended to the shore. Two more torches blazed and then two more, two more, and on and on to form opposing parallel lines that ended atop a high dune on my left. It was a flame-lit corridor—but for who, or what?

The drumming continued and the head and shoulders of a hooded form appeared within the corridor above the top of the dune. The robed figure crested the rise and came on, proceeding down the corridor while behind it another individual arose, followed by another, and then another. A seemingly endless, single-file line of robed men marched in lock-step down the slope toward the ship, their paces keeping cadence with the sound of the drum; thrum-thrum, thrum-thrum, step-step, step-step...

I knew them, although how I knew I cannot say—the ghosts of the dead of Dún Ailinne. White spirit faces frozen like those of granite statues were framed within the hoods of their robes. It was with relief and gladness that I could not recognize the stone-like faces, for I did not wish to.

The line progressed before me and each figure, in turn, walked up the ship's gangplank and disappeared aboard. At last the final figure mounted the top of the dune and there could be no mistaking it—Master Tóla.

My eyes held him as he followed the others down the dune and I waited in breathless anticipation until he came abreast of me. I called out to him, "Master Tóla!"

The throbbing of the drum stopped, as did the procession of the dead. He turned to me with unseeing eyes. His was the face I dearly remembered, though immobile like the others, as if graven in the rarest alabaster.

His lips did not move though he answered in his familiar voice. "What's that? Did someone call to me?"

"Yes, Master. It is Ossian."

"You say so? Should I know you?"

"Of course. I am or was your student."

"I'm so very sorry. I do not recall."

He did not recall? The strangeness of it held my tongue at bay.

He continued, "Are you the Druid who called for the ship lying there? If so, we whole-heartedly thank you. We have been waiting for it within this darkness for ever so long."

It was with a sense of shame at my negligence that I replied, "My apologies. I should have prayed for your deliverance much sooner. Only now have I performed the sacred ceremony that might bring you final release. Since the very night of your...that is...um...since the night of the attack my thoughts were for your comfort and peace."

"Your kind thoughts are appreciated. However, seek neither comfort nor respite within these halls of the dead, for you will find none here. Such bliss may only be found among the Golden Ones on the shores of Tír na nÓg. There by the aegis of the Lordly Ones all become young for all time."

"Yes, Master, of course. Paradise awaits you on the shores of Tír na nÓg. Before you sail there, I would that you know that plans are already underway to bring vengeance against those who struck Dún Ailinne."

"That may very well be, though vengeance holds no value to me. The world of the living embraces no actuality for the dead. It is the world of what was and might have been; a dream world that died with us. For the moment we of Dún Ailinne exist between worlds, only within the here and now on this lonely strand beside this sea. Yon ship waits to transport us all to our final reality, to the islands of Tír na nÓg—all save two still held within the dream."

"Yes, Master. All save two. I am one of them, the other being the bard Laoidheach. Do you not remember our final night together upon Knockaulin?"

"Again I am very sorry, but no. I have forgotten that dream if such there ever was."

"It is said that those at Tír na nÓg well remember the living and await their arrival."

"Yes? Perhaps you are right, but that is not the case here." He bowed before me. "Your pardon. I must go; the ship waits. May the gods' blessings be upon you, Druid."

I bowed in return. "And you, Master Tóla."

Cymbals again crashed and the drumming recommenced. The Master turned away as the procession resumed shuffling toward the beach. My eyes followed him until he disappeared aboard the ship. Then the gangplank was pulled aboard by unseen hands, and the ship backed away from the shore to be swallowed by the night.

All became silent as the throbbing of the drums ceased and the echoes died away. The torches atop the dune wavered and went dark as became the case for all the others, as two by two in line toward the beach they flared and winked out.

Blackness returned as did the moans and shrieks, but the earth once more shifted below my feet and I staggered to keep pace with the motion. My head swam as the fresh aroma of the sea was replaced by acrid smoke. Before me sparks swam in the night sky above my fire within the Sacred Grove.

I swayed and fell to the ground, gratified by the clean smell of the earth as my fingers grasped the firmness of it. I smiled as I lay there. My remarkable encounter with the Underworld had been a beneficent gift from the Lordly Ones and I thanked them for their revelation and generousity. Peace filled me knowing all would be well with Master Tóla and my Dún Ailinne friends. Exhausted sleep found me.

* * *

I awoke to the grayness of the morning. Grass and leaves clung to my robe; my muscles were stiff after a night spent sleeping on the ground and they complained as I sat up. My hands scrubbed my face to wash the sleep from it.

A sense of being watched consumed me and I spun around to discover Aine sitting on the nearby bench, her hands clasped in her lap.

"Pardon me, brother, for disturbing you." The anxious expression on her face arrested my attention. "You've been here the entire night and…so if…if this isn't a good time we can speak later."

I yawned and stretched; my stiff legs tingled as I extended them before me, kicking leaves. "No, you aren't disturbing me." Visions from the night before attempted to creep into my thoughts and I shook my head to clear them away.

A smile formed on my lips as I absorbed her poise. Her one-piece green and white floral dress covered her trim figure from her throat to the tops of her small leather shoes. "You wish to discuss Laoidheach?"

Her face flamed and she nodded. "Are my feelings toward him so obvious then?"

"I wouldn't—"

Her hand flew to her mouth, covering it in alarm. "They must be since you knew my thoughts without asking! It's shameless I am. What must he think of me?"

"He's—"

"And don't you make excuses for him!" She extended her hand forward, demanding silence. "He's a man with his own thoughts so don't you tell me that he hasn't mentioned me."

Puzzled, I tried again. "Yes, of course he has, but—"

"He's a man who likes women and has much to say about them, I'm thinking. Women have a way of knowing such things about men. Hah!" She wagged a knowing finger at me. "You men think you're so smart. Let me tell you, brother. Men have few secrets that women can't see through, and you can rely upon it."

I remained confused. What had I done to deserve such a lecture? "I thought you wanted me to tell you about Laoidheach."

"And what have you just now been doing?" Her hands returned to her lap and she resumed her prim pose.

I grinned. "Did I mention that his grandmother was a changeling child?"

An incredulous smile crept across her face as the wonder of it dawned upon her. "He is? I mean, she was?" She leaned forward, eager to hear more. "Tell me."

She would want to know everything so I laid on my back, clasped my hands behind my head and stared upwards into the crowns of the tall trees. There was little I knew about Laoidheach's life before his arrival at Dún Ailinne. Much I knew though little I would share with her about his activities after he arrived.

"Well?" she persisted.

I told her about his father and mother, his training as a bard, and repeated his claim that he was descended from the Fire God, Belimawr.

"Oh, it must be true!" she exclaimed. "That explains everything about him, don't you see? He is so handsome with his long, golden hair—and he's very tall, like you and father. Just think of it, his grace, charm, wit and magical voice—only the gods could have given him so much. It is no wonder so many women have loved him."

Now how was it she knew about the women? There are times when it is best to remain silent and I determined this was one of them.

I realized that my silence had become my undoing when she said, "Aha! I knew it! Your lack of words tell me I am right. Not that any of those women matter now, for they are all in his past. His future is all I care about."

I sat up again. "His future? And just why is it you care about his future?"

She turned up her nose and peered down at me. "Because I'm in love with him and shall become his wife. He simply doesn't know it yet."

"I should say he doesn't know it! And I must also say that for a girl who wants to marry a man, you've treated him rudely."

"What would you have me do, fawn all over him like a little girl? Long ago you told me to learn the ways of women from Fainche, may the gods continue to rest her soul. Well learn I did, so don't you be telling me how to treat a man!"

Whether the ways of women were blessed or cursed by the gods I could not say, though I could never make sense of them. "So, you are rude to Laoidheach because you want to marry him?"

Her eyes rolled and she shook her head as if she must explain a simple thing to an idiot. "I will not be like the other girls he has known and cast aside. Men desire most that which they cannot have. When the proper time comes Laoidheach will realize he wants and loves me above all others. Soon after we will be wed."

It was not my place to tell her Laoidheach already loved her and had his own marriage plan. Little it mattered. He would have inevitably become ensnared within her sly trap anyway.

"You do not ask my blessing on your marriage?"

"Of course not. You love us both and would not wish ill against either of us. Besides, you approve of the idea of our marriage, do you not?"

"Of course I approve of it. Come," I rose with a smile and offered her my hand. "We will walk back to our home. I will fill my empty stomach while you continue to taunt Laoidheach."

* * *

"How many warriors have you?"

"Eleven mounted and twenty-four men afoot," I replied to my father's question.

Candles burned low as Laoidheach, my father and I gathered about a map spread flat on the surface of the table. Aine sat quietly in a far corner knitting, her work lighted by a low flame within the hearth. From time to time my friend's eyes darted across the room towards her.

"It's a small army you have to begin a war." My father relaxed in his chair and sipped wine from a copper mug. "Still, King

Domhnall was reluctant to allow more men to leave the village during these troubled times."

"Aye, but those who volunteered are good men all." My eyes moved from the map to meet his. "I will gather more as we travel the country. It was generous of King Domhnall to provide us with rations."

"Yes, but you must forage for your own after they are gone. Our granaries here are still plentifully stocked. Only by carefully allocating the stores to our people will they barely meet our village's needs before another crop comes in; provided the Dagda's message was correct that the darkness will prevail for nine months."

"You doubt it?"

"Of course not. During the three weeks since you arrived here we can already see considerable improvement. In only three more months, and perhaps sooner, the sun should reappear."

"We may only pray that it might be sooner. The fields have remained fallow these many months. Now, men must turn to removing most of the fallen ash before planting can begin. Much work will be needed."

"That is true." He pointed to the map. "So, you travel north to strike first at Kilcullen?"

I rose and stood silently for a moment. "Kilcullen? No. Sure, it was from there that the attack fell upon Dún Ailinne, but I have no desire to return there. No, not to the pain and bitterness I left there, at least not right away."

Worry showed on his face. "A traveler visited the village today. He spoke of widespread depredations against us. In addition to Dún Ailinne, Christian zealots are razing important shrines across the entire country. I fear you face a general uprising, my son."

"Then the sooner we face it the better." My hand slapped the tabletop. "We leave on the morrow with but a single thought in mind; to drive the Christians back and while so doing revenge those who have fallen! By the will of the Lordly Ones, we shall succeed."

* * *

Villagers gathered 'round as I walked down the column of twos speaking words of encouragement to each man. Laoidheach and I would lead the march aboard our horses, followed by the men on foot. Mounted warriors and pack animals would bring up the rear.

Amid the bustle, Aine emerged from the crowd and ran to stand beside Laoidheach where he sat astride his horse. Her small, tear-streaked face turned upwards and she waggled a finger at him. "Don't you go about getting yourself killed. Come home to me. Come home soon!"

Chapter 9
Blood for Blood

𝕴 positioned the wolf headdress upon my head as I stood on the ridge crest. The shouting warriors in the mist-shrouded meadow below were anxious for a fight. More than two hundred jeering men massed in two solid ranks, their distant insults sweeping uphill toward us. Behind them stood a Christian church and, nearby, a small village.

During the past month I had seen their like in nine other Christian villages. No doubt some of the men had experienced more than one battle, but regardless, they were farmers, not proper warriors. The majority wore no armor and a few carried nothing more than sharpened wooden spears.

A black-robed priest waved a crucifix on high as he paraded back and forth before them shouting encouragement, but why would he not? My men stood in a single row behind me and the priest could see we were a small force.

I leaned upon the death's head staff as my eyes roved beyond the enemy to a shadowy woodland in the background. There was no sign of movement. The foolish priest and his followers had no concept of the ruthlessness of the battle that would soon consume them. The Christians determined the manner in which this war would be fought by massacring every living soul at Dún Ailinne. As was the case in the nine previous villages, repayment would be in kind.

Fifty-three confident warriors afoot waited behind me, men of Rath Raithleann and villages nearby. They were volunteers all, not enough to wage a major war but well armed and sufficient in number to prick Christian skins.

Laoidheach looked to my black-painted face, a question in his eyes. At my nod he struck the leather-clad drum a single beat, paused, and then began a slow rhythmic pounding that grew in volume and echoed within the valley below.

"Remember lads," I called out to the men over the throbbing of the drum, "'quick' is the word, and fight as a team! Watch the backs of those around you. Fight to bring honor upon yourselves and your tribe. Fight to defend the almighty Lords of the Sidhe. By the time this day has ended only heroes will be left standing." Bitterness filled my heart and rang forth in my wild cry, "For the glory of Fea, Nemon and Badbh; in the mighty name of Macha— death to all Christian priests and those who stand with them!"

The men roared as one and my staff waved them forward. Stepping in cadence with Laoidheach's drumbeat I led them down the slope towards our enemies. At fifty paces from the Christians' front rank I stopped and waved my archers forward.

Twenty-four bowmen stepped to the fore, knelt and unleashed a salvo of arrows that rained down upon our foes. In the manner of the veteran warriors that they were, they reloaded, aimed and released a second flight. My warriors began shouting their own taunts as Christians fell back in disarray under a relentless shower of arrows. Now and again one of our foes was struck and fell, though whether wounded or killed I knew not.

At my nod Laoidheach picked up the cadence on the drum until it became a steady roar. My twenty-nine mounted warriors erupted from the distant woodland accompanied by eight chariots. Feral screams filled the air as they raced toward the rear of the enemy's left flank, which melted away before the ferocious onslaught. Horses reared, their hooves flailing the air while the swords of their riders struck the Christians down.

Chariots, wheels stirring great clouds of dust, swept among the Christian ranks, their armored passengers hurling iron-tipped javelins among the enemy with deadly accuracy. What but moments before had been a solid front of opposition dissolved into individual frenzied groups swirling about to face riders who slashed at them from every side.

Again I lifted my staff high, motioned my warriors forward, and we went among them with the sacred names of the gods escaping our lips. The battle was won before it began. Christians by the dozens dropped their weapons and fled toward the false safety of their church and village. My men afoot swarmed and battered those few who stood firm while mounted warriors pursued and hacked down every man who would flee.

I strolled unarmed and unconcerned among the fighting as stout men of both sides grunted, cursed, bled and died about me. Distinct images—a raised shield, a brawny arm holding a sword high, a rearing horse, arrows hanging suspended against the gray sky.

The Christian priest was among the fallen. I stood above him as he gasped away the waning moments of his life, his profane blood corrupting Mother Earth's hallowed soil. Grasping fingers clawed toward a small golden crucifix lying where he had dropped it just beyond the abilities of his feeble reach. His pleading eyes locked onto mine.

The crucifix was no larger than my finger, but solid gold it was and it would join the growing pile of plunder that would purchase provisions for my men. The trinket quickly found its way into the leather purse at my belt and I strode away from the priest as light left his face forever.

The fighting continued until not a Christian was left standing. My men walked among the fallen ensuring that none still breathed. Afterwards they gathered about me, some grim, others holding expectant grins on their battle-grimed faces.

"Bring our wounded there," I pointed to a tree, "and I will treat them. You there," I nodded to a young warrior, "do you hurry back up the hill and bring down my bundle, for there are medicines and bandages in it."

I rubbed the tension and tiredness from my eyes before continuing. "The rest of you—burn the church and make a good job of it." I pointed to one of men. "Aimhirghin knows this village well and he tells me that a few of its people remain loyal to the Lordly Ones. Oak-leaf wreaths hang upon their doors. Remember that, for they must not be molested or disturbed in any way. As for everything else in the village, it is yours. Take what you will."

I walked toward the tree to serve the wounded; my heart long since hardened against that which would befall Christians within the village. As was custom, the children would come to no harm, though all males capable of wielding a sword would be killed. As for the fate of the women, few if any would be killed, but they knelt before priests and I regarded them no higher than their men.

* * *

The merchant stood in the back of his open wagon and heaved a bag of barley to the ground atop a gathering pile. Behind him the rolling grasslands of the midlands stretched into the distance. Our supplies were low and I had anxiously anticipated his arrival at our camp. Word of our mission and victories spread across the country. During the past month ten to twenty new warriors arrived every day and my small army had swollen to six hundred fighting men.

He glanced down at me as he reached for another bag. "I'm telling you, sir, it's not easy finding folk willing to sell their stores in these hard times. Some kings are selling off everything in their granaries at high prices. It's a crying shame what they're doing if you ask me."

I leaned against his wagon, my arm propped atop a wheel. "So kings enrich themselves while their people starve?"

"Right you are, sir. Such treatment of their people is inhuman, I say."

My eyes roved from the man to the meadow in the background where there was stirring within our camp. "Inhuman? I think not. Humans come in many forms and are capable of many things, good and bad."

I pointed into the wagon. "What are those boxes?"

"Empty wine bottles, sir. Now as I was saying, and you can mark my words. Cruel kings seal their own fates. In the end a king serves at the will of his people. The people rise up against tyrants and fools. Such will be the case now, I'm thinking."

"Maybe, maybe…but if so, it will be too late to do any good." I nodded toward the bags. "You guarantee the barley is fresh, now?"

"Fresh?" He was reaching down for another bag but stood up and stuck a thumb in his chest. "You think I would cheat you? Of course it's fresh and you'll find none better."

"We will see."

"You'll find it to your taste well enough." He grabbed a bag and tossed it on top of the others. "Now, what did you mean when you said it will be too late for the people to rise?"

I shrugged. "Even during times of desperation an uprising requires organization, and it is the nature of people to act slowly. Food is needed now, today. Many will starve before the people finally rise."

"Aye," he nodded, "on that I agree, sir. Indeed I do, though it's a sad thing that."

Though outwardly I showed little interest in the discussion, in truth my heart sank. While I fought Christians, a new, perhaps wider war was beginning; the war King Túathal Máelgarb greatly feared—war to acquire food.

"Only the dead have seen the end of the war," I murmured.

"What's that, sir?"

"Nothing." I shook my head to drive away memories. "I merely quoted Plato."

"Plato?"

"No matter. Listen carefully. We've heard rumors that Christians have formed a large force and plan to move against us. Do you know of it?"

The merchant's wide eyes were innocent. "I'm sorry, Wise One, I am a simple trader and know little of such important things."

No doubt my warriors could get the truth out of the man, but I opened my purse, removed a silver coin and tossed it to him. "Now perhaps you remember something of the Christians' movements?"

He grinned. "Yes sir, now that I think on it I believe I do. I heard they've put together near a thousand warriors and are moving this way even as we speak. I should think that in no more than a fortnight," he pointed toward the north, "they'll be cresting yon ridge."

My hand absently tapped the wagon wheel as I considered his news. It matched what I had heard from other sources. Although my forces had grown considerably, we would still be outmatched by the Christians and this time we would face more than farmers.

"Excuse me, sir." The trader motioned toward the grain. "I delivered the fifty bags of barley and, if it's all the same to you, sir, I would be taking my pay and heading off." He pointed to the west. "As you can see, there be storm clouds gathering and I would make a start towards home before the rains arrive."

"Certainly," I threw my thumb over my shoulder, "go to the first tent and see the man there. He'll see to it you're paid."

"Thank you sir, I'll be doing that very thing. Before I go, would you be wanting to order more supplies?"

"Aye, that I would. Deliver us fifty bags of rye, twenty barons of beef, twenty smoked mutton shoulders and hams, and twenty barrels of ale. Also toss in all the vegetables and fruit you can fit aboard. Have all that here a week from today."

The merchant scowled. "That I'll do, sir, but be warned prices are going up and I can't guarantee what it'll cost ye. Now would there be anything more? Salt, seasonings, wine, oil, anything of the like?"

I had been watching the skies and he was correct: Rain was coming for sure. His mention of oil while I was thinking of rain brought a small smile to my face. "Oil you say? What manner of oil?"

"Ach, sir, it be the finest grade of flaxseed oil. It's good for cooking of course, but if you're thinking of lighting, it burns with a bright flame and will serve you well for the purpose. Allow me to say too that I've a fine stock of wine—"

"No. No wine, thank you."

From behind me a woman's voice whispered, "Oil, Ossian, oil. Remember Master Tóla's manuscript, the one about Alexander the Great."

I whirled about—but no one was there.

"Remember," the voice whispered again.

Once more I spun around. The merchant seemed to be paying me no mind and I asked, "Did you just now hear a voice? A whisper?"

He cocked an eyebrow. "A whisper? No sir, can't say as I did."

"That is very odd. I heard it clearly."

"If you say so, sir." His uncertain nod said more than his words.

There was no doubt I heard it—a woman's voice but how could that be? Who whispered? What did she mean? I thought for a moment and the importance of her message came to me along with the remembrance of the manuscript. It contained ancient knowledge told within a story of Alexander the Great and the Persians. Of course! If that knowledge could be properly brought against our enemies, the shock might even the odds and turn the tide of the coming battle in our favor.

I turned around toward the spirit voice and whispered, "Thank you."

The decisive outcome of the battle might well depend upon this merchant, and I pointed into his wagon. "Would you be so good as to hand me one of those empty wine bottles?

"The man watched me, a question in his eyes. "Why, of course, sir."

He handed me the bottle and I hefted it in my hand. It was made as baked pottery, though it felt light enough. I hurled it as far as I could, where it fell and shattered upon the ground.

"Sir, I must say!" He was red in the face. "Those bottles cost money, you know!"

"Of course they do, and I will pay you for that one. Now, do you have pine tar at your disposal?"

He was confused. "Pine tar? Yes, that is, I know where I can acquire it."

"Good man. I wish to order one small keg of pine tar, two barrels of your flaxseed oil and one thousand wine bottles."

"Very good sir! I can assure you I will deliver some of the finest wine—"

"No. Not wine. Only the bottles."

He stared at me as if he was now firmly convinced that I was dim-witted. "You want one thousand empty wine bottles, sir?"

"Yes. The bottles along with all the other items we've discussed. Can you deliver all those things here by next week?"

It would be understandable if he still questioned my sanity but I could see his mind swirling and he came through like a champion. "Yes sir! Absolutely sir, though it will require several trips." His lips turned down in a scowl. "These be troubled times so I shall need payment in advance."

"You may have ten percent of the payment before you leave here. The remainder you will receive upon delivery."

"You do not trust me."

"As you say, I do not trust these troubled times or the sense of a man who would travel alone in a wagon, his purse stuffed with gold."

"As you say, sir. You understand that all this special…well, my regular customers will suffer a bit, don't you see, and I'll—"

The cost of such things remained a mystery to me but much looted gold, silver and similar treasures resided in our treasury. I had a good man who would see to proper payment. "Say no more. You will receive special compensation."

Chapter 10
The Battle of Lough Derg

My soft leather shoes swished through the wet grass as I walked from camp towards a small nearby mound. Behind me men were donning armor, saddling horses, preparing for the fight of their lives. Hidden behind a wall of morning fog swirling across the prairies from Lough Derg, warriors in the enemy camp would be doing much the same while hearing the words of Christian priests speaking of their god.

I climbed the mound to its crest and shivered slightly in the cold, damp air. Overhead, misshapen skeletal branches of a long-dead tree jutted into the gray sky. Face upward, arms spread wide, I offered up prayers to the gods for their aid and protection during the coming battle.

It was while I was standing just so, that amid a fluttering of wings, a carrion crow lit upon a limb immediately above my head. The branch gently swayed under its weight. I could have reached up and touched it.

The crow cocked its head in the manner of birds and squawked, "So Druid. Do you prepare a feast for me or shall you become a part of it?"

Glaring black eyes and the raucous voice sent a chill down my spine and struck me mute. My outstretched arms fell to my side and I stood there, spellbound.

"What say you, foolish man? Are you too feeble-minded to speak?"

Calling upon the gods for their aid and protection is a natural thing but to have them magically appear in such a form no man would expect. Within the manifold gods and goddesses this one I knew on sight; it was said she appeared in many guises, including the one roosting before me silhouetted against the gloomy sky, her crow aspect. I knew her as the Morrigan, as well as who and what she was. Mór Rígan, mighty Queen of the Sidhe, descended from the Tuatha Dé Danann themselves—goddess of war, life and death. Though awed by her appearance I was also wary of her.

Well known for her wrath, she fed upon the souls of the dead. I tried to wipe the horror of such things from my mind, swallowed hard and bowed before her. "Pardon me. Yes My Queen, of course I can speak. Your presence here is an unexpected honor."

"Hmm, yes. But, you haven't answered my question."

A wind gust ruffled her feathers while I gathered my wits at her miraculous arrival. "As for your question, it shall be answered soon enough." I pointed across the rolling grasslands where the fog was lifting. "Look for yourself. There is stirring within the enemy's camp. Already they plan to launch their attack."

"You are outmanned, Ossian, two of theirs for one of yours. Are you prepared for that?"

"You know my name, My Queen?"

She sat on her branch and ignored my foolish question. Of course the goddess knew my name and I flushed with embarrassment for asking.

I swiveled my head around for my neck grew stiff from staring up at her. "I finalized my battle plan last night. We intend to surprise the Christians with new weapons. My most seasoned warriors offered their thoughts and all believe we have at least a chance to succeed despite the odds."

Her talons gripped the branch and it bounced a bit as she sidled back and forth along it. "So, you understood the meaning behind my message, eh?"

"Yes, we…wait. I see. Yours was the voice that whispered in my ear while I spoke to the merchant."

"And who else's would it have been?"

New confidence filled me. The Morrigan, goddess of war, was guiding me. "I sincerely thank you for planting the seed for the idea in my ear."

"Your gods stand beside those who uphold them. Meanwhile, Druid, you may keep your thanks until after you have won the battle...if you win it." Her wings rustled and without another word she took flight. My eyes followed her until she disappeared in the gray western sky.

* * *

Laoidheach and I, eyes upon the ground, picked a cautious path as we slowly rode forward through the late morning gloom to meet the robed priest and armored warrior who cantered toward us from the Christians' massed ranks. Our horses danced as we reined them in at a distance of three paces from our adversaries.

The priest stared at us as though we had emerged from the Underworld. We were naked, our bodies painted black. I wore the wolf's headdress and carried the death's head staff.

He cocked an eyebrow and sneered. "So, pagan," he gestured towards me with an open hand, "I expect to meet a worthy adversary and find only a heathen. I should have known you would appear as such after the manner in which you pillaged defenseless villages."

His insults were expected and I replied in kind. "And you are precisely what I expected, priest—an arrogant bastard like those who massacred our innocents at Dún Ailinne. Say your piece and be on your way. We have many Christians to kill this day and you waste my time."

The warrior stiffened, his hand reached for his sword. "Hold your tongue you blasphemous horse turd or your head will come off here and now."

The priest waved him to be silent. "Druid, God in His infinite majesty may yet grant your warriors mercy. I wished to meet with you and share His message. Go among your men, tell them to recant their pagan ways, tell them that if they will throw away their weapons and come to the One True God, then today their lives will be spared. As for you, well…you understand there can be no mercy for you and," he nodded toward Laoidheach, "your friend there."

A yellowish glob splattered on the priest's shoulder and he almost gagged as he sputtered, "Upon my word!"

Circling above was a single carrion crow. I laughed aloud. "Oh ho, priest, how do you like the mercy of my gods?"

My attention turned to the warrior. Was there doubt in his eyes? "What say you now, big man? You know an omen when you see it, do you not? Go back and tell all your warriors of it if you dare!" I pointed to the sky. "See the Morrigan above. She shits on your priest and his god. The goddess of death waits there to feast upon your corpse. The gods have ordained this day is lost to you, and well you know it. I urge you all to leave while you still can."

Fury filled the warrior's eyes. "I know foolish talk when I hear it, Druid. I'm done with you and your filthy insults. Prepare for your death!"

They wheeled their horses and trotted back toward their men. I glanced upwards once again and winked. The importance of signs from the gods was well known to me, as well as an understanding of how they might be perceived by common men standing in the ranks. Doubt would fill superstitious Christian hearts as word of the Morrigan's omen swept among them. My eyes met those of Laoidheach and, despite the coming battle, we both laughed aloud.

* * *

Laoidheach stood beside me, an ornate carved cattle horn hung by a cord against his chest. To his right three eager lads waited behind tall, leather-clad drums.

At my nod he swirled a hand high with a flourish and then dropped it to point to the drummers. A single unified beat thrummed once across the wide-open landscape.

The drummer's signal sent one hundred selected archers forward to form a single line at three-pace intervals. Bows and quivers filled with arrows were in their hands, bulky leather bags draped from their shoulders. Behind the archers stood fifty warriors equally distributed along the line. The fifty held burning torches.

A grim smile touched my face, the brightening of midday adding to the spectacle that unfolded to my right. Colorful banners streamed throughout the throng as my almost two hundred mounted warriors and chariots trotted their horses' forward en-masse and then held them in check fifty paces behind the line of archers. Further back and painted for battle, four hundred warriors chanted, shrieked and waved their tribal flags on high.

To my front an equally colorful mass of shouting Christians advanced towards us across the wide-open meadow, their mounted warriors in the lead. Earlier my scouts reported the Christian army consisted of twelve hundred men, perhaps a few more. These would be no mere farmers we faced this day—they were well-armed, well-armored and well-led warriors.

My experienced war council had assured me this battle would consist of little sophistication. Knowledge I had gained through years of studying traditional methods of warfare supported their opinions. The open landscape offered nowhere to hide enveloping forces and since we were badly outnumbered the Christians would see no reason to divide their large army for feinting maneuvers. They would simply hurl their vastly superior numbers directly at our front and bludgeon us into the ground.

Our battle plan was devised accordingly. Now it would be tested as our long, thin line of archers offered an obvious target. Nervous sweat ran down my still naked body etching streaks through the black paint.

Horns blew and cymbals crashed among the Christian ranks a quarter of a mile to our front. It was beginning.

* * *

I muttered last prayers to the Lordly Ones knowing as I did the Christians would be offering up prayers to their god as well. Whether men or gods would decide the battle I could not say with surety, but only the corpses of warriors would litter the field at the end of the day. There was no time to worry that my own might lie among them.

Distant horns blew again. Mounted warriors massed into a compact horde of at least three hundred riders and chariots cantered forward from the Christian ranks. They gained speed until reaching a full gallop as on they came in a solid wave toward my thin line of archers.

I nodded to Laoidheach, who removed the horn from around his neck, placed it to his lips and blasted out a single long burst. Without thought I took a few steps forward, my eyes locked upon my bowmen.

Upon hearing Laoidheach's signal, archers dropped their unwieldy leather bags, knelt, nocked arrows in their bows and waited. The Christian riders came on, more than a thousand hooves pounding the ground like rolling thunder, showering dusty clouds and clods of earth into the air. Banners streamed against the gray sky, swords swirled high as on and on they raced.

I wondered at the riders' horror when they reached our carefully sown field of iron caltrops. For some their thoughts would be brief as they were thrown from the backs of their falling, screaming horses and crushed underfoot by those coming on from behind.

Pandemonium broke out among the Christian ranks as more horses and riders fell while those following smashed into one another as they slowed to avoid their fallen comrades and the sharp-spiked caltrops. The momentum of the enemy's charge was broken though they did not stop. The vast majority of Christian riders kept coming but much slower than before.

My bowmen required no order to begin unleashing their arrows. They were told beforehand to shoot as soon as the horsemen came within range. Now hundreds of arrows were flying through the air as the archers lofted arrow after arrow into the massed riders. The steady deluge of iron-tipped missiles had little effect on the armored enemy so onward they rode, now at little more than a walking pace like a deadly, indomitable wall of iron.

Again I nodded to Laoidheach and again he blew the signal horn. Archers dropped their bows and opened leather bundles. Each man withdrew a wine bottle filled with flaxseed oil containing a linen fuse and sealed with pine tar. The fifty men bearing torches stepped forward to within arm's reach of the archers.

My eyes fixed upon the scene, gauging distances. I raised the death's head staff and Laoidheach blew his horn. Bowmen lit linen fuses on the torches, turned and hurled their flaring firebombs among the enemy's tight-packed ranks.

The resulting terror defied description—one hundred fragile bottles shattering against armor, flaming oil showering amid horses and riders, screams of animals and men filling the air. I swung the staff above my head again and another one hundred firebombs lobbed through the air to sow fiery ruin among the enemy.

Never had I expected to witness such a scene of chaos and pain—flaming horses bucking, blazing men falling, dreadful wails mingling to form a single mournful moan. Those who escaped the fire raced to the rear, many of those falling as once again they encountered the caltrops. How many were down? Half perhaps? No, more—two-thirds, no less than two hundred men.

Laoidheach stood transfixed, his mouth agape. I nudged him with my elbow and then pointed to the horn. He spun around, giving it three long blasts.

Archers scattered as our mounted warriors raced forward yelling wildly, falling upon the disorderly remnants of the enemy's riders, most of who were on the ground, burned, injured or wounded. Our warriors went among them, slashing Christians down. I winced when a few of our own horses stepped upon caltrops but my men began a thorough job of dispatching the entire enemy force, all except the lucky ones riding frantically back toward their own battle line.

My horse was being held for me so I looked back, waved and turned to Laoidheach. "This battle is far from won. Tell your drummers to beat the rally. Later I will want a marching cadence with flourishes. Now we take the fight to them."

Jubilation lit his eyes as Torcán, leader of our mounted troops, cantered across the fields to join me. "Beat 'em for fair, we did. Two hundred dead ones, I'd say, and us with but a few scratches."

A warrior led my horse forward and I took its reins. "We caught them by surprise; that is all. They will be prepared for us now."

He snorted as his heavily bearded face turned toward his warriors still riding among the enemy fallen, searching for signs of life. Injured horses were dispatched alongside their riders. "Aye, that they will, Wise One. They'll be prepared to burn."

"Don't forget they still outman us almost two for one. The Christians are experienced warriors and will not turn their backs on their god so readily as you think. What can we expect from their remaining horsemen?"

Fearlessness and the experience of countless battles etched lines across his face. "Not much, I'm thinking." He pointed toward the distant enemy. "Many who escaped were injured or burned. No doubt a few still have a bit of fight left in them but not enough to make a difference."

So far everything had gone even better than planned but we had only passed the first test of the day with many more to come. "Very well, divide your men and swing around both flanks of their line as planned. They will have to turn portions of their line to face you, so stretch them out, stretch them until their line grows thin. Then hold. Do not strike until you hear my signal."

"Aye," he grinned. "The bastards should have quit when the Morrigan shit on their priest." With a casual wave he turned away to gather his men.

There was much danger in leading my warriors across open ground to assault a far superior force holding a defensive position. In fact, it was altogether likely they would mass their men and counter-attack as we approached. I breathed a prayer that the Morrigan would remain beside us and leaped to the back of my horse.

Laoidheach now held his horse as well and led it to stand beside the drummers, where he offered instructions. The drumming commenced and he gave me a wry smile. "You realize bards aren't trained for fighting battles?"

"You're not dead yet. Besides, you've promised to marry my sister. I'll be holding you to it. Get your ass up on that horse; we've a battle to fight."

Bowmen were gathering their arrows on the field as we rode towards three hundred warriors standing in solid ranks waiting for the call to join the battle. Their wild enthusiasm rocked the earth as we approached.

My horse snorted and pawed the soil as I reined to a stop before them. Two men stepped forward from the cheering ranks. One of the two, a gangling lad, handed me a circular wooden shield plated with a thin coating of bronze; painted a brilliant yellow, in its center a coiled, black serpent displayed bared fangs.

He bobbed his head and then stared at the ground as a bare toe drew a circle in the dust. "The shield be a gift from us all, Wise One, though it was Meallán worked the most on it. Arrs 'll soon be a'fallin' amongst us thick as hailstones, we're thinkin'. The shield there with its sacred serpent, it'll do a proper job of protectin' ye."

During almost two months of fighting I never felt the need for protection other than that offered by the gods. The coming battle would be far different, though, and the youngster was right. "Arrs" would be falling like hail. The shield was cleverly designed for a horseman. I slipped my left forearm through hoops attached to its back, leaving my hand free to grip the reins.

To my left Laoidheach accepted a similarly designed shield. A black crow, wings extended, spanned its surface from edge to edge, the background blazing crimson.

The lad reached forward and took my hand as I leaned down and offered it while saying, "They are fine shields and timely gifts. We thank you both, Meallán, and everyone."

There remained a battle to fight so the death's head swirled and the serpent shield flashed as I held them high and shouted, "The gods are with us this day!" I swiveled around on my horse and pointed the staff towards the distant enemy. "The Christians are there confident in their great numbers and they wait for you. Will you take the fight to them?"

Wild cries and shrieks filled the air as warriors danced, leapt about and waved their tribal flags. Again I raised the staff, twirling it above me, stoking the fires of their battle fury.

"Stay together," I shouted over the din, "fight together and remember—a man who fights alone is a dead man. Listen to the drums, listen for the signal horn and heed your captains' whistles. Now prepare yourselves to stand tall. Show those bastards your hearts; let them feel the keenness of your blades. Captains, prepare your men." I raised a fist in the air. "The Morrigan stands beside us this day. Who among you stands beside her?" Amid renewed cheering I shouted, "Death to the Christians!"

I spun my horse around to the face the enemy and kicked its ribs. Laoidheach pointed to his drummers, who began pounding the marching cadence. Whistles blew and our force moved forward through the scene of the earlier fighting.

* * *

A sense of bitterness followed by an onrush of despair filled me as I walked my horse through fire-ravaged carnage, the horrid stench of it all filling my nostrils, coating my tongue. Charred, grotesque figures of horses and men sprawled all about me, mute testament to the effectiveness of our strategy, stark evidence of its unrepentant brutality.

Since leaving Rath Raithleann I had seen much of fighting, though never slaughter on the scale of this. Now there would be more butchery. Revulsion engulfed me at the knowing of it.

Unbidden, doubt entered my mind. What purpose would be served by going forward with this horrible thing? In the name of the gods, what were we doing?

It was not the time to wonder at the reasons for the fighting so I shook my head to dispel my doubts and concentrated on the action to come. Without question the Christian leader originally intended that his horsemen would ride us down. How would he react now after witnessing the holocaust that consumed them?

My greatest fear as we marched across the fields was the Christians might strike at us first—mass together and charge among us. If so, firebombs could again be used to break up their initial assault. Regardless, they could easily maneuver their men on the open ground and envelop us within their greater numbers. Many Christian warriors would break through. The bombs would prove useless within a swirling melee of close quarters fighting.

We left the enemy dead behind us as we crossed the meadow in line of battle, four hundred men three ranks deep, drums throbbing, flags flying. My thoughts turned from worrying over the plans of my adversary to consider my own. Eight hundred firebombs remained from the original one thousand. Each of Torcán's two hundred horsemen rode with two bombs in a pouch attached to his saddle. Archers still carried four firebombs within their bundles and they had their orders.

My attention rested on the distant Christians, their flags, banners and an occasional crucifix held high. At both ends of the enemy's main line of battle Torcán's horsemen followed orders. The harassed Christians responded exactly as we anticipated. Their flanks turned back at right angles to their front. Battle lines lengthened and thinned as warriors were positioned to stand further apart. Yet even as I watched, Christian horsemen galloped along the lines and their men began falling back, crowding together.

My stomach churned. They were massing for an attack. I motioned to Laoidheach, who waved a signal to his drummers. The drumbeats stopped and the whistles of my captains sounded up and down the line as our advance halted in its tracks three hundred paces from the enemy. Bowmen would be needed to stem the coming assault but before I could turn in my saddle to motion them forward the Christians' strategy became clear. They were forming a defensive box and I was stunned by the stupidity of it.

Laoidheach nudged his mount next to mine. "What's happening?"

"The Christians sealed their fate." My staff pointed forward. "Behold their funeral pyre. Signal Torcán, for I would speak with him."

* * *

Some men are born to fight, pure warriors who relish the call to battle. Such a man was Torcán, the richness of his armor and weapons reflecting his trade. As his horse cantered toward me, his face turned to the sky and he howled like a wolf.

"We have them," he roared. Exhilaration and the lust of his battle fury flashed in his eyes. "The dumb bastards withdrew inside an oven of their own making to be roasted like a side of beef."

"Aye, that's the truth of it," I nodded though again my heart sickened, seeing already the bloodbath to come. No matter, there was nothing to do but press on.

I stood in my stirrups and pointed. "See for yourself; they've created a four-sided box, four men deep on each flank. Instruct your riders to distract the enemy on the three sides facing away from us. Race past them and hurl fire into their ranks while we attack those to our immediate front. Begin upon hearing three blasts from the horn."

His teeth flashed as once more he raised his face skyward and howled. Part hero, part rogue, and fully a fighting man, Torcán leaned back in his saddle and jerked his reins hard—his leather-armored horse reared, its iron-shod hooves flailing the air as it spun about. A broad grin crossed his face and a wave came over his shoulder as he galloped away toward his men.

Four hundred pairs of eyes followed me as I turned my horse and rode back and forth in front of my troops. "Archers—at fifty paces, stop and unleash two flights of arrows into the enemy directly facing us. Afterwards be prepared to throw two firebombs into their ranks as you lead our charge upon them. Save your other two bombs for use against the Christians' other flanks as the opportunity presents itself. The rest of you. Your time has come. Are you ready?"

A roar swept up and down our ranks. Laoidheach motioned for the drums to begin thrumming. I raised the death's head, reined my horse and, with Laoidheach beside me, trotted directly toward the enemy's line. Behind me, my warriors followed and began a chant in time with the drums.

"Morrigan!"

"Morrigan!"

"Morrigan!"

* * *

The Christian crosses fell within a whirlwind of fire. Flaming men spinning 'round and 'round, their sightless eyes staring, open mouths screaming silently—arrows singing, swords, axes and war clubs swinging, javelins flashing, horses racing, firebombs bursting—cheer upon cheer, roar upon roar, horror upon horror.

Just as a bird selects twigs, one here another there, to create its nest, so too my senses selected colored images, sounds, odors and the feel of the battle to weave a singular nest, defined as one by unimaginable anguish.

My horse snorted and danced near the edge of the fighting. An iron-tipped arrow "tinked" against the surface of my shield, one more among the many that had already struck it.

"Ossian!"

It was Loaidheach. His ashen face was turned to me as he cried out, "Ossian. They've killed me." He slid off the far side of his horse and I glimpsed an arrow protruding from him as he fell from view.

Grief overwhelmed me and my heart threatened to burst as I leaped from my horse and ran to fall on my knees beside him. He lay on his back; his still naked, war-painted frame stretched long and unmoving, eyes closed.

Tears streamed down my face and I brushed them away with the back of my hand. My old friend who I loved like a brother, indeed, he was to become my brother-in-law, now lay—wait! There was something odd about the arrow penetrating him.

I pulled his right arm away from his side and straightened up with a snort. The arrow had barely skewered the fleshy inner part of his upper arm. Laoidheach wasn't dead. He fainted.

An arrow swished past my head and I ducked instinctively, as, grumbling, I hurried to my horse and retrieved my small medical bag. Returning to Laoidheach's side, I snapped the head from the arrow and drew the shaft back through his arm. Three quick wraps with a clean linen cloth bound his slightly bleeding wound and I gave the knot an extra hard jerk as I tied it off.

Rising battle clamor caused me to glance toward the fighting. The enemy had fallen back under our initial assault but were attempting to rally. Five long strides took me to the goatskin water bag hanging from the side of Laoidheach's horse. With a sense of evil satisfaction I emptied its contents onto his face.

"What?!" he spluttered as he shook his head and sat up. Confused, he looked up and saw me standing above him. "Ossian. Are you dead too?"

"Of course I'm not dead, you idiot, and neither are you." Looking about, I spotted his shield, stalked over to it and then tossed it to him. "Stay behind that thing—don't make me report your death to Aine. Now get back up on your horse. You have duties to perform."

The Christians' rally was short-lived as firebombs continued to splatter among them. For them the battle was lost. Indeed, they had no chance from the very beginning in the face of our new weapons and strategy. Their lines were beginning to break apart as their warriors fell while others began to turn and flee before our savage onslaught. Our horsemen slashed down all who attempted to run away.

The battle was ours and the bitter thought of the slaughter to come became more than I could bear as, once again, unbidden the question came. Why? My horse cantered into the fighting. I pointed my staff at Christians fighting alone and in small groups, and shouted, "Yield! Will you yield?"

Desperate, grimy faces lifted to mine, amazed and uncertain at my remarkable offer. Clemency was an unheard of thing. Precious time elapsed while more men fell, but I was determined to stop the fighting. "Drop your weapons and back away." To my own men, I demanded, "Give quarter to all who will accept it."

Throughout the battle scene, amid the swirling, fighting groups, time and again I repeated my offer and demands. My captains, hearing my words, echoed them, taking up the cry.

"Yield!"

"Yield!"

"Quarter for all who yield!"

Many Christians immediately grasped the opportunity to live and dropped their arms while others, their faces snarling like cornered beasts, continued to fight until they were battered down. In the distance our horsemen struck down all who tried to escape to the rear and I galloped toward them.

"Stop it! Let them go!" Back and forth I rode, repeating my order. Horsemen drew up, staring at me in amazement as battle lust faded from their eyes.

A horse raced towards me. Torcán, his face taut with fury, raged, "What are you doing? We kill them today or face them again tomorrow."

I laid my staff across my lap, leaned forward in my saddle and met his glare. "You will do precisely as I say—do it now, and without further said about it."

His fury turned to wonder as he tried to divine my thoughts before he turned his horse, galloped away and, like any good man, obeyed my orders. Relief flooded through me, my shoulders sagged. Perhaps Torcán was right, perhaps we must fight against those same fleeing men again, but I prayed otherwise.

I walked my horse back to the battlefield where Christians stood in dispersed groups, uncertain of their lot as prisoners. My warriors surrounded them, unsure of what to do with prisoners. Dead and wounded lay everywhere—hundreds of them.

Within a group of prisoners, I spotted a black robe. As I rode closer I recognized the Christian priest who met me prior to the battle. He sat upon the ground, head down, and didn't look up as I reined-in my horse beside him.

"So priest, you sit there like a lump while your followers suffer?"

For a moment he remained motionless, and then he turned his head and spat upon the ground. The hatred filling his face reached out to me as he looked up. "Damn your cold heart. You cannot chastise me, pagan. Only God Himself can do that."

"I will chastise any priest, Christian or Druid, who idles while men urgently require his aid." The death's head staff pointed 'round the battlefield. "See for yourself. Your wounded and ours call for water and care. Stand up like a man! Treat your men, pray over your dead, but do something of value!"

It wasn't until he stood and staggered in doing so that I saw that the lower portion of his robe had been burned away. His exposed leg, cherry red and covered in large blisters. My staff gestured to it. "See me later. I have burn salve and herbs to allay the pain."

A Christian warrior stooped, picked up a javelin and handed it to the priest, who grasped it and leaned upon it with both hands. His stoic face turned to me. "Keep your magic potions, for I will have nothing to do with them. God will provide all I need."

He turned his back to walk away, and I asked, "What is your name?"

"Joseph. They call me Father Joseph."

Chapter 11
The Brightening

The graves of our dead stretched across the meadow in three long rows. Each warrior lay buried with his weapons, that he might have them in the afterlife. I offered up prayers as I proceeded down the rows, naming each man in turn and invoking the gods' blessings upon him. The ceremony ended with my brief, final prayer.

> Gods of our fathers,
> O Lords of the Everlasting,
> We humbly ask your blessings
> on one hundred thirty-four of our comrades,
> Valiant warriors all, who fell fighting for you.
>
> We ask for their release from the darkness,
> We pray they might all arrive safely,
> And become one with the Golden Ones,
> Upon the blessed shores of Tír na nÓg.

* * *

Warriors massed about the small group of captains gathered around a central fire. Two days had passed since the battle, two nights during which I remained awake, my heart torn by all that had occurred and what might lie ahead. Of one thing I was convinced. The fighting must stop, not through our surrender but through a truce with the Christians. If such a thing were possible, it would be my responsibility to bring it about. First though, I needed support for such a thing from my own men.

I revealed my thoughts to them and a warrior shouted, "The Christians must turn their backs on the new god before peace can be restored. I say if they do not, we kill them all!"

"You would impose religious tyranny upon our people? Kill all whose beliefs differ from your own?" I shook my head. "No, dear companion. That is not the way."

"It is the way of Christians who began this war!" another warrior shouted.

"Yes, but it is not the right way. People will and should fight when their right to live and freely believe as they choose is threatened." I pointed into the distance. "Our dead lay buried there, men who fought to defend our freedom to worship our beloved Lordly Ones. However, to deny others the right to worship Christianity or any god of their choosing would make a mockery of the freedom those men died for. That is not a vision for the future for our land that I could support."

Torcán stood nearby, arms crossed over his chest. "What is your vision?"

"It is vague at best, though shamed I am to admit it. However, this I do know. I see the futility of continuing a war wherein both sides merely strive to enslave the other. Innermost beliefs are not a matter to be decided upon a battlefield but within individual souls. I pray that yesterday's battle and all those that came before will finally reveal that truth to our enemies. Perhaps the best we can hope for, though, is that the horrible consequences of the battle will give them pause, cause them to consider that now is a time for reason, not further fighting."

An older warrior, a captain with graying hair and somber eyes, slumped by the fire. His son fell in the fighting and the personal tragedy of it weighted his words as he spoke to the others. "I share Ossian's hope for the future, for what other choice is there? To fight on and on with no hope of winning by either side?"

A great sigh escaped him as he paused. "What manner of men are we?" His hand swept 'round to capture the group. "We fought to defend our honor and our beliefs in the Lordly Ones. Those are good causes and righteous ones, I'm thinking. Now? There is no righteousness in continually killing others because of what they

110

hold in their hearts. If the Christians learned by their defeat that we are men who will rise up to defend our gods, and if they stop their depredations against us, then I say there have been enough deaths. Let this battle be the end of it."

Around the fire the old warrior's words were greeted with silent nods, and I looked to Torcán. "What say you, my friend?"

He looked up with a shrug. "If the war ends today, then so be it. Call upon me later if you need me and I will be back. Otherwise," he rose to his feet with the effortless grace of a superb swordsman, and, ever the warrior, continued with a grin, "somewhere there will always be a need for a man with a horse and a sword."

"I shall send a message to the Christian bishop at Tara, relate to him what was said here today and request there be a truce between us."

* * *

I stood upon the massive bole of a fallen tree. Before me more than two hundred captive Christians massed together under the gray afternoon sky, their faces sullen as I carried my message to them.

"Do not mistake my words. They are not offered in kindness, repentance or as an offer of friendship, for I hold none of those things in my heart. You are my enemy. You fought against me, you killed my friends and, most importantly, you dishonor my gods.

"I ask you this. What have you gained by coming here to do battle? What did you hope to gain?" My staff gestured toward the distant battlefield. "Hundreds of men fell upon yon fields, your men and my men, but to what purpose? Battles do not change men's faith regardless of their outcomes. You surrendered because of your good sense and desire to live. However, despite all the deaths and the horrors of battle you did not surrender your trust in the Christian God, and my men remain true to the Lordly Ones.

"You fought gallantly so I hold you are honorable men. Again I ask you, where is the honor in killing without purpose? Ask yourselves that question again and again as you return to your homes."

For the first time, faces brightened among the prisoners and they turned, chattering and slapping one another on the back. Until this moment they undoubtedly assumed they would be massacred or enslaved.

I raised the staff calling for silence. Then, I gestured to Father Joseph, who stood among the throng, and motioned him forward. That his burns pained him greatly was obvious, as, once more leaning on the javelin, he slowly hobbled to the front of the prisoners where he stopped and looked up at me.

I spoke loudly that all might hear my words to him. "Priest, your men are free to leave at your discretion. I leave it to you. However, there are many wounded among you who cannot be moved and require care. If you abandon them here, they will not be treated for they are not my concern."

His face was as cold as his reply. "I do not need a Druid to remind me of my Christian duties."

A heated retort almost escaped my lips but I held it in check. "Perhaps you think now to rebuild your army and return to attack us again. If that be the case, then so be it, for you have already seen we do not fear facing you. We fear only the wasteful necessity of doing so."

My attention shifted back to the mass of prisoners. "This war began in the darkness, never-ending night that clouded minds and sowed fear throughout the land. Now each morning dawns brighter than the day before. I ask that each of you pray to your god as I do mine that, with the return of the light, wisdom will replace fear, a desire for peace will overwhelm hatred and understanding will lead to tolerance, one for the other."

My words met utter stillness. Maybe I was wrong in freeing these men. Helplessness filled me for by their silence it seemed likely I would confront them in battle again.

* * *

"Joseph." I rolled the foreign-sounding name on my tongue and turned to Laoidheach. "My friend, I am placing much hope in the priest Joseph. I pray the gods will give me the wisdom to sway him."

He sat cross-legged on the ground under my canopy running a tiny bone needle and thread through a rip in his tunic, and looked up from his work with a grunt. "Baile of the Honeyed Speech blessed you with the gift of the Blarney. If you cannot sway him, such a thing cannot be done."

I settled onto a wooden bench with a sigh. "I fear it will take more than the Blarney to convince him. He has complete trust in the words of his god and none in those of Druids. Now we soundly defeated him in battle and his heart is hardened even more against us."

"Then, you must melt his heart." He squinted in the dim light cast by a single candle, and stretched the thread to its full length as he drew the needle through his tunic with practiced ease. "Augh. Now my patches have patches. I fear that I will soon be forced to remain naked for more than just battles."

"If that be your condition, please favor us all by completing your needle work. Tell me, 'O bard among bards, how would you suggest I melt the priest's heart?"

He lay his mending aside. His long legs stretched before him and crossed at the ankles as he leaned back and rested upright upon his elbows. "You recall the story of Tea, daughter of Lughaidh?"

My mind reached back. "I remember a bit about her. It was the Age of the World 3502; Tea demanded the hill Druim Caein as her dower from her husband, King Eremhon. Later the hill was renamed Teamhair in her honor, for therein she was buried. Of course we now call that same hill Tara."

"Aye, that's the same girl, though there was much more to her story." He reclined onto his back, clasped his hands behind his head and spoke upwards to the canvas canopy. "It seems Tea, daughter of Lughaidh, son of Ith, was chaste, beautiful and well known for her sweetness. She was desired by all who saw her. Her father had great hope that she might marry well and took her to meet Eremhon, who became king of all Eire after he defeated Emhear at the Battle of Geisill. Eremhon was known to despise all women and he greeted Lughaidh and Tea in his chambers with great rudeness. Forthwith, they were dismissed."

I fidgeted at the open entrance to my canopy as Laoidheach told the story. "So in the end, Tea overcame Eremhon by her loveliness and sweetness. I doubt I can do the same with the priest."

My interruption of his story was met with a snort. "You've a vile temper. Shut up and listen." He paused a moment, still staring upwards, recapturing his place in his story. "Lughaidh was angered and embarrassed by Eremhon's reception of them but wondered at the king's hatred of women. Therefore, he went to a Druid and asked that he divine the cause behind Eremhon's bitterness. Through incantations, the Druid called upon the goddess Aebhel, who, as you know, is wise in the ways of lust between men and women. Aebhel responded to the Druid, saying, 'Within the shee near Dun Deilginnsi in the territory of Cualann, you may hear the whisperings of the fairy queen, Sorcha, who has King Eremhon's ear and loves him. Her love for a mortal can never be satisfied, so in her resentment and sorrow she cast a magic spell upon him that he would detest all other women.'"

The sky seemed brighter this night. Perhaps the moon gleamed behind the high clouds of ash. It was a thing unseen for many months. I stood staring upwards, my mind following Laoidheach's story. I feared there would be little point to it.

He sighed. "It would be a sad thing, I think, to be a fairy and love a mortal. There is a story—"

I threw my hands up in despair. "Would you please complete your first story before beginning another one?"

"What? Oh, yes, of course. Now where was I?" Still lying upon his back, his right arm shot upright and he shook a knowing finger in the air above him. "Aha, I have it. Lughaidh loved his daughter above all else, and thought there could be no finer future for Tea than that she become wife to the king. Yet such a thing was impossible unless Sorcha relented and removed her spell. So it was that Lughaidh traveled to Dun Deilginnsi and climbed the grassy mound that held the fairies' shee.

"He called Sorcha's name down the entrance to her magical underground palace. Again and again he called until finally she answered him. Lughaidh pled his case to the fairy queen, expressing his love for his daughter and hopes for her, but Sorcha remained unmoved. 'I shall not relinquish my hold on Eremhon,' she replied, 'for I love him more than any mortal woman ever could.' He acknowledged that might be true, but explained, 'Because of your spell, Eremhon has become a bitter, lonely man. He is king of all Eire, but, due to you, he shall never sire an heir to replace him on the throne. You may well love him, but you love yourself more, for by your spell you place your happiness above his. Only by releasing him can you prove the truth of your love.'"

Laoidheach sat up, hunching forward and wrapping his arms around his knees. "Of course, Sorcha heard Lughaidh's sincere words and released Eremhon from her spell. Soon after, the king was married to Tea and their story you know." He cocked an eyebrow, and asked, "Now do you know how to melt a priest's heart?"

The candle burned low on its unadorned dish, yet the warmth of its glow filled me as I turned to stare into the darkness. Yes, my way was clear.

* * *

The morning fog was lifting as Joseph hobbled into my canopy. He collapsed upon a rough bench with a long sigh, his hard dark eyes on me.

A yellow-stained linen bandage was wrapped around his leg, the stench of the foulness beneath it evidence of spreading sickness threatening to kill him. Fever touched his face and I hoped his senses remained untouched as I spoke.

"Thank you for coming. Had I known the condition of your leg I would have come to you."

"My condition is not your concern." He leaned the javelin he still used as a staff against the bench beside him. "My life is in God's hands. Go ahead; speak your piece, for my proper place is with my men."

His manner was neither more nor less than I expected. "There is much that separates us, you and me, though also much we hold in common."

"I doubt it."

"We are men of faith who stand beside our gods. On that you must agree. We speak to the people telling them of our gods' truth."

His eyes blazed. "There is only one truth, the truth of the one God, the only God. It is Him I bring to the people. As for you?" He snorted. "Your pagan demons, if they exist at all, are Satan's tools. Now what is it you want of me, Druid? I tire of your presence."

I squatted that I would be on a level with him. "I want you to tell me why we are fighting. I fear I no longer know."

He leaned back and squinted. "What manner of trickery is this? You ask a foolish question."

"Foolish? Yes, perhaps so. Yet I ask it honestly, so I would appreciate you answering it."

A hiss escaped his lips. "You fight for nothing…nothing, unless it is to spread Satan's words. We fight and sacrifice ourselves for a grand and noble cause by spreading the Word of God Himself. We fight to protect the one true faith. Hah. You cannot say the same."

"Oh, but I can say the same. We sacrifice ourselves for our gods for the same reasons."

"You know nothing of the need for sacrificing for a cause greater than yourself. Hear me, for the Scriptures tell us, 'For God so loved the world that He gave His one and only Son, that whosoever believeth in Him shall not perish but have eternal life.' That, Druid, is a greater sacrifice than any mortal can ever make."

My legs grew tired from squatting so I settled myself on the ground, cross-legged before him. "It is no small thing, I know, for a father to give up his son. Yes, your god sacrificed his son for a great cause, but today my thoughts turn to the many fathers," I turned my face and looked toward the distant hills, "who gave up their sons on yon battlefield for far less. You say sacrifice is necessary in all grand things. Now you sit there, I sit here, and we talk of our sacrificed warriors. What grand end did their sacrifices serve?"

Sweat beaded on his flushed brow, a sign of the sickness within him brought on by his rotting leg. "Mine stand for the Will of God by ridding all Eire of the likes of you."

"You wish to kill all Druids?"

"I came here to take you by the throat and kill you. It was the devil's own luck I did not succeed."

"Yes. But that was not my question. Your god demands the deaths of all who oppose him? Is that your mission, Joseph, to carry out your god's will by sacrificing your men while murdering us all?"

"Of course not." A hand wiped the fevered sweat from his brow. "You have Satan's voice and twist my words."

"I merely wish to understand them as I hope you will understand mine. Will you hear them?"

"Have I a choice?"

"Certainly." I shrugged and gestured outward. "You may walk back to your camp, as you will, though I hope you will not until you've heard my offer."

"I will not bend to your threats or bargain with you, pagan."

"Threats? I did not ask you here to threaten you. Have I not already promised that you and your warriors may leave at any time? Hear me. I wish to beg a favor."

He snorted. "A favor? I am your prisoner and have nothing to favor you with."

The time had come and I opened my mind before him. "I want a truce between us. As to our faiths, we will never agree, but this war is an injustice for our people and the killing must stop." I withdrew a scroll from inside my robe. "The favor I ask of you is that you present my offer for a truce to your bishop at Tara."

"A truce?" Skepticism crowded his face. "Even if I were to agree, how can I trust your word? The word of a pagan? No, they are Satan's words meant to tempt me."

I shook my head. "They are my words, Joseph." I gestured outside. "I am sick of this, the killing, the misery, the horror we bring upon this land. As spokesmen for our faiths we can end it if we can only agree that Eire's future lies in the hands of gods, not on a battlefield. Let us carry out our fight on a field of ideas, allow the people to choose which gods to follow within their hearts."

"Those are pretty words, snake worshipper, but they couch your deceit." He folded his arms across his chest and looked away. "Waste no more upon me, for I will not hear them."

"But you must hear them if you care about the people of this land."

The full measure of his hatred filled his eyes as he turned back to me. "I care well enough. For the glory of God I shall continue to fight to rid this land of you and all like you, and the people will be all the better for it."

The message within Laoidheach's story returned to me. "Better for it? Better because you choose to continue the fighting and killing though I offer a truce? Why? Is it bettering the people you care about most or your own thirst to rid Eire of all Druids? Would you place your wants above those of the majority who crave peace and prosperity? Look into your heart for the answer."

He tilted his head, his stubbornness unabated. "I fight for righteousness, that all might come to see God's True Light."

"Yes, and in your mind that is a noble thing. Yet how many families must sacrifice their loved ones before you finally attain what you want?" His hatred weighed upon me and my hands scrubbed my face to wipe away the burden of it. "I will tell you this, though why I do so I cannot say, for you are my enemy. You will never defeat me, Joseph, until first you defeat yourself."

Perhaps he heard me, though understanding is a tenuous thing. His eyes remained hooded as again I proffered the scroll. "The truce I offer here is a thing we can do, should do and must do for the greater welfare of our people. I pray you will accept it."

He licked his parched, cracking lips, his eyes fixed upon the scroll. A sigh escaped him and his shoulders sagged. "You think me a fool, a man indifferent to the deaths about me? You think I do not yearn for peace?" Resolve returned as he straightened up. "If I were to agree to your request, it would be as you say, as a boon to our people. Even so, make no mistake, Druid, I despise you and the demons you stand for. My quest to rid Eire of the likes of you shall never end."

Hope surged through me. "You agree then?"

"I agree only to consider it. I shall need God's divine guidance on this matter." His hand shook as he reached for the scroll. "Call upon me at my camp tomorrow."

I grunted as he took the scroll and inserted it inside his robe. "What I must do next cannot wait until tomorrow." I ducked from under the canopy, waved to Laoidheach, nodded and then stepped back inside. My medical bag lay against the canopy wall. Inside it was a bronze knife with an evil, curved blade, its edge keen as a razor.

Joseph's eyes grew wide when I removed the knife from the bag. Four burly warriors strode in and I motioned to the priest.

"What happens here?" Joseph glared as warriors grasped his arms. "I agreed to consider your offer."

"Aye, but you will be of no use to me if you're dead." I gestured to his leg. "Your leg is rotten. If it is not treated right away, it will kill you. These men are here to hold you motionless while I cut away the foulness and apply curative herbs. Pray to your god for his mercy; scream if you must, for none will blame you. But by the Dagda, I will heal your leg!"

* * *

Our wounded lay under canopies nearby and it was there I spent my nights, tending their needs. Therefore, I awoke to the brightness of morning and Laoidheach bursting through the closed flaps of my canopy. "Ossian! Wake up. Come. See for yourself, the sun has returned, and oh, what a glorious thing it is too. Hurry now!"

My shadow fell across the ground as I stepped outside. The magical prophecy held within the song of the Dagda, sung in the voice of Master Tóla, returned to me. Nine months of darkness there would be, the Dagda had said, and so it had been.

Throughout the camp tents were coming down; men gathered in groups, packs slouching from their shoulders. A small group approached, Christians, two of whom carried a litter bearing a wounded friend.

They stopped and a ragged, bearded man faced me. "Father Joseph spread word of your offer for a truce and we thank you for it. We return to our homes praying to God that such a thing comes to pass. May God's blessings be upon you." He gestured to the others and they continued on their way.

Three days had passed since I began healing the priest's leg. If he now spoke of a truce, I wished to hear it from his own lips, so hurried to his camp where I found him in his tent.

Joseph laid quietly, the feverish flush already gone from his face as he gazed up at me. "It is a bitter thing for a man to owe his life to his enemy. I know God works His Will in mysterious ways. To Him I offer thanks for my life that I might continue to serve Him, and to you though you be merely a tool in His wondrous hand."

"Do not thank me, Joseph, for I did not heal your leg out of a sense of kindness or as an offer of friendship. Neither shall ever pass between us. But, tell me. I heard just now that you speak of a truce."

"It is true I have spoken of it. You truly meant what you wrote in the scroll, did you not?"

"Aye. I meant it well enough. May the Macha strike me dead if I did not. So tell me now. Will you do it? Will you carry my terms to Tara and speak with your bishop?"

He shook his head in disbelief. "Are there other Druids who feel as you do?"

"Within my message to your bishop I promised to write Druids across the land asking they honor a truce. Yet, today, I speak to you only for myself, though there was another…a great man who taught forbearance, understanding and reason."

"Was? What happened to him?"

"He is dead. Christians murdered him at Dún Ailinne."

"Dún Ail… Oh, yes. I see." He sat up to lean back on his elbows. "A bad thing that…Dún Ailinne. A stupid, unnecessary thing that brought naught but shame upon us."

"Yes, well—"

The light of understanding filled his face. "Of course! That's why you are here, isn't it? You fight to avenge Dún Ailinne."

My shoulders slumped and I nodded, visions of that night once again returning to torment me. "Yes, though I have learned that vengeance is a deceitful master. Hope for victory under its name is merely an illusion."

Tears welled in his eyes and he wiped them away with the back of his hand. "So many deaths, too many… Why was I so stupid when God's Own Light was there to lead me? You fought me to avenge Dún Ailinne, and I fought you to avenge your depradations against my fellow churchmen. I see it now, yes, it is quite clear, vengeance upon vengeance, the waste and futility of which you speak." A wince crossed his face as he rolled over and grabbed the javelin lying beside him. He reached up a hand. "Help me to stand. I have lain here long enough."

I did as he asked and he rose to his feet, leaning heavily on the shaft. The linen cloth bound around his leg was a bright white, a sign the leg was healing.

"The people call you Druids the Wise Ones. Now I understand why that is so. Would that you might see God's True Light and use your knowledge on the side of Christ."

It was little I cared about his judgement of me, good or bad, though again hope surged through me. "You will do it then? You will carry my message to the bishop?"

"Yes, you are right. This horror must end. Upon my solemn word to the Lord God Himself I shall travel to Tara and urge the Reverend Bishop to agree to your truce." He sighed, and shook his head. "And in God's name I thank you for it."

* * *

Thoughts of peace crowded my mind while I strolled back to my pavilion. Laoidheach idled nearby, strumming his lyre. He looked up as I drew near.

Sunlight warmed my shoulders. Though it would be foolish to hope too much that Joseph would succeed with the bishop, relief was flooding through me and I smiled as my face turned to the blue, cloudless sky.

A twang from Laoidheach's lyre was followed by his question. "What did the priest say?"

I walked close and slapped him on the back. "Pack your things old friend and see to our horses. Let's go home."

Chapter 12
Tomorrow Comes Today

Shadows accompanied our line of march as we rounded the final bend in the trail to see Rath Raithleann on the hillcrest before us. Laoidheach rode at my side, and behind us all thirty-five of the warriors who left the village with us were returning home—yet another blessing by the Lordly Ones.

Black smoke smudged the sky above our village, more than expected from the daily cooking fires of the women, and I wondered at the reason for it. I felt a tinge of concern but the gods had always smiled upon Rath Raithleann.

The warm sun of the spring afternoon touched emerald fields that stretched into the distance. Nearer the village herds of cattle, horses and sheep grazed within paddocks enclosed by low, stone fences with sturdy wooden gates. Beyond the village the stately trees within the sacred grove were again turning green, and I smiled at the sight. The splendor of it all was a forgotten scene, its serenity filling my throat after nine months of darkness, including the past three months of constant fighting.

Thatched roofs showed above the ancient protective earthen wall encircling the village though nothing could be seen of the people or events inside. My warriors were muttering behind me, wondering at the absence of the many folk who should be seen going about their daily work. I motioned to pick up the pace, the dust of the trail rising around us. The daily grit of it in my teeth was now a natural thing, no more noticeable than breathing. Finally, the large wooden gates leading into the village stood wide open before us. Beyond the gates all were there, the laughing, cheering, clapping people of Rath Raithleann.

Joyous faces turned up to us, eager hands reached out to touch us, exulting voices called out our names as we progressed through the throng toward the village center. There we discovered a low wooden platform, its background draped with green, yellow and red pennons, the tribal colors of the Eoghanachts. King Domnhall was there. Resplendent in a brilliant blue linen robe edged with fox fur, he sat upon a high-backed wooden chair, a welcoming smile on his age-lined face. Beside him stood my father in the Druid's traditional black-striped robe.

I turned and waved my warriors forward, motioning for them to mass behind me. Then Laoidheach and I dismounted, knelt in the dust and bowed before the King.

The tempting aroma of roasting meat wafted past my nose as my father stepped forward and began to invoke a prayer of thanks to the Lordly Ones for our safe return. Prompted by the enticing smell, my unruly stomach rumbled and Laoidheach quietly snickered as he knelt beside me.

Word of our victories had spread across the land and reached the ears of King Domnhall, who now stood to address us. "Today Rath Raithleann welcomes her sons to their home. You have honored us by your courage and many victories over the Christians, so we gather here to honor you. A great feast has been prepared in celebration of your safe return."

His eyes swept the crowd and then he nodded toward my father. "The Wise One thanked the Lords of the Sidhe for returning you to us and I add this, for I know it to be true. Your many triumphs were a blessing from the gods' themselves and for that we shall be forever grateful to them."

Silence gripped the villagers crowding near to hear their King's words. Distant cries and laughter broke the stillness from children frisking within a world ruled by kings and gods of their own making. It was an idyllic scene as the king stood upon the dais, framed by a blue sky. In that moment the horrors of the past few months fled from my mind, replaced by hopes for a grand, tranquil future for the people of Rath Raithleann and all Eire.

"It is altogether fitting," King Domnhall continued, "for a king to bestow favors upon those who bring honor to his realm. Therefore, Ossian, rise and stand before me."

I did as he bade, wondering at his intentions. Though he stood upon the platform our eyes met on a level.

"Despite your youth it was you who led our men and others who joined you in defeating Christian forces. No man could have done better and it speaks well of the man you have become. Now let it be known that you will join your father as a Wise One in my royal court. In keeping with your position, you are hereby awarded two parcels of land and an annual stipend of twenty-four pieces of silver. Furthermore, you shall be permitted to erect a home at a location suitable to you near your father's. May the gods continue to bless you."

I bowed and mumbled, "And you my King. I am most sincerely humbled by your kind generosity."

The King turned to Laoidheach and motioned for him to rise. "Laoidheach, though you are new to my kingdom it is proud I am to have you among us. Word reached us that, though you were grievously wounded in battle, you remained at your post and by your valor a great victory was won."

My eyes beheld my friend and I snorted quietly. It seemed he should at least have the decency to blush at the King's exaggeration.

"Now," the King continued, "let everyone know that, henceforth, Laoidheach shall be known as bard of Domnhall's court. In keeping with his position, he is hereby granted one parcel of land and an annual stipend of twelve silver coins. Furthermore, he may choose a proper location on the west side of the village to erect a home."

The King's generosity toward my friend was gratifying, though surprising. I smelled my father's hand in it. Given the right to build a home on the west side of the village was no small favor as it was a preferred location. Prevailing winds would keep away much of the smoke and latrine odors emanating from the village.

Each warrior who accompanied me received three silver coins as a token of the King's appreciation for their service. When the coins were added to the booty they looted from Christian villages the men and their families would fare well, indeed.

A stray wind gust again pushed smoke from the cooking fires past my nose, and my mouth watered in anticipation of the feast to come. The King was kind, generous and, perhaps best of all, a man of few words. After his brief closing comments we were dismissed and I hurried toward long tables piled with roasted meat, breads and savory dishes.

* * *

People crowded about enjoying the festive atmosphere. I sat alongside my warriors at a long table laden with food while laughter and delectable aromas filled the air.

A side of pork ribs lay upon the polished oak trencher before me, roasted to perfection by knowing hands. A hint of charring surrounded its edges, smoke-enhanced juices oozing to the surface. It was while I was tearing the first rib away from the slab that I heard, "Ossian." It was Laoidheach. "Have you seen Aine?"

A stab of guilt passed through me when I realized that my thoughtless absorption with food prevailed over higher obligations to my family. Reluctantly I laid the rib on the trencher. "No. I am sure she is here somewhere. Keep looking, you will find her."

"I've already looked everywhere, asked many others about her, but no one seems to know where she is."

"Did you ask my father?"

His face reddened. "No, he… That is, well, he is sitting there," he pointed, "engaged in a quiet discussion with a lady. I sensed he would not appreciate my intrusion."

A lady? My gaze followed Laoidheach's pointing finger but I could not see my father through groups of people seated around tables and milling about. Unbidden, my foolish, unruly hand snatched the rib from the trencher and shoved the succulent thing into my mouth.

A wee, chattering bundle of swirling black linen emerged from the crowd, hurtling directly toward Laoidheach. Grease dribbled down my chin and I wiped it away with the back of my hand, a grin on my face. My mother's eldest sister, Luiseach, who we lovingly called Aunt Lou, bustled forward to confront Laoidheach, her wagging finger pointing upwards directly towards his nose.

"And who gave you leave to be mentioning my niece's name in front of all these big ears and wagging tongues?" A shawl wrapped Aunt Lou's head, her thin, lined face protruding forward. Tiny as she was, she was like a sparrow harassing a Hugh's hawk as her finger continued to wag beneath his nose. "My niece is a good girl, she is, and I'll not have you bandying her name about among these," she paused and gestured toward the table where I sat among my warriors, "these ruffians."

Laoidheach, his eyes wide, stammered, "Madame, I...I assure you—"

"Madame? Paugh! And don't you be denying it, boy 'o; a dozen people reported to me that you've been asking after her." She took a step closer. Fisted hands on hips, her neck craned as she glared upwards. "And what manner of gentleman would be mentioning a maid's name in such company as this, I ask you? Not much of one, I'd be saying."

Alarm filled his eyes as he peered down his nose at his tiny antagonist. "I assure you, I was merely concerned, as she—"

"Concerned? Concerned indeed." She took another step forward, her finger wagging again. "Who would you be to have concern for my niece? Have you spoken to her father of your concern?"

"Well...no, but—"

"Aha! I suspected as much." He took a quick step back as she advanced, her finger upward pointing like a deadly lance. "You've no right to be speaking of her at all without there being an understanding between you, which there is not."

He tried to explain as again he retreated when she took another step forward. "I thought there was an understanding, you see—"

Finger still wagging she charged forward and he continued to fall back. "Maybe in the heathen land you come from men speak openly of maids without their fathers' approval. You will find that is not the case in Rath Raithleann. Here, all the proprieties must be observed."

A ridiculous log that he failed to see blocked Laoidheach's line of retreat as he backed away from his tiny tormentor. Inevitably, his heels made contact with the log and backwards he flopped onto the ground with an, "Oomph." He lay stunned, his long legs looping across the log.

Victory gleamed in Aunt Lou's eyes as she cackled over him. "It's said you are the King's new bard." With a snort, she added, "Are you his bard then, or his new court fool?"

Puffed with triumph, she turned to walk away but for the first time noticed me sitting at the table. She scurried over and patted my grease-streaked face. "Oh Ossian, it's glad I am to see you safely home. You must be sure to come by and visit. I'm certain your sister will be happy to see you, too."

"Aine is living with you?"

"That she is. She came to live with me after we heard you were returning home." Aunt Lou gestured to Laoidheach, who now rested upon his elbows. "Aine couldn't remain living under the same roof with that barbarian friend of yours. And the two of them having no understanding with your father. It would be unseemly, don't you see? Just think of the scandal of it."

* * *

Beside my father stood the widow Riona, a lovely, soft, blond-haired woman I guessed at ten years younger than his age of forty-five. Had his red beard been streaked with gray before I rode away to face the Christians? I could not recall, though sad I was to notice it.

A gentle smile accompanied her curtsy upon being introduced to us by my father. Laoidheach and I bowed, he with a gallant hand flourish. I liked her immediately and saw why my father would be interested in her, which I suspected was the case. Many years had gone by since my mother passed away and I thought it a fine thing that my father might find comfort in this woman.

"It is proud of you both I am," my father began, "and I welcome you home. I congratulate you on your positions within the King's court."

"Thank you, father. The King's generosity was unexpected, yet grateful we are for it."

"Aye, but I hope you know this grand feast he ordered in your honor might be his greatest gift of all. It was a risk to serve so much food when our granaries run low. Famine stalks the land. There is much unrest as people of other tribes starve. No doubt they will continue to do so until the next harvest which I pray with the gods' blessings will prove bountiful."

The famine and unrest of which he spoke we regularly witnessed first-hand while traveling the land fighting the Christians. Images of thin, drawn faces and the swollen bellies of children returned to me. During these times food became more precious than gold and my thoughtful gaze returned to the joyous people gathered about tables still laden with the celebratory feast.

Shuffling and throat clearing erupted beside me as Laoidheach bowed. "Wise One, with your permission I should like to speak with you at your convenience."

My father scowled. "And I know what it is you wish to discuss. Very well. We will speak of it tonight."

* * *

Firelight flickered in the room as my father considered Laoidheach's request to marry Aine. Already my friend had responded to the many ritualized questions posed to him as required by the sacred laws.

Finally my father nodded. "Very well, you have my blessing. You may marry my daughter, for I know Aine's feelings on it."

Relief flooded Laoidheach's face. "Thank you, Wise One."

"Yes, well… Now, young man, as to the dowry. I feel two gold coins and a plot of arable land is appropriate. By such a dowry, as well as through your service to the King, you shall soon become a wealthy man. Do you agree?"

"I'm not sure—I—"

"Very well," my father grumbled. "Three gold coins but not a scrap of copper more."

"You misunderstand, Wise One. You're original offer is more than generous and I thank you for it."

My father glared at him from beneath a raised eyebrow. "What? Why didn't you say so the first time? We are agreed then, two coins and the land?"

"Yes, Wise One, of course." Laoidheach cleared his throat. "When do you think I might speak with your daughter?"

"Send a messenger to the home of my sister-in-law, Luiseach, and request an audience. Work out all such arrangements through her. If all goes well, you should be married within four months."

"Four months?" My friend groaned. "Must we wait so long?"

"Of course. The courtship rituals dictated to us by the gods countless centuries ago must be followed precisely. There is no other way."

* * *

Candlelight brought life to the *men* arranged upon the fidchell board as I contemplated my opening move. Laoidheach had gone to bed much earlier and now my father sat quietly across the table watching my hand hovering above the board. We both had won two games and this one would determine the match. A strategy that worked for me earlier in the evening would be employed again and I hoped for the same outcome as I moved my bronze-coated *man*.

His copper mug clunked on the table surface as my father hunched forward and countered my opening. With a contented sigh he leaned back in his chair. "There is a matter I wish to discuss."

My eyes remained riveted on the board as I suspected a ruse, that he merely wished to distract my attention from the game with idle chatter. "And that is?"

"Next year, if the gods will it, I shall receive the honor and title of Master Druid. At that time it is my plan to step aside in my role as chief advisor to the King."

My contemplated move fled my mind at my father's surprising words. There could be no misunderstanding them and I leaned back in my chair, waiting for him to continue.

A small smile flickered across his face. "So, you do not ask the obvious? Why, eh?" His hands came together on his chest, his fingers flexed, forming a cathedral. "I have considered stepping aside for some time, but more so after the fall of Dún Ailinne. In fact, only recently the gods favored me with a proper plan for my future."

He leaned forward, elbows on knees. "Despite your efforts and resistance by others, Christians continue to gain strength month by month. Our old gods, the Lords of the Sidhe, are being evermore pushed aside by the the new god and his son the Risen One. Dún Ailinne was a disaster for us. Almost one hundred bright young Druids were slain in a single night. Other schools were similarly attacked then and later, where more students were killed. Don't you see? Almost an entire generation of Druids has been lost, so where lies our future? In the years to come, who will stand for our gods and time-honored traditions?"

The enormity of his words left me breathless, for this was a vision I had not considered. My hands reached forward and gripped the edge of the table as the layers of his reasoning piled higher and higher in my mind.

"You see the future you describe clearly," I replied, nodding, my teeth clenched. "Yet now more than before I do not understand why you would step away from your duties to King Domnhall. Every Druid must stand forward to resist the Christians."

He rose to his feet, palms flat atop the table, and leaned toward me. "You are here now, on our King's court. You can capably take my place. Never worry, I shall not relinquish my responsibilities as a Druid. Dún Ailinne must be replaced and I think to begin a new school here. After I receive the title Master it is something I can do and I believe must do. We must begin to rebuild what we have lost."

A school for Druids here at Rath Raithleann with my father as its Master? It was an amazing idea...a grand idea. "You discussed this with the King?"

"I did. Indeed, he is in accord with all I told you." Lifting the pitcher of ale from the table, he refilled my mug. "When the time comes, King Domnhall will help sponsor the founding of our new school."

Long it was we talked of his plans, pausing from time to time, listening to the songs of the night birds. The ale pitcher was tilted often, most commonly toward my mug. So is it a surprise then, at the end, my father easily won the deciding game of our fidchell match? Oh, a sly one he was.

Chapter 13
Golden Summer

𝕿 he sun's golden rays streamed across the morning sky, an omen promising a bright future. I awoke with a thick head and tongue, yet filled with eager anticipation. My position in the King's court was assured while my father pursued grand plans of his own.

Hopes, dreams and aspirations reside within the minds of mortals but are guided to their certain ends by the hands of the gods. It was knowing this truth that held me in prayer to the Dagda that he might influence the spirit of the bishop of Tara to accept my terms for a truce between Christians and Druids.

In keeping with my plans and promise to Father Joseph, I wrote letters to noted Druids across the land asking their forbearance toward the Christians, pleading for a cessation of the fighting that all people might dwell and prosper within an atmosphere of peace. Each letter was written on vellum using the Ogham characters and rolled into a scroll for delivery by trusted messengers of my choosing.

And then I awaited a response from Tara.

* * *

Beneath the thatched roof of an open-sided pavilion workmen rolled away the heavy stones covering the village's six in-ground silos. Each circular pit contained locally grown grains—oats, barley, wheat, rye and flax. Livestock and poultry were important to the village, but in truth it was the grains that stood between the people and starvation.

King Domnhall stood in the narrow lane behind me flanked by two burly warriors. I felt his anxious eyes on my back as I lowered a weighted line into each silo and made a note of my measurements.

Eyebrow cocked, arms crossed over his chest, he was awaiting my report when I turned around.

"I must conclude my calculations, Your Highness, but it seems the levels are dropping as predicted." The workmen remained near with their big ears. I dismissed them with a wave and added, "Provided we continue rationing the grain, the stores should be more than sufficient to meet our needs until this summer's crop is harvested."

His hands went to his face as though to wipe the tension from it. "That is good. That is good, Ossian. You've seen the refugees?"

I winced at the thought of them. "Yes, Sire. I treated a few suffering illnesses. They are a pitiful lot, I'm thinking."

"Aye. They are that, but there is not enough food to continue feeding them and our own people. To every party of refugees I authorized giving one handful of grain for each family member. Afterwards our warriors escort them down the road."

"It's sad for them, I am, Your Highness, and a generous thing it is you are doing. During this famine what king could do more, eh? In fact, a month ago I heard a rumor that some kings are selling their stores for great gains while their people starve."

"It is no rumor, Ossian. I regret to say it is true, may the White Lady devour their souls."

A growing concern in mind, I leaned a shoulder against a squared piling. "Sire, I recommend you post additional guards until this time of hunger is past."

"Why?"

"The number of refugees is increasing. Some say they heard that food is plentiful here. Such false reports could prove dangerous for us. Others may come to demand more than your generosity."

"Our men are needed in the fields now." He looked into the sky as though seeking inspiration, and shrugged. "I will consider your suggestion. Now then, continue to monitor—" He paused, interrupted by the approaching tittering of women.

A broad grin spread across my face. Laoidheach and Aine walked side by side along the narrow lane winding among small cottages, Aunt Lou and a small bevy of her aged cronies in close pursuit. It is said the gods decreed the courtship rituals. Perhaps it's true, but if so, surely they were inspired by the wiles of women, for no man could conceive such things.

The King, a lopsided smile on his face, excused himself with a soft "harrumph," and hurried away in the opposite direction. I leaned away from the piling and straightened up, awaiting the arrival of the happy couple and their ancient, giggling escort. When they drew near I bowed low, my sweeping hand almost brushing the ground. "Good morning mighty bard and fair lady. Please allow your poor servant to wish you a very fine day."

Aine, nose in the air, ignored my teasing. Laoidheach cocked an eyebrow on his haughty face and returned my banter. "And who would be giving you permission to speak to your betters?" He gave me a dismissive, backhanded wave. "Away with you, scoundrel."

Aine murmured, "My brother would play the fool. Don't you be encouraging him."

I bowed again. "My sister would deign to notice her lowly brother? May the gods be praised for it."

Again her nose went into the air and she grabbed Laoidheach's arm to hurry him past me.

"None of that," Aunt Lou reprimanded. "There'll be no touching between you."

Again a grin spread across my face as the grand procession moved on, clucking biddies in tow.

* * *

It was with the knowledge of roast duck in mind that I accepted Aunt Lou's invitation to dinner. If Aine was still irritated at my teasing two days earlier, she gave no sign of it as she busied herself preparing the table.

The delicious aroma of roasting fowl mingled with the perfumed incense favored by women to create a heady mixture that permeated the small room. I relaxed in a chair near the fire, sipping a mug of hot apple brandy. The women prepared a small feast for the three of us and I asked the reason for it.

"You'll be knowing soon enough," Aunt Lou smirked. "There is a favor we'll be asking of you after we eat."

"And that would be?"

Aunt Lou wagged her finger. "After dinner and after the other ladies arrive." Her eyes swept the table. "Well then, it seems all is ready. Bring your brandy and sit there," she pointed to the head of the table.

I should have known. Whatever Aunt Lou's wily plan, I was fairly trapped in it. Nevertheless, the duck was roasted to perfection, sided by stewed cabbage, black pudding and thick slabs of buttered rye bread. The women kept their plans a mystery throughout dinner though now and then knowing glances passed between them. Finally I pushed my grateful stomach back from the table.

Soon afterwards, Aunt Lou's plans progressed as women began arriving. Most I knew as friends of Aine or Aunt Lou's elderly cronies. However, there was one guest I had not met, a likely young lass with bold green eyes and shimmering black hair falling across her shoulders.

Aunt Lou stepped over to a shelf, removed a linen bag and then laid it on the table before me.

"What's this?" I prodded the bag with a finger.

"Chicken bones."

"Chicken bones?"

"Certainly. Every girl deserves a prophecy before she marries. So, Wise One, we gather here that through your reading of the bones you may foretell what the future holds for your sister."

So that was the reason behind the excellent meal and why I was there: to provide the evening's entertainment. Still, the ceremony would serve the purpose. The women gathered to honor Aine while enjoying an amusing evening. What harm could there be in playing my part? A sly plan formed in my mind, a prophecy certain to bring laughter among the group.

The reading of bones involved a simple ancient ceremony, one I learned at Dún Ailinne though Master Tóla held it in little regard. It was a common practice among charlatans to conduct such readings and I hid a smirk as I tilted the bag and dumped its contents onto the table before me.

"Divination was known to the Old Ones, a gift to humans from the goddess Cethlion." My attention swept the faces of the group, though I paused for a moment at a pair of green eyes. "It was she who predicted the fall of the Formorians to the Tuatha De Danaans. Therefore, it is to her prayers must be offered that a prophecy might appear."

Firelight guttered within the silent room and I cleared my throat. "You must all join hands as I begin the divination ritual." Eager hands clasped amid subdued giggling as I leaned forward, palms flat against the tabletop," and continued,

"O'er winds' howls and moans and shrieks,
The goddess of tomorrow speaks,
Of things that might the future hold,
Or could, or should or must unfold.

O Cethlion, your wisdom flows,
'Tis only you who truly knows,
A sign that will the future tell,
Tomorrows wherein spirits dwell.

O Cethlion your prophecy,
Of sights, and sounds and what will be,
Within the mists of time concealed,
At last through you the truth revealed."

Eyes closed, the forced scowl on my face hid the mirth threatening to bubble to the surface. My hands felt for the bones, scooping them together until I cupped them all within my palms.

"O Cethlion, O Cethlion, see before you the girl Aine, daughter of Ciann Meghan the Druid, betrothed of Laoidheach the bard. See about her family and friends who gather now that you might divine her future life through these poor bones."

> For Aine I pray, for Aine I plea,
> You shall reveal her truth to me,
> Through these poor bones two worlds entwine,
> O Cethlion, I pray your sign.

Bones rattled as I dropped them onto the tabletop and opened my eyes. Despite believing the ceremony utter foolishness, to my astonishment a vision truly did appear. The mirth within me melted away in an instant as a ghostly image formed within the scattered bones—a grassy knoll, at its crest a single tree, shaded beneath its branches a lonely cairn. The vision existed for only a moment and I jerked back gasping as it burst apart in glittering, colorful shards.

My fists scoured my eyes and I looked up to find Aunt Lou staring at me. Firelight flickered across her face, playing across deep, crisscrossing lines etched there year by year, decade by decade, memorializing her life, each a record of some great joy or sorrow. The hissing and crackling of the fire filled the silent room while her eyes questioned me as if to say, "You saw something, some fearful thing. What?"

I pushed the hilltop vision from my mind. Apparently the others merely expected my startled reaction so I forced a smile and returned to playing my game.

My finger pointed to the scattered bones. "See there, thigh bones cross symbolizing the union of Aine and Laoidheach. Close about them," finger moving above the table, I counted, "fourteen smaller bones representing the bounty of their marriage."

Teasing laughter erupted within the room as Aine shrieked, "The bounty? Fourteen children?"

"Aye," I nodded, my eyes solemn, "and only a year apart their ages."

Amid continuing laugher and women's chatter Aine pretended to swoon, the back of her hand to her brow. Questions from the group came to me.

"What are their names?"

"How will poor Laoidheach feed such a brood?"

"How many will be boys?"

I waved the questions away with a dismissive hand. "The bones do not speak to those things. They are questions worthy of divination in their own time. However, the revelation offers assurance that Aine and Laoidheach will share a long, joyful, prosperous life together."

Perhaps the vision of the lonely cairn would have preyed upon me had I not remained otherwise distracted throughout the long night in the presence of a delightful young lass with black hair and bold, green eyes.

* * *

Sickness was common among the villagers, especially the children. Often I was called upon to provide medicines and healing prayers. It was during such a mission that a messenger came and bade me report to the King's longhouse.

The child I visited had a slight fever so I handed a small bag of crushed willow bark to his mother as I gave her instructions on its use, and hurried away. My father, Laoidheach and a number of stone-faced village elders sat upon benches facing the King.

"Ossian, a messenger brought this from Tara." Sitting relaxed in his chair, King Domnhall leaned forward, handing me a scroll closed with a wax seal. "Likely it's your reply from the Christian bishop."

The room remained silent as I took the scroll from his hand, for all knew the prospect for peace hung in the balance. Breaking the seal and unrolling the document within my sweating palms I discovered it consisted of three individual pages, and then looked up in disgust.

"Sire, your pardon, but the message is written in Latin, the language of Christian priests."

"You can read it?"

"Aye, but poorly. It's a foul language, ill-suited for Irish tongues, and I may stumble a bit." Greek was the accepted written language of the well educated. The Christian's insistence upon Latin was another sign of their arrogance. I looked to my father but he shook his head in response to my unspoken question.

At the King's urging I took a seat on a bench alongside the elders and began translating the first page of the bishop's message as I read it aloud. He began with a flourishing greeting, bestowing his god's blessings upon me. My hopes for peace waned as an extensive list of the Christians' grievances followed, blaming Druids and their followers for the turmoil sweeping the land. As he had done during the synod at Tara he held us responsible for the onset of the recent darkness, saying that it was his god's retribution for our stubborn adherence to our traditional beliefs.

My father cleared his throat and I glanced at him, though he remained silent. On the message's second page the bishop went on to claim it was Druids who initiated hostilities while Christians merely defended their faith and themselves against our depredations.

Red faced, Laoidheach leaped to his feet. "Does this bishop truly expect us to believe his damnable lies? Does he think we have forgotten Dún Ailinne?"

"Be seated, Laoidheach," the King admonished. "No one here is misled by the bishop's words." He nodded, "Continue Ossian."

The message went on to list villages and Christian churches that fell which fell to our Druid forces. Sweat trickled down my back as I ignored the satisfied mumbling within the group and turned to the final page. Throughout the first two pages the bishop's tone expressed anger. It was with small hope remaining that I prayed that I might yet find words of conciliation.

I continued to read aloud. "Father Joseph tells me you are a sincere man whose words can be trusted. His conviction of your sincerity holds no sway with me, for I have no faith in the words of a demon worshipper."

Again Laoidheach leaped to his feet. The King would have none of it and bade him return to his seat.

A lump filled my throat as I translated the following paragraph in my mind and resumed. "However, I agree that your proposed truce between us is in the best interests of this land's people and, in God's Name, I shall not stand against it. Therefore, word shall be sent across the land under my seal declaring God's truce." With my hands trembling I concluded, "Christian forces shall defend themselves vigorously against pagan attacks but under no circumstances shall they be the first to violate this truce lest they face the certainty of excommunication. I hereby decree by God's Own Hand, let everlasting peace be restored to all Eire."

King Domnhall rose from his chair to stand before us, arms crossed. "It seems the bishop is an arrogant bastard but at least he appears to hold some measure of common sense." A smile flickered on his face. "Congratulations, Ossian. You have won your truce and proud I am of you. Everlasting peace the bishop decreed. Now let it be so, eh?"

Relief flooded through me as I sat there, humbled. Much work remained to ensure a lasting peace, but for now at least our people could pursue their lives without living under the cloud of possible Christian attacks. A contented sigh escaped my lips as my father stood and offered a prayer of thanks to the Lordly Ones.

Chapter 14
Beware the Open Hand

here was much to do as the midsummer festival neared. For one thing, we must call upon the goddess Aibheaog to bless the wells and springs. With this in mind my father directed me to groom the spring in the Sacred Gove.

My head shook at my father's odd behavior as I walked through the village. Granted, my return to the village relieved him of his most tedious duties, yet he seemed to grow more distant and indifferent to his responsibilities each day. Still, my confidence in him remained unshaken and I grinned, remembering the cause for his distraction. A man could easily daydream in the presence of the widow Riona.

Songbirds trilled in the early morning air as I followed the well-worn path into the Grove to perform the cleansing ritual. The gentle strumming of a lyre blended with the birdsongs and I grunted in surprise. It was early for Laoidheach to be awake and stirring.

As I came into view he glanced up from the bench where he sat and grinned. His brilliant yellow tunic stood out against the shadowy wooded background. "Is there no place a man can hide?"

"Just what is it you've done now that requires hiding?"

He stretched mightily, arms above his head, stiff legs outstretched before him kicking the air. Then he drooped, elbows on knees. "It isn't what I've done, it's what I haven't done. Aine told me, you know."

It seemed an odd response, as if I might divine his meaning. "Know what?"

"About our fourteen children, of course. How is a poor bard supposed to care for so many?"

Laughter sputtered from my throat. "Poor bard indeed. Hasn't the King favored you? Besides, as for the children—"

"That he has. It's true the King has favored me and thankful I am for it. Yet even through his beneficence I cannot feed such a brood."

"As to the fourteen children—"

Waving a dismissive hand, Laoidheach rose from the bench. "It isn't that a bard cannot afford so large a family. It is simply that I can't, at least not yet."

Fists on hips, elbows wide, I tried again. "Will you stop for a moment and hear me out?"

He ignored my words as if they were chaff in the wind and continued his pacing back and forth, hands clasped behind his back. "I'm not blaming you that Aine shall bear so many children. No, you merely foretold the future while well I know who will be responsible for creating them." He stopped, glancing toward me. "I have a plan. Will you hear it?"

Snorting my disgust, I gave up and nodded.

"Good." He resumed pacing. "Your future is assured. As a Wise One, wealth will come your way like butterflies to a floral garden. The same can be true for me," he stopped, raising a wagging finger into the air, "provided my name becomes known beyond the walls of Rath Raithleann. We can both recite the names of famous bards who earn vast riches by accepting invitations to perform in villages across the land. It is in my thoughts to become one of them."

If he was going to pace about, I intended to sit, and plopped down on the vacant bench. "You've the talent for it, to be sure." I nodded. "Yes, your plan can work, but I must remind you that becoming a noted bard relies as much on luck as talent."

"Thank you my friend. And right you are about needing luck." He stopped pacing, and stared into the sky. "Noted bards have something more I lack; new, original songs and ballads all their own." He glanced toward me. "I think to write a ballad about our fighting the Christians. Many heroes fought with us yet I must select the deeds and valor of one such man. Can you suggest someone?"

I thought for a moment and nodded. "Torcán perhaps? He is a fearless warrior and great horseman."

A grin spreading across his face, Laoidheach snapped his fingers. "Torcán. Yes, of course. He is a perfect choice. He's a dashing character and no man fought harder or with greater skill. Torcán it is then."

"Good." I began to rise, but dropped back down as Laoidheach continued.

"Of course the warrior's ballad is only a beginning. No matter how original the story, I cannot rely upon it alone to catch the attention I'm seeking. No." Shaking his head, Laoidheach frowned. "I need something more, something new, a tale of gods and men. Tell me Ossian, do you know such a story that remains untold?"

Yes, I knew such a tale, though hesitated to tell it. Nearby stood the altar where it began and ended. Memories returned of my visit to the Underworld, of speaking with Master Tóla and of a ghost ship bound for Tír na nÓg. Now my friend stood waiting, hoping that I might help him, so slowly, haltingly, I told him of that night and his eyes widened as I spoke of it.

His mouth fell open, and he swallowed hard. "Why have you not spoken of this before?"

"Perhaps because I felt it was a gift, a personal gift given me by the gods. Much there is I do not understand about the reason behind that night. But it was real enough. Of that you can be sure."

"If you say it is true, then I am sure of it." Excitement radiated from his face. "Just think of it, a visit to the Underworld. It is the stuff of an epic poem, a hero's tale begging to be shared."

"You make too much of it." I snorted. "A hero's tale indeed."

"Quiet. It is you who makes too little of it. There are old stories, ancient tales of men encountering such things. Yet, yours is a new one, a miracle within our time."

Shaking his head he began pacing again, and I waited for him to speak. Finally he stopped before me. "Words cannot express my feelings at this moment. Yet, make no mistake; they shall come, yes, they shall come in the form of a song. By that song I promise you, your name will live forever."

* * *

The cleaning of the spring entailed stepping among the stones and pulling up weeds by their roots. Muttering prayers as I worked alone around the pool, tossing the weeds into a wicker basket, the morning sun beat down on my uncovered head.

With the thought of a handful of water in mind I knelt upon a stone at the water's edge and leaned forward. My reflected image peered back up at me, bringing a wry smile to my face. Red braids fell below both ears, the remainder of my hair pulled straight back to form the thick plaited strand falling down my back. A close-cropped beard framed my tanned, angular face.

A wind gust stirred the air as I leaned further forward, stretching outward to capture a handful of water. Ripples formed upon the surface of the pool and I paused, hand suspended. A moment later the waters stilled and I found myself staring into a pair of piercing gray eyes. That the head and shoulders image within the spring was that of a Lord of the Sidhe I had no doubt. The hood of his scarlet robe shaded much of his bearded face.

Transfixed, I remained frozen, hovering above the pool's edge like a stone statue. Most certainly he was a god, but which one? Lugh? The Dagda? Mac Lir? There was no way of knowing. I remained silent, humbled, fearing to ask.

The god began to speak, his voice like rumbling thunder,

> Within the copse atop the rise,
> A stag proud with antlers wide,
> About him, does, fawns his like,
> His sovereignty unquestioned there.
>
> Hunters keen with spear points bright,
> Surmount the hill, creep through the trees,

146

The herd serene, unknowing, graze,
Unaware as peril nears.

From within the wood a spear is thrown,
Behind it fly half a dozen more,
The herd entrapped, senseless fall,
Their king struck, dead eyes glaze.

Sweat beaded my face as his eyes lingered on mine. I blessed my years of Druid's training that allowed me to hear and remember his every word. He continued,

War horns blare as banners wave,
Hunters of men, swords aflame,
Warriors all, tranquil prey in flight,
The peaceful ones fall and burn.

Hunters of game, hunters of men,
Feed their bellies or stock their folds,
Wise men beware the open hand,
For peace is a fool's delusion.

Overhead, leaves rustled while a light breeze brushed my cheek. Stirred by the wind, again the waters rippled and the image vanished as quickly as it came. The handful of water forgotten, I rocked back on my haunches, the words of a god echoing in my mind.

I was awestruck, but then could any man not be astonished and honored by confronting a god? The experience held me spellbound, my mind on fire, remembering his face, his every word and nuance. My stomach knotted as the import of his words took hold.

Rising to my feet I began pacing. My thoughts darkened as his warning grew clear. *Beware the open hand*, he said, and *peace is a fool's delusion*. Sickness filled my belly as I wondered if I was acting the deluded fool to trust the bishop's truce.

Again I knelt beside the pool, this time filling both cupped hands, splashing the cool water on my face, trying to bring clarity to my judgment. I pieced together key phrases hidden within the message and gasped as the god's warning became apparent; *Hunters of men, swords aflame, The peaceful ones fall and burn, Their king struck, dead eyes glaze.* We were going to be attacked. Domnhall, King of Rath Raithleann, and his people thinking now to live in peace were going to be attacked.

I raced up the path toward the village, torn between speaking with my father and going directly to the King. The message came as a matter of gods and men so I chose to first seek my father's counsel. He would not be home at this hour so I hurried directly to the longhouse. The sentry outside the door told me my father had stopped by earlier but was already gone. I knew where next to look for him.

Footsteps and stirring within the widow Riona's dwelling responded to my urgent rapping. My father opened the door, stepped outside to stand beside me and nodded with questioning eyes.

"As you requested," I began, "I visited the Grove to begin preparations for the midsummer ceremony. While there a vision appeared within the pool, speaking a warning." I went on to describe the vision, recite the message and tell him my interpretation of it.

His head shook, his face grave. "By your description the vision in the pool was none other than the great Lugh himself. It had to be, as it matches descriptions passed down from the Ancient Ones. Ossian, sometimes you…" He paused, his head again shaking. "You have a special relationship with the gods." Hands sliding inside the sleeves of his robe, arms crossing over his chest, he added, "However, I heard no words within the message that spoke to an imminent attack."

"Father, you must listen—"

"Ossian, I heard you. Lugh's message was for your ears, that you not be overly trusting of the Christians. That was all he was saying to you." Head lifting, he paused and gazed into the cloudless sky. "I confess, however, that a voice whispered a word of warning in my ear during my morning prayers."

My sense of urgency heightened. "What voice? You heard it today?"

"No. It was more than a week past. Indeed it was on the same morning your message from the bishop arrived. The voice was feminine, one I did not recognize."

Relief flooded through me knowing my father already took steps to avert danger. "How has the King responded? What protective measures is he taking?"

"I said nothing to the King. That day it seemed your truce was more imperative." He swayed and shrugged. "Since then many important matters take my time and I have been busy you see..." His voice trailed away.

His behavior was baffling. Was it not a Druid's foremost duty to protect his King? "Then you understand we must report to the King, that he might raise the guard."

A growing premonition of danger weighed upon me as he merely responded, "Of course." His eyes moved to the widow's door. "Perhaps later. Yes, tonight during dinner we will speak of this."

"No, father, not tonight." I hesitated, fists clenched at my sides, amazed by his indifference. "We must speak of it now. The King must be warned right away. Scouting parties must be dispatched, sentinels posted—"

"Not now, Ossian," he insisted, "we must discuss this at length. This moment I am..." Again his anxious eyes moved to the door. "Tonight will be soon enough. Afterwards I will decide if the King should become aware of it."

"Father, if you are busy, I will go now and speak with the King."

I turned to go and he grabbed my arm. "No. We mustn't alarm King Domnhall and the villagers needlessly." He placed his hand upon my shoulder and gave me a comforting smile. "Remember the bishop's message. He promised peace, did he not?"

Was it me or himself that he reassured? "Aye, he did that, though Lugh's warnings now speak otherwise."

His tone was gentle. "I ask you again. Did Lugh warn of a Christian attack?"

"No, but little it matters who might bring it."

"Who?" A small smile touched his lips. "What nearby tribe must we fear? We have no enemies now that we have a truce with the Christians. We must think this thing through, you and I, eh? Tonight. I promise we will decide a proper course tonight."

Foreboding filled me as he turned his back, re-entered the cottage and firmly closed the door behind him. It was the thought of disobeying his orders and hurrying off to warn the King that turned me toward the village longhouse. Yet, my footsteps faltered, for the ropes that tie a son to his father's will are strong.

I stood there, gripped by uncertainty, absently rubbing the serpent ring, a prized possession that never left my hand. Disrespecting one's father was a shameful thing yet I remained torn between my duty to him and my King. Spinning slowly about, I reflected upon the widow's cottage. My father was almost certainly right; we should discuss it. Spreading an alarm without cause would be a foolish act.

With my mind still busy with indecision I turned away, my steps leading toward my father's home. As I walked, a shadow crossed the ground before me and I glanced up. High aloft, a solitary crow rode the wind, circling the village.

* * *

Wood chips flew as the axe head bit deep in time with the rolling of my shoulders. Little time I owned to spend to my own ends. The fields given me by the king produced overgrown brush. Following my conversation with my father, I chose to spend the afternoon hacking away my frustration along with the brambles and small trees. By the following summer my fields must be ready for cultivation.

The rhythmic pounding of the axe against a tree almost drowned out the distant cries.

"Corcu!"

"Run!"

"Attack! Attack!"

"Horsemen!"

"To arms! Raid!"

The sun's glare fell upon my face as I straightened up, stretching my work-stiffened back. Sweat soaked the ragged kirtle I wore to the field. Squinting, hand shading my eyes, in the distance swirling banners erupted from the forest's edge amid onrushing horsemen and chariots followed by swarming warriors afoot. A huge warrior led the way; two horses pulling his racing chariot while below his gleaming bronze skullcap long red hair flowed freely. Within the charging horde I counted one…two…three crucifixes held high.

My white-knuckled hands gripped the axe as fear, desperation and the awareness of my earlier failure to raise an alarm crowded my mind. I remained transfixed for only a moment more, cursing my stupidity for trusting the promises of the Christian bastards.

I turned to flee as sounds I knew well, war horns and drums, clamored within the onrushing enemy. Even as I ran I realized it was too late. Horsemen would overtake me long before I reached the village.

Behind me screams and shouts grew louder. Glancing over my shoulder, farmers working farther afield fell beneath the swords of galloping horsemen. Mounted warriors gained on me and I recognized the colors and banners of the Corcu Duibne tribe who dwelt far to the west alongside the sea.

Two warriors reined toward me and there was no hope for it. I turned to face them, filled with bitterness, resigned to defeat. Axe head held at the ready at shoulder height, I waited.

The horsemen rode in tandem, the one on my right wielding a sword, the man on the left a war club. Onward they came, armor gleaming, eyes fixed upon me, bared teeth flashing within heavy beards. The warrior on the right canted over, arm cocked, holding his sword low as if to use it as a scythe to cut me down. It was he I chose as the target for my axe.

They came upon me in a rush of pounding hooves and I whispered a final prayer that my soul might be welcomed at Tír na nÓg. My axe swept down to counter the swinging sword—

* * *

The aroma of soil and grass first touched my rousing consciousness. Awareness took a tentative hold on my mind though I knew not where I was or why I was there. My eyes flicked open. Moon glow lit the field. I lay face down, lacking the strength or desire to rise.

Pain streaked through my skull like a lightning bolt and I stirred only enough to roll onto my side and violently retch, stomach cramping, I retched again. My senses whirled and I struggled to maintain my grasp on reality or such little reality I could muster.

My hand reached to my throbbing head and came away covered with sticky, sweet-smelling blood. The thought came that I lay dying but I was completely indifferent to it. A black cloud developed in the back of my mind and rapidly swept forward to re-envelop my senses.

* * *

"Ossian."

The word came clearly though at first it held no meaning for me.

"Ossian," the soft, coaxing, feminine voice continued. "Rise up, Ossian."

A groan escaped my lips, faint awareness returned and I wished the voice away.

"You are gravely injured, Ossian, but can stand if you will."

Again a groan and once more my eyes opened to confusion and darkness.

"You must stand. Do it now."

It was a kind voice, a caring voice, a voice begging compliance. "Yes. Of course." Was it my response I heard? I wasn't sure but placed my palms against the ground, flexed my legs and pushed myself upward until I rested upon hands and knees. Lights flashed before my eyes and I barely stifled a shriek as insufferable pain streaked throughout my skull.

"You are doing well, Ossian," the voice encouraged. "Now, rise. Stand to your feet."

My senses swirled 'round and 'round. Remaining suspended on hands and knees, again I retched.

"Overcome the weakness. You must battle against it. Stand. Stand."

Once more I pushed upwards, fighting my own frailty until I stood upright. Flashing lights and whirling senses returned and I staggered backwards, falling where I lay gasping.

"Again," the soft voice pleaded. "You must try again."

The source of the voice meant nothing. Be she goddess, fairy or mortal I thought only to reward her encouragement. Great weariness weighed me down but I renewed my fight against it, finally rising to my feet. Again my head ached and swam. Once more I staggered about though this time managed to remain upright.

"Now, you see? You did it, Ossian. You did it."

"So it seems, yes." My hand went to my pounding skull.

"You cannot remain here. You must go, go now."

Mind reeling, I whispered, "Go? Go where?"

There was no response so I repeated, "Go where?" But I stood alone under the stars in utter silence. A memory came, Corcu Duibne warriors streaming across the fields toward me, and suddenly I remembered. I remembered everything. How much time passed since the attack? Had it come earlier today? The day before? I had no sense or knowledge of how long I might have lain in the field.

Supported by trembling legs I turned about, surveying my surroundings. Uphill in the general direction of where I thought Rath Raithleann should lie, an orange glow lit the dark sky. My heart heavy with the thought of what I might find within the village, I took a tentative step forward, a second and third. At twenty steps I rested and then tottered twenty paces further.

By the time I leaned against a post at the ruined village gates I had a reasonable idea of my injuries. The source of the blood was a deep gash within a large area of swelling just above the base of my skull. Apparently during the attack my lunge with the axe against the swordsman thwarted his blow, but the other rider smashed his war club into the back of my head. The shoulders of my kirtle and plaited braid down my back were stiff with dried blood.

The stench of mixed wood smoke and charred flesh permeated the air and my heart near burst at the sight of the burning village. Nothing remained untouched during the Corcu Duibne raid. On unsteady legs I bent down, picked up a broken lance shaft to use as a staff and hobbled forward.

Only the crackling flames overrode the deathly silence. Onward I went, my searching eyes finding ghostly figures churning within acrid smoke, shadows darting among smoldering cottages—horror exposed by flickering firelight—black blood and death at every turn. Faces, dead eyes staring—known, unknown, might have known—contorted, swollen, charred.

I stumbled down narrow lanes throughout the village seeking someone, anyone…probing for life while my desperate eyes quickly turned from grotesque piles of the dead. My rasping voice called out, the snapping and popping of flames the mocking reply. Time and again I fell, crawled and then rose only to stumble and fall again.

Ceara was there; sprawled on her face near her home. Her small boys lay beside her. Aunt Lou's home, a tumbled pile, blazed in the night, though whether she and Aine lay beneath rubble I could not see.

My father was at the longhouse, his head atop a tall wooden pike alongside that of the King. Eyes glazed, mouth agape, he hovered over me and I fell to my knees, head throbbing, staring upwards toward him.

Unreasoning maniacal hatred seized me, and I shouted at him. "I loved you and respected your wisdom above all others. Now look at you. Why are you there? Answer me! You would ignore my question now as you did my warning? I say you are up there, foolish man, because you paid no heed to the gods and now you are dead, your family is dead, your King is dead and your village is dead."

I clutched my head in both hands. Mind reeling, I shrieked, "I trusted your judgment. Oh, how I trusted you as a son should trust his father. Now the burden of this tragedy lies with me as well, for I knew. Yes, I knew and did nothing. Because of you I did nothing."

A smoldering fire burned through the base of the pike at that very moment and it toppled, its gruesome burden falling to the ground—rolling, rolling, rolling across the scorched ground toward me. Screaming, I lurched backwards from the horrid thing, scrambling away on hands and knees, on and on, my fingers clawing the earth as my father's head seemed to pursue me across the warm, ash-covered courtyard.

Searing pain cloaking my mind, I staggered to my feet and ran. Consumed by terror I stumbled away from the village into the night, a cowering, mewling, half-dead creature blind to all but the crushing pain blanketing my mind.

How many days, how many nights did I flee the ruins of my life? What matter, for does a mindless brute measure time? If I stole food from farmsteads by which to survive, what of it? Is an animal seeking only to remain alive a thief?

155

An evening arrived with the smell of the sea in the air, and above the rock-strewn shoreline a cave—a miserable hole within which to crawl as a wounded beast would creep into a hidden place to die away from prying eyes. Such were not my thoughts then, for I had none, nothing more than a dim awareness of my existence.

* * *

Days, weeks, months passed, my mind dominated by pain, driven to madness. That I survived was not by my own hand but by the will of the gods. I ate, though what or how often I cannot say. During more lucid moments I found myself surrounded by the shells of creatures living at the sea's edge, the bones of fish and remnants of nearby plants.

At last the day came I sat hunched, cross-legged before the cave mouth, rain drawing a gray curtain across the panorama of the sea. Though my head still throbbed my ability to remember and reason was returning.

Desolate were my thoughts, for all I had ever known or hoped to be ended on that final, terror-filled night at Rath Raithleann. Perhaps the gods favored me by leaving me alive as they had at Dún Ailinne, though the hollowness filling me little resembled life, and I found no meaning in it.

Memories and the grief bound within them overwhelmed me as I bent further forward, arms wrapped around my knees, sobbing aloud like a woman. Tears streaming, I rubbed the serpent ring, now a worthless trinket from my past. My future as bleak as the rain, I would remain hidden within my cave, for where else was I to go?

Book Two

Chapter 15
Brendan

$\mathfrak{J}$ lay on my bracken bed staring at the cave's smoke-smudged ceiling. Thoughts of the past crowded my mind, memories brought about by the Morrigan's visit. Had she truly come? Had I actually spoken with her? On many days my mind still grew confused, clouded, but then her words returned. Words I well knew to be true just as her presence in my cave must be true. "Your wounds are healed, your father will not rise from the dead, nor will your sisters."

Yes, they were dead, but death is such a small thing. That I had learned. Still, a man strives to survive even when it is senseless to do so.

There was much to do so I rose and busied myself. Mussels must be pried from the rocks now that the tide was out. They would be added to seaweed I gathered, by which farmers might enrich their fields, and a bag of carrageen, the kelp prized by women for the thickening of their broth. All to be traded in the nearby village for a moldy loaf and scant jug of ale. It was a village of simple farmers with but a few head of cattle and sheep, merely a place to be.

At midday I started off under a sunlit sky, the seaweed strapped to my back and two woven bags of mussels in hand. Reaching the village required an exhausting walk across high, boulder-strewn ridges.

There was a priest there, one who claimed that Patrick himself had ordained him, but he was old and gave me little trouble. Yet, some in the village still held to the old ways.

When I first came and showed the serpent ring the priest made the villagers drive me away, but some would still sneak to my cave for what little divination I could give them and ask me to read the stars for planting time. Their gifts were meager but many were as poor as I was.

As I came in sight of the village, Beagan came running toward me.

"Go back, Wise One. This is not a day to be here. A new priest has come, a man called Brendan with fourteen followers. He preached last night against the Druids and he will not welcome you!"

He stopped and watched me rub the serpent ring.

I raised my eyes to meet his. "So, Beagan, you have come to drive me away? You, who brought your child to my cave for blessing? And was it not I who gathered herbs for you when your wife was stricken?"

"To drive you away? No! I come but to warn you of the priest's presence."

No priest could make me fear him, for there is little to fear when you have nothing. It was not a thing Beagan would understand.

Still, I would know more of this new priest. "So, why should this man come to your little village, which could hardly feed his people for one day?"

"Right you are, for it is little food any of us have following the dark times. Still, he has laid a tithe on us and on all the villages within a day of here. We are to build him a boat and provision it, for he plans to sail to the Northern Isles to carry Christ's word to them."

Christ's word? I knew all too well about Christ's word. Did Eire not have gods enough already without bringing forth this new one?

I un-strapped the seaweed from my back and set it down beside my two leather bags. "Take these, Beagan, and go through the fields to the back of the village. Find Gair, who I deal with. Give it to him and bring me back my bread and ale."

Beagan nodded, shouldered the pack, took the bags of mussels and set off.

"Two loaves for the carrageen!" I shouted after him

Exhausted by my trek to the village, I sat beside the trail on a gentle rise above the village and waited with my back against a rock. In the valley below the men worked their fields around the small village, a cluster of wattle and daub, thatched roof huts. Smoke plumes rose from the women's cooking fires fueled by wood collected from the distant rugged ridges covered in oak, beech and linden trees. Gulls swirled above Trá Lí Bay, suspended against the bright sky, but I could not see the curraghs I knew to be there.

Presently, a man came walking toward me. He carried a staff and was muttering to himself.

"Good day, stranger," he greeted me. "You are not from here, for I have met everyone in the village."

I shrugged. "I am but a simple traveler."

"Well, so am I a simple traveler."

I glanced at his undistinguished, bearded face. He wore a common wool robe but I sensed he was considerably more than a common man.

He sat down beside me, pointing to the west where the sun slid into the sea. "It's late for further travels, come to the village and eat with me. The women have made a good stew and baked fresh bread today."

"I would rather not, but thank you for your kindness. There is a priest of the new religion there that I would not meet."

He looked at me and chortled. "And why would you not meet him, traveler?"

Again I shrugged. "I have my reasons."

"Reasons will not fill your belly." He stood up. "Come, I insist. You have my word this new priest will not harm you."

It was with no intent to mock the man I replied, "And who would you be to guarantee protection against priests?"

161

"You doubt my word, traveler?" Laughter filled his eyes.

"Not your word, nor your sincerity in giving it. I say again, I am but a poor traveler, a man of little virtue to judge such important matters as words and intentions. I fear you would little value my company."

"I will judge the value of those I meet. Come, I assure you again there will be no trouble in the village. There is food aplenty and I would share it with you."

My belly was in conflict with my judgment. "I admit I am tempted by you."

His staff nodded toward me. "Is it the serpent ring on your hand that creates the conflict within you?"

"You noticed it, then. Yes, in part it is the ring. I was told this new priest speaks strongly against the meaning of it."

"The new priest is to be feared for his intolerance of the old ways?"

My head shook as I warily chose my words. "Feared? No. But avoided, as must all priests be avoided for those of us who would cling to the old knowledge and the old gods."

"A time of great change, a wonderful change is sweeping this land, traveler. The priests do but herald the change and in so doing bring new knowledge to replace the old, and the one true God to replace the many pagan gods of the past." Face turned to the evening sky, arms spread wide, he spun in a slow circle before stopping, his eyes radiating exuberance. "The change to the Truth of which I speak is as inevitable as the winds and the tides."

I understood then, for the light of his beliefs shown brightly on his face. "You are Brendan the priest...you must be. No other man hereabout could speak such things. Yes, of course...that is how you guarantee my safety in the village."

"Yes, I am Brendan, I am a priest and I am still hungry." His eyes once again reflected humor. "Come traveler. Let us eat while we talk of the old times and the new."

I placed no confidence in the promises of Christians, but Brendan I felt I could trust, not as a priest, but as a man of his word, a man worthy of respect. And the lure of the stew was irresistible.

* * *

Firelight reflected from the hovel's stone walls as a woman, her woolen shawl drawn taut to her face and slumped shoulders, flitted like a spirit around our rough table. She brought bowls of stew, fresh bread and mugs of ale.

Brendan sipped his ale. "Who are you, traveler?"

"I am called Ossian and I live in a cave near the sea."

"Ossian. Ah, but that is merely a name, and a cave is merely the place where you live. I asked who you are."

"I fear the answers you seek are of no more account than fancied phantoms in yon evening's mist. I am what you see before you and no more—a poor man, a fisherman and gatherer who lives alone and strives only to survive."

Brendan shook his head. "A poor fisherman who wears the serpent ring?"

"The ring is not for you to speak of."

"I think not. I am a Christian priest, yes, but well I know the old ways too, and know that the serpent ring may only be worn by a chosen few."

I sat quietly, sipping stew from the bowl.

"Ossian." Brendan rolled the name on his tongue, "Hmm. It is said long ago a man of that name stood alongside Finn Mac Cumhaill to found the Fianna at Almu. It is also said that same Ossian was a renowned Druid leader, a man of ballads and songs. Are you, Ossian of the serpent ring, such a man yourself?"

I ignored his question. The stew was good, the best I had eaten in many months. "Have you tried the stew? I believe you will find it fine and to your taste."

Brendan's eyebrows lifted and his humor returned. "Hah! A Druid and man of ballads and songs you may possibly be, but even if so, you are a hungry one."

"I thank you for inviting me to join you. It is a rare treat."

Brendan spoke as he munched his bread. "I merely invited you to the table. God provided the meal. A timely meal it is, too, from the looks of you. You are overly thin and stooped. Are you ill?"

Earlier, as I stood beside him, it was necessary to raise my eyes to meet his though he was but average height. Still, I cared nothing about my stooping posture and would tell little to this priest. "I am recovering from…that is, yes, I have been ill."

"Then I shall pray for your speedy recovery. Tell me, Ossian the fisherman, have you a boat?"

"A crude curragh I found abandoned on the shore. I made a few repairs to it and take it on the sea when the weather permits."

"You fish the nearby bays and inlets?"

"Yes."

The priest swiped his bread through his bowl to capture the moisture of the stew. "You travel beyond the sight of land?"

"At times, depending upon the weather."

"Are you afraid of being lost at sea?"

"There is the sun." I shrugged. "What is there to fear?"

"You know the positions and movements of the stars, as well?"

And so. It wasn't fishing that held his interest; he knew of the Druids' preoccupation with the stars and would gauge my knowledge. "I know no more and likely far less of the stars than most who fish these waters."

"The villagers here are building a large curragh for me and my followers that we might sail to the Northern Isles to spread the word of Christ there. Perhaps you've heard of this?"

"A little…no more."

"The voyage will require several days. Which stars would we follow to reach the Isles?"

It was another of his tests. "You will have a pilot aboard. He will know better than one such as I, who has never been to the Isles."

"God is my pilot in all things—"

A light rap at the door interrupted Brendan's comment, and a cowled monk entered. "I apologize for interrupting your meal, father, but—" and then he noticed me.

"Yes, Brother Erc, what is it?" Brendan asked.

"I'm sorry, father. I didn't realize you had a guest."

"Indeed, Brother. This is Ossian, the fisherman."

"Ossian!" Erc hissed. "Father, this is the Druid the old priest warned us about."

"Of course he is."

So, the ring had been telling enough. From the beginning Brendan had known who and what I was, that I had earned the right to bear a Druid's staff.

Erc was a slender, swarthy man. His uncompromising hatred of me and all that I represented radiated from black, burning eyes as he turned to me. "What evil wind brought you here? The Holy Saint Patrick, may God rest his immortal soul, banished all of you pagan snake worshipers from Eire."

"Brother Erc," Brendan interceded, "please restrain yourself. This man is here because I invited him to eat with me."

"But, father! I urge you beware this man. Patrick himself invoked all of the virtues of the Holy Trinity to,

> guard against the black laws of heathenism,
> against the spells of women, and demons, and Druids."

Brendan nodded. "Indeed he did, dear Brother, though I do not need you to remind me of it. But, Patrick intended so much more when he invoked the Trinity to support his true mission here, that Christ may be seen and cherished,"

in the heart of everyone who thinks of me,
in the mouth of everyone who speaks to me,
in every eye that sees me,
in every ear that hears me.

Place your trust in the Lord God, Brother Erc," Brendan added with a soft voice. "I would that this man see, hear and come to Christ through me."

"Yes, father, though I would prefer to see this blasphemous Druid in chains."

"And I would prefer to have him embrace Jesus Christ as his Lord and Savior! Now Brother Erc, you had a purpose in coming here?"

"Yes, father, it's the villagers, they claim..." Erc hesitated, his eyes slanted toward me. "Father, please accept my apologies for disturbing you. My message is not urgent. With your grace I shall leave you now that we may discuss the matter tomorrow."

"Thank you, Brother, that will serve me well." As Erc turned to leave, Brendan added, "And Brother, please hear this and share it among all my followers. Ossian the fisherman is not to be disturbed. He shall be free to leave the village at his will. Do you understand?"

Erc bowed. "Of course, father. I will tell the others and it shall be as you say."

The door closed as Erc quietly shut it behind him. Brendan turned to me. "Don't worry, you are safe here under my sanctuary. So, shall we now discuss...hmm, how did you phrase it earlier? Oh, yes, now I remember. Shall we discuss your phantoms in yon evening's mist?"

I sat quietly for a moment before answering. "What matter phantoms even if such exist? We banter words, you and I, but to what good end? We are as unlike as the ox and the whale, and follow far different paths."

Brendan nodded. "Yes, there are differences between us, but with God's help I hope to wash them away. With the Light of His only son, Jesus Christ, I shall find the way to deliver you into the Grace of the Holy Trinity."

"I am but one man, insignificant, and unworthy of your efforts."

"Not so small, I think, and what's more, every soul is worthy in the eyes of God. Yes, and I would that you will see His glory and come to Him."

"What matter? Beyond this evening's meal we will speak no more." I pushed my empty stew bowl away. "After tonight your thoughts will turn again to the Northern Isles where there are many who might hear your words and be swayed by them."

"After tonight I shall not forget you. Even though my brethren have spent scores of years in the Northern Isles spreading His word there remain many who might be converted to the True Way."

"Yes, you and your brethren are relentless in spreading your faith. I fear even the Golden Ones of the Blessed Isles shall not be spared your incursion."

Brendan was an eager listener. "The Blessed Isles, you say? It is a familiar name known to me though I know nothing of them. Where lay these Isles?"

I pointed vaguely outward, beyond the hovel's walls. "Many weeks sailing across the western sea near the River Oceanus. Or so Mac Lir said."

His disappointment showed on his face. "Mac Lir said? Mac Lir is but a blasphemous pagan sea spirit. Your Blessed Isles and the people there are but a heretic myth, then."

"A myth? Think so, if you will, but I know them to be otherwise. The Blessed Isles have been called many things but perhaps are best known among us as Tír na nÓg, the Isles of the Ever Young. Much has been said of the Isles by others who proclaimed them a paradise."

"Tír na nÓg?" Brendan shook his head. "It is merely spoken of in legends. But the Ever Young? Who are they?"

"They are the Golden Ones, the spirits of the dead. There they remain until called upon by the gods to return here and be reborn."

"You describe a Heaven here on earth? Such a thing is not possible and is contradicted in the Scriptures by God's Own Word.

No, your beliefs are founded in the ancient stories of the old ones, for spirits live on only by the grace of God Himself."

I would not mention my encounter with the spirits of Dún Ailinne as they boarded the ghost ship enroute to Tír na nÓg. Perhaps he would believe my story, perhaps not, but it was not something I would share with him. "As you say, priest, but The Blessed Isles are there, you may rely upon it."

"You have proof of them, then?"

"No proof, but I have faith and that is something a man like you should understand. There is an old song of our people that tells of the Isles. Though I am a poor singer I will tell it to you."

> Fair are the blessed,
> The Isles of the Ever Young.
> Far to the West.
> Where live the Golden Ones.
>
> They have no want or care,
> Soft breezes soothe the Land.
> The springs run crystal clear,
> Where the sacred Rowans stand.
>
> They have no guilt or fear,
> And nothing gives them flight.
> There is no darkness there,
> Only the soft moonlight.
>
> My heart cries out for the West,
> And the touch of the Ever Young.
> Where no man is oppressed,
> And the songs of the gods are sung.

Brendan remained silent for a moment. "Your voice is not poor. I hear the training in it. Do your people have other tales of this land?"

"There were many. Within the Isles are four great cities: Falias, Gorias, Murias and Findias. Within each city dwells a powerful Druid, and within each a potent magical treasure. Now the old ways are vanishing and there are few left who know the details and the old songs. I know but a fragment of one other, from the song of Nihil."

> She takes my hand at the sea marge,
> She whispers low on the wind,
> She sets her sail for Tír na nÓg
> And leaves worn life behind!

I rose from my bench. "I do not wish to be impolite but it is late and I would go back to my cave. I thank you for inviting me to eat with you, for the food was well done."

Brendan was surprised. "You go now? So late? Stay that we might talk more of these Isles of yours. You are unwell and are welcome to sleep here that you may depart more comfortably in the morning."

"Thank you, but you will be busy tomorrow and I would not burden you. I have kept a man waiting for me and there are things that I must do beside the sea, things important to my meager existence best done in the early morning."

I walked to the door, opened it and glanced back at him. "I wish you a safe journey, Brendan."

"I think we will meet again, Ossian." The priest rose, placing his palms together before him in the manner of prayer. "But go if you must, go with God's blessings upon you."

Chapter 16
A Path to Tír na nÓg

𝕿he evening sun, a dull orange orb, sank toward the distant rim of the western sea. Only a few shorebirds that frequented the rock-strewn beach below me remained. Soon they, like others of their kind, would end their daylong search for the tiny shellfish hiding beneath the sand. My own daily search for food began early that same morning. First was the gathering of knotgrass and goosefoot seeds to prepare a poor porridge, and, as I tired of sea fare, later I hiked the banks of Cumeenduff Lough to fish for the trout there. Time and again I cast my baited hand line into the sparkling clear water and sat on a stone, anticipating a reward. At days end I returned with three fish, a small one and two others of pleasing length and girth.

I turned from my view of the birds and darkening sea and entered my cave to bake the small fish for my dinner. The two larger ones were suspended above the smoke to be preserved for later. Many of my days were spent in such a way.

A fortnight had passed since last I visited the village and spoke with the priest, Brendan. Soon he would sail to the Northern Isles. I doubted to see him again as he would stay long in the North to spread his religion. His movements were of little interest to me. I would remain in my cave beside the sea until I felt safe to move on.

* * *

I awoke from a deep slumber to the spirit voice of the Morrigan. My low-burning fire cast dancing shadow figures upon my cave walls, and her voice, no longer the harsh croak of a crow, came softly from the night, a refrain in the sigh of the wind.

"Wake up, Ossian," she was saying, "you sleep soundly while your gods are displeased with you."

Wary of her, I sat up and replied, "What, My Queen? The Lordly Ones are displeased, you say? Why?"

"You traveled to the village and spoke to the new priest, Brendan, at length."

"Yes, we spoke at length. What of it?"

"We fear you were swayed by this man. He is becoming prominent. Someday he will assume the place of the eminent priest, Patrick, who banished all followers of the sacred serpent from Eire's shores."

It was troubling to hear that even gods know fear. "Brendan did not sway me from the beliefs instilled in me by my father. The Lordly Ones need not be troubled so long as there remain those of us who still believe in them."

"Gods cannot exist in an empty void. What purpose do gods serve in the absence of conscious thought if there are no mortals who know and worship them? The god of the Christians gains greater supremacy each day as more and more mortals convert to the new religion. The new god acquires strength while your gods continue to fade."

"You, all of you Lordly Ones must come together to resist the new god of the Christians and reverse the tide of the new religion."

"We did resist in the beginning, Ossian, but now it's too late...too late. Much has happened while you lay idle in this cave. The new god has won Eire. Because of this, many of us have already departed this land for Tír na nÓg, the Isles of the Ever Young. Hear me,"

> The Age of the World, was 3303,
> Edarlamh and his Tuatha De Danann
> Overcame the Firbolgs at Magh Tuireadh,
> And secured this place, this Eire, for themselves, Forever.
>
> Forever, I say...but what is that? Forever...
> It was wife, we thought, not mistress, honey not bittersweet.
> We held it close in hand, ever dreaming foolish dreams,

While we gathered about the fire to sing the songs of
Forever

This land was ours Forever, we said, your Lordly Ones,
For two thousand plus four hundred years.
Tomorrows beyond imagining,
lives beyond lives, time without end,
Minding not that in a universe with a beginning, there can
be no Forever.

The sun sets now; I see it setting, on our Forever.
The Father, Son, and Blessed Mother are here.
New Holy Ones have won this Land and its people.
Their sun rises as ours sets, and so begins their time of
Forever.

Tír na nÓg, the Blessed Isles are our final Forever,
Enchanted, enshrouded in the mists of the western sea.
They must not fall to the new Father and his followers,
Lest all be lost to us, your Lordly Ones, lost upon this earth,
Forever.

It was an astonishing thing. "The Lordly Ones are leaving Eire?"

"Some will remain and live in the Underworld, but yes, already many have gone. As for the remainder of us...we shall see."

"Why tell me this? I am no more important than the small fish I ate for my dinner."

"Perhaps that's true, perhaps not. Once you showed great promise. As of now, you still are of some consequence to the old and the new. Brendan sees this and understands the significance of seizing your mind and will, that others might follow your lead."

Bitterness welled within me. "Of consequence am I? Once I hoped to become of consequence. Look about you, My Queen, and see that I have nothing—nothing! Of what consequence is that? Of what consequence am I to anyone?"

The voice of the Morrigan sneered. "I see...you lost your vanity most of all. You thought yourself important and looked to the time when you would gain even more favor. Now look at you, thin, starving and hunched over like a cowering puppy. Stand up straight before me!"

"My Queen, I've been ill and—"

"You were ill but the injury to your head is past. Stand up, stand up straight. At least try to look like a man!"

I stood as she ordered and rose upward to my full height though my long unused neck and shoulder muscles cried out as I did so and my head swam with the effort.

"Now," she continued, "that is much better and a small beginning, though you hide in this loathsome place, frightened to return to the world of men."

A forgotten, fearsome memory flashed through my mind; firelight from the burning village illuminating my father's head on the end of a pike alongside that of King Domhnall. "My Queen, perhaps you forget...my father—"

"Your father... Your father...," she scoffed. "The stupid man was so smitten by a woman he failed his king! You heard our warning, Ossian, and you knew the attack was coming, didn't you?"

"Yes. Yes, of course I knew." My head drooped and I held my face in my hands. "Do you not think I feel the weight of it? It preys upon my mind like maggots on rotten flesh."

"Of course." Her scornful tone held no touch of sympathy. "Your father ignored his gods' warnings as well, didn't he?"

Long since I made peace with my father's ghost and would not speak ill of him.

At my silence, she raged, "I asked you a question! Did your father ignore his gods?"

My face flushed as I nodded.

"Yes! Your father foresaw the attack on your village and neglected to sound an alarm," the Morrigan hissed. "And now he is dead. His king is dead. Your entire village of Rath Raithleann is dead! Think of it, an entire village of believers gone, dead at the hands of Christian followers."

My face remained flushed but she would never break my faith in my father. "My father was a good man, a wise man and ever faithful to his King. The Corcu Duibne attacked our village; the destruction and death is on their heads, theirs alone!"

"Your loyalty to your father remains strong though misplaced."

She was silent for so long I thought her spirit departed, but finally she sighed. "What is done is done, is it not? Now, will you take part in the future? You, Druid, were raised in the special knowledge that is as old as the world itself. You have understanding and abilities far beyond common men. You led men in victorious battle. And yet you lie here in your squalor and self-pity. True, you have lost much, but have you lost yourself as well?"

"I have lost all! Yes, the special knowledge of which you speak was meant that I might advise kings. I fear—"

"You fear everything and cower here in this lowly cave." Her derisive voice echoed in the darkness. "You even ran from an old priest who drove you from his village. Is that now the path of the mighty Druids who speak for their gods? To run and hide from the new religion or perhaps even succumb to it out of fear?"

My spirits sagged. "Do not ridicule me, My Queen—"

"You forget yourself! I can ridicule you, torture you and even kill you if it serves my purposes! You know that, do you not?"

"Of...of course, My Queen." I had been careless with my words. "Please, I meant no disrespect, but why do you come to me now? I am of little value to the Lordly Ones."

"Hmm, so finally you think to ask, eh? I am here to weigh your value, and as you freely admit, there's little I have found of it. As for your future, we shall see. I also came to find if you remain true to your gods."

"Why would you doubt me? I will remain true to my gods unto death. I said as much to Brendan himself and he was tolerant in his views toward me."

"You are wrong. Have you already forgotten the fate of Master Druid Tóla? He too thought he found tolerance among Christians. Brendan possesses great patience in converting you to his faith through his teachings, yes, but no tolerance of your gods and beliefs."

"Little it matters now. Soon Brendan will sail to the Northern Isles, so I shall speak to him no more."

"Your gods will decide those things that matter. Be not so sure that you and Brendan will not meet again, be not so sure."

* * *

Another week passed and I drifted upon the sea, fishing in my curragh. Soon I must return to the village to trade for bread and ale. Truth be told, I sometimes grew weary of my own company and wished to talk with men.

I was concentrating on my fishing when a porpoise surfaced beside my boat, saying, "I have been to the village. You told Brendan of the Blessed Isles, of Tír na nÓg?"

I knew the Morrigan could change her shape at will and came in many guises—a crow, a crone, a wolf, a beautiful red-haired woman, but it was a startling thing to see her appear beside me in the sea. My mind spun as I sought a proper response. "What? Uh…that is…yes. It was a meaningless conversation between two men, My Queen, no more. I spoke of the Blessed Isles to Brendan as simple amusement. I scarce think he believed me."

The porpoise extended its head above the water. "You spoke too well, for the priest did believe you. Now he thinks of little else."

"And so? To what end?"

"To go there, Ossian! To go there! Even now he prepares to sail to the Blessed Isles to convert the Golden Ones living there to his religion."

To go there, she said? It was an astonishing thing! How could Brendan ever think to find them? Even with all my knowledge of the movements of the sun, the moon and the stars, I would at best hold only a slim hope of reaching the Isles…though I had no reason to try.

"You are surprised, are you not?" the Morrigan asked. "Yes, he is going and if he is successful in finding Tír na nÓg, the fault will be yours."

"The fault would be mine, My Queen? What fault?"

"I told you, many in the Sidhe have gone to Tír na nÓg and others will soon follow. This new religion has already swept Gaul, Pictland, Dalriada, Calchfynedd, Dumnonia…the list is endless, and now it has captured our sacred Eire. The Blessed Isles are the last sanctuary of your gods. Brendan must not be allowed to find the Isles and convert the Golden Ones."

"Yes, of course. I…I see it plainly now, but who would have thought Brendan would be so foolhardy as to…" My voice trailed away as I considered the enormity of it.

"Make the attempt? Oh yes, he will certainly make the attempt. We look for you to travel with him so that he does not succeed."

"No man can find Tír na nÓg on his own." I pointed out to sea. "Only the gods can lead him there."

"And you think Brendan's god could not show him the way?" The porpoise head nodded. "He can, you know. Oh yes, Brendan can most certainly find the Isles, so now you must stop him."

An immense wave rose from the surface of the sea, rocking my boat violently. My grip on the gunwales tightened while the Morrigan hovered unaffected on the water's surface.

"You demand that I go with him?" My shaken mind reeled; my eyes swept the sea, the shore and the sky in confusion. "My Queen, surely you can't be serious? I say again, Brendan's quest is foolhardy and I would be equally foolish to accompany him."

"No, Ossian. It is foolish for you to remain here trembling in your cave. It is foolish to think that a Druid can survive here in the old ways in the face of the Corcu Duibne and the growing number of intolerant Christian tribes like them who would in the end destroy you. You, like your gods, must leave Eire and go to the west. Your future is there, not here."

I wasn't convinced, her words made little sense. "Yes, I see, but if I were to agree to go—"

"No, you shall go!" The fixed smile on the porpoise-face belied her temperament. "Your gods face a crisis, and forget not it is a crisis caused by you. We offer you no option but to go with Brendan and foil his plans."

My gods were leaving; running away in the face of the Christian god? And hadn't the Morrigan herself just now chided me again for running before the Christian tribes? I held my tongue at the pretense of it. Yet how could I hope to prevail where the gods themselves could not? She offered me no choice. Though the gods' powers might be waning, well I knew the penalty for defying their wishes…especially hers.

I looked into her gray, porpoise eyes. "My Queen, it was not my intention to question the desires of the Lordly Ones, but rather Brendan's. He will fill his boat with fanatical monks to spread his religion. Why would he allow me, a known Druid, to accompany him?"

"Brendan's *why* is not our concern. You must find a way to persuade him."

She made demands though offered no guidance? "Of course I understand—" But the porpoise had disappeared beneath the waves.

* * *

During the following week my thoughts often returned to the Morrigan. Had I truly seen her and heard her voice, or was it only the mad imaginings of a solitary man? Would Brendan truly journey to the Blessed Isles? It was unlikely, and yet…augh! The gods had their own plans and twisted words to their own ends. They were a wily group and could not always be trusted.

Of one thing I had grown certain. Whether real or imagined, the Morrigan was right. Inexorable change was sweeping the land and, if my gods were leaving, Eire no longer held anything for me other than certain death by the Corcu Duibne or another Christian tribe like them.

If it was also true that Brendan planned a voyage to find the Golden Ones, I must find a way to sail with him. Such an unheard-of adventure could bring unimagined rewards, though it was far more likely to end in disaster and my own death. It mattered not. Why remain here and die at the hands of Christian zealots when I might yet serve the will of my gods?

* * *

I spent three days gathering all I might to trade within the village. It was night as I sat by my fire thinking to travel there the next morning.

A large wolf prowled outside my cave mouth and sat down to stare at me. I knew it for the Morrigan even before she spoke. "So, you would obey our wishes and go to the village to speak with Brendan?"

I was no longer surprised by her magical appearances. "Yes, My Queen. I leave in the morning."

"What will you offer that you might convince the priest to allow you to travel with him to the Blessed Isles?"

"I have nothing to offer but myself and my knowledge."

"Your offer will not be enough. Brendan will demand higher payment of you. He is a priest of the new faith and knows you as a pagan. He will not allow you to accompany him to spread his religion unless you first come over to his Father."

"That may be so; yes, that will likely be Brendan's demand. I must think on this."

"Think on this, Ossian? So like a merchant you would think of trading your gods in exchange for the slender hope of reaching the Blessed Isles?"

"What? My Queen, you suggest that I would barter my own gods to further myself? No. Never would I consider that, and a poor man I would be if I did. I shall go with him as you commanded."

"So," the Morrigan cackled, "perhaps at last you have found your lost spine?"

My face flushed in the firelight. "Perhaps I am remembering who I was before the Corcu Duibne...before I came here."

"If that is truly so, I might help you after all."

"Thank you, My Queen. You are right; Brendan will demand high payment of me. I must convince him of my knowledge of the stars. I could be valuable in plotting his voyage."

"Brendan is not a man of the sea. Your offer will seem of poor value in exchange for a voyage to the Isles of the Ever Young. You must put forward much more. Hear me,"

> If you search for Tír na nÓg,
> Treasure will avail your quest.
> Gold will speak where not the truth,
> For a journey to the West.
>
> When you voyage to Tír na nÓg,
> A sacrifice must be made.
> To the throne of Paradise,
> A sacrament must be paid.

My hands scrubbed my face and I shook my head, stifling a yawn. "You speak in riddles, of treasure and sacrifice. Look about you, My Queen. You see treasure here? Have I anything of value to sacrifice?"

"You must try to remember."

"Remember what?"

"Remember everything...back to before the Corcu Duibne came. You knew many things then, things taught you by your father and the Master at Dún Ailinne. You stood in your father's shadow then, but no more. It is time you stand alone under your own sky."

I nodded, understanding the truth in her words.

The Morrigan continued. "Should Brendan allow you to go with him, how will you prevent him and his followers from influencing the Golden Ones?"

"It will be hard, My Queen, and I have not thought on it. There may come a time when I must but it matters not without I go on Brendan's ship."

"Remember what I told you," the Morrigan sighed, "but this much I owe you as a warning, for I see it is true. Should you go search for the Blessed Isles you will embark upon a voyage from which you will never return."

Chapter 17
Trá Lí Bay

It being a strenuous trek to the village, I left early in the morning, my trade goods on my back. As I walked the Morrigan's words haunted me. "You must try to remember." It was true. I had chosen to forget much, beginning with the many painful memories of the attack on my village. I forced myself to think back. The Morrigan spoke of treasure and sacrifice, but what was I to remember?

I rested on a ridge crest and the memory came. Of course! There were the sacral ornaments hidden beneath the hearthstone of my father's home—the golden headband of Etain who was once poet to the Tuatha beneath the Earth; the jeweled collar of Druth the cupbearer; the thirty golden coins bearing the visage of an emperor of Byzantium. My father's bones would have no use for them and Etain and Druth were now ghosts.

Was the treasure still there, or had the Corcu Duibne found it when they sacked the village? It could be sacrificed in exchange for a voyage to the Blessed Isles…if need be. I still thought of these things as I came to the headland and looked down on Trá Lí Bay.

The village little resembled the quiet community I knew, for there were plumes of smoke rising everywhere. As I walked down the hillside my nose puckered. There was a reek compounded of rotten things and excrement. Men scurried about laying lathes of wood on the ground. Women tended fires over which fish hung to be smoked, and an annoying stench rising from long pits dug in the ground wafted toward me.

As I neared the beach I found the rough shape of a boat pegged out on the ground. I hardly recognized it at first, for it was larger than any craft I had ever seen. Men were hacking at oak planks with adzes, shaping them to size and fitting them to the outline scratched on the ground. Others shaved bark from two long oak logs seemingly meant for masts.

The selection of trees for the building of boats was no small thing. Not only should trees be chosen for their strength and character, but their individual spirits judged as well to ensure their affinity for joining with the sea. No doubt the Christians ignored the vital selection ritual and it was discomforting to think that Brendan and perhaps I would come to rue their negligence.

Two arced beams that would join together to form the bow of the boat lay side by side, and I gazed at them with puzzlement. A ball of twine was nearby and I used it to take simple measurements of the boat's width and length and the curvature of the two beams. I took up a scrap plank, found a piece of charcoal and sat down on a log. A smile touched my lips as I wrote the equation, all the while offering blessings to the ghosts of my instructors at Dún Ailinne.

Erc strode over to me while I was completing my calculations. "And what are you here for, Druid?" he hissed.

I stood and gazed down into his burning black eyes. "Brendan wished to hear more of me about the Blessed Isles."

"We know enough. They are to the west. We go there to bring the Lord's Light to your Golden Ones."

I paused. So, it was true. The meaning within my dreams of the Morrigan…it was all true.

Little it was I cared about Erc's opinion of me, though I knew it well enough. "I thought you planned to sail to the north to Patrick's Islands."

"Aye, so we did until you," he pointed a finger at my nose, "befuddled Father Brendan's head with your songs. For a week after you left he thought of little else."

Erc crossed his arms, rocking back on his heels as he glared up at me. "Then he called a meeting of the chief men in every village within a day's walk from here and told them that the Lord had called on him to sail west. He bid their aid in building a great curragh for the voyage, and in laying in enough provisions to feed thirty men for ninety days. The villages have been stripped bare and there is much resentment."

He took a step closer to me, fists clenched at his sides, his hatred blazing. "I blame you for all this, Ossian the unbeliever, for filling his head with these wild dreams. He bade me not to molest you and to let you pass if you came again, but if I had my way, I would throw you in yonder tanning pits."

Perhaps he thought I would quail before his wrath, but the silly man failed to understand that revealing his emotions before his enemy merely exposes a laughable weakness. I wished only to be rid of him. "And where is Brendan now? I would speak with him."

"He is there by the sea," Erc pointed, "in prayer. You are not to disturb him."

I ignored him, tossed the plank aside and walked on to find Brendan on his knees, gazing out to sea. He rose when he saw me.

"Ossian!" he exclaimed, though now it was his face that lifted to mine. "Something has happened; you are no longer stooped, and stand upright. Your illness is passing then?"

"Yes, thank you. I feel much better."

"Praise God. I am glad to see you here. I sent Erc to fetch you weeks ago but he said he could not find you and thought you had moved on."

No one had come to find me but I said nothing of it. "It is true what they say? You sail in search of the Blessed Isles?"

Excitement glowed on his face. "Of course it's true, and a blessing upon you for the inspiration for it. Think of it, Ossian, think of it!" His gesturing hand swept the ocean's wide expanse. "They are there; your Blessed Isles are there! There can be no doubt, for the truth of it was revealed to me by none other than God Himself."

"Your god spoke to you about the Isles?" My heart sank, as I remembered the Morrigan's warning that Brendan's god could guide him to Tír na nÓg.

He was almost dancing upon the beach like a gleeful child. "Yes! Yes! Listen. I was intrigued by your description of the Isles and you convinced me of your sincerity, but still I doubted their existence. Therefore I fasted for three days, and prayed for God's counsel. Finally, at the end of those three days, God spoke to me. Yes, He spoke to me and commanded that I sail west, west to find your Isles. And I shall find them by following the Guiding Hand of God while sailing under the protection of Jesus Christ. I know I shall!"

I could not share in Brendan's joy, for I very much feared he would find them, and, if so, the fault would be mine. His god commanded that he find the Isles, while my god, the Morrigan, commanded that I saw to it that he did not. The Druid in me recognized the irony in the manner gods manipulate men for their own ends.

Brendan took up his staff and bade me follow him. "Come. I have much to show you."

We walked together through the village. "Look there!" He pointed to the tanning pits where four men were peeing into clay pots. "The hides of sixty bullocks nearly tanned already. Urine mixed with the oak bark speeds up the process. And over there, flax being retted for our linen sails. The women of three villages are weaving for us. Praise be for Erc, he used to be a curragh builder in the Aran Isles before the Lord called him."

Brendan paused. "He does not like you. Erc sees Druids and people who hold to the old ways as a threat, where I see them as those who can be led gently to the Lord. But he gets things done and I depend upon him."

I dismissed his comment with a wave as I told my lie. "Little I know Erc's thoughts whether about me or my beliefs. It is good though that he is able and can be trusted to carry out your wishes."

"Erc carries out God's wishes. I am merely the messenger."

The time had come. I must gain a position upon Brendan's boat. "It is a bold adventure you dare take. Who will guide you to the Blessed Isles?"

"Why, a fisherman much like you. Our own Lord and Savior Jesus Christ Himself will show us the way."

What kind of man was this Brendan? He would go to sea and simply trust that his god would lead him safely to his destination? For a moment I questioned the wisdom of joining such a man even if he would agree to it.

Yet my obligation to the Morrigan left me no choice. "Your god was a fisherman?"

"Yes, our Lord Jesus Christ was a fisherman and also a carpenter."

I briefly wondered why Eire's old gods, the Lordly Ones, would flee to Tír na nÓg in the face of this common god of the Christians. "Is your god, Jesus Christ, familiar with piloting the western sea?"

Brendan shook his head. "Jesus is not a god; he is the Son of God, unified within the Holy Trinity of the Father, Son and Holy Spirit. Jesus knows all seas better than any man."

A Holy Trinity was not new to me, a Druid, whose business it was to know of such things. The Goddess Morrigan was also a trinity. Indeed, she was a trinity within a trinity. As the Goddess of War she incited warriors to riastradh, battle fury, as Fea, Nemon and Badbh.

Brendan would have no interest in my gods, those he considered pagan, so I spoke again of the sea. "Your Jesus knows the dangers of the Red Wind of the east? He knows the movements of the tides and currents? He understands steerage that relies upon the position of the sun and the balance of the stars around Polaris during each season?"

Brendan was looking uncomfortable as the monk, Erc, walked over to join us, saying, "Father, I told this heathen not to disturb you."

"Ossian is welcome and he is not disturbing me."

Erc looked at me. "I overheard your last words. You were making a point?"

I nodded, but turned to Brendan. "The work on your boat is not complete. Perhaps I can help you."

Erc sneered. "We have no need of your help."

"Perhaps not, but the design of the boat is flawed."

His dark eyes pierced mine. "And who are you to say such a thing? I built many a curragh, have you?"

"No, but see here." I knelt down and began writing an equation in the dust. "The beams hewn for the bow of the boat will not join properly. I have already calculated—"

Erc stepped forward, his foot swept across the dust to erase my work. "What manner of evil is it you attempt with your magical signs?"

Still kneeling, I looked up. "Magical signs? Did you not recognize the Greek lettering? I simply meant to show the calculation of the curvature of the two beams. As they are they will miss joining by a full three hand-widths."

Brendan looked to Erc, his eyes wide. "Is what he says true?"

"He speaks nonsense," Erc snapped, his face flushed. "The hewing of the beams he speaks of requires great skill. Sometimes several attempts are necessary before they are properly met. He simply saw our first attempt. I predict they will join, but if not, I will have the men hew out others until I am satisfied."

I hid a smile as I rose to my feet. "Yes, I can see how that can be done, but Euclid devised a simple mathematical calculation that will ensure they fit properly the first time."

"Euclid?" Erc snarled. "Another of your pagan demons, no doubt."

The monk's ignorance was insufferable but I kept my voice calm as though explaining some important thing to a child. "Euclid was among the most learned Greek mathematicians. His works on geometry are well known."

"Stories of the Druids' great knowledge are also well known," Brendan said, "and perhaps you can make the measurement predictions you say. However, I know better Erc's abilities and place my reliance in him and the Lord."

Brendan's own lack of understanding of mathematics was confounding. I gave up on it and sought another way to gain importance in his eyes. "You will need a pilot aboard your ship when you sail. Yes, I understand your reliance upon your Jesus Christ. But when have the gods not demanded that men also contribute to their own needs?"

Erc raged, "You would dare tell the father what Jesus Christ demands of him?"

Brendan raised his hand for silence. "Ossian, you have said much about tides, the sun and stars. What are you truly saying?"

"I wish to assist you in any way you deem necessary and serve as your pilot when you sail to the Isles."

The priest's eyebrows jerked upward, his mouth fell open. "You wish to go with us? Ours is a mission to spread God's Holy Word, while you are a —"

"A devilish pagan!" Erc spat. "Father, this man's impudence is beyond belief!"

"Erc is correct." Arms crossed, a scowl on his face, Brendan continued, "You are a non-believer and your presence upon our boat would be a distraction and serve little purpose. However, if you would hear my words and come to the true God, perhaps I would consider your request."

"Father," Erc's hand swept toward me, "you cannot trust this man's word! I urge caution in dealing with him. He will steal your soul and from it prepare a feast for his demons."

Again I turned to Erc, little believing I might alter the cruel hatred in his heart. "You can trust me when I say that I will not bargain my gods and beliefs against a position on your ship." Cool shrewdness glimmered in his eyes as I continued, "You know who I am. Yes, well I know the Tuatha Dé Danann and can cite all their names, but I also know the changing of the seasons by the sun, moon and stars. I know the movements of the sea and sky. I can predict changes in the weather and calculate numbers in my mind beyond the abilities of most men. I can lay a course for a long voyage at sea. Would not these abilities prove valuable on your journey to find the Isles?"

The monk's face showed understanding, but hardened as he ignored my truth and turned to Brendan. "You see, father? He has the devil's own voice. He tempts us with his demon's tongue, and black magic."

Brendan shook his head. "He does not tempt me, Brother, though he might very well be able to do all he says." He looked at me. "Without you honestly come to Christ, you may not accompany us on our voyage."

"But enough of this!" Erc snapped. "If this man is evidence of the legendary wisdom of the Druids, we will have little problem being rid of the remainder of them. Father, we have a real problem. The village chiefs say they have had enough. They say they have been stripped bare, that we take the men from their fields and that they have not enough to feed themselves or provision us for the voyage."

Brendan's face fell. "But we cannot give up now; we have come so far."

"They are adamant, father…maybe next year we can—"

"Next year, next year…we must sail within two moons! You must find a way."

The villagers' burden was not a thing I had considered and I would have my say about it. "Families starve? Children go hungry so you can provision your voyage? Brendan, you are a priest of the Christian god and the people deserve better from you."

Brendan's hand went up to silence Erc, who bit back his rage. "The people suffer. Yes, I do not deny that's so. Yet, God's true followers gladly suffer to serve His Will. They will manage somehow, and the most important Being within all the Universe requires that we sacrifice for Him."

Erc's eyes glinted as he cocked an eyebrow. "Sacrifice; that is not a new concept for a Druid, is it?"

My face flushed. "If you refer to human sacrifice, you know full well it was an ancient rite that Druids haven't practiced for untold generations. Now, as for the needs of the village. Would gold help to ease their obligation to you and buy passage for me aboard your boat?"

The monk eyed my torn kirtle and scoffed. "And where would a tattered hedge wizard like you find gold? Yes, bring us a bag of gold and you will be most welcome on the voyage. Now leave us. Father Brendan and I have much to discuss."

There was coldness within me. "Someday I shall not ignore your ill-bred insults."

My attention turned to Brendan. "This man has said that gold will purchase my passage with you. Do you agree?"

He glanced uncertainly toward Erc. "Yes, it will be as Brother Erc said. I prefer otherwise and think it a poor bargain, but it will be as he said—provided you have gold."

It was troubling to learn that even the will of a man like Brendan might be bought for a handful of gold. Regardless, as the Morrigan predicted, treasure would open the way to Tír na nÓg.

I left them to exchange my trade goods for the journey north to Rath Raithleann, the place I had fled from in shame and sorrow. Few villagers were willing to part with the meager food left to them and I left Trá Lí Bay with only two stale loaves and a bit of dried fish.

If only my father's treasure remained…if only.

Chapter 18
A Journey to the Past

𝕿 he next day I set out early to continue north. It was a journey that I would fain not take. I cut a cudgel from a blackthorn bush along the way and chanted a charm of traveling to myself to keep my spirits up.

It was an ancient forest that I made my way through. Giant moss-encrusted boles and gnarled limbs of towering oak, beech and ash trees loomed over me. Waist-high ferns and bracken made the traveling harsh, with the trail sometimes disappearing into patches of thorn and briar bush.

After the arduous trek, I came to a small clearing with a shallow spring running through it, and decided to rest for the night, for I still had some four days journey to my old home. With some dry tinder from my pouch, and after striking a spark from my flint and ironstone, I soon had a good fire blazing.

As dusk began to close, I cast about at the clearing's edge and found two young hedgehogs. They were soon gutted with a sharp stone; their bellies stuffed with burdock leaves and young nettles, and rolled in wet clay from the bed of the spring. Raking fire coals over them, I sat and waited as the dusk rolled over me.

Fear and shame had kept me from making this journey for too long, fear of the Corcu Duibne warriors and shame that I had slunk away and lived for so long without purpose. Now, I would follow the old gods where they led me, even in company with Brendan and the new god on the cross. I rose and kicked the coals aside, cracking the hot clay, pulling the hedgehogs' skin and quills away from the tender flesh.

I slept well with a full belly and that night she did not come to me.

The second day was easier for the forest fell away as I came down from the hills to the river valley of the Blackwater. The land was fertile and good pasture for cattle. It was from here local farmers would bring tribute to King Domnhall, and pay service to my father for the charms he gave them and the blessings called upon their children. I skirted around the farmsteads that I came to, fearing I would be recognized. I did not know how strong the Corcu Duibne had become here.

I was nearing the Galtees hill country and climbed to a ridgeline. Small wooded mounds dotted the landscape and I was wary of them. Such places could be shee mounds, the haunted places of the fairies, beneath which they were known to live in elaborate, underground palaces. It was unwise to disturb them.

On the fifth day, I came upon a barren rise at twilight from where I could see the earthen wall encircling Rath Raithleann. The Sacred Grove still stood beside the fort's perimeter. Within the evening's stillness all looked as it was before the Corcu raid. I decided to rest and go upon it in the early dawn, so bedded down without a fire lest the enemy remained about.

At the first gleam of morning light, I went down from the ridge and made my way toward my old home. Nothing moved, no fires burned; there was no sound of cattle or children, only the screech of a hawk, high overhead, broke the silence. Fearing the main gate be guarded, I climbed the outer earthen wall to look down upon the lifeless, charred ruins of the village within.

The long hall of King Domhnall still stood, its roof burned out, but the stout oak beams and lintels had resisted the fire, which had swept through everything. I made my way across to the Sacred Grove, for it was in that holy place I knew that I must make peace with my father's ghost. Yet when I came to it, I fell upon the ground and wept...for all was desolation.

Some trees had been outright felled while others had bark rings cut from them so that they stood bare and lifeless. Crude crosses had been cut on the trunks of many, and in the center of the grove, where the holy spring emerged from the ground, lay the bodies of two red deer. I could see the bones of many others. I went to the edge of the rock pool and saw the rotting remains of plants strewn in the water. Monkshood, wolfsbane and nightshade. The Corcu Duibne had not only assaulted our people, they had made war against Mother Earth, herself.

Anger took me as I sat against a dead rowan tree, as a wolf would take a young calf by the throat. *I will have blood for this*, my mind cried out, and, through a red mist, the Corcu fell to my sword, their women shrieking as I raged among them.

Drumming in my ears cleared my vision and a vague form appeared before me that coalesced into a terrifying figure all wings and claws and fury. The Hugh hawk's head eyed me balefully and shrieked, "Vengeance is not yours to give, Ossian. I will feast upon their eyeballs soon enough. There is nothing here for you but dreams, Ossian, and you must follow your gods. To the west, Ossian, to the west."

Flowing wings wide, she soared upwards and vanished in the clouds. She laid a burden on me that even my rage could not overcome.

I looked for a last time upon the ruined grove that had once held my soul, and thought of Beltane. It was the time when the young girls wore white hawthorn in their hair, and the great fires lit to welcome back the sun. And it was then we would lead the cattle to their summer pasturage and return to feast and dance among the sacred rowan trees.

The pleasant memories were like so much dust, and I shook them away to trudge up the old familiar path to the village of the dead. Even after so many months, the rancid smell of death still hung in the air, the bones of my people lay ravaged by weather, scattered by scavenging animals. Little I wanted or wished to see of the village. It was with only one purpose in mind that I hurried past the remains of haunted cottages.

Where my father's roundhouse stood, only jumbled stones and charred oak beams remained. I cleared away debris and found the hearthstone where the fire-pit had once been. No amount of scrabbling in the dirt would move it.

A tool of some kind would move the stone, so I searched through the rubble. A bit of red caught my eye, a shawl, Aine's shawl. Taking it up with a smile, I held it to my face that I might yet catch her fragrance. The stench of mold mixed with old smoke assailed my nose, and, disgusted, I threw the lifeless thing to the ground.

Returning to my original task, I took a charred beam and sharpened the end with a broken stone. After much effort, I finally raised it and levered the stone aside to reveal a large leather bag. They were still there, the collar, headband and golden coins. Beneath them in a separate package lay a prized Druid's robe woven for my father by the Weavers of Screeban. Threads of silver and gold shaped a serpent's head, its body coiled across the emerald green linen.

The robe I shoved into the bag with the treasure, slung it all over my shoulder and made haste to depart, all too ready to leave the stark ruins, the old ghosts and hopes of things that might have been. My future, whatever it might be, now rested with Brendan and his improbable voyage.

Chapter 19
A Twisted Way

$\mathcal{A}$ fast pace brought me down from the hill country just before dusk. It was an empty land. Wooded mounds dotted open grasslands where but a few isolated groups of cattle and sheep grazed. I made ready to bed down beside a cairn of stones when I saw a chariot in the distance. Presently, two Corcu Duibne warriors aboard the chariot approached, long ropes towing two men behind them.

Probably slave takers, I thought, crouching behind the rocks, but there was little I could do against them with only a blackthorn cudgel. They passed within a hundred paces of me and, as they did, I heard one of their captives singing an old ballad and knew that voice. My heart thrilled as joyous tears crowded my eyes, for no man could sing with such a voice but my friend Laoidheach.

I waited until they had gone well past and followed them at a safe distance, knowing they would soon make camp for the night. I was no warrior and lacked skill in the use of weapons. Yet, Laoidheach lived...by the hands of the gods he lived, and I was determined to try to free him despite the risky nature of it.

Sure enough, they halted by the riverbank and lit a fire after pasturing their horses. The men tied their captives to a tree and made ready for the night. These were brutal, battle-hardened warriors, and I prayed silently to the Morrigan to aid me in her battle aspect. I thought my best plan was to sneak upon them in the dark and club them while they slept.

Hidden within the brush, I waited until clouds had stolen the moon from the night sky. It was late when I kissed the serpent ring for luck and began creeping as silently I could though the long grass to where a warrior lay sleeping. The firelight revealed a giant of a man with bright red hair. He wore a leather jacket with studs of iron.

I crept up to him and was lifting my cudgel when he rose up to his elbows and grunted, "You would murder me as I slept? Well, now it's three to sell to the salt mines in the north," and grabbed for his sword.

The spirit of Macha, the battle fury aspect of the Morrigan, was in me, and I struck the warrior a mighty blow on his head. He fell back, so I struck him again and heard his skull break.

I dropped my cudgel, seized the sword lying on the ground beside the warrior's body and ran to where his companion was stirring awake. The man staggered to his feet, a war club in his fist, and I thrust the sword through his belly. I then slashed him, then again, again and yet again.

"And so, Ossian," Laoidheach called softly. "We thought you dead, and that one certainly is. You cannot kill him twice."

The grotesque, broken bodies of the warriors lay sprawled on the ground, and I tore my eyes from them as a spiritual sickness overwhelmed the battle rage within me. I threw the sword to the ground. Yes, more than once in the past I had given orders that men be killed, and always they were my enemies, the enemies of my faith and people. There was no joy now in my personal triumph. My hands trembled and I stared at them, wondering at their weakness.

"Ossian! Ossian, come cut us free!" Laoidheach called again.

I went and released Laoidheach, who wrapped his arms around my shoulders in a firm embrace. Firelight revealed his watering eyes. "I thought you dead. I was certain of it, but now, just now you come out of the night to save me from," he gestured towards the dead warriors, "those bastards there. How is that possible?"

"We will discuss it later." I pointed to the other prisoner. "Who is this?"

"He is Goban; a smith from the drumlin country to the north."

The smith was a short, bald, stocky man with arms the size of young oaks. Taking up the sword, I cut him loose and he too embraced me.

"Ye have me life," he said, "and I, Goban, will not forget it."

I nodded a somber reply.

He pointed to the bodies of the Corcu's and then peered up at me intently. "It is no small thing to kill men, eh? But, those two swine needed killin'. I'm thinkin' they were your first?"

"Yes. Yes, they were..." I hesitated as I struggled to find the proper words.

He nodded. "No man with a sound mind finds killin' an easy thing. I am honored that ye chose to shoulder such a heavy burden that I might be free. Yet, I know too, that as a man of honor, ye will not permit tonight to weigh on ye, for what ye did was the right thing. Ye saw the need for it, did ye not?"

"Yes," I nodded, "had I not seen the need, I would not have acted."

"Ye acted as a true man," he beamed, "and there ye have it. Again I thank ye!"

"Yes, yes, we thank you again and again, but we need food," Laoidheach urged. "Those bastards have not fed us for two days."

We found some barley bread and a bag of rancid beef in the men's pouches. My nose wrinkled at the odor of the beef, and I poured it onto the ground.

"So, ye know each other, do ye?" Goban asked.

"Yes," Laoidheach said, "we have been good friends for many years."

"Well then, I will leave two old friends to talk. If I might have a slice of bread to take with me," he pointed to the bodies, "I will drag these two pieces of offal into the darkness and check on the horses."

I gave Goban bread, and he went to work. I was curious about the man. "Tell me about Goban, Laoidheach."

He shrugged as he sat down beside the fire, cross-legged. "There is little enough I know other that what I said earlier. He is a good, solid man, I think. Have you nothing more to eat with you?"

"Satisfy your hunger for tonight with the bread, old friend. Our breakfast waits there." I pointed into the darkness toward the river. Even as I said it, I was hoping that my old skills had not deserted me.

Seating myself beside him, I continued, "So, we have much to tell each other. How is it that I find you here a prisoner?"

Laoidheach was chewing the bread, but glanced towards me. "First, quickly. Tell me of Aine. Have you seen her?"

"No, my friend, I have not seen her, but I know she is dead."

His expression did not change as he urged, "If you have not seen her, how can you be certain?"

"It was told to me by..." I hesitated. How could I explain the Morrigan? "It was told to me by someone who was there and knew her for dead."

He hung his head quietly for a moment, and sighed. "I knew it for the truth, though I held small hope... She was not among the other captives, you see, so yes, I suspected as much."

"We both lost much to the Christians that day, my friend. Much more, I fear, than we can ever replace. So, tell me of the other captives."

The names he cited were people I knew, or had known, though he didn't know all their names or if they all still lived. I nodded as he spoke of them, and, when his list ended, I asked, "How was it you were taken?"

"I've a simple story," he shrugged, "with little to tell. I was in the long hall with the King when the Corcu Duibne came. Their attack came as a surprise; as you know. We were not prepared to defend the village or ourselves. Mounted warriors streamed into the village as our men ran to their homes for their arms."

I nodded. "Aye, I was in the fields when they struck and was knocked senseless early in the raid. The big man there, with the red hair," I nodded toward the corpse, "I remember seeing him. He rode his chariot and was among the leaders."

"Yes, his name was Ó Scannláin, and he was their most beastly killer. You see, the Corcu Duibne took me and a hundred or so others of our village prisoner. They insisted we march under guard to pay homage to their king. Those who were grievously wounded during the battle, or were too young, ill or feeble to make the march were slaughtered without delay. Ó Scannláin took great glee in the killing of our innocents."

The image of it filled my mind, and my guilt over killing the man turned to dust as I spat. "His death was well done then, though small penance for our many dead."

"True. The man was an animal."

"But Laoidheach, they left you alive. Why?"

"Their king liked my songs and ballads…at least he did for a while. Later, he demanded I learn the songs of the Christians, songs exalting their God and Jesus Christ. That was all very well; it makes little difference to me what I sing, so long as I am alive and fed. So, I sang their songs of piety, the songs of their beliefs."

"And yet, I find you here, a slave on his way to the salt mines in the north."

"Yes. Is there more bread?"

I reached into the bag and handed him another piece.

Wiping crumbs from his mouth with his tunic's filthy sleeve, he continued, "A few weeks ago, I forget the day, the king said I was to make up a new ballad to praise his greatness. He insisted the ballad include verses to honor his raid on our village. I could not do it, Ossian; I would not."

"You said as much?"

His eyebrows shot up. "Of course I did no such foolish thing! The king would have lopped my head in a moment at such arrogance. I found excuses to delay creating his ballad, citing a lack of inspiration, you see, that sort of thing. Finally, the king grew weary of waiting…in fact, I believe he grew tired of me generally, and decided to be rid of me. So, here I sit."

* * *

Sunrise had not yet chased away the morning mist when I made the short walk to the river where I cautiously peered into the cold clear water. Two fat salmon not yet spawned rested in a pool beneath an alder tree and I sang to them as I sank my hands into the water and gently stroked their bellies. I quickly jerked them onto the bank and they were soon roasting on a spit.

Laoidheach walked over and eyed the salmon. "Aren't those fish cooked yet?"

I smiled. "Patience, my hungry balladeer friend, just a bit longer."

Goban lounged beside the fire and pointed to the bodies of the Corcu Duibne warriors. "We must bury those pieces of shit soon. They will begin to stink and attract the carrion birds that will draw attention to this place."

He was right. "Yes, the bodies might be found, but we must be far from here when they are."

"The chariot can be burned here on our fire, and we must search their belongin's for things we might use. The big bastard there," he nodded, "wears a kirtle studded with iron. I would take it if it suits ye."

"Take it," I shrugged as I eyed the short, almost gnome-like man, "though it be overly large for you."

"It's true I haven't the son of a bitch's height, but the shoulders and girth will fit me well enough."

"Tell me Goban, you are a smith? How is it you came to be here, a captive?"

"My home is Tara—"

"The city of the High King?"

202

"Damn it man, and what other Tara is there? I am a smith, as was me father and his father before him, and came to Tara from the drumlin midlands some twenty years ago. I work silver, gold, copper, bronze…metals of all kinds, ye see, though I prefer the working of iron. I was among Tara's best smiths." He straightened up. "No, I was Tara's best smith. No man can equal the strength of me iron."

Laoidheach glanced at him with a grin. "Tara's best smith, you say? What manner of great smith and tradesman are you that that you lie here and starve alongside us? Speaking of starving, Ossian, see to the fish. Aren't they yet ready?"

"No, my friend. Bide a while longer, for the salmon will taste all the better for it."

"It is not I that is impatient; it's this unruly stomach within me."

Goban was a man who interested to me. He was a difficult man to age, but I thought him only a bit younger than my father. "As a smith at Tara, you must have been a man of respect and wealth. How is it you became a slave?"

"Humph. I worked many years, and, as ye say, accumulated wealth in gold, land and cattle," Goban growled. "Then, foul priests branded me a sorcerer who practiced black magic, and demanded the High King banish me from his city forever."

The King had shown his support for priests in the past, so I was not surprised. "Why should they do such a thing? Why would they take offense against a common smith? Are you also a sorcerer as they claimed?"

"I am a man! I am Goban! I am what and who I choose to be! I choose to be a common metalworker who plies his craft in the age-old ways of his father…in the ways known to smiths long before the priest Patrick arrived in Eire and began convertin' our people to the new religion."

He waved a dismissive hand. "The foolish priests overheard me citin' the ancient prayers to Lugh, Go fannan and Ebhlinne during the making of me fire and the meltin' down of metals. They declared them to be spells, they did, invokin' profane magic. When the priests speak through their asses, the King smells nothin' else. Bah! I waste words speakin' of it."

Images of a blue flame, molten metal and white-hot sparks spiraling into the sky filled my mind. How could there not be enchantment behind it? "No, Goban, your words are well said, and yet it would seem the King showed poor judgment toward you in relying on the priests' nonsense."

"There was more, Ossian, for in his eyes, the King showed great judgment. You see, the King's Gatekeeper's cousin's son-in-law is also a smith there. The son-in-law was envious of me success and the Gatekeeper knew of it. When the priests brought up me name in court, the Gatekeeper whispered in the King's ear, and that was the end of me."

"The end of you? I don't understand."

"It is all very simple. The King's power rests upon the shoulders of his most trusted supporters, don't you see? He strengthens his power by occasionally bestowin' gifts upon them. By means of the priests' accusations, my removal became a gift to the Gatekeeper's family, no more, and now they are even more beholden to the King."

The truth of it was plain to see although so was the injustice. "But the Gatekeeper's gift was small compared to the shameful thing the King did to you. How can a King treat his people so unfairly, and still—"

"Unfairly? Unfairly, Ossian? Powerful men offer fairness only when they have nothin' to gain by withholdin' it, and that's a bitter truth. This was not a matter of fairness as you and I judge it. Ye see, I meant nothin' to the King, and yet, through me, he could appease the meddlesome priests, delight the Gatekeeper's family and, as an added measure, take all me possessions into his treasury. In his beneficence, he left me alive when he had the power to do otherwise…which I admit was no small thing. Oh yes, Ossian, the King likely considers his actions most fair."

Laoidheach could no longer remain quiet. "You both chatter away while my stomach is treated unfairly. Surely, the salmon are well done. See for yourself, they are beginning to char."

Though Goban's words still stirred me, I nodded. "Very well, yes, it seems the fish are ready."

We sat down beside the fire and ate greedily.

"Needs butter," grunted Goban, stuffing pieces of fish into his mouth. "Salt too!"

"Food, food," muttered Laoidheach, "that's all you ever think of."

"And who was it, me harpist friend, just now whinin' over the cookin' of the salmon?"

"It's called a lyre," he cocked an eyebrow, "and I merely wished to be sure the salmon was cooked properly."

Goban licked his fingers. "In a goat's ass."

Chapter 20
A Hero's Journey

We buried the Corcu Duibne warriors that morning. I walked the riverbank and found two rowan seedlings, transplanting them atop the graves. In keeping with tradition, I muttered a plea to the seedlings that they hold the warriors' ghosts in their graves lest they escape to haunt me in coming years.

We inspected the warriors' gear, but found little of use. Goban retrieved his heavy smith's hammer, iron tongs and hand bellows, and Laoidheach found his lyre. The chariot we would burn as Goban suggested, but we would keep the two horses for our travel.

Goban tossed a leather purse to me. "Look there, the big man carried it. It contains coins, I think."

I emptied the contents of the purse into my hand—nine copper coins bearing the image of an old Roman. I tucked the purse inside my kirtle.

Laoidheach absently strummed his lyre, and, without looking up, asked, "So where go you from here, Ossian?"

"I will return to Trá Lí Bay. A Christian priest is there, his name is Brendan, and I will go with him on a voyage to the west."

"To the west of where?"

"We sail west to find the Blessed Isles."

Laoidheach almost dropped his lyre. "To Tír na nÓg? Are you daft, man? No mortal can sail to the Blessed Isles. Everyone knows that."

"Beware what everyone knows, Laoidheach, lest you know it too."

"What?" Laoidheach shook his head. "Listen Ossian, this priest, Brendan, has he bewitched your mind with his Christian ways that you would attempt so foolish a voyage?"

"Perhaps it was I who bewitched him. My old friend, this is not merely a voyage I would make, it is a voyage I must make."

"You speak in riddles, but I suppose that is the Druid in you."

"Ossian is a Druid?" Goban was surprised.

"Of course he is...oh wait, we forgot to mention it, did we not?"

"Yes, but it explains much." Goban nodded toward me. "So, Ossian, tell me more about this voyage of yours. Do ye think there might be a place for a smith on your ship?"

Goban seemed a solid, reliable man, and I found the suggestion in his words agreeable. "The decision would not be mine alone, I'm afraid, but yes, if I have my way, you will be welcome."

Laoidheach shook his head in astonishment. "Crazy men! I am in the company of crazy men!"

Goban's eyes glinted. "Ye say so, Laoidheach? And where go you from here? Ye think to sing sweet songs to a king while he blows in your ear?"

"Well, I hadn't actually thought upon it...that is, I haven't considered the future. I am a bard, and as such will be welcomed in many circles."

"No, me fine lad." Goban shook his head. "Once ye would have been welcome, but now? Ye're an escaped slave and filthy murderer. Ye'll be hounded by the Corcu Duibne when their warriors fail to return. They are Christians and have much influence among all the clans. Can ye say as much?"

"I killed no one!"

"Yes, Ossian killed those scum, but it will make no difference. Ye'll be sought after as a killer."

Laoidheach stood and began to pace. "I...I still have friends who will hide me. After a while, I can travel to new provinces and…" His voice trailed away as the enormity of his changed status dawned upon him.

"Yes, ye can travel the land until caught, and then…krrrrk!" Goban grinned evilly as he drew his index finger across his throat.

Laoidheach stopped, clasped his ashen face in his hands and then peeked at Goban through his fingers. "So, if I stay here, I will have my head lopped, but if I go with you, I will surely drown in the sea?"

"Those seem to be your choices, yes," Goban smirked.

"You have the dark heart of a slave trader, Goban, and take pleasure in tormenting me."

"If so, it is because ye are so easy to torment, Laoidheach. But if I was a motherless slave trader, I'd not be wastin' my time on the likes of ye."

"Hah, and what would you know of such things?"

Goban scowled and shook his head. "I've seen much of slave traders and their ways. On me way here, there was a girl…"

His mood swinging in an instant at the mention of a girl, Laoidheach grinned. "A girl you say? Tell me of her."

"She was a beautiful thing, young, fifteen or sixteen years I would say, with long reddish hair, and the world's bluest eyes. She sat in chains, surrounded by a group of dick-head slavers, though she held her head high."

"Who was she? How did such a girl become a slave?"

"I was not permitted to speak with her, of course, but she is called Aine, and I learned she was captured months ago when the dog filth Corcu Duibne raided her village."

"Aine!" Laoidheach spun to face me. "Ossian, you heard Goban? Aine! Think of it, our Aine captured and a slave; it must be her, for there cannot be two such girls in all Eire!"

My mind swirled at Goban's words. They could not be true. Aine was dead. The Morrigan had said to me…*your father will not rise from the dead, nor will your sisters.*

"Ossian!" Laoidheach urged. "Listen to me, listen to Goban. My betrothed, and your sister Aine is alive and a slave!"

It was impossible. I fought back the hope that surged in my heart. "No, my friend, Goban describes another girl, though her name and description be altogether the same as our Aine. There can be no doubt of it. Our Aine is dead."

"How can you be so sure? Ossian, you didn't see Aine yourself after the Corcu Duibne attacked our village, and you didn't witness her lying dead."

"No, I did not see her." My hands scrubbed my face, a hundred thoughts battling within my head. How could I explain my conversations with the Morrigan to these men? "I say again, there is no doubt of it."

"I say there is doubt! How can you give up on your sister so easily? I will not. I leave immediately to go to her, and you can damned well come or go as you will!"

Aine was dead. Had not the Morrigan, the goddess of death herself, said exactly that? Yet, Laoidheach was right. Goban's description of the girl planted a seed of doubt, one I could not ignore.

Rising to my feet, hands clasped at my back, my eyes closed as my thoughts raced. How could I go in search of the girl and thereby be certain about her without breaking my vow to the gods that I would return to sail with Brendan? He planned to sail within two months, and already much time had passed since last I saw him. I could not break my pledge merely on the possibility that my Aine lived.

A promising solution came, my eyes opened and I pointed to a nearby hill. "I will go there alone. At the crest of the hill, I will build a sacred fire and call upon the gods for guidance. Will you wait for me here, my friend, until I return?"

Laoidheach nodded. "Of course I will wait, but how long will it take for the gods to answer?"

"Who can say? Today, tonight, tomorrow…perhaps never. The gods speak when they will and no sooner."

"It had best be the sooner, for I will wait for you until morning, Ossian, but only until then."

Goban had been watching, and now offered caution. "I know ye for a Druid, Ossian, and know your powers. Still I warn ye be wary. Humph, ye may be favored by the gods, but as for me," he spat into the fire, "I would have nothin' of it."

Picking up the sword taken from Ó Scannláin, I left them with a nod to walk up the hill alone, thoughts on the ritual before me. My Druid powers had waned during my long months of isolation, though I hoped my mission would succeed. Praying to all the gods for illumination would do no good. One god must be called upon, the god most likely to care about the well-being of a desperate woman. The names of the many gods and goddesses swam in my head until I settled upon Brigid, goddess of all feminine arts.

The day was in the eighth month, the month in which holly ruled. Therefore, it was fitting to kindle my fire with holly branches. Casting about the hillside I came upon a holly tree and lopped branches from it with my sword until my arms were full. I muttered my apologies and appreciation to the tree as I did so.

Upon the summit of the hill, I created a small fire, and sat stiffly erect, cross-legged beside it. Soon a column of smoke spiraled upwards, and I reached my hands outwards toward it. Only then did I begin my prayer to the goddess, Brigid.

> I call upon the Earth Mother,
> I call upon all the Lords of the Sidhe,
> I call upon all the Mysteries of our land,
> I, Ossian, a Druid of the faith, call upon you.
>
> I call upon you Brigid, O goddess of women,
> I call upon you Brigid, O goddess of prophecy,
> I call upon you Brigid, O goddess of divination,
> I, Ossian, a Druid of the faith, call upon you.

I pray that you might hear me,
I pray that you might answer me,
I pray that you might guide me,
I pray that you might bless my quest.

I come to you, dear Brigid, offering all that I am.
I offer my mind, that I might hear you,
I offer my heart, that I might understand you,
I offer my soul, that you might see all that I am.

I ask that you hear me now, dear Brigid,
Though I come not with empty hands.
Demand of me what you will in return,
Demand payment for my poor appeal.

Must I prostrate myself before you?
If so, I shall willingly do so.
Must I create a shrine to you?
If so, I shall eagerly build it.

Must I offer my blood to these flames,
That you might absorb my passion,
That you might taste my sincerity?
If so, my blood will be spilled, and gladly.

I come to you, dear Brigid, that I might see more clearly,
I come to you for a girl who cannot speak for herself,
I come to you that you might offer guidance,
I come to you that I might best serve
　　　the will of the Lordly Ones.

My prayer was repeated, time and again, as the sun crept by overhead. I remained seated before the fire, desiring neither food nor water. A fresh holly bough was positioned on the fire as needed to feed its flames.

The afternoon was growing late when Brigid answered, her voice coming from the center of the pillar of smoke rising above the fire. "I hear you, Ossian, though I wish I did not. I answer you only that you might stop calling my name."

Hers was not the response I had expected. "Thank you, dear Brigid, for answering my prayer. I am humbled in your presence."

"And humble you should be. Hurry now, what is it you want of me?"

"There is a girl, dear Brigid, a girl taken into slavery. Her name is Aine. It is said she could be my sister, Aine, daughter of the Druid, Ciann Mehigan. I ask your aid that I might see her, hear her and thereby discover if it is truly she."

"And if it is she?"

"Then I will go to her and deliver her from the slavers who hold her captive."

"And if it is not?"

"The Morrigan has laid a geas on me. If the girl is not my sister, I shall promptly accede to the Morrigan's wishes.'

Brigid's gay laugh emanated from the smoke. "Poor Ossian. You are in quite a dilemma, aren't you? But, let us assume that I will allow you to see and hear this girl, Aine. What do you offer in return?"

"I said in my prayer—"

"No, no. You offered mere trifles, Ossian. I demand more."

"Of course, dear Brigid. If it is mine to give, it shall be yours."

She laughed again. "Be not so eager, Druid, else I raise my demands. Let me see, what do I want from you? Hmm…oh yes, I have it! It has been long since I lay with a mortal. I wish to do so tonight. If you agree to send a man to me here on this hill tonight, I shall grant your request."

I was shocked. The goddess wished to lay with a mortal? I had heard of such things, but her demand came as a complete surprise. I ventured cautiously, "Dear Brigid, I must admit you have surprised me, and since I am already here, perhaps…"

Brigid chuckled. "No Ossian, though I find you very handsome, and believe you capable of satisfying me. But no. Your offer is too simple a solution, don't you see? No, I insist you must convince someone else to come here, a man I will find agreeable."

Laoidheach! Did he not claim to be descended from a changeling? Women found him irresistible, and he made a sport of attracting them. I nodded. "I know such a man. He is nearby, and I am certain I can convince him to come here tonight."

"You *are* accommodating, aren't you, Ossian? Very well, I accept our bargain, but I warn you, do not break it. I have had men castrated for less!"

I believed her, and nodded, silently praying Laoidheach would not fail me.

She continued, "So now you will see the slave girl, Aine. Keep your eyes on the smoke, Ossian; keep your eyes on the smoke..."

The smoke swirled 'round and 'round, and gradually a face appeared, my sister Aine's face...small, wan and all alone, though it was all the same as the smoke. She could not see me, her searching eyes wandered as she called forth, her plaintive voice a resonance in the still air. "Father! Father you must find me! You must help me... Ossian, are you there? Can you see me? Can you hear me? Please, Ossian, please come soon for I can bear no more of this!"

"Aine!" I cried, though I knew she could not hear me. "I'm coming, Aine. Bear your torment just a little longer, for I shall find you."

The smoke swirled again and another face appeared—that of a crone, the Morrigan. Her dark eyes pierced mine as she spoke. "And so, Druid, you would forsake your vows to us, the Lordly Ones? You would allow Brendan to sail while you search in vain for your sister?"

"You told me my sister was dead, My Queen, yet have I not just seen for myself that she still lives?"

"She breathes, it is true, but she is dead, Ossian, dead to you and all men other than the scum holding her. Even they will not permit her to breathe much longer."

"She lives!"

"She is a slaver's whore! A woman sold time and again only to spread her thighs before all comers. From this point forward, she will be despised and ridiculed by all, men and women alike, and nothing you can do will change that. Hear me now. She is dead to you. Remove her from your mind and fulfill your obligation to your gods. I bid you immediately travel to meet Brendan."

My spirit sickened beneath her harsh words, but I shook my head. "Sadly, My Queen, forgetting my sister I cannot do. I hear the horrible things you say about her, but I measure and cherish Aine for who she is, not by what she was forced to endure. I must find her and save her if I can."

Flute-like fairy voices emanated from the air around me, and my heart jumped into my throat as they screeched,

"Kill him!"

"Kill him, My Queen!"

"Kill this insolent mortal!"

"Silence!" the Morrigan shrieked at the unseen fairies.

"Kill him...kill him...kill him..." the voices chanted.

"I said silence!"

She glared at me. "You heard them. You heard the little people who live here. They spurn your impudence, as I do, so perhaps I shall grant their wish. I have warned you before of the penalty for disobeying me!"

I had unwittingly climbed atop a shee mound. Shuddering and glancing about, fairy voices echoed in my mind. "Of course, My Queen, you may take my life at your choosing, but I ask you. What manner of man, god or mortal, would turn his back upon his own sister to save himself? Were I to do such a thing, what kind of man would I be to serve you?"

"Bah! Men and their absurd sense of honor..." The Morrigan hesitated, finally saying, "Go then! Go find that wretched sister of yours, though I tell you again, it will do you no good." She paused again, and then hissed, "Just pray you that Brendan does not sail before you return to Trá Lí Bay."

The Morrigan's face disappeared within the smoke and I sat alone, sweat soaking my clothing. I had dared challenge the goddess of death herself. Well I knew that it was only by the greatest good fortune that I survived my impertinence. I rose to my feet, tossed dirt upon the fire and kicked the brands apart to prevent them rekindling.

The sun was setting as I descended the hill to rejoin my companions who stood waiting. I stopped before them. "Yes, it is true. Aine lives and I will go with you in the morning, Laoidheach, to search for her. Goban, you will travel with us?"

Goban nodded, so I turned to Laoidheach. "Tonight, though, there is a great favor I must ask of you."

"A favor? If it is within my power, I will do it, for you saved my life."

"You are a good friend, and I knew I could rely upon you." I turned and pointed back up the hill. "You must climb the hill, where you will find a woman waiting for you."

His eyes narrowed. "What? You say a woman waits for me? What woman?"

"Her name is Brigid, and you will find her most fair. She asks that you stay the night with her."

Arms crossed, he leaned back on his heels, eyebrow cocked. "What manner of joke is this? You can't be serious."

"I am most serious, my friend, oh yes, very serious. You see, I gave my word to her you would come."

"On your solemn oath, she is lovely?"

"Lovelier than any woman you could ever imagine."

Laoidheach looked to Goban with a questioning glance, and received an evil leer in reply.

"You must hurry," I urged, "for it will be dark soon, and you will be unable to find your way up the hill."

"But..."

"Hurry now," I repeated, "and do not worry. I assure you that no harm will come to you."

"Very well," he sighed and started to move, but stopped in mid-turn. "Wait. No harm, you say? What manner of no harm?"

I hid a smile. "Will you just go on?"

He nodded his glum acceptance and began to trudge toward the hill, head sagging like that of a man knowingly walking to his doom.

* * *

Sunrise found Goban and me sitting beside our fire casting frequent glances up the hill, hoping to glimpse our friend. At last, we spotted movement. Laoidheach slowly wended his way down the slope.

Finally he drew near, waddling straddle-legged and leaning against a walking stick like an old man—hair disheveled, face gaunt, eyes bloodshot.

Goban began to chuckle and then fell over backwards roaring with laughter. Dust clouds billowed about him as he pummeled the ground with his hands and kicking heels.

Laoidheach staggered over to him and spat upon the ground. "I spit upon you and your ancestors."

Goban rolled from side to side, and roared all the louder.

My friend never spoke of his night atop the fairy mound with the goddess, though Goban often goaded him about it. I could only guess that my obligation to Brigid was fulfilled, for I heard no more of her.

Chapter 21
Blinne

We began our journey that same morning. Earlier, I asked Goban where he had seen Aine.

He looked towards the horizon and pointed. "There, to the north, in the lands of the Uí Néill at a village called Quirene."

Laoidheach rode one of the horses, for he remained incapable of walking, while the other carried a pack containing our few possessions. We trekked all day, avoiding the main trails and those who traveled upon them. Toward nightfall, we came upon a clearing and a small, thatched cottage nestling among the trees alongside a whispering stream.

An old woman came to the door, watching us with open suspicion. She drew a black shawl over her head, holding it tight to her plump cheeks and round shoulders as we neared her doorstep. "If it is my husband you wish to see," she pointed, "he is yonder, working late in the fields."

I stepped forward, and bowed slightly before her. "We are but weary travelers, mother, hopeful of finding a safe place to spend the night, and perhaps food if you have it to spare."

She placed her hands on her hips, squinting eyes measuring us. "Perhaps you may camp here tonight if it pleases my husband. As for food, it is little we have for ourselves and none to share with vagabonds the likes of you."

"As you say, of course, mother. But, we ask not your charity. We can pay for our meals if it serves you well."

"Pay, you say? Pay with what?"

"With a copper coin, mother."

"Show me."

I opened the purse, withdrew a coin and held it forward in the palm of my hand. "It is wise you are to be wary during these times, but my friends and I are honest men, and wish no harm come to you or your family."

She stared wide-eyed at the coin. "I have seen such coins in the market, and heard things said of their value." She looked up. "You offer this in exchange for food?"

"Yes, mother, if it is satisfactory payment."

"Perhaps you are honest men, as you say, but the decision will be made by my husband. I warn you now, he is a hard man."

We tied our horses to a nearby shrub, and sat down to wait for the woman's husband to arrive from his fields. Presently, a small, stooped man approached. His was a lined, care-worn face, and he stopped, surprised by our presence.

"Good evening, sir," I greeted him. "Your good wife said we should have words with you."

The woman heard me speaking, and came from the house to stand beside her husband. He glanced at her, blinking his eyes.

"These men wish to stay the night here," she told him, "and offered to pay for food with a copper coin."

The man blinked again, nodding his understanding.

"They seem to be honest young men," she continued, "though I must say the disgraceful state of their clothing does not speak well of them."

The man nodded.

"I believe they can be trusted, and we should allow them to stay the night. We can spare them some of our food in trade for the coin, don't you think?"

The husband blinked, shrugged and nodded his agreement.

The woman gave me a hard stare. "Didn't I warn you my husband can be a difficult man? And yet, he has agreed to let you stay and share our food."

A smile teased the edges of my mouth, but I bowed. "You warned us for fair, mother. We thank you, sir, for your gracious hospitality."

The man nodded.

"I am called Blinne and my husband here, Quillen. Now then, what be your names?"

I introduced my two friends and myself, after which Blinne invited us into their single-room cottage. A smoke-stained copper kettle hung above the fire pit behind the hearth. Blinne boiled a stew for their dinner, but scurried about adding more cabbage and peas to the kettle. Quillen reached to the rafters above his head with a knife and sliced a large piece from a smoked ham. It was diced, and then added to the stew.

"Quillen," Blinne ordered, "go you outside now and wash. You are covered with the dirt of the fields. Afterwards, I want you to come straight back, for it is time for your rowan berry tincture." She looked to Laoidheach with a knowing wink. "He has the piles, don't you see, and the tincture is good for him."

Laoidheach flushed. "Yes, I see. I'm sorry to hear...that is...ahem, I had best go and wash a bit myself." He looked to Goban and me. "In fact, I think we should all go wash away the dust from our travels."

I turned to follow the men outside, but Blinne called, "Wait Ossian, I would speak with you."

She waited until the men were gone, and then continued, "I know you now, Ossian. That is, I visited your village many times and knew your father. He was a good man, and offered my family medicines and many blessings. I saw you with him once or twice, and the serpent ring on your hand helped me recognize you. It was a bad thing the Corcu Duibne did there, a bad thing."

"Yes," I nodded, "it was a bad thing."

"Humph, raised as you were, and now look at you, a shabby scarecrow if I may say so."

"Yes, well I—"

"Hush and wait there a moment." Walking across the room, she stooped to open a small wooden chest. After rifling through folded clothing, she turned and straightened up, holding a fine, cream-colored linen kirtle, and tan leggings.

"These were my son's," she said, "and him now dead of the flux these three long years. He was tall and thin like you, and they should fit you well. I would that you will wear them."

"But mother, I—"

"Don't you 'but mother' me, young man!" Wagging a finger at my nose, "A man in tattered rags is in no position to refuse new clothing."

It was no small thing for Blinne to offer the clothing of her dead son. And too, she was right. I was in no position to refuse.

"Thank you mother, the clothes honor me." I took them from her outstretched hands. "Please accept another copper coin in payment for them."

"No, Ossian, you owe nothing for the clothing. Consider them payment for your father's many kindnesses to me and my family. Now, before you go outside to wash and change clothes..." She reached atop a ledge and removed a shining copper mirror, wooden comb and small knife. "Take these things of Quillen's with you and shave, or at least trim that shameful beard."

I glanced down shuffling my feet. "Yes, mother." And then scampered through the door.

* * *

A dense mist obscured the early morning sun. Blinne regarded me with approval as I sat astride the horse. "You look well, Ossian, with the new clothing and your trimmed beard."

"We thank you, mother, for your kindness. Would that the gods provide your home with prosperity and comfort."

Blinne nodded. "Quillen and I give thanks to the Earth Mother for our good fortune. What of you, Ossian? Where lies your future in these trouble times?"

"My future? It is a question I have asked of myself many times of late. I cannot see my future, mother." Face lifted to the sky, I shook my head and sighed. "I cannot see it."

Chapter 22
The Cave of the Tuatha De Danann

We rode hard in the early dawn, letting our horses have their heads. Our few possessions were loaded aboard my horse that Laoidheach and Goban might ride double. Laoidheach chanted as he galloped, his long flaxen hair streaming in the wind and, in truth, I felt he had more than a touch of the Tuatha about him.

The sun had reached the center of the sky when we stopped briefly to rest the horses, and then traveled on 'til we came to a rim of rugged hills.

"Enough," I called to my companions as nightfall approached. "Let's find a place to rest until the morning. Tomorrow we will cross the hills while the horses are still fresh."

We found a spot beside a cliff face and made our camp among some broken boulders. I removed the sack of gold from the horse and tossed it on the ground where it landed with a loud clank.

Goban glanced at it, eyebrow cocked. "Ye've carried that bag since we met. What have ye there, Ossian?"

"Gold. I fetched it from my village. It will go to pay for outfitting Brendan's voyage."

"Gold?" Laoidheach's mouth fell open. "May we see it?"

I reached to the bag and poured the contents onto the ground.

He fell to his knees, gawking at the treasure, and then looked up. "Where did you get this?"

"It was my father's, the cup and headband gifts received by my grandfather. I had just retrieved it in Rath Raithleann before I found you and Goban prisoners of the Corcu."

"Good," Goban nodded as he inspected the gold with an assayer's eye. "We will have need of it on our journey to find your sister."

"No, Goban." Laoidheach was sporting the headband and I grinned at his antics, but continued to Goban, "Again I tell you, this gold is for Brendan."

"And how do ye propose we eat in the meanwhile? We have need of another horse, perhaps two, for we will need a pack animal. And with what do ye propose to purchase your sister from the god-cursed slavers? Do ye think the few copper coins remainin' in your purse sufficient to provide for our needs?"

I had little knowledge of the value of such things, for my wants had always been provided for by my father or others. Ashamed of my foolishness, I wagged my head. "Of course you are right. I had not considered those things. Is there gold enough here to do all you suggest?"

Offering a wry grin, Goban replied, "I think this will do nicely, yes. In fact, we can purchase the two horses and live like bloody kings for more than a month in exchange for only three of those gold coins. As for the cost of ye're sister—"

"I would offer all for my sister!"

"Um, yes, well as for the purchase of her, we simply must wait and see, but her cost will be a trifle compared to the treasure I see spread before me. Ye needn't worry, your priest Brendan will have more than enough remainin' to provision his ship."

"Now, to more urgent matters," Goban grumbled, patting his hard stomach. "Not much to forage for around here. We must make do with the dry barley bread and gnats' piss for ale the old woman gave us. I'll be starving tonight rather than again desecrate me stomach with her vittles."

"Ah yes," Laoidheach jibed as he shoved the headband into the bag. "A great smith such as you is more familiar with finer fare. Hams, great barons of roasted beef, young lamb turned on a spit, great stews of pork, venison baked with berries—"

"Stop! May ye're pecker rot and drop off," Goban groaned. With that, he gathered bracken for a bed and was soon asleep.

We settled down around our campfire, and ignored Goban's snoring. Laoidheach sliced the bread, took a sip of Brinne's ale and grimaced. "Goban was right. This ale does taste like gnats' piss."

"You say so, Laoidheach? I cannot judge it so, since I have no experience with drinking gnats' piss."

He gave me a small smile. "I haven't spoken of it, but I see a great change in you, and not for the better. When last I saw you, in the days before the Corcu Duibne raid, you stood tall among your peers, and held an air of supreme confidence about you that I fail to see now. It's as though some piece of you is missing. Is it that you have lost all faith in yourself and the gods?"

I paused for a moment as I considered his words. They were not spoken as criticism, but rather in the gentle manner of a concerned friend. "There is truth in what you say, though now I can say openly, only partially so. Yes, looking back on it, following the raid on our village I did lose myself. I lost myself totally. Not only were our king and village defeated on that tragic day, but I was also defeated, utterly defeated in all that I was and ever hoped to be."

"I thought you dead, for you disappeared and there was never word of you."

"Perhaps I did die, at least for a while." I stared into the fire, remembering. "You see, my friend, it is little I recall about the day the Corcu Duibne struck, though sometimes I am haunted by fleeting memories of the horror of it. Somehow, I staggered away from the village, my head pounding from the blow I received, and wandered far until I found myself in a lonely cave beside the sea. I huddled there like a wounded beast, all the while my head shrieking with pain. It was as if a curtain cloaked my mind. How I survived, I cannot say." I leaned forward, picked up a twig and stirred the fire. "Like I said, perhaps I was dead for a while, for I have no memory of what I did or how I lived during those months."

Laoidheach leaned back, hands clasping a bent knee. "All of us, all the survivors of Rath Raithleanne, died a bit that day. I wonder what has become of the others now."

"They are all slaves in one capacity or another, somewhere. But it is Aine who captures all my thoughts." I tossed the twig onto the fire, glancing at his somber face. "You know her circumstances? You know what they have done with her?"

He sat up, cross-legged, hands scrubbing his face. "You think I do not? You think I have not thought of it and lain awake tormented by wondering, fearing?"

"Your betrothed will not be the same as when last you saw her." It was with no intent to distress or even test him that I continued. "There will be those who will call her unclean and unworthy to be wed now. What are your thoughts, knowing as you do all that has happened to her?"

Elbows on knees, he stared into the fire. "You ask if I will remain true to our betrothal?"

"Aye, though it is a hard thing I ask of a friend and brother."

"I will not lie and say I have not thought long about it. What man would want his wife to…?" A hand wiped tears from his eyes. "Ach, I weep like an old woman."

He straightened up and sniffed. "I made my pledge to Aine with my soul and mind and I shall not go back on it."

My heart warmed, yet I understood the storm that raged within him. "If it is because you feel honor-bound to do so, as Aine's brother I release you from your pledge."

Within the firelight's glow, his twisted, anguished face turned to me, and he gasped, "It is because she owns my heart and I still love her more than life itself." Finger pointing toward me, his face hardened. "And I say this as well. Do not worry about spending your treasure to purchase Aine back from those bastard slavers. I intend to kill them all, every one."

* * *

Something woke me, and I sat up, startled by a quavering moan that seemed to come from the cliff. I rose, taking a flaming brand from the fire, and made by way through the boulders. Around a sharp turn a small cave opened, from which the sound seemed to come.

A vibrating drone, it rose and fell in a high pitch and came from no man nor animal I knew of. Some unseen force propelled me forward and I could not fight it even though I knew it was the Tuatha under the earth that summoned me.

A tunnel spiraled downwards and I followed it, unnerved though drawn on by the irresistible summons. Down and down I went, my elbows brushing cold damp walls, my feet feeling for steps carved into the stone until I arrived at a huge cavern. This was no mere fairy palace. Millions of fireflies lit the glistening cavern walls. Filled with the musty smell of a place long empty, it seemed the Tuatha had abandoned everything; chairs, tables, cooking pots littered the floor. There was treasure, enough to supply a hundred voyages, and I gasped at the sight of it. Horn drinking cups encrusted with precious stones, scabbards of silver, rings and armlets of gold.

At the far end of the cavern, a simple wooden stave stood erect, somehow inserted into a great stone. It shivered and moaned with the eerie sound that woke me. I made my way to it and reached to touch it.

"Stop!"

I looked down. A small brown rat glared at me with beady red eyes.

"I see you Morrigan," I whispered. "What would you have of me?"

"My gift, Ossian. Do you think I would send you to the other shore without defense?"

"Is this the sacred staff of the Druids, the Slatnan Druidheacht?"

"This is not a simple Druid's staff. This is the Staff of Nuada of the Silver Hand! Look upon it well. See it is made of birch, the axis upon which the universe spins. When you withdraw it from the stone it is dead wood, a staff that travelers would carry."

It was an amazing thing, the Staff of Nuada himself, first king of the Tuatha. "But My Queen, I have no knowledge of the use of such power."

"Look underneath the stone, my Ossian, and see what you find there."

I cleared away the rubble at the base of the stone and came upon a small chest made from oak and covered with lacquered silver. Curious as to its purpose, I laid it on the rock beside the stave, and the rat scuttled over to it and struck it with its paw. The chest sprang open. Inside it lay a silver pommel in the shape of a coiled serpent.

She gestured toward the Staff. "Now pay heed. The Staff of Nuada is a powerful charm, even in the hands of a poor mortal such as you. The Serpent and Staff must never come together except in a time of dire need, for when you raise it the Serpent Staff will draw the very life force from you if you keep it raised too long. Keep the pommel hid about you and let no one know of it."

I took the gleaming Serpent, hid it in my kirtle and then lifted the Staff from the stone. It shrieked once as I withdrew it, then shuddered and was still.

It was an awe-inspiring gift. "Yes, I understand, but how will I command the power of it?"

"The Staff itself will direct you—otherwise call upon your gods for guidance. It can aid you much during your voyage to Tír na nÓg."

"And what of you, My Queen? Will you too withdraw to the west?"

The rat looked at me and shimmered, expanding into a burst of light. Eldritch laughter echoed through the cavern as the light coalesced into a looming, terrifying figure. She was Macha of the Morrigan's Fate Trinity—Macha, goddess of battle and death—Macha, a woman with harpy's wings, sagging breasts and talons dripping blood.

She settled her wings and spoke. "So you ask if I go to find peace in the Isles of the Blessed? Never! I am War Goddess of the Tuatha, and, though my powers grow weak, I would pass quickly in the idleness of the West. I crave the thrill of battle, the clash of steel on steel, spilled blood and the fear of men. I will stay and feed upon the souls of my enemies until the God of the Christians claims them all. Now go, but take nothing else from this place or the earth will take it."

Without warning, she vanished and I was alone in the great hall.

Staff in hand, I made my way back through the tunnel bringing nothing else of the Tuatha, though the riches lying there sorely tempted me.

Back in our camp, I could not sleep so I lay awake until the first gray of dawn and saw Goban stir and rise.

He made his way over to Laoidheach and poked him with his foot. "Come on, minstrel, stir yourself. I spent the night dreaming of your taunts of food. We must make haste."

Laoidheach went to water the horses, while Goban muttered he had to piss and wandered 'round the cliff.

We mounted and were waiting for him to finish his business, when there was a dull rumble and a cloud of dust billowed into the air.

"Goban," I called. "Are you all right?"

A sorry figure appeared through the dust, covered in dirt from head to foot.

"Wha…what happened?" he stammered.

"Goban did you find a cave and did you enter it?

"Yes I did," he snorted, nose in the air, arms akimbo. "It looked a nice quiet place to crap, so I was squattin' down when I saw a dagger lying on the ground, and a fine one at that. I just picked it up to take a look at it and the earth fell on me. I was lucky to get out alive."

"That you were. Have you the dagger with you?"

"No," he mumbled. "I must have dropped the damned thing."

"It's well you did, for it would have brought bad luck to us. Now pull up your britches, we've far to go."

Chapter 23
The Wiles of Gods and Men

I rode alone, the Staff of Nuada across my thighs, while Laoidheach and Goban mounted double. Midday found us riding into a village and soon we had a crowd around us.

Village children ran beside us, whooping and yelling. "Strangers! Strangers!"

A man emerged from a stacked-stone cottage, a Christian priest clad in a black robe. Three warriors idling nearby joined him and the group approached us.

"We must be careful," I whispered to my friends, "lest they know of us. We must not use our own names."

The priest came near, and made the Christian's sign of the cross. "May the Lord smile upon you." His eyes passed over us. "So, strangers, there are few who pass here during these troubled times."

"Right you are, father," I replied, "and we would not be traveling except that we have been called to Tara by the High King."

"You call me father. You are Christians, then?"

"Aye, we are but poor servants of the Heavenly Father, and His son Christ Jesus."

The priest clasped his palms together beneath his chin. "'For even the Son of Man came not to be served but to serve, and to give his life as a ransom for many.'" Again he made the sign of the cross in the air before him. "May He watch over each of you during your journey. Few come here, though we must guard against the vile Druids and their pagan following who have once again brought God's wrath against this land."

"Once again, father? I'm sorry. I know of the darkness, of course, but has God wrought yet more vengeance upon us?"

"You have not heard? Yes, you must not travel to the villages nearby the coastline for there is a deadly plague there. Many hundreds, perhaps thousands of people have already died of it."

A grizzled warrior stepped forward, a grim-faced, stocky man sporting a close-cropped beard. "One moment, Father. Many brigands roam the land, and I would know more of these strangers." He glared at me. "Who are you? Where are you from? State your business here."

I matched the man's stare. "I am called Ó Scannláin, and," pointing to Laoidheach, "this is my friend Bran, and behind him sits Fintair, a smith from our village. We are of the Corcu Duibne."

Another warrior spoke up. "I know the Corcu Duibne warrior Ó Scannláin, and you are not him."

I kneed my horse close beside the man. "The warrior Ó Scannláin of whom you speak, he is a massive man?"

The warrior nodded. "That he is."

"And does he not have red hair, the same as mine?"

The warrior nodded again. "That he does."

"Then you speak of my cousin, for the red hair is common in our family. Now, know all of you, we travel to Tara at the High King's bidding."

The first warrior spoke again. "Something smells amiss here. Three tattered men, and but two horses? Of what use would King Máelgarb have for the likes of you?"

Goban leaped from the rear of his horse, eyes blazing, chest out. He strode forward, and faced the warrior; burly arms stretched wide, hands bunched into iron-hard fists. "Ye dare question Master Ó Scannláin? He and Master Bran have more cattle between them than ye can count. Though I doubt ye can count beyond ye're own fingers, toes and the insignificant piece of meat hangin' between ye're legs that ye fondle into the night."

He turned to me. "Master, perhaps ye and Master Bran would care to rest in the shade of the grove over there while I treat with these minions."

I almost laughed aloud at Goban's audacity, but remained where I was lest he stirred trouble.

Goban looked again to the warrior. "It is no god-cursed business of yours, pokin' your impudent nose into these gentlemen's affairs, but I will tell ye we lost two horses and most of our possessions while crossin' a swollen river only four days past. A regrettable thing it was, but now we are here to replace what we can." He glanced about. "Though, I doubt this pigsty of a village has much of any account."

Hand dropping to his sword hilt, the warrior's face glowed red. Goban grasped the hammer at his belt.

The priest stepped forward, arms outstretched. "Let us have no trouble here."

To Goban he continued, "I'm certain there was no intention to insult your masters. Tell me man. What is it you need that you might travel on?"

"We require horses, clothin', blankets and food." Arms folding over his chest, eyebrow cocked, he added, "And we have gold to pay for it all."

"Gold you say?" The priest turned to the warriors. "You have done your duty, and may leave us now. The Church will attend to these Christian gentlemen's needs."

* * *

We traveled through an area of rolling green meadows separated by low stone walls. Now, we rode our individual horses. A fourth horse carried our supplies, packages of food, drink, spare clothing and blankets, everything needed for our journey. The packhorse would later serve as a mount for Aine when we came upon her.

Thunder rumbled in the distance, storm clouds gathered and a stiff wind swirled the high grass around us. We rode through an area I knew, for we were nearing Dún Ailinne, though it was a place I would avoid.

Watching the troubling skies, I said, "We must find shelter soon. There is a place I know, an isolated Druid chapel, a shrine dedicated to Accasbel. If we hurry, perhaps we can arrive there before this storm arrives."

We changed course, turning onto the main trail to Dún Ailinne. A bit further on, a narrow lane turned east between stone walls toward the chapel. Soon the place came in view, but I was dismayed at what I saw — the shrine was in ruins.

Again thunder rolled across the sky and large raindrops pelted us as we rode up to the burnt-out stone structure. Walking our horses through the small courtyard, we dodged debris while the evidence of what happened there grew clear. Christians had been at work to erase the memories of our gods and beliefs.

"There!" Goban gestured. "A bit of roof still covers a corner of the chapel. It will offer ample shelter for us."

We tied the horses to a burnt timber, and piled our supplies under the small covering of unburned roof. A campfire was soon burning and we satisfied our hunger with dried venison and berries.

Afterwards, Goban reclined back on his elbows, but sat up and pointed. "May I see your sword, Ossian?"

I handed it to him and he tapped the blade with his fingertip as he held it close to his ear. "It's poorly made, Ossian, poorly made," he grumbled. "I will make ye a new one, not a butter spreader like this, but a proper sword sanctified by the gods, a sword that sings in the hand of the man who wields it. Within only three months, I can—"

"Three months?" Laoidheach scoffed. "You haven't three days. We leave again in the morning to find Aine."

I agreed with Laoidheach. "He's right, Goban, I will make do with this sword."

Goban grinned and pointed to the Staff of Nuada. "Ye should fight with your Druid's stick, then. It will serve ye as well when the fightin' begins."

"Speak no more of the Staff, for it is…" I hesitated. The Staff was a personal gift from the gods, a magical object of unimaginable power, not a thing for discussion or speculation. "But why do you say I should favor it?"

"I watched ye use the sword against that Corcu warrior holding his battle club when ye saved us, and ye showed no skill with it. Ye were fortunate to catch the man unawares. He was still half-asleep or otherwise he would have quickly killed ye."

He was right, though I would not readily admit it. "You think I can be killed so easily?"

"I think ye would fight hard, or try, but ye're clumsy with a sword." He waved a casual hand. "So yes, even a novice warrior with little trainin' could kill ye quick enough."

No man wants to be thought an easy victim. "Clumsy am I? Hah. You are a tradesman, a smith, what would you be knowing about fighting?"

"I told ye before, I am no mere smith. I am a master smith, a maker of swords. To understand the qualities of a fine sword, one must also be skilled in its use."

Laoidheach smirked. "First, you are a master smith, and now, a master swordsman. Is there no end to your talents, Fintair?"

"Fintair? Fintair is it!" Goban turned to me and growled, "Why did ye tell those men back there in the village me name is Fintair? It is a dog's name and a silly name for a man."

I hid a grin. "I'm sorry my friend, but I had to think of a name quickly, and Fintair came to my mind."

"Well think of another name, for I will have no more of it."

"What would you have me call you, then? You choose."

Goban thought for a moment. "Ye can call me Aonghus before others, if ye must. It is a fittin' name for a man."

Laoidheach laughed. "So I say again, is there no end to your talents, Aonghus?"

"Bah, ye laugh at nothin', for I have never been to a school and cannot read or write me name. I cannot sing the songs of our people or tell their stories. I do not know the stars or the meanin' of them. I do not know the many gods, and I cannot divine the future."

He stiffened, his expressive hands working to make each thing as he described it. "But, I can create a golden bracelet to grace the fairest arm, mold an iron kettle to hang above a common hearth, shoe twenty horses in a single day and, yes, stand confidently before men with a sword in me hand."

A thought came to me. "You would stand before me with a blade?"

His jaw dropped. "Ye wish to fight me?"

"No. You are right; I have no talent with a sword. I want you to teach me to use it."

"Very well, I will try to teach ye. There," he pointed toward the ruined courtyard, "an iron fence stile will serve as my sword."

He then glanced at Laoidheach. "What of ye? Ye wish to learn the use of a blade as well?"

"I know the use of a blade." My friend's hand flashed to his kirtle and, as if by magic, a dagger appeared in his hand.

Goban cocked an eyebrow. "So. Ye're a knife man, eh?" He gestured toward the dagger. "Where did ye get it?"

"You two weren't alone in rifling through the trappings of the two dead Corcu warriors." He remained seated, took the dagger by the blade and threw it the length of five paces, where it stuck, quivering, in a charred wooden beam. "If you wish to practice fighting," he yawned and reclined on his back, "please do it quietly, and let a man rest."

Three days it rained while a gale blew in from the sea. Hidden we remained under our bit of cover while Goban taught me the use of a sword.

Chapter 24
Brógán O' Tolairg

F ields lay fallow about us as we neared the edge of the village of Quirene. I shook my head as I gazed about. The idleness of such good land when so many went hungry represented a vile waste of the Earth Mother's bounty.

A roughly dressed, bearded man stepped from behind dense shrubbery and held up his hand. "Stop! What do you here?"

"We are merely passing by your village," I said, "but require information, and hope to replenish our supplies."

The man gave us a haughty glare. "Information you say? And why would we likely give it? You are not welcome here. Stay the night here on the trail if you must and water your horses in the stream, but remain together and do not wander into the village. We have little, with nothing to offer strangers, and the men here are jealous of their women."

Goban chuckled. "If ye're any example of the men of Quirene, I should think the women safe enough, though I don't doubt the farmers closely guard their sheep into the night."

Pointing a finger toward Goban, the man replied, "Watch your tongue, little man! Do you not know that Quirene is the home of Brógán O' Tolairg? He does not abide strangers, and would cut your tongue from your impertinent mouth."

"Little man, is it?" Goban began to dismount. "Perhaps ye should recall the sayin'; an open mouth often catches a closed fist!"

"Wait!" I held up my hand. "Remain on your horse, Aonghus." I looked to the man on the ground. "So, why are you here? Are you a village sentry?"

"I saw you coming, and did no more than any man of our village would do were he to see strangers approaching."

"So your village would deny us entry while you entertain vile slavers?"

His eyes flitted about like those of a caged rat, but he muttered, "I know nothing of slavers."

"No? Oh, but I think you do. In fact, I think you know quite a bit about them. Tell your master we will pay well for information if it proves useful."

He straightened, pointing to the ground. "Do you wait here. Perhaps someone will come for you, perhaps not. If no one comes soon, I would advise you to leave quickly."

The man disappeared into the shrubbery, and I motioned to my friends to remain silent. They nodded their understanding while their eyes swept the area. Perhaps the man had been alone, but others could be lurking nearby.

We had a short wait, for the same man returned. "Brógán O' Tolairg bids you welcome to Quirene. Follow me, if you please."

We walked our horses into the village. It was arranged in a familiar manner, thatched-roof huts surrounded a common area of hard-packed earth. Four men stood beside a pit, a fulacht fia filled with water. Into the pit they were dropping hot stones from a blazing fire, boiling meat. All around, armed, roughly dressed men sat in quiet groups, trying hard to ignore us. Under my breath, I whispered to my friends, "See to your weapons. Something is amiss here."

The man led us to a large cottage where he stuck his head inside the door and muttered something. Then he turned to us. "Please dismount and enter. Brógán O' Tolairg wishes to speak with you."

The Staff of Nuada was never far from my hand, and I had it now as I stepped from my horse and walked toward the cottage. Laoidheach and Goban followed as I strode through the door and stopped in surprise. The man at the far end of the room seated on a large wooden box was not what I had expected.

240

"Come in. Come in all of you!" the man laughed. Huge and grotesque, he was, without doubt, the most corpulent being I had ever seen. His head and face meticulously shaved, he beamed with good humor. "Please, come in and be seated! Would you care for ale? I do not wish to brag, but I have perhaps the finest ale in all Eire!"

I shook my head. "No, though we thank you. We are…"

"Oh, don't bother with names. No one uses his true name during these times; while I," he chuckled, "well you already know who I am. Please do sit down."

Two benches were aligned before him so we seated ourselves, and I continued, "We are sorry to disturb you, Brógán O' Tolairg, and request only a brief moment of your time."

O' Tolairg again chuckled, his eyes squinting through rolls of fat alight with humor. "Yes, so I've heard. You want information."

Then he pointed to Goban, and laughed. "You are the one who mentioned the sheep, I think. You have a sharp wit about you, one I appreciate, but," he placed a finger before his lips and whispered, "shh. The men here wouldn't want their little secret to become known." His head rolled back on his thick neck as he roared at his own joke.

I began to grin as well, but then froze, seeing the wooden cross hanging on the wall behind him.

O' Tolairg followed my gaze and turned back to me. "You find the thing distasteful, I think? Yes," he nodded, "it is an offense in your sight."

"No, I—"

"Do not deny it. You think I don't know the meaning of your serpent ring? Take the damned cross off the wall and throw it through the door if it suits you. It serves no purpose here, although a few of my rare guests find it comforting."

He was a strange one. "You are not a Christian, then?"

Again he laughed. "A Christian? Hah! No, I'm no Christian, and far from it, though sometimes it's wise to appear otherwise. Now, you wanted information?"

I nodded. "Yes, and I will gladly pay for it if it pleases you."

His fat jowls jostled as he chortled. "Let's discuss the value of my information after I've provided it, shall we? You mentioned slavers to my man. Now, tell me. What do you wish to know?"

"There were slavers here a few weeks ago. They held captive a young girl, a beautiful girl with long, auburn hair by the name of Aine. Do you remember?"

"How could I not?" the fat man beamed. "Such a girl is to be remembered. It is she you are interested in?"

"Yes, she is… That is, what became of her? Do you know?"

He waved a dismissive hand. "She was here, held by a mangy dog named Scannlon and his flea-ridden friends. Now she and they are gone."

"I see. Yes, but did they say where they were going?"

For the first time, O' Tolairg frowned. "Yes. Scannlon is a great fool, and planned to travel east to Saithne."

"Saithne, you say? I do not know it."

"Humph, no doubt. It is a small village north of here, near the coast. Ships from distant lands have brought poisonous plague to some coastal villages and certain death for all who encounter it. The plague is in Saithne, and it is a place to be avoided."

Laoidheach gasped beside me, and, concerned for Aine, my heart sank at the mention of the word…plague, the Black Death. I looked to O' Tolairg. "Why would a man deliberately travel to a village poisoned by the plague?"

"I've already told you. Scannlon is a fool. He thinks to capture youngsters there for slaves after their parents die of it. It is a stupid plan, one that will no doubt kill him."

"And one that will kill Aine too, no doubt," I mumbled.

242

"What is the girl to you? Your wife perhaps?" He shook his head in answer to his own question. "No, not your wife. I have it! She is of your blood. Your hair is red while hers is auburn. She is your sister! Am I right?"

I nodded. "Yes, she is my sister."

O' Tolairg beamed. "I knew it from the very first. I'm very clever, don't you see, and I always know how things will be in the end. So tell me, was my information useful?"

I tired of the fat man. "Yes, you were very helpful. Now tell me how I can repay you."

He pointed to Goban. "I want him."

"What? But that is ridiculous. Oh, I see. It is another of your jokes."

"Oh, I love my jokes, yes I certainly do, but regrettably this is not one of them. You see, he is an escaped slave, but of course you knew that already. I well remember he came through here at about the same time as your sister, only he was a captive of Corcu Duibne warriors. I think they will pay a fat reward to have him returned to them. Wouldn't you agree?"

The dilemma we now faced was my fault. I should have realized that Goban might be recognized in Quirene. The gaze O' Tolairg fixed upon me was no longer that of a jolly fat man.

I rose and faced him. "This discussion is meaningless. I would not give you the man, even if he were mine to give. I have two pieces of silver. They are ample payment for your information."

O' Tolairg snickered. "You have silver? That is good, for I will have it and the man. To be sure, I will take all you have, and, if you are very fortunate, you and this other one beside you," he pointed to Laoidheach," can walk away from my village to find your sister."

"You are a pig."

He leaned back and yawned. "So I have been told before, but you begin to bore me. You and your friend have two choices. You can walk through that door and continue walking, or I will hold you and sell you as non-Christian slaves to the Corcu alongside the little man here."

I drew my sword. "You forget. We are armed and we have you. You will follow us outside to our horses."

"No, I think not." He called, "Oh, Osgar!"

The man who led us to the cottage appeared in the doorway. "Yes, Master O' Tolairg?"

"You heard what was said here?"

"Yes master."

"Be a good man, then, and go tell the others to gather before my cottage, won't you?"

The man disappeared from the doorway, and O' Tolairg sneered. "You see? You have no way out. Oh, I understand you might kill me, yes indeed, but I have more than fifty men out there who would then kill you. There's no profit in that, now is there? No. I suggest you all lay down your weapons, and accept my offer. Leave the small man with me, and you can simply walk away."

"I have no need to kill you. Goban will."

"Of course. But then my men will kill you just the same, don't you see, and your deaths will be on his head. What say you, Goban? Do you want to be the cause of your friends' deaths?"

Goban looked to me with sad eyes. "The bastard has us trapped for fair, Ossian, and that's a fact. Go with Laoidheach while ye can. I will deal with this fat pig afterwards."

O' Tolairg was already gloating over his victory, but my mind was on fire, seeking a way out.

"Let us just cut this swine's throat," Laoidheach urged. "His men might cut us down afterwards, but we cannot give up Goban."

"You are a man of honor, eh, pretty man?" the fat man grinned. "Be very cautious, for I think my men would enjoy capturing you to use at their pleasure in the place of their women," he winked, "or sheep. Where is the honor in that?"

"It is not a thing you would understand, you filthy pile of shit," Laoidheach snapped.

Laugher filled the room as O' Tolairg leaned back his head and roared.

The Staff of Nuada trembled in my hand, at first so slightly I scarce noticed it. It began quivering again, more urgently. An unknown energy raced up my arm from the Staff, a vision of unimagined power filled my mind, and suddenly I knew precisely how to confront this evil man and his henchmen.

I pointed my Staff at O' Tolairg. "Stand to your feet."

O' Tolairg grinned. "I think not."

Goban rose, strode over to him and slapped his face hard with the flat of his calloused hand. "My friend said stand to your feet, ye stinkin' offal!"

The fat man cringed under Goban's blow, but his shifty eyes found mine. "I offered you a way out of here, but now I take it back! You will die here, or be sold as a slave!"

It was now my turn to smile. "Will you stand, Brógán O' Tolairg, or must Goban encourage you once again?"

He sat motionless for a moment, and then sighed. Two wooden canes rested on the floor beside him. He took them in his hands and heaved his enormous bulk upright. The man stood there, leaning upon the canes, glaring. "And now?"

"Now you will lead us through the door."

"You are foolish men." His eyes captured Laoidheach and Goban. "And very soon you will be dead men."

I gestured toward the door. "Proceed."

Laoidheach whispered in my ear. "What are you planning? Are you certain this is a good idea?"

"Stay behind me and watch our backs, my friend." I then handed my sword to Goban, and pointed to O' Tolairg. "Prod him and keep him moving through the door."

Goban walked behind the man and slapped him across his broad ass with the flat of the sword. "Ossian told ye to proceed. Start movin'!"

The huge man took a hesitant, shuffling step forward, his massive weight much supported by his arms and the canes. Another step was taken, and, slowly, a third.

"You are an inconsequential scoundrel," I said to him. "You think yourself important because the scum in this filthy village cower before you. Know me for who I am, Brógán O' Tolairg, for I am Ossian, son of Ciann Mehigan, and a Druid among the Eoghanachts. You will release us unharmed, or, by the gods themselves, I shall unleash a power against you such as you cannot even imagine."

He glowered at me and hissed, "You think my men and I tremble before the idle threats of wizards? You Druids flee before the Christian priests, and scatter like leaves before the wind. Even your old gods, the Lords of the Sidhe, fall back in the face of the irresistible incursion of Christian priests and their Holy Trinity. You cannot defeat the Christians, and you cannot defeat me! When we step through that door you will taste my power, Ossian of the god-cursed Eoghanachts!"

Eyes narrowing, I pointed at him. "You are foolish to forget. You will die with us, and as you said, where is the profit in that?"

"Foolish am I? You think I will die so easily?" His lips curled. "It will take more than the likes of you to kill Brógán O' Tolairg."

Goban again slapped him across his buttocks with the sword. "Keep moving! Ossian didn't tell ye to stop walkin'."

O' Tolairg grunted, and resumed his slow shuffle like that of a monstrous, four-legged brute. He walked past me and the stench of him assaulted my nose, the foul odor of a creature long unclean.

Goban stepped forward, opened the door and told the fat man, "Ye go first. If an arrow comes, ye take it."

246

Perhaps there was truth behind Goban's words, for O' Tolairg hesitated, and then called out, "Wait! I am coming out!"

He began shuffling forward again and stepped outward into the sunlight. Goban followed closely behind, his sword at the man's throat.

I reached to the pouch at my belt, removed the silver coiled-snake pommel and placed it upon the Staff. At once, power surged through me, so I hurried through the door to discover fifty or more armed men of the village clustered twenty paces away.

My eyes swept the crowd and I held the Staff high as I called to them. "There need be no trouble here! Stand back, and my friends and I will simply ride away."

O' Tolairg bellowed in return. "Stop them! Archers forward, archers forward! Kill them!"

The Staff shuddered violently in my hands and I clenched my fist around it. "Stay back!" I yelled as eight bowmen stepped to the front of O' Tolairg's men. "Do not raise those bows, for you will suffer the wrath of the gods, the wrath of Nuada himself!"

The archers ignored me as they nocked arrows on their bowstrings. Behind them men raised weapons above their heads, shouting insults.

Laoidheach gasped and then stepped beside me, poised, knife in hand.

I understood the power of the Staff since it first trembled in my hand. Now I held it level, and pointed the pommel at the archers. A force like lightning showered from the pommel, shrieking like the tortured soul of a banshee, striking and searing the eight archers who stood directly before it. It was a scene of horror, of screaming pain by all touched by the power of the Staff.

The remainder of O' Tolairg's men fell back, dropping their weapons to race away in panic. I raised the Staff vertically and the lightning stopped.

Eight men lay upon the ground before us. Two writhed, emitting agonized groans.

Goban stared at me, the horror on his face plain to see. He could not find his breath, so whispered, "When I told ye the Druid's stick would serve you as well as a sword, I did not know the terrible truth of it. It is an evil thing, possessed by an unspeakable demon."

"A demon possessed thing, Goban? No. This power far exceeds that of a mere demon. This is the staff of a king, the Staff of Nuada of the Silver Hand! Through it, the Tuatha De Danann established an empire, yet until now, little did I truly understand that it possesses the power of the gods themselves."

O' Tolairg had slumped to the ground, and now lay there quivering, mewling with fear. Goban stepped over and kicked him in his ribs. "This was all your fault ye stinkin' pile of cow shit. None of this should have happened. None of it!"

He raised his sword to take the man's head, but I ordered, "Stop Goban! That is not the way. Wait."

I looked across the village, but saw no movement. "Osgar!" I called. There was no answer, so I called again, and yet again.

Finally, there was a distant response. "I hear you, wizard! What do you want of me?"

"Come forward! On my word, no harm will come to you!"

There was motion at the edge of the distant grove of trees, and then Osgar staggered into view as though pushed into the open by unseen hands. He glanced once over his shoulder, and then began walking hesitantly toward us to stop five paces away. Face pale, he avoided looking toward the charred bodies of his former comrades.

He stared at the ground. "I am here."

I pointed to the fat man who still lay quivering upon the ground. "Look there. Is this man your master?"

Osgar shook his head, and then spat upon the ground. "Brógán O' Tolairg is no master of mine. Go ahead; kill the fat bastard, and all the better for it."

I shrugged. "I have no further interest in him. He can continue to lay there, you can select his fate; it makes no difference."

The man squinted. "Who are you?"

"I am Ossian, a Druid from the lands of the Eoghanachts. As for you, you are a bandit who lives in a village of bandits. Your former chieftain is discredited. What will you and the men of Quirene do now?"

Osgar gestured outwards from the village. "Before the darkness, we were farmers. Then our crops failed and our fields lay fallow. O' Tolairg convinced us that the only hope for our families was to turn to banditry."

"Yes, but the sun has long since returned, and yet you haven't returned to your fields. Your friends there," I pointed to the bodies, "were farmers, but are now dead bandits. What say you?"

"What happens here next isn't up to me. As for myself, I will return to my fields. The others must decide for themselves."

"Then it is two things I say to you and the men of Quirene." I pointed to the charred bodies. "First, take the wealth of O' Tolairg, all of it, and share it equally among the women of the men who lie there. Do you understand?"

He nodded.

"The second thing is that my friends and I will ride east from here, but will be coming back this way soon. When we do, if we find bandits here, we will kill all who oppose us and burn this village to the ground. Do you understand that as well?"

Osgar's smile was grim. "It would be difficult to misunderstand you."

"Good." I turned to my companions. "Come then. We can be far from here by nightfall."

Chapter 25
The Black Death

ver north we rode, and then east toward the coast. It was there we would find Saithne, and, somewhere near there, Aine. We came upon a farmer in his field, and asked that he point the way.

He gestured eastward. "There's a cart track leading to Saithne. Do you know the Black Death is there?"

I nodded.

"It is foolish you are to go there then." Leaning on his hayfork, the farmer shook his head. "It is a village of the dead, as you will be too if you do."

We traveled on and found the track; narrow, winding and rutted through years of travel. Soon a man came toward us pushing a cart. A woman and three children walked behind him. It was as if we were invisible spirits, for they never looked up as they marched by. Like ragged ghosts, they were, the wheels of their laden cart squealing as the family plodded silently onward, away from Saithne.

It became a familiar scene, a promenade of the lost, straggling along in family groups, in twos and threes, or alone, all escaping a dreadful tragedy behind them. Then we began to find the others, those lying quiet in the tall grass alongside the road, those who carried the poison within them, those whose attempt to escape came too late.

Swarms of carrion birds, fat from feasting on the dead, chattered and fluttered among the scattered trees lining the track. We tied linen cloths over our noses to fight away the stench of bloated bodies and hold the poison of the plague at bay. I chanted prayers as we rode along to protect us from the Black Death and ghosts of the dead.

Further on, a small knot of men squatted in the shade by the roadside, Christian monks all by the looks of them. One of their number lay on his back in their midst, his eyes moving within a face swollen and blackened by pustules, proof of the plague that spelled his doom.

We rode wide of them, until the prone man croaked, "Ossian. Is it truly you?"

I reined my horse around and stopped at what I hoped was a safe distance from the fatal disease dwelling among them. "Who is it that asks?"

"It is I, father Joseph. Do you not know me?"

His inflamed face was unrecognizable, but I knew him well enough. "Aye. I know you." I leaned forward, resting my crossed arms on the horse's neck. "It was you I trusted to carry a message of peace to your demon bishop at Tara. And well my entire village felt the full measure of his lying response."

"But the bishop agreed to your terms, Ossian, and that's the truth of it." His voice was weak, and one of his aides raised him up to place a flagon of water to his lips. Joseph drank in large gulps. Panting, he continued. "A truce now holds between us throughout the land."

Bitterness welled within me. "A dying man should tell no lies, priest. Your bishop and his Corcu hordes offered no truce to Rath Raithleann. That's the truth I know."

Angry glances and muttering came from the monks gathered about Joseph, but he waved them to silence with a frail hand.

"The bishop had no hand in that. He sent word to all the tribes that depredations against you were to cease." Joseph paused, gasping for air like a landed fish. "It wasn't until afterwards he learned of the Corcu raid on your village, and heard you were killed. By God's Grace, I see you now before me, and thankful I am for it. Upon my honor and sworn faith in my Holy Father, what I say is true."

No doubt Joseph believed his own words, but I had seen too much of Christian deceit. "The Corcu ignored your bishop's command? It seems unlikely."

Joseph's words fell to little more than a rasping whisper, and I leaned forward in my saddle that I might hear them. "It was your food the Corcu were after. Their people starved, they attacked your village to fill their bellies. The fact you were a heathen tribe merely eased their souls, don't you see? The bishop was furious when he learned of it. As was the case following the raid upon Dún Ailinne, again I am ashamed of God's followers, and may only humbly ask your forgiveness of them as I ask God to forgive them as well."

"Forgiveness?" Venom born of deep-held hatred filled my mouth. "You dare ask that I forgive that which can never be forgiven? As for your bishop, will his fury bring back my King, my father, my family, and all the people of my village? His fury earns him no merit with me."

"My friend," Joseph pleaded, "Jesus Christ himself teaches forgiveness—"

"Enough! This land has known naught but fire and blood since the first Christian set foot upon its shores." My hand shook as I pointed a trembling finger toward him. "Your faith is like the plague that now consumes you. Too much has passed that I shall never forget or forgive."

My heart hardened against him, I wheeled my horse around toward the distant village and kicked its ribs.

Behind me came Joseph's weak call, "Ossian—"

* * *

The sun was high overhead when first we saw the smoke. Black as ink it was, like three grotesque beckoning fingers coiling and twisting in the wind, thick columns soaring to incalculable heights within a cloudless sky.

We followed the smoke until we crested a hill and Saithne appeared downslope before us. A tremor ran through me as I gazed

253

down on the hamlet. It was like wolfsbane—small, lovely and deadly. A colorful ocean-side village bordered by emerald fields, dying as its people died. Nearby, a handful of men tended the sources of the smoke; three pyres piled high.

"They're burning their dead," Goban muttered.

Horses abreast, holding dread in our hearts, we proceeded down the dusty track to the village edge, taut hands gripping reins, ready to fight or flee from men or ghosts. No one was in sight. An oppressive silence weighed upon us, our horses making soft footfalls as we walked them past the first cottages. Open windows like vacuous eyes stared at us.

Breaking pottery crashed in the hut beside us. Instantly, Goban's hammer was in his hand. We swung our horses 'round facing the threat. Presently, a whining yellow cur slunk from the hut, dashed around the corner, and was gone from view.

Laoidheach laughed at our timidity as we turned back on our original course. Though Saithne was a small village, finding the slaver Scannlon and Aine would require time within a place we would fain not be.

The gods were smiling, for we had gone but a short distance farther when a crone tottered from a sagging hut. Clad in a ragged black dress, a shawl screening her face, she stooped far forward grasping a walking stick taller than her down-turned head. I urged my horse forward, and stopped beside her.

Twisting her wrinkled face around to peer up at me, the hag's gap-toothed mouth opened as she cackled. "If it's robbing me you have in mind, you've found a poor bargain."

"No mother, it's information I seek. I look for a man and a girl."

"Look upon the burn piles then," her ancient voice quavered. "It's likely you'll find their ashes there."

"The man's name is Scannlon, a low dog of a slaver. Do you know him?"

"Scannlon, you say? Do I look like a woman who would know a slaver?"

"No, mother, though I thought you might have heard mention of him."

I was turning away when she added, "That I have."

Had I heard her right? "What's that?"

"I said I've heard of him."

Leaning down to her, I held my eagerness in check. "Would you know where I might find him?"

The crone's eyes squinted, and she shrugged. "Let me think. I can't seem to recall. An old woman's mind fails when she's hungry, you know."

I nodded. "Half a loaf?"

"And a wee bit of beef?"

"Aye, though we've lamb instead." I waved Laoidheach forward, pulled a bag from our packhorse and selected the food.

She removed her shawl and held it forward in trembling hands, eager eyes watching my every move.

I nodded toward the empty cottages. "I should think food would be abundant within the homes of the dead ones."

"Ach. It disappears quickly into ready hands after the family dies, and I'm not so agile as I once was."

It was a full loaf and large piece of lamb that I wrapped tightly within her shawl, and she accepted it with a smile and nod. "I thank you, sir. May the spirits keep you safe from the evil that dwells here."

"So where is Scannlon?"

"Keep going the way you are," she pointed, "and then left at the second lane. Past three cottages and a bit beyond, a path turns to the right. Follow it to the end. A poor hovel is there where you'll find Scannlon if he still lives."

Laoidheach jerked his reins, his wide eyes haunted. "Let's go get Aine."

We rode on, each man's face solemn at the prospect of facing Scannlon and his slavers. But it was Aine that mostly filled my mind.

At the lane where we were to turn left, we reined aside as a man driving a slow-rolling, horse-drawn wagon crept toward us. Its wheels screeched under a heavy burden, a death wagon, and we drew further away, averting our eyes as the gruesome cargo rolled past.

Again, Laoidheach urged us on. We walked our horse down the lane and turned onto the path described by the crone. At its end squatted a hut, barely visible behind overgrown shrubbery. A filthy, wiry man leaned against the side of the door.

I was in no mood to talk and wasted no time. "I seek the man, Scannlon. Are you him?"

Eyes dropping, he spat upon the ground. "No."

Beside me, Goban growled deep within his throat.

I goaded my horse closer to the man though he appeared unconcerned. "Very well, then. Is he within the hovel there?"

He was an indolent scoundrel. "Maybe. Who are you to be asking?"

I dismounted, shouldered the man aside and strode into the hut's dark interior. There was but a single small room, the stench of the place enough to make a man retch. Three men lounged on the floor, and an alarm bell pealed in my head at no sign of Aine.

I glanced at each man in turn, a surly lot, and then demanded, "Which of you is Scannlon?"

A burley, gray-haired man leaped to his feet and bowed in the obsequious manner of a peasant standing before his lord. "I am Scannlon, young master, and how might I be serving you this fine day?"

"I hear you are a trader in slaves and that you have a young girl to sell."

"It is true I sometimes trade in lowly humans, those of little value you understand, but a young girl?"

"That's right, a girl. I was told her name is Aine and I wish to purchase her from you."

Another of the men, still prone upon the floor, snickered.

Scannlon avoided my gaze as he frowned. "Aine? I'm not familiar with the name."

My hand rested upon my sword hilt and I drew the blade partially from its sheath. "Do not play games with me, slaver. I will have the truth from your lying mouth."

"Of course, young master." He rubbed his chin with a grimy hand, and then grinned. "Ah yes, I remember the girl now. Please believe me when I say that girl was not for you. Granted, she was a fine piece of ass at first, as all of us can attest, but later, well...." He raised a finger as it suddenly inspired. "Listen, if it is a woman you want, perhaps—"

"I rode here for the woman Aine!"

The snickering man on the floor laughed aloud. Instantly my sword was in my hand, its blade at the man's throat. "Where is she, dog? Where is Aine?"

The man recoiled in surprise. "She's gone...dead."

Laoidheach gasped behind me and my heart sank. "Dead, eh? How did she die?"

He clamped his mouth shut, so I flicked my wrist and the man's left ear fell into his lap.

His shriek filled the hut as his hand clasped the side of his head. Eyes clamped shut, he began rocking back and forth, wailing.

A quick step brought me close, where I kicked him and sneered. "I asked you a question, slaver! How did she die? Answer, lest you wish to lose your other ear."

Quailing before me, blood running down his arm to drip from his elbow, he pointed to Scannlon, and whimpered. "He killed her just last night. He strangled her after she scratched his face. Look closely, you can see the scratches."

I didn't have to look for the scratches. I had already noted them. Both hands gripping my sword's hilt, I swung the blade through the air like a scythe. It seemed to encounter no resistance at all as it severed Scannlon's head from his shoulders.

Behind me came a shout from the man who previously stood by the door. He was coming at me, his knife but an arm's length from my throat, when his skull seemed to burst in a crimson cloud. Goban entered, leaned over and retrieved his hammer.

He grunted, "The man wanted to fight, eh?"

The scraping of metal on metal turned me around to find the no longer wailing man drawing a sword as he began to rise. Once more, I swung my own and the man sat back, gaping at the stub of his wrist. I offered him the quarter he intended for me and swung the sword one last time, striking his neck.

Panting in fury I looked to the final man, who until now remained silent. "The girl, Aine, her body, where is it? Speak quickly if you value your life!"

He was a churlish bastard. "It's gone. Only moments before you arrived we pitched it upon the wagon that collects corpses."

The death wagon! I recalled the fires beyond the outskirts of the village. If I hurried, perhaps I could stop the wagon before it reached them.

Laoidheach stood behind me, face taut, tears streaming. I was striding toward him and the door when his hand flashed to his belt. He grasped his dagger, and hurled it past my head.

An agonized gasp turned me around to see the final slaver standing wide-eyed, Laoidheach's dagger protruding from his chest. He panted, "But, you said—" and collapsed.

258

Walking across the room, my friend retrieved his dagger, wiped the blade on the dying man's filthy clothing and shrugged. "And now it is done. The bastards are dead, every one."

Dead, yes, but what matter such filth? Now, Aine! Through the door of the slaughterhouse of our making, I ran, and leaped upon my horse. One thought filled my mind—to stop the corpse-laden wagon before it reached the fires!

I kicked my horse in its ribs; its thundering hooves echoed against lifeless cottages as I galloped back in the direction from which we had come. Tears stung my eyes, blurring my vision, and I wiped them away with my forearm. Soon, the trundling wagon came into sight; it was nearing the edge of the village.

The wagon driver, cloaked in a black robe, gaped in toothless surprise as I reined my horse beside him shouting, "Stop! Stop the wagon!"

The man squawked, "Stop you say? Who would you be to be saying stop to a man who is going about his own affairs?"

My eyes had already found Aine atop the pile of corpses and my mind screamed its anguish. No matter, there was nothing for it now but to concentrate on the driver. "You have a girl there and I would have her from you."

"You would have her?" A queer light shown in his eyes as the wagon rolled to a stop. "No, you cannot have her. She's mine, all of them, the dead ones, they are mine now."

"You must understand. The girl is my sister and I would see she is properly buried."

"Your sister?" He cackled in the manner of a madman. "She is no one's sister now, boy 'o. You cannot have her. They will give me food when she is delivered to the fires."

I would bargain with the foolish man if I must, but, in the end, I would have Aine's body. "See here, man. I will trade you the corpses of four men for the girl. What say you?"

"Four men you say?" His mad eyes were shifty, skeptical. "Where are these four men?"

"We have a bargain then? I will tell you if you agree."

"Yes, yes, we have a bargain. Hurry now, tell me."

Laoidheach and Goban wore grim faces as their horses trotted up to me. Laoidheach leaped from his horse and strode toward the wagon.

"Stop!" I yelled. "Go no closer. The corpses there, all those people but Aine died of the plague and you will likely get it too if you touch them."

I turned to the cart driver. "You there. My sister is the small girl atop your ghastly pile. Pick her up and lay her gently here on the road beside me."

He was wary of me. "And the corpses of the four men you promised me?"

"You remember the cottage where men put her body on your cart?"

The driver nodded. "That I do."

"Go there. You will find the men inside."

The driver grinned. "Four for one. I will dine well tonight."

The man did as he was told and I rolled Aine's poor naked body within my thin woolen blanket. Then Laoidheach and I laid her across the back of our packhorse. All the while my thoughts swung from anguish to raging fury with the bitter realization I had arrived just one day late to save Aine's life...one day...one day...one irrevocable day that would burn within my soul forever.

The wheels of the death wagon squealed anew as it resumed its grisly mission toward the fires, and I looked to Laoidheach and Goban. "We must find a safe place away from here and you will wait there. I will take Aine into the hills where I will perform a proper burial rite over her."

Laoidheach's face flamed. "No, Ossian. I will not stand aside while my betrothed is buried. I will go with you."

There was a thought in my mind, one that could be dangerous, and I said as much. "My friend, I plan a ceremony, one that could spell extreme danger for anyone nearby. No. You must stay away that no harm will befall you."

"I said I was coming with you and come I will." He mounted his horse and leaned toward me. "You think to use your Druid's magic to invoke spirits of the dead? You think to perform a ceremony that will frighten me? You are right." He nodded. "Under those circumstances, I would rather not come with you, but on the memory of my mother, you will not stop me from standing one last time by my Aine."

I looked with exasperation to Goban, but the smith surprised me. "Laoidheach is right. Ye would be wrong to deny him his final chance to stand beside his beloved. You two are me only friends now. When ye go into danger, I will be with ye."

Simple sincerity shown on his downcast face, and a lump formed in my throat. "No man ever had a better friend, Goban, and I thank you for it. Very well, but listen you, both of you. If you come with me, you must do no more or less than I tell you."

I paused, my hands scrubbing grief and weariness from my face. "If all goes well, you will witness a thing seldom seen except by Druids themselves, and you must never later speak of it."

Chapter 26
Beneath a Lone Alder

A soft evening rain spattered against the makeshift oilskin canopy covering us as we stood atop a grassy hill beside the open grave. Overhead, the boughs of a lone alder, the most sacred of all trees, would offer shade and protection for Aine's bones.

Already, the gods of death and the Underworld had been made aware of Aine's altered state, and the conventions of the burial ceremony satisfied. A gold coin nestled in Aine's hand so that all would know her as a woman of means when she arrived on the shore of Tír na nÓg. Now, only one rite remained, one likely to utterly fail or even sow destruction about us.

Laoidheach, eyes red and watering, and a grim-faced Goban stood beside me, Aine's blanket-enshrouded body at our feet beside the grave. Only her face was exposed; delicate, serene and lovely.

"Go there, both of you." I pointed into the distance where the horses stood tied to a bush. "Do not come near again unless I call for you."

"No." Laoidheach shook his head, "Goban can go. I will remain here beside you and Aine."

I laid my hand upon his shoulder. "My friend, please go as I asked. This is no place for you. I will call upon the gods, that they might awaken Aine."

Hope lit his eyes. "You will bring her back to life? Back to us?"

"No." I shook my head as I gazed down on Aine's still face. "That I cannot do. Aine belongs to the gods now, and they will not give her up. If she awakens, she will be neither dead nor fully alive. She will reside somewhere between. It is said the guardians of the dead are jealous of their wards, so at best I might revive her for only a short while."

"What power could do such a thing?" Goban whispered.

I raised my Staff. "Once again, my friend, the power exists here within the Staff of Nuada." Pointing to them, I warned, "Should anything happen to me during the ceremony do not approach me or touch the Staff. Ride away. Ride away quickly."

Shoulders slumping, they drew blankets over their heads against the light rain and strode away. My attention turned from them as I concentrated on the sketchy plan developing in my head. It was a thing I never before attempted, but lessons taught by Master Tóla on calling forth the dead returned to me. Settling upon the ground cross-legged beside Aine, I remembered back, piecing together the complex ceremony.

A fire would be needed, one that would attract the attention of the gods, and I peered out from beneath the canopy at the rain and water-soaked hill. A small smile touched my lips as I offered a blessing to the memory of Master Tóla. Rising while removing my knife from its sheath, I reached overhead and sliced off a piece of the oilskin canopy. Taking the knife and a piece of flint from a bag at my belt, I soon had a spark, and then a tiny flame consuming "that which cannot burn."

Then, everything rested within the powers of the Staff, though whether it would serve in what I was attempting, time would tell. Yet, it contained powers unknown even to the Master, so if I called upon them, perhaps my plan would succeed even if every step of the ritual wasn't followed precisely.

Aine suffered unimaginable abuse and died alone, far from home and family. For all that, I carried a great responsibility. Though I could never hope to set things right for her, perhaps I might capture this one moment that she would know she remained loved and remembered.

Taking the serpent pommel from its pouch I placed it atop the Staff. At once, the Staff shuddered, and I placed my right hand on Aine's shoulder that its power might pass through me to her. Eyes closed, concentrating, imbued with seemingly limitless power, I opened the necromancy ritual,

> Within the darkness where spirits dwell,
> Ghosts of those who came before,
> Lost to all but the gods of death,
> Abides one there whose name I speak.

> Aine, daughter of the Druid, Ciann Meghan,
> Spirit child of Rath Raithleann, now lost.
> I speak of Aine, whose faith remains unbroken,
> Within the glory of the Light of the Sidhe.

> I call upon you, O Cromm Cruaich,
> Ruler of the Land of the Dead,
> Guardian of the Underworld,
> I call upon you, O Cromm Cruaich.

> Hear me, O Cromm Cruaich,
> Feel the power of the Staff of Nuada of the Silver Hand,
> Through this power, I call upon you,
> Release the ghost of Aine, that I might speak with her.

> Release her, O Cromm Cruaich,
> Release her spirit in the name of Nuada,
> Release her while the power of the Staff endures,
> Release her upon my promise she will be returned to you.

For a moment, nothing happened. And then Aine's body rose to a sitting position. Her eyes opened, and she stared at me without comprehension. My hand remained on her shoulder, energized by the power of the Staff. No doubt, my hand trembled, as, awestruck, the full wonder of it swept over me.

Uncertain of how to proceed, but holding hope in my heart, I leaned close and whispered, "Aine, it is I, Ossian, can you hear me?"

"Ossian?" she murmured. "Ossian?"

"Yes, Aine, yes." A chill ran down my spine at the sound of the voice I longed to hear. "It is Ossian, your brother. Do you not know me?"

Her clouded eyes fixed upon me, her voice like that of someone rousing from a deep sleep. "Yes, Ossian, I know you. I waited for you, you know. I prayed that you might come, and waited ever so long."

A tear ran unchecked down my cheek as I nodded. "I know, dear sister. Within a vision, I saw and heard you calling for me. I…that is, I am so sorry that I arrived too late."

Her face, like graven stone, revealed no expression. "Too late, Ossian? Too late for what?"

"To save you from the monsters who held you. To save your life."

"To save my life?" Her voice was hollow, lacking tone or inflection. "Am I dead, then?"

She didn't know. How could she not? Unsure of what to say, I continued with caution. "Have you no final memory of what became of you?"

"I…oh yes." Her voice strengthened. "I was in a place of terrifying darkness when you called, and remembered nothing. Now that I am here beside you, yes, I remember. The man Scannlon held me, and then there was only silence and total darkness. Oh, I see. Yes, I see now. How very odd it is to be dead. But, I am speaking to you, Ossian. Are you dead too?"

"No dearest, I am not dead, but have called upon the gods that we might briefly speak together one last time."

"I see; how very wonderful." She paused, and in a tiny voice murmured, "When I was very small, I asked that you teach me necromancy. Do you remember?"

My mind returned to that long ago night as I remembered, but the tragic story I recounted to Master Tóla years earlier of another lost girl, Ailinne, for whom Dún Ailinne was named, rushed back as well—two seemingly isolated occurrences that now seemed to point to this very moment.

"Well I remember...yes, well I remember. Now I must ask your forgiveness, sister, for your death was my fault. Mine alone."

"Your fault, brother? I think not. No, there is no blame upon you."

"I should have come for you sooner, but I thought you killed during the raid upon our village. I should have made certain, I should have searched for you and been certain. I might have saved you much torture. I might have saved your life."

"Ossian, you must stop." A dim light glowed on her face as the power of the staff took greater effect. "There is no blame on you. None. What is done is done and there can be no changing it."

"If it were only that simple, Aine. No—"

"Hush, dear brother. My fate was sealed when the Corcu Duibne raided our village. I was dead from that moment forward, and there was nothing, nothing you could have done to prevent it." A small smile lit her face. "Now, because of you, we have this final time together to say goodbye. Let it be a pleasant time for us. Let us share our love, not bitterness, for there has never been such between us."

I captured movement from the corner of my eye. It was Laoidheach drawing near. I shook my head to bade him stop, fearing the effect of the power of the Staff upon him.

Aine asked, "What is it, Ossian. I cannot see very well. Is someone there?"

"Yes, it is Laoidheach. I bade him stay away—"

"Laoidheach? Oh, Laoidheach," she called softly. Her face flushed, fully revived, and her voice returned, Aine's voice. "Laoidheach, my beloved!"

There was no stopping him then. He ran to us and fell to his knees by her side.

Tears stained his face. "Aine, my dearest one. I could not stay away. I had to come to you, hear your voice...see your beautiful face."

"Oh, Laoidheach, my love, my love... Oh, but that I must not leave you, though we could never be together now. I have shamed you so."

"Aine, my darling, Aine, you never shamed me, you could never shame me...never." His hand went to her face, caressing it. "It is an unbelievable thing, don't you see? You honored me, me the poor fool Laoidheach, with your love. I wish to shout it to the skies. See before you the man who loves Aine, and earned her love in return! What other man can say such a thing? What other man ever received so much?"

"Oh my beloved, but had I lived, our betrothal would have—"

"Say no more of it, darling, I pray you, say no more." Urgency filled his voice as he spoke quickly. "Listen to me closely. I want that you be my wife. Do you still agree?"

"Of course, my love, but now? It is too late, too late."

"I say it is not too late!" He turned to me. "Ossian. You can perform the marriage ceremony. Marry us now, this instant."

I sat speechless for a moment, astonished by his audacity. "Marry you? But that's impossible."

"Why is it impossible? I say again, marry us, Ossian. Quickly, perform the marriage ritual that we might be wed."

Aine was dead. Such a marriage was unthinkable. Rather than merely denying his earnest plea, I sought a simple solution. "Well you know the marriage ceremony is conducted over a period of three days."

"Bah! Simply forego the many silly rituals and banns. Unite us in spirit as man and wife, for that is all that remains to us. Unite us as one for all eternity. Please, my friend, do it now."

Still I sought to discourage him. "The banns are important, the dowry most certainly so, for it is our law."

"The dowry, yes, I had forgotten it. Your father is dead, so as Aine's brother the matter of the dowry now rests with you." He held forward his open palm. "Quickly, do you have another coin?"

"Well, yes, I have several..."

Shaking his empty hand, he urged, "One will serve as the official dowry. Give me the coin and let's proceed."

"I cannot release Aine or the Staff. You will have to get it from the purse at my belt."

His hand went for my purse and withdrew a coin.

My resolve weakened, and I looked to Aine. "Are you certain you want this? You understand the...er, extraordinary nature of it?"

Happy tears glistened in her eyes. "I understand it most well, brother. Yes, though I be dead, and know your reluctance to continue with it. Yes, I know it seems foolish, but if it is his will, I wish more than anything to leave this world for the final time as the wife of my beloved Laoidheach. Please, Ossian, please say it can be so."

My heart was tearing apart as I looked upon them. They had such a short time together, these two, and suffered unspeakable horrors. Now they asked one simple thing of me that would ease their sadness and gladden their hearts forever.

My reluctance vanished. I could not refuse them. "Yes, Aine, of course I shall try to make it so, though it is not within my power alone to bless your union. Only the gods can do that."

There were vows to be made, and I turned to Laoidheach. "You know the vows?"

He shook his head. "No, but tell them to me quickly."

"Very well, repeat these words," and Laoidheach did so as I began,"

> Aine, you are blood of my blood, and bone of my bone,
> I, Laoidheach, give you my body, that we two might be one.
> I freely give you my spirit in whole,
>   'til our life shall be done.

You cannot possess me for I belong to myself,
But I give you all that is mine to give.
I shall serve you in all ways for all time,
Our livestock in the paddocks and grain from our fields,
All that I am or hope to be I offer you with loving hands.
So I pledge by the gods of my fathers.

Laoidheach's eyes watered as he completed his vows, and I turned to Aine. "And now, Aine, repeat these words,"

Laoidheach, I, Aine, vow you the first cut of my meat,
the first sip of my wine.
From this day it shall be only your name
    I cry out in the night,
and into your eyes that I smile each morning.
I shall be a shield for your back as you are for mine.

May the children I bear prove the truth of our union,
Above and beyond this, I will cherish and honor you,
Through this life and into the next.
So I pledge by the gods of my fathers.

Drifting mist mingled with my tears, my eyes shifting between the two as I concluded, "By our Druidic laws, the dowry is paid and you have sworn the marriage vows, but they must be sanctified by the gods. I cannot speak for them, but promise that I will do all I can for you."

Laoidheach implored, "Then call upon them. Quickly now, call upon them."

"Very well, I shall try." I closed my eyes. The Staff trembled in my hand and bade me pray to Danu, the Queen Goddess of the Tuatha De Danaan themselves.

I call upon you, O Queen.
I call upon you, Danu, Goddess of prosperity,
    magic and wisdom,
to see the young people before you who
    pledged themselves,
one to the other for all time.

I pray that you ease their distress,
and shower everlasting happiness upon them.

See us, O Queen.
See us here, and offer your blessings,
upon the unification of these two young lovers,
lovers knowing they are already lost even as they begin.

Hear us, O Queen.
Hear our pleas, and take pity,
that the man, Laoidheach, and the girl spirit, Aine,
might become as one for all time,
and so that someday they will reunite in paradise,
at Tír na nÓg, as man and wife.

Bless these poor lovers, O Queen.
Their time together is so very short.
I beg you show us a sign of your sanctification
    of their union,
so that from this point forward,
all men will know them as man and wife forever.

A spiritual union is tightly bound within the minds of those who hold to it and I would not deny this marriage whether blessed by the gods or not. Even with the power of the Staff in my hand, I held little hope Danu would reply. Regardless, I had already decided that a sign would appear, one I would note even if it was an obscure thing such as a bird in flight, a mere gust of wind, anything I could point to that in the minds of Laoidheach and Aine would consecrate this extraordinary ceremony.

And yet, wide-eyed, I caught my breath as a most magical thing happened. The soil fractured beside the kneeling Laoidheach, and he gasped and shrank away as a plant sprouted and grew tall before our amazed eyes. The leafy stem formed a single bud, and the bud expanded to form a perfect scarlet rose.

Never again would I doubt the power of the Staff. As gratitude swept over me, I closed my eyes.

> We thank you most sincerely, O Queen.
> We thank you for hearing us,
> and for consecrating the union between
> Laoidheach and Aine.
> Now know all men they are man and wife,
> for by your blessing,
> it shall forever be so.

Laoidheach hesitated but a moment longer, and then plucked the rose, brushed it with his lips and presented it before Aine. "My wife, my dearest one, I offer this blessing from the gods, a single rose bespeaking our eternal unity, as a token of my love."

"Keep the rose, beloved husband." Aine's eyelashes glistened. "I pray you keep it always as a remembrance of your loving wife. Remember too, I will be waiting for you, waiting on the shore of Tír na nÓg where we shall be Ever Young together."

My entire body trembling, my eyesight dimmed. The Morrigan had warned that the Staff would draw the life force from me. Now my strength was waning fast, as did the energy sustaining Aine.

She whispered, "Kiss me once, my love, for I grow terribly weary and fear I cannot remain beside you much longer."

Laoidheach leaned forward, gently kissed her lips, and Aine sighed. "Sing to me, my beloved. Sing to me as I return to sleep."

Her eyes closed, and, with tears streaming down his face, Laoidheach sang softly,

> What matter the moon, my love,
> If you aren't beside me?
> What matter the stars,
> When I stand alone?
>
> I bear the night's silence,
> A night without splendor.
> I wander...

* * *

I dwelt in nothingness, a place of serene quiet. How I arrived there, I neither knew nor cared. It was a warm place, a place of comfort, a haven removed from my world, a world of unspeakable sadness, a world in flames.

"Ossian?"

From somewhere my name was called—an annoyance. My mind and body were at peace and I did not wish to be disturbed.

"Ossian? It is I, Laoidheach. Ossian?"

Bah! The bother of it! There was no reason why Laoidheach should—a hand was on my shoulder, shaking me.

"Ossian!"

My eyes opened to discover Laoidheach's face above me, pasted against the background of a bright blue sky. It was strange. My last recollection was of dark clouds, of falling rain.

"Laoidheach What...that is, speak to me of Aine."

He pointed. "Aine lies there. At least, there lies her form. I pray her spirit has already reached Tír na nÓg."

I rose on my elbows and looked to where he pointed. On the grassy knoll beneath the alder where I last saw Aine was a mound of fresh earth covered by a cairn of stones. My mind flashed back to Aunt Lou's cottage and the vision I received the night I foretold Aine's future.

Laoidheach still knelt beside me, his hand resting upon my shoulder, when a new image raced through my mind. Perhaps it was the lasting effects of the Staff, or my final moments alongside Aine, but it was then I saw it, the horror of it...I saw my friend's death.

A twisted smile touched his face, his voice soft. "It is a very odd thing, is it not? Yes, it is quite odd."

It was appalling to know I brought forth the dreadful image at such a time. "You mean you saw it, too?"

"Aye, but do not be troubled by your revelation, my friend. Possibly, it was because I was touching you when your vision came,

273

but whatever the reason, I saw it clearly." He shrugged. "There will be no help for it, will there? No, of course not, for it is destined to occur exactly as you foresaw it. But, I say again; please don't worry, for you see, I feel no fear, none at all. When that time comes, whenever and wherever it may come, Aine, my beautiful wife, Aine, my love, will be waiting."

Chapter 27
The Woman at the Window

Before returning to Brendan at Trá Lí Bay, I would fulfill my promise to the men of Quirene. Uncertain of what we might find there, our eyes swept the woodlands and shrubbery as we neared the village. Yet, unlike our previous visit, we found men clearing fields or tilling the soil.

Nearby, a man stopped working, holding a hoe waist high in his fists as we rode up to him.

Sweat streaked the man's soiled, bearded face and I nodded to him. "You know us?"

He was tall, his long muscular arms and stooped back spoke to years of tending his land. Iron lived in his eyes, though his straightforward gaze was wary. "I know you."

His field evidenced much effort went into its clearing. I pointed toward the truth of his work. "You are a good farmer, I think."

No doubt banditry lingered in his past, as it did for all the men of Quirene, but his full, unwavering attention held me. I knew him then as a proud, serious man who rightly cared little what I thought of him. He shrugged. "I farm, though the season grows late for planting. In good years my family fares well."

My hand swept 'round the fields near and far. "We seek the man, Osgar."

"You will find him there," the man pointed further down the trail, "beyond the sixth stone fence."

I reined my horse to proceed, but paused when he asked, "You would have burned our village?"

"Aye, that I would had I found bandits here."

A grim smile twitched the corners of his mouth, matching his humorless chuckle. "I thought as much."

Faces turned toward us as we rode the trail, and Osgar saw us coming. Like the first man, he carried a hoe as he strolled through his field and joined us.

"So, Osgar," I greeted him. "No bandits?"

"No bandits, Ossian." He shrugged. "After you left we held a vote." He cocked an eyebrow and jammed a thumb into his puffed chest. "It was I who spoke for abandoning our evil ways and returning to our fields."

Perhaps that was true, though it was likely blather, for I knew him as Brógán O' Tolairg's minion. "All the men agreed?"

"The few who did not are now gone, as they were no longer welcome in Quirene." He shrugged and gave me a knowing wink. "You see, I knew you would come back. It's little we have in our village, but we'd no interest in seeing it all burned."

Crossing my arms across my horse's neck, I leaned forward. You gave O' Tolairg's wealth to the women of the dead archers as I directed?"

"Aye. That we did, and all now wealthy because of it." He winked. "There is one, not a comely lass, poor thing, but I make a special effort to visit her often and offer what comfort I can. I believe we will soon come to an understanding, so to speak."

The larceny in Osgar's soul was never far from the surface, but I had no interest in his plans for the dead archer's widow. "And your master? What of him?"

"I have no master, but if you speak of Brógán O' Tolairg, the man is dead. His bones lie buried in an unmarked pit there," he pointed toward the village, "beyond those trees."

Goban grunted. "Serves the bastard right, I say."

"Aye, right you are." Osgar glanced down and took an idle whack at a weed with his hoe. Then he leaned on its handle, hands lapping over its end, and turned his attention back to Goban. "Well we heard Ossian's message, so we dug a deep pit and threw Brógán O' Tolairg into it. The man had four dogs, enormous wolfhounds they were, that stood so," he raised his hand to his chest, "at their shoulders. O' Tolairg personally trained the beasts to become ferocious man-killers. They were fed by his hand alone and only he could control them."

Leaning back in his saddle, Goban scowled, crossing his arms over his thick chest. "And so?"

"And so, the dogs were thrown into the pit with him. Each day we fed the man but not the dogs. After only three days, Brógán O' Tolairg fed his hounds for the final time."

Laoidheach winced as the three of us exchanged glances, and then Goban asked, "The dogs, where are they now?"

Osgar raised his hoe, pointing it toward the village. "They share the pit with their master forever."

* * *

Old men idled upon benches, watching as we traveled through a tiny hamlet in the lands of the Ui Failgi. A young woman with toddlers playing around her skirt glanced up from gathering vegetables in her garden.

I nodded to her as we rode by. "May the Lordly Ones bless and keep your family safe, and may the Earth Mother bring forth bounty from your garden."

Eyes wide, her face wary, the woman made the sign of the cross and backed away toward her doorstep, motioning for her children to join her.

Sagging in my saddle, I sighed, for a moment feeling very old. What had become of my land, my Eire?

At the edge of the village stood a lone cottage, seemingly abandoned, its grounds unkempt. We would ride by it, following the trail leading toward the southwest and our still distant destination. Movement drew my attention; an impossible vision stood framed within the cottage's only window.

Yet, she was no vision. Indeed, she was real enough. Flowing, dark red hair curved about a fair, oval face, and the world's darkest violet eyes held me as though I sat before her judgment. She nodded to me, a tantalizing half-smile curling perfect lips as she stepped from view.

Unmindful that my friends rode on, I reined-in, my heart skipping as I waited, hopeful she might reappear at the window.

"Ossian. Why have you stopped? Come on, me stomach's already griping and we've far to ride before we camp tonight." It was Goban, looking back over his shoulder, waving me forward, concerned as always with the food around which his days revolved.

I ignored him, my attention returning to the window.

Laoidheach walked his horse back to me, his hand hovering above his knife's hilt as he scanned the shrubbery surrounding the cottage. "What is it?" he whispered.

"You mean you didn't see her standing there," I pointed, "in the window?"

"See her who?" Then a grin broke out on his face. "Oh, I see." He shook his head as demons danced in his eyes. "No, I didn't see her, but if you'd like, Goban and I will travel on and set up camp while you remain here to conduct business with the...um, lady of this house."

"Ach, your evil tongue wags like a viper's." Dismounting, I tossed him my reins. "Do you wait here. I will be only a moment."

Pursued by his chuckling, I was striding toward the cottage when he called out, "If it's meeting her you plan, when the door opens I'm thinking you'll be meeting her husband's hairy knuckles."

It is a dark day, indeed, I was thinking, *when a man's friends...* My steps faltered. Perhaps Laoidheach was right. Perhaps she was married. Then I remembered her face and straightened my shoulders. I would soon find out.

Five quick steps brought me to her door, heart racing, and I gave it a rap. There was no response. Weight shifting from foot to foot, I raised my fist to rap again and hesitated. If she were to open the door at that moment, I would look like an over-anxious, foolish adolescent.

Forcing my mind and body to remain calm, I delivered three solid knocks. The force of my blows swung the door wide, hinges screeching, to reveal a single, empty, dust-covered room. A simple chair sat in a corner, festooned with cobwebs. A lump formed in my throat, born of dismay and confusion. Without doubt, no one had entered the cottage in months.

* * *

Day after day we traveled, avoiding people to the extent possible, and potential trouble. We made a hasty stop in a village of the Corcu Ochae to replenish supplies, and pushed on. More than once over our evening fire we discussed the mysterious woman in the window, but none of us could make sense of it.

Morning mist shrouded the mountain valley as we followed a trail single file beneath towering ancient trees. Only the soft hoof-falls of our horses broke the silence. It was a familiar trail, the same one I had followed a month before when I left Brendan to journey to Rath Rathleann. A long day's travel would bring us to Trá Lí Bay.

Wrapped within our own thoughts, we proceeded at a slow pace. I led the way with Goban close behind and Laoidheach trailing, leading the packhorse.

Back from the trail, within a small clearing in the undergrowth, she appeared again, fog swirling about her, standing alongside a massive, moss encrusted tree. Long red curls tumbled across bare shoulders, her blue gown draping to her feet. Her face, eyes and small smile I well remembered, and I stopped, filled with wonder.

"Blast!" It was Goban. "Why are ye stoppin'? I almost rode into ye."

I pointed to the clearing. "There, you see her?"

Leaning forward in his saddle, Goban stared toward where I pointed, but just then, dense fog swirled about her, and she vanished in the mist.

He tilted his head. "I'm not sure. For a moment I thought I saw... No. It was merely a wind gust churnin' the fog, nothin' more."

Dismounting, I turned to hand him my reins. "I shall soon find out."

"No." Unmoving, he did not reach for my reins. "Ye mustn't go in there. Perhaps ye saw a woman, perhaps not. But if ye did, it is said that banshees, evil creatures that they are, sometimes transform themselves into beautiful women to lure travelers from the trails. Those who follow never return, for they are devoured by the banshee."

Little I believed him, my hand gesturing towards the trees. "That was no banshee, and I sense no danger from her. I tell you it was a woman, the woman in the window."

"And so, how is it possible that the same woman who mysteriously disappeared in an empty cottage a few days past, just now reappeared alongside us in the forest?" He leaned down and placed a hand on my shoulder. "How well will your *senses* serve ye while you're turnin' on a spit above her fire? Don't you see? If she's not a banshee, then what manner of spirit is she?"

She is a woman of indescribable beauty, more lovely than I could ever hope to imagine, I wanted to say, but I held my heart and tongue in check, for Goban was right. What manner of spirit was she? My very essence told me she posed no threat and drew me towards her. For a moment the fog raised, and I sighed. She was gone, and it would be foolish to wander about in the forest seeking her.

"Little it matters," I nodded and pointed, "for you can see she is no longer there. Perhaps she is a banshee, though I think not. Regardless, whoever or whatever she is, she's gone now." Turning, and mounting my horse, I nodded. "Come. We should arrive at Trá Lí Bay by sundown."

* * *

The sun, a glowing orange ball, sank into the western sea as we rode into the village. A few people went about their business, ignoring us.

Eventually a crowd of monks came toward us with Erc at its head.

"Ride on strangers, we have nothing for you here," he called, waving his hands.

"Brother Erc," I replied, trying to remain cordial in the face of his insufferable arrogance, "it is Ossian. Do you not know me?"

"So," his eyes squinted, "yes, of course. Satan returns, eh?" He turned and spat on the ground. "What do you want?"

"We had a bargain, remember?" I pointed towards the bay. The unfinished boat remained where I last saw it, though there were no signs of work taking place. "Have you given up on making the voyage, then?"

"Given up?" Erc snarled, "Hardly. The fools hereabouts, they..." He paused. "What they or we might do is no business of yours."

"Oh, but it is. I remind you again of our bargain. My companions and I have returned to fulfill my part in it."

"Companions you say?" Erc's lips curled. "You mean the girly looking one and the dwarf who has taken a mud bath?"

Goban bristled and reached for his hammer. I motioned him to be still and dismounted.

"Brother Erc," I said, stepping close, my eyes bearing down on his. "What you say to or about me is of absolutely no importance to me. However, when you belittle my friends, then I am going to look to you, not as a religious man, but merely as a man. What say you?"

There was much he wished to say, his hatred of me burned in his eyes, but he glanced away, and growled toward my friends. "My profound apologies for my ill-considered insults. Your pagan friend, he... His views are an abomination in the eyes of God."

The monk was insufferable. Fortunately, only Brendan's views mattered. Stepping to our packhorse, I removed a leather satchel. Much I had learned from Goban about the value of gold. Opening the satchel, I displayed the wealth within, though not all the gold — only the headband, cup and a few coins. "I have brought you and Father Brendan gifts."

Erc's eyes nearly popped from his head when he saw the gold and he snatched the satchel from my hands.

"Yes," he chortled. "Yes, yes, I'd like to see those petty chieftains faces when I show them this. I could buy their villages with this. No more…'O Erc, we can't afford to give you this, O Erc, we can't afford to give you that, O Erc, our men are too busy to help with the boat.' They'll move their asses now, they will."

He made to scuttle off without even a thank you, but I called after him. "We have ridden hard to get here and need to eat and rest."

Erc turned to the monks behind him. "Give them whatever they ask for."

He ran off, doubtless to tell Brendan how percipient he was to send me off to search for treasure.

We made our way to the cottage that served as the monks' dining hall, settled beside a good log fire and immediately Goban took charge. He turned to the monks who had followed us and held up his hands.

"Now ye heard what that fellow Erc said. One," he said counting on his fingers, "we need beef. Big pieces of beef, cooked just right; two, some venison would be nice; three, kill a young pig and roast it until the skin crackles, and, while we're waiting, bring two whole hams with mustard relish, and none of your barley bread, but three wheat loaves and your best butter. And ale, not the stuff the villagers drink, but bring it from Erc's own store, a whole barrel…no, two barrels."

The monks' jaws dropped. "But sir," one protested. "That's enough food for an army, and such food you demand...not even Father Brendan eats so well."

"More than enough for an army but just enough for us, now be off with ye and tell the women to light their fires for I swear I could eat a horse."

"You want a horse, too?" another of the monks wailed.

"Be out of here," Goban snorted, "and I want those hams on the table before I finish taking me boots off."

I couldn't help laughing. "Now Goban, you know the Christians believe gluttony is a deadly sin."

"Well it's lucky I'm no Christian." He spun about and roared, "Where's me hams?"

* * *

I woke to the morning sun, a burned-out fire and my stomach churning from too much food and ale. Goban was lying flat with an empty ale mug in his hand and grease still smeared on his chin while Laoidheach was curled up cat-like.

Goban's eyes opened at that moment, and he sighed, rubbing his bloated belly. "For the first time in these many weeks I'm not hungry."

Nodding, I growled, "I should hope not."

He cocked an eyebrow as he sat up, cross-legged. "You're angry?"

Rising to my feet, arms folded across my chest, I stood looking down on him. "And why shouldn't I be after last night?"

"Last night?" He scratched his chin. "Just what was it that happened last night?"

Rocking back and forth from heel to toe, I pointed my finger at his nose. "I suppose you don't remember your behavior toward Father Brendan? I suppose you don't recall sitting at the table when I introduced him to you," groaning and scrubbing my face with my hands, "that you hiccupped, opened your mouth and belched in the man's face?"

Eyes wide, his jaw dropped. "I did no such thing."

"You did precisely that." My finger stabbed at Laoidheach. "And as for him, he sat slumped in a chair and didn't even bother to wake up." My eyes rolled as I threw up my hands. "Oh, and a fine impression it was the two of you made on the priest."

There he sat like a stone until he raised his hands to cover his face. I thought him sobbing as his shoulders began bobbing up and down, but then a roar of laughter erupted from his throat. Rolling onto his back, legs flailing the air, his laughter filled the room.

Captured by Goban's mood and antics, my anger melted, replaced by a smirk, a chuckle, until at last I was laughing aloud with him. Slumping over at the waist, my hands pounded my thighs as laughter poured from my throat. Yet, even during those few moments of uncontrollable merriment, I knew my laughter was born of more than my friend's antics. Many of the shackles formed during my journey spawned by tension, horror and misery were falling away, and I was reveling in my release.

Standing erect, hands wiping laughter's tears from my eyes, I watched Goban roll over and crawl on hands and knees toward Laoidheach. He shook the bard awake, who groaned and held his head between his hands. "Leave me alone, I'm dying."

"Good ale that was," Goban chuckled, "but I fear ye had too much of it. I need to bathe myself, and a good dip in the sea will clear that head of ye'rs."

He took the protesting minstrel by the collar and led him from the hut.

Wiping the last remnants of a smirk from my face, I considered my next move. It was time to confront Brendan about finding space for my two companions on the voyage. Without doubt, before the passage to Tír na nÓg ended, I would have desperate need of them.

* * *

I found Brendan on a short rise above the village, and pleaded my cause. He sighed and shook his head. "I am truly sorry, Ossian, but it is just not possible. Your gold helped us, of course, but there is simply no room for them on the boat. Besides that, brother Erc and many others would not stand for two more nonbelievers on the voyage. I had trouble enough persuading them to accept you."

"But Father Brendan—"

"Enough! Now let that be an end to it, for we have work to do." He pointed down to the village, and his hand swept the busy scene. "As you can see, already the people returned to work. The sails have still to be finished and the oars cut, fish and hams to be smoked, ale brewed. You needn't worry. We'll find a place for your friend Goban in the village when we leave, for there is always work for a smith."

He paused. "As for Laoidheach, I am not sure what we can do for him. Perhaps he can find a girl in the village who will have him and he can settle down and farm the land or learn some useful trade. He will have to lay up his harp, for there is no place for his songs among our Christian folk."

"Finding a girl who will have him won't be a problem for Laoidheach, but you could easier take his life than take his harp away from him."

Brendan's impatience reflected in his words. "His problems are of no interest to me, I have God's work in mind. Now go, for Erc and I have many plans to make."

I curbed my anger as I left Brendan, but was determined of one thing: The voyage would not take place without my friends.

Chapter 28
Planting the Seeds of Trickery

$\mathfrak{B}$ rendan stood before his small cottage, the early morning sun gleaming upon the quiet gathering of twenty-nine monks massed before him. Though I knew many of the monks by sight, this was the first time I had seen the more recent arrivals. The eyes of every man fixed upon Brendan as he began speaking to them.

"It has been asked by some," he began, "why God would direct us to sail to a place called Tír na nÓg. Is it not a pagan place? Is it not said to be a place where heathen spirits reside? Is it not said that those spirits pray to their demonic gods?

"It is has been asked by some, why God would permit such a heathen place to even exist. They ask why He would create a Heaven on Earth, the Blessed Isles, where Druids and the pagan spirits of Eire known as the Golden Ones cavort and mock his very existence.

"To those who ask such questions, I reply, why did He create an entire world where, at the beginning of time, none knew or came to Him? Was He not present while the ancient Greeks, Romans and even the pagans here in our beautiful Eire prayed to their demons? And yet, did He not in His Own time and in keeping with His Own divine plan, bring His Word to those lands so that the people there might at last come to know and worship Him?

"Hear me, Brothers, for by His Own words I know this to be His Truth. The Grand Master Himself, the Creator of All Things has called upon us to sail to Tír na nÓg that we might shed His Light, His Wisdom and His Grace upon the pagan spirits of Eire who dwell there, that they may find salvation upon the island paradise of His making.

"Think of it, Brothers! We few gathered here today were selected by The Lord of Hosts Himself to carry out His bidding.

Think of it! Through His Divine Providence, you were chosen to be a part of His plan, so that in His time, all peoples throughout His world may see and come to Him. Throughout history, from the time of Christ Himself, may His many blessings be upon us, few men have been so honored by the Father of us all.

"Fall upon your knees, Brothers! Fall upon your knees! I call upon each of you this day, this hour, this instant to begin a three-day period of thanksgiving, a three-day period of fasting and prayers that we may come together as one to offer our thanks to the Lord God Almighty for His benevolence toward us!"

> O Lord of Creation, O Father of us all,
> Your unworthy servants come to You on our knees,
> Groveling in penance for our many sins beneath the majesty
>   of Your Light.
>
> O King of Kings, O God of the Universe,
> We ask that You might see Your poor followers
> and have pity upon us,
> That You forgive our many weaknesses, as we blindly
>   strive to serve only You.
>
> We thank You, O Heavenly Father,
> For Your Son Christ Jesus, who sacrificed Himself
>   on the cross for us.
> We thank You for Your guidance that we might
>   find our way to the Blessed Isles.
>
> We thank You, O Lord of Mysteries,
> For hearing our unworthy pleas as we open
>   our hearts to You.
> We ask that You bless us now, and on our journey
>   to carry out Your Will.
>
> We ask all these things in the name of the Father,
>   the Son and the Holy Ghost.
>
> Amen

* * *

Goban stood scowling within his rough lean-to; his work-hardened fist gripped the hammer. He swung the hammer downward with a mighty blow and it clanged against the long, glowing iron rod resting on his anvil, showering hot sparks about him, and then glanced up at me. "It is good for a man to have useful work, though food alone is small payment for it. Why is it Brendan can't see the worth of me skills and allow me to join his voyage?"

We had discussed this many times in company with Laoidheach. "Yes, I too would that Brendan might grant you passage, but to his mind, each of his monks will serve his god's purpose as well as man a paddle. The ship's complement is full and there is no place for you and Laoidheach even if Brendan would permit two more non-believers to join him."

Goban squinted. "Brendan plans to sail soon, I think."

"Within a fortnight."

"And if something were to befall two of his monks during these last days, would there not then be room aboard, and would he not need willin' replacements at the oars?"

His question smelled of intrigue and I lowered my voice. "It may all be true as you say, but what calamity might come to pass that the monks could not be present for the sailing?"

"Calamity?" Goban shrugged. "I said nothing of a calamity, and wish ill on no one. Still, if Laoidheach and I are to join ye, then the solution appears very simple—two places must become available aboard the ship."

"How could that be possible?"

"Perhaps, in these last days, two monks will see the dangers they will surely face on such a voyage, lose their courage and so flee from the village in the middle of the night."

I was suspicious of Goban, but shook my head. "And thereby break their word to their god and Brendan? By their beliefs, the monks might save their lives but lose their souls in so doing. No Goban, Brendan's monks would not conscience such a thing."

"So you say, but many men will barter certain death today against the loss of their souls tomorrow. Little it matters. Nothing will befall Brendan's monks. I was merely reflectin' about a possible future."

I knew better. Goban never spoke idly. "Perhaps you think to encourage such a future?"

He inserted the iron rod into a pile of glowing coals, and began to squeeze his hand bellows. Fresh air flooded the bloodred flames, turning them yellow, blue and then white. "And if so?"

This was a new side to Goban, one I had not seen. "For the most part, Brendan's monks are good men, and I would see no harm come to them."

"Humph. First, ye speak of calamities, and now of doing harm. Do ye not know me at all? Again I say I wish no harm come to anyone...no real harm."

I glanced about. No one was near to hear our words, but I kept my voice low. "You have thought how two monks might be encouraged to abandon Brendan?"

"Encouraged? Hah! Yes, you were right to say that none would willin'ly leave. The encouragement I have in mind will require force on our part, but I see how two monks might disappear just prior to the sailin'."

I could not divine Goban's plan, and plan he must have, or at least the beginnings of one. There would be great risk in attempting such a thing, but then, was not the voyage a great risk in itself? To have stalwart, trustworthy men at my side would be worth much risk.

Caution was needed. "You know it would mean much to me if you and Laoidheach could join our quest. But, if you think to remove Brendan's monks by force, there can be no mistakes made. It must be done quietly, without undue injury to them."

Goban mumbled, and turned to his fire. The iron rod was glowing red and he pulled it from the coals. He handed me a leather pad. "Take this and hold the rod over me anvil."

I did as he asked, and he measured two hand widths from the rod's glowing tip. He then placed a sharp iron wedge at the point of his measurement and struck it sharply with his hammer, and then struck it again. A short section of the rod broke away, and he grabbed it with his tongs.

Goban dropped his prize into a water-filled oaken bucket where it cooled with a loud hiss. He gave me a fleeting glance. "And so, Brendan has another iron pin to hold fast the floorin' in his ship. Ossian, I think to capture two of the monks and keep them tied-up in your old cave near the sea. Your friends here in the village can release them after we sail." His eyes spotted movement behind me. "Someone comes near. We must speak of this later."

* * *

"Father, the villagers strive hard," Erc was saying as we stood inside Brendan's quarters, "but many of the special provisions I have ordered may not arrive for several weeks. I fear our voyage must be delayed an additional fortnight, perhaps two."

"More delays, Brother Erc? There seems no end to them, we must—"

"There can be no more delays," I interceded. "Listen to me, Brendan. We must sail within the next two weeks whether all of Erc's provisions have arrived or not."

Erc glared at me, but turned his attention to Brendan. "Father, do not listen to this man. Again, his words shall lead only to folly. To leave without all of our supplies would spell disaster."

Brendan nodded. "Ossian, what Brother Erc says is true. While I cannot countenance more delays, we cannot sail until we are fully provisioned."

"There can be no more waiting!" They paid little heed to the lessons to be learned from the ancient knowledge of their native land. "The signs favor us now during this month of the autumn equinox. To delay beyond another fortnight will mean we begin our travels in Agant, the only month of the year in which one must never travel. It will be a month of thirty-one days, ill-omened in and of itself, and the month of Sanheim, Lord of the Dead."

"Signs and omens," Erc scoffed. "Father, Ossian adds no merit to our discussion, but speaks only of foolish pagan superstitions and profane demons. I speak for the welfare of all those who will sail with us. We must not depart before all is in order, and there is food enough aboard our ship to ensure a safe journey."

"They are much more than superstitions, monk, and had you not forsaken the beliefs of your own people, you would know well that what I say is true. The signs—"

"The signs...the signs! You should huddle safely ashore if you fear so much."

"I would be wise to do so if you insist upon more delays." I continued with a smile. "Of course, in good conscience you would then be obliged to repay all of the gold I gave you. Can you do that?"

"You know full well that most of the gold is gone."

I turned to Brendan. "You demanded a high payment of me to partake in the voyage and now I expect that my opinions will be heard."

"Yes, Ossian, of course," Brendan sighed, "but Erc says that all of our provisions have not yet arrived. We must be prudent despite our impatience to sail."

"Erc said we wait for special provisions." I faced the monk. "Tell us, Erc, what special supplies delay our departure?"

A bare smile touched Erc's lips. "Capon by the dozens from the Deisi, barrels of the finest wines from the Ui Maine, smoked trout is even now en-route from the Tethbae—"

I had heard enough. "You demanded gold from me that you might acquire luxuries?"

Brendan was thunderstruck. "Brother Erc, ours is a mission to spread the Word of the Lord God. Christ and his Disciples were but poor men with simple tastes, and yet see how they have changed the world! I thought only to supply our ship with basic foodstuffs; grain, meat, vegetables and the fruits that are nearby and readily available."

Erc was untroubled. "Father, we embark on a long, difficult, dangerous mission unlike any the Disciples could have imagined. We owe it to ourselves to acquire foods that fill not only our bellies, but enrich our souls."

"And you have my gold to pay for it," I chided.

"Brother, there is gold remaining?" Brendan asked.

Erc nodded.

"That is well, Brother Erc. You will fill the ships larders with the common foodstuffs local to this area and there shall be no further delays. We depart for the western isles ten days from today with or without your special provisions."

* * *

Only two days remained until Brendan's sailing, and rain pattered on the roof of my rough, stacked-stone hovel. I sat before the fire alongside Goban and Laoidheach. Our voices remained low, though the steady rain would mute our discussion should anyone pass near in the night.

Earlier in the day, my friends had carried out their plan to abduct two of Brendan's monks, though I had no hand in any of it aside from keeping Brendan distracted. "So, Goban, tell me how it was with the two monks."

"Everythin' went well." His eyes glinted in satisfaction. "The two are now trussed in your old cave."

"They were injured?"

Goban grunted. "Not at all, though by now they are likely awake with achin' skulls and thick tongues."

Leaning forward, I rested my elbows on my knees. "Tell me what happened."

He nodded. "That I will." Pausing for a moment, he stroked his chin, and then began. "A small wooden wine keg balanced on me shoulder as I hiked along the stony path above the village. Soon, two monks neared; two good-natured lads I had carefully selected among Brendan's group and planned to meet."

A smirk threatened the corners of his mouth as he continued. "The monk named Finnén laughed like the jolly lad he is, as he walked to me, and asked, 'So smith, what manner of goods are you smuggling today?'

"I slumped unhappily, I did. Oh, I played me part well, if I do say so. I says to him, 'There was a mistake made. Too much wine was ordered for the voyage. I was told to dispose of this keg, and take it yonder,' I pointed up the hill, 'to a man who would have it. It's an unfortunate thing though, as I fear the man is a drunkard and bane to his family.'

"Finnén proved the clever man I thought him to be and he knew an opportunity when he saw one." Goban rubbed his hands together as he proceeded with his story. "'It would be a sad thing,' Finnén frowned, 'for such a treasure to fall into the hands of a drunkard. Do you not think so, Brother Aodhán?'

"Aodhán agreed right away, saying, 'In truth it would, especially since it was first intended for the voyage to carry out God's work. Perhaps,' he winked and gave his friend a sly smile, 'the disposition of this keg should be left to the work of God's servants.'"

"Wait." I raised my hand. "Brendan's monks drink wine as we all do, but I cannot believe their faith would permit these two to drink so much as to become affected by it."

"It takes little to be affected," Goban chortled, "when it contains hemp powder."

"Hemp powder!"

"Aye, when mixed with wine, it puts a man to sleep."

Eyes alight, Laoidheach leaned forward, a grin conquering his mouth. "You see how simple it all was. I was—"

"Quiet," Goban muttered. "I'm tellin' this story and ye'll make a muddle of it."

Crossing his arms over his chest, Laoidheach cocked an eyebrow, and grumped, "My apologies. Please proceed O' master storyteller."

"Indeed," Goban nodded. "Ye'll kindly remember Ossian asked me to tell it. Now where was I? Oh yes, now I recall. The monk Finnén grinned and scratched his chin, thinkin' of the wine. 'Oh yes, Brother,' he said to Aodhán. 'You are absolutely right, and by so doing we would prevent further misfortune from befalling the poor sinner who lives on yon hill.'"

A smile still threatened Goban's lips as he continued. "The monks responded exactly as I anticipated, you see, but I feigned reluctance. 'Hmm,' I said to them, 'I'm not sure about your offer, Brothers. I do not want to get into trouble by failin' to follow me instructions.'

"'Trouble?' Aodhán was chucklin'. 'What manner of trouble? Brother Finnén and I will accept the responsibility of ridding you of the contents of your keg, will we not, Brother?'

"'It is a responsibility I shall joyfully assume.' I told you they were a good-natured lot.

"So, I relaxed and smiled, knowin' I had them, you see. I asked them, 'Would ye then, have me stand the keg on end and remove the bung so that ye might begin your work?'"

Stiff-faced, Laoidheach asked, "May I speak now?"

Goban reclined back, propping himself up on his elbows. "Go ahead. There's little more to add."

"Little more? Little more you say because you had little hand in it."

Goban yawned. "Mine was the most important part."

"It was no such thing," Laoidheach growled. "If it wasn't for me—"

Exasperated, I slapped my knees. "Will you please stop bickering and tell me what happened?"

"Yes." Laoidheach stiffened his back and glared at Goban. "The sun was still high, and the two monks lay snoring in the grass when I rode up the trail leading three horses. We bound and gagged the two men, and hoisted them onto the backs of the horses. As you know, it's a difficult ride to your old cave, but we hurried to reach it and then return here at nightfall."

Though all seemed well, I worried about the monks. "You made arrangements with my friend Beagan so the monks will be released after we sail?"

"Yes, Beagan agreed to travel to the cave on a matter of life or death. Now, we may only pray that Goban and I too will sail with Brendan. But, that wasn't the end of it. This is the most important part."

Goban grunted, and yawned again.

Laoidheach ignored him and continued. "Darkness was well fallen when we returned here to the village earlier tonight. Fortunately, rain wasn't falling as I stood near the open window of a local man who is friend to Finnén. It was then I stood in the dark and assumed the voices of the two monks, and spoke aloud that the man inside could plainly hear me."

He cleared his throat and again glared at Goban. "The most important part of our plan, you see, was that someone here in the village knew, or at least thought they knew, the two monks feared to voyage with Brendan and intended to run away."

I smiled, recalling his almost magical skill at mimicry. Laoidheach often amused students at Dún Ailinne by imitating Master Tóla's voice. "You think the man believed what he heard?"

Laoidheach shrugged. "We will know for certain tomorrow, won't we?"

Chapter 29
Betrayal

ray clouds scudded overhead and a stiff cold wind buffeted us as we stood in the village center. Villagers carried bundles towards the curragh nosed against the nearby shore.

Brendan's voice echoed with the sadness weighing upon his heart. "Brothers Aodhán and Finnén fled in the night? I know them both well; they are men of stout humor and are devout servants of the Lord." Wrinkles creased his brow as he shook his head. "They would not desert our mission."

Grim-faced, Erc nodded. "I'm afraid it is true, father. A villager who knows Finnén overheard him speaking of it with Aodhán in the darkness." He turned to me. "I was told they stole your horses to hasten their escape."

I smiled inwardly. "Two of my horses are missing." Goban's plan had worked as well or perhaps better than we had hoped.

Brendan shook his head, clearly amazed by the actions of the two monks. "What measure of fear must have overwhelmed our Brothers at the thought of facing our quest? Think of it, Brother Erc. We sail tomorrow, and, at almost the last moment, they lost sight of their duty to God. They quailed in fear when in truth they should have seen only glory in spreading His Word. We must all fervently pray for the salvation of their souls."

"You are right, of course, father," the ever-practical Erc replied, "but their desertion now threatens our sailing. The curragh is heavily laden, and will be unwieldy at sea. Every man will be needed at the paddles, especially if we encounter storms. For the safety of all, we must find replacements for Brothers Finnén and Aodhán before we sail."

The priest was unbending, his arms crossing his chest. "You again recommend a delay? I think not, Brother. We sail to convert the Golden Ones on the Blessed Isles at God's bidding, and sail we shall! I will agree to no further delays. We sail at dawn as planned."

"But Father—" Erc pleaded.

My time had come. "A moment please. I know two men who—"

"Yes, yes, I know," Erc snapped, "the smith and the bard; both friends of yours, both snake worshippers, and both murderers."

Brendan's eyes opened wide, his eyebrows leaping upwards. "What is it you say, Brother? You say Ossian's friends committed murder?"

Erc turned to me with a smirk. "You thought your friends' secret was safe, didn't you?" Then, he faced Brendan, "Yes father, I recently learned that Ossian's friends were prisoners of the Corcu Duibne, and murdered two Christian warriors so they might escape."

The priest turned to me, a question in his eyes. "Is this true, Ossian? Your friends killed two men?"

"No, Brendan, it is not true." That Erc knew of the two slain warriors came as a complete surprise. Yet, truth is a steadfast ally. "Laoidheach and Goban were captives of the Corcu, yes. They were taken to be sold as slaves to the salt mines in the north. They didn't kill their captors. I did."

"You did?" Brendan cocked his head. "You did, Ossian? By what right did you kill those men? There can be no excuse for murder. It is a mortal sin in the eyes of God."

"I killed them by right of warfare! Is it a mortal sin before your god to kill my enemies and in so doing free my friends from slavers?"

"Warfare? You war against Christian tribes?"

"No! Christians war against me! This is no war of kings against kings where men face men in honorable battle. No, this is a war of beliefs, a war of annihilation!" My attention turned to the sound of children playing beside a cottage. It was little notice I took of them, but it gave me pause while I curbed my anger. "Months ago, before I came here, the Corcu Duibne attacked my village without warning. They slaughtered my family and many innocents. Those they did not kill were taken as hostages to be sold as slaves, Laoidheach and my own sister among them."

"Your sister? Then where is—?"

"She's dead." My eyes held his. "A chaste delicate flower, she died in chains, the prisoner of slavers allied to the Christians who had their way with her time and again before they killed her."

Brendan closed his eyes. "I hear you, Ossian, and yes, slavers are a blight upon all humanity, regardless of the cloth they wear. May God forgive them. I shall pray mercy for their souls."

"Your god would forgive such wicked men? For what possible reason?" Again my anger grew. "No matter, their filthy souls are all that remains of them, and your god can show them mercy, as he will. The gods of my people and I did not forgive them, and they received no mercy from us."

"You mean...?" Brendan sighed, as he saw the truth of it in my eyes. "I see. This is too much, and I shall ask God's mercy on you as well. I accepted your gold, and agreed that you may accompany us, but now—"

"Now you must stand by your word, priest, or are you a man who would turn his back upon it?"

"But, you have since killed; you have openly declared yourself an enemy of the One True Faith. How can I now permit you to join us on a mission to spread His Word?"

"You knew me for what I was before you accepted my gold, Brendan, a Druid and Irishman who lives by the ancient laws of his heritage. I remind you again of our bargain."

Erc jabbed a finger toward me. "You have broken the bargain by sinning before God, and admitting to your crimes."

299

"Crimes?" The foolish man was an annoyance. I took a step towards him and he backed away. "Again, I tell you I carried war against my enemies. Now I ask you. Why was a Christian priest, bearing a cross, the symbol of your god, leading the Corcu Duibne warriors when they streamed into my village and slaughtered our innocents? By your judgment, would that not also be a crime, or is perhaps killing acceptable in the eyes of your god when it is performed by Christians?"

"What?! You...you again dare question God's Will?" Erc sputtered.

Why would he think his god's will mattered to me? "I dare question you. In fact, perhaps we should put the entire question before a council of the elders of the villages hereabouts." I smiled at him. "Erc, you have made it no secret that you accepted my gold to outfit your boat, and I think they hold you in little regard. Yes, let us put the question to them, for they are fair men who understand the importance of an agreement, and I will lay claim to your boat if you cannot repay me."

Erc's teeth bared as he hissed, "You bastard, you are Satan himself."

No man who hates so much can own a soul, I thought, but I was done with his arrogance. "I am a Druid priest! I am a spokesman for my gods and my people, equally the worth of you or any man on a quest to find Tír na nÓg!"

Erc stood trembling with fury, as I turned to Brendan. "What say you, Brendan? Does our bargain stand?"

He nodded. "I gave you my pledge. Yes, our bargain stands."

"Very well. Now as to Laoidheach and Goban, they will replace your missing monks at the oars?"

Brendan crossed his arms on his chest, stepped back and looked me up and down. "I have seen you anew today, Ossian. You are no longer the timid traveler I first met. Do not mistake my words. I do not fear your threats. I fear only the displeasure of God Himself.

Perhaps I made a poor bargain with you, and perhaps you are Satan, as Erc said, but I will stand by our agreement."

I offered a small smile and nodded. "And you have not disappointed me. You are the steadfast man I knew you to be. Now...my friends?"

"Bah!" Brendan waved a dismissive hand. "You may not be Satan, but you have his tongue. Yes, your friends may come on our mission, but warn them that they had best pull hard at the oars or I will have their lazy carcasses thrown overboard."

The faces of nearby villagers and monks turned to us, as Erc screamed, "No! I will not permit it! Father, you cannot succumb to this pagan and his followers. I beg you remember the gospel of Luke. 'Behold, I have given you the authority to step on serpents and scorpions, and over all the power of the enemy, and nothing shall hurt you.' I daresay you not only have God's authority to step on this," he pointed at me, "serpent, but also a duty to Him to do so. I demand you rescind your decision immediately. This snake worshipper has openly proclaimed himself our enemy and cannot go on the voyage!"

"You demand, Brother?" Hands folded before him, Brendan cocked an eyebrow. "Ossian has fulfilled his bargain with us, and I see—"

"You see what? You see nothing!" Erc trembled with fury. "You stand for nothing, not even God Himself!"

Brendan raised a hand, shaking his head. "Brother Erc, please! I beg you call upon His Grace and calm yourself."

"Bah! Your grace...God's Grace...you ask that I calm myself in the face of your meek submission to the demands of a devil worshipper? Have I not stood by you even though you insisted upon proceeding with this ill-considered voyage? Have I not silently borne your blundering leadership and blind obedience to every foolish edict handed down by the Holy See in Rome? Brendan, I waste my time and words with you."

Lines furrowed Brendan's brow, reflecting his sorrow. "Brother, your views of me matter not at all, but you must fall on your knees and plea for forgiveness for even considering slighting God Himself and the Holy Father in Rome."

"Dare you not to question my relationship with God!" Erc's finger jabbed at Brendan as his eyes spit fire. "You haven't the right! My adoration of Him equals or exceeds your own, as is made plain by your dealings with Satan. As for the Pope, he spews vile unholy rhetoric against all who question his secular views and authority."

"The Pope speaks the words of Christ Himself. That you openly disagree with him could be interpreted as heresy."

Erc clenched his fists; his black eyes glowed. "Heresy in whose eyes? The Pope's? Yours? The great and wise Pelagius was also branded a heretic by the papacy and its followers, but that did not lessen the truth of his words."

"Pelagius, Brother?" Brendan gasped and stepped back. "But, he has long been branded a heretic for speaking against the Scriptures and the Holy Father. Surely, you do not follow his teachings!"

"Yes! Pelagius, wise and indomitable man that he was, stood against the rule of Roman doctrine, as do I."

"Why have you not mentioned this before?" Brendan's shoulders slumped. "We could have discussed it, and I would have happily led you toward God's True Light."

"Why? Why indeed! Now I am done with you!" Erc spat at Brendan's feet, and turned to me. "As for you, Druid, I say this; be wary, always wary. It was you who sowed Satan's disharmony among us! You are the devil's own, and now I am free to renew my mission from God to rid the world of the likes of you. I will come for you, Druid, the same as I went after others of your kind at your pagan temples and the demon's school at Dún Ailinne."

My heart turned cold. "You were at Dún Ailinne?"

"Of course I was there." He smirked, hands on hips. "It was I who led the attack and rallied our men by," his hand swung in the air above him, "waving the Cross of Christ in the center of the courtyard that all might rejoice upon our victory! And it was I who burned the high demon himself in the midst of his blasphemous school. I who lit the kindling at his feet that he might scream out his agony in life as he does now within the fiery bowels of Hell."

Erc fell to the ground with a squeal as I leaped upon him, my hands wrapped 'round his throat. Firelit images and the anguish of that dreadful night filled my head as I straddled him, hatred strengthened my hands as I squeezed the life from the perpetrator of it all.

Hands were upon my wrists, those of Brendan and monks who rushed from nearby to aid their fallen Brother. I tried to shrug them off, striving to finish what I had begun, but was forced to relinquish my grip on Erc's throat. The weight of their combined efforts pulled me from my position atop him.

Kicking and shouldering my way to my feet, straining to free myself, I attempted to again hurl myself upon my enemy. Brendan's face appeared before me, a blurred image seen through my hate-filled eyes.

"Ossian! Ossian, stop this, I beg you!" His hands rested upon my shoulders and he gently pushed me back, away from the still prostrate Erc, as I continued writhing within the firm grasp of his monks. "Listen to me, you cannot do this thing, you must not kill him."

"He..." I gasped. "He killed Master Tóla, the wisest, kindest, most gentle man to grace this earth." Tears streamed down my face. "He burned him...he burned him..." Unable to say more, clenching and unclenching my hands, I sobbed aloud.

Again, Brendan laid his gentle hands upon my shoulders. "It is much you have seen of death, I'm thinking. Too much. Would that you could find Christ, that he might comfort you."

"It isn't comfort I seek." Still in the grasp of the monks, I jutted my jaw toward Erc. "It is vengeance, and the opportunity to rid my people of a cruel killer."

"No, I cannot permit you to kill him. You are a good man, a much better man than Brother Erc, it would seem. Would that you could see your duty as Christ would ask of you."

He turned, gesturing to Erc. "Do not defile your hands with Erc's blood. He is a traitor to his own faith, don't you see. Erc is our responsibility, my responsibility. Please, I beg you. Allow me with God's Light to do what I must with him."

A roar like that of a charging bull burst through the ring of monks and villagers gathered about us. Goban, hammer poised in his upright fist, rushed to my side, Laoidheach close behind him.

"What happens here?' Goban growled. Pointing the hammer towards the monks still holding me, he muttered, "Let go of me friend if you value your skulls."

The monks turned anxious faces to Brendan, who waved a dismissive hand. "Let him go."

My eyes found those of Laoidheach and I pointed to Erc, who now sat upright, rubbing his throat. "That son of a whore led the attack on Dún Ailinne and murdered Master Tóla. He burned him."

Laoidheach's face turned deathly white, and then flushed red. "Then repayment is due in kind, I say." His knife appeared in his hand as he stepped towards Erc.

"Stop!" The bard hesitated as I turned my attention to Brendan. "You said Erc is your responsibility. What say you now? What will you do with him?"

Brendan shook his head, and then stood erect, his stern gaze falling upon the fallen monk. "You aren't injured. Stand up like a man."

Sullen-faced, Erc returned the priest's stare and rose to his feet. "Brendan, you—"

"Silence!" Brendan shouted, and Erc stepped back, eyes wide.

The priest strode forward to face him. "By your own words you have confessed to being apostate and in so doing you are an avowed heretic in the eyes of God. You are hereby banished from my presence and the fellowship of your Brothers here. However, before you leave you shall be scourged for your profane thoughts and behavior."

Motioning towards the monks who had been holding me, he said, "Take Erc there." He pointed to a lone ash tree at the edge of the village. "Strip him of his clothing and tie him face-forward to the tree."

Upon hearing Brendan's words, Erc's face turned ghastly white. Then he tensed, turned away and attempted to flee. Goban hastened forward, grabbed the hood of the monk's robe and gave it a solid backwards jerk.

"Think ye to hurry off, me boy 'o?" Goban chuckled. To Brendan he added, "Maybe I'd best accompany your men to yon tree. It seems this lad here," he gave Erc another hard jerk, "objects to your plans for him."

* * *

A mournful wail escaped Erc's lips as the lash fell across his back, opening yet another long red tear in his flesh. The rope binding his wrists to the tree trunk high above his head prevented him from collapsing to the ground. Blood streamed down his naked body as he hung there sobbing and moaning.

His face revealing his disgust, Brendan threw the lash to the ground and turned away. Fifty lashes delivered, though if the whip had been in my hand, I would have gladly given no fewer than fifty more. No, I would have continued lashing the monk until he breathed his last.

It seemed every villager had arrived to witness the spectacle, forming a half-circle alongside Brendan's monks. He turned to face the gathering, his hands and robe spattered with Erc's blood.

"See before you God's justice on one who chose to turn his back on Him. For this man, there can be no salvation and he shall now be cast out into the wilderness, naked and alone. Let his name not be spoken aloud, for such an end shall befall everyone who betrays the Word of the One True God."

Brendan's eyes roamed across the assemblage before him. "The voyage must again be delayed for a few days. Before we can sail, I must write the formal decree of heresy, which will be delivered to our bishop at Tara, that it may be entered into the official annals of the Church. I will advise you all when I select another departure date."

* * *

My comrades accompanied me as, slumping, I strode through the village towards my hut. While Goban's plan had done its work and they would accompany me on the voyage, there was no joy in the knowing of it. The emotional encounter with Erc had drained away any joy I might have chanced upon.

"I'm thinking," Laoidheach muttered, "Erc deserved to die after all he did at Dún Ailinne. Still, he is a proud, arrogant man, and word of his public humiliation will spread. Perhaps Erc will actually suffer more by his life than by his death."

I stopped, gazing towards the nearby mountains. "The flames of Dún Ailinne have not died away within my mind. They still burn brightly, and I regret not killing him. You are wrong about leaving Erc alive. Likely it is because you did not come to fully understand him—he rejoices in killing. The man is a hater, and his hatred will only grow stronger from his punishment. Brendan, good man that he is, made a mistake. This land would all be the better for it if Erc was dead."

Chapter 30
Never-Ending Sadness

hree days passed, yet Brendan remained silent about a new sailing date. It was understood by all that he was in prayer, and not to be disturbed. With little to occupy my hands and somber thoughts, I climbed to a high point above the village, perched upon a stone and gazed out to sea. When we sailed I would leave Eire, knowing it to be forever; from that point and throughout all eternity, it would be as though I had never existed.

It is a sober moment when a man realizes his entire life, all his hopes and dreams, had come to nothing. My many failures haunted me. What tracks had I made upon my homeland? What memorable thing had I accomplished to leave my mark?

Regrets solve nothing, prove nothing, create nothing, yet knowing that provided little solace—

I started at rustling in the heather behind me and spun about. My breath caught. She was there, she of the lovely face, flowing red hair and immaculate blue gown tracing her slender woman's form as it draped to her feet.

"So, Ossian, we meet again." Her husky voice sent a shiver down my back. "Why do you idle here in this lonely place? You look to the sea. Do you see your future there?"

I knew her then, as I should have immediately known her. Leaping to my feet, I bowed. "You honor me, My Queen. As for my poor musings, they remain here with our people on our green island."

Mincing steps brought her to my side where she gracefully settled upon my stone. Motioning for me to retake my seat, she asked, "Here? Your future lies with Brendan's voyage. You must think on that."

Her nearness brought a flush to my face as I sat like a statue beside her. Never could I have even dreamt of a more desirable woman. A wind gust stirred a stray curl, and I resisted the urge to reach out and touch it, all the while cursing my foolishness. We were as far apart as life and death, she and I. Was she not Goddess of Death?

"Ossian, did you hear me?"

Flushing again, I regained my wits. "Yes, you are right, of course. Today my thoughts remain here along with my desire to stay and stand beside my people."

"You would stand beside your people?" A sad smile crossed her perfect face. "I honor your courage and well know you would willingly do so, though it would mean the end of you. I have watched you more closely than you know, and never found your boldness lacking. No man but you ever had the courage to stand up to me and it is one thing I have come to…to admire about you."

It was a remarkable compliment, and my heart warmed, though I remained respectfully silent.

Slender hands clasped in her lap, she shook her head. "I'm very sorry, but you must realize you would stand alone. The people have abandoned you and your ways as they have their gods. All but a few think only of the new god and the words of Christian priests. It's too late. Your time has passed here, as has mine. You have lost, Ossian. Nothing remains here for you, so now your future lies to the west."

I leaned forward, burying my face in my hands, realizing she was right, knowing how thoughtless I had been to cling to my beliefs in a time and place where I no longer belonged. Voice rasping, I replied, "Things are changing so quickly now, and I wish…I merely wish to return to the old ways, to a time when my life made sense."

"I wish that too." She rested a soft hand on my shoulder and I trembled under her touch. "I wish it very much, more than you know. I wish too that you needn't...but how silly, wishing will not make it so."

Her hand returned to her lap, and I fought against the urge to reach out and take it in mine, to wrap my arms around her and hold her close.

She tilted her head back, eyes closed. "The Dagda says that immutable laws exist within our universe, laws such as change that are far more important than gods. He was the first to see the change coming to us, just as change will always be coming." Opening her eyes, she smiled. "So then, change makes sense, does it not? How else are the people to grow? Without change, how can Eire grow?"

"The Dagda's wisdom exceeds all others, so it must be true." It was my turn to smile. "Please excuse my melancholy. Today I am flooded in memories. I think of my father and mother, Ceara, Aine, Master Tóla and all the others who leave their bones in this land. The people of Rath Raithleann built homes, raised families, cleared and tilled fields that will remain in use for all time. Though their names and faces be forgotten and their voices forever stilled, my family and friends' presence will be still felt throughout all the generations to come...like waves in the wind."

She nodded. "I see. You fear by leaving you will be forgotten."

I was surprised. It was as though she read my thoughts. "Something like that."

"You are wrong. I...your gods will not forget you. Of that you may be certain. You will be remembered as the Druid who stood beside us during these dark times, who dared risk all that Tír na nÓg shall remain our haven forever."

"It is a humbling thing to be held within the thoughts of my gods. I know of no greater honor and I thank you for it."

She cocked an eyebrow. "But, that is not enough, is it?"

"Of course—"

"You are a poor liar." Wagging her finger and shaking her head, she smiled. "No. You wished to leave your mark that the people might remember you. That is understandable. Those of merit desire to accomplish great things, memorable things."

"You are right. I hoped to be remembered for doing some great thing, though it sounds a bit silly when I look back on it now." I grinned at my own foolishness. "It is the purest form of vanity, is it not? You were also right about what you said earlier: The Christians have won Eire and I lost, we all lost. Now I will sail away forever leaving nothing behind to show for my trouble."

"No. Striving to make one's mark is not silly. For an honorable man to reach towards immortality might be a vain thing, but it is not a bad thing. Throughout all you have endured there is one thing you never lost—yourself. You have overcome much, and no man could have done more, cared more. It is another trait I have come to…to admire about you." She flushed and hurriedly added, "All your gods admire you for it."

Rising and stepping away, her hands pressed against her glowing cheeks. "I must go. Soon you sail and we will speak no more." For an instant it appeared as if tears crowded her dark, violet eyes. "Goodbye my Ossian." She vanished in a glittering burst of golden light.

Emptiness captured my heart at her sudden disappearance. My head was spinning; for an incredible moment it almost seemed that she…no, I was mistaken. She would never shed tears over me. She was the Morrigan.

* * *

The morning sun crept through the doorway of my hut when a monk appeared saying Brendan wished to speak with me. It was but a short walk to the priest's cottage and he bade me enter when I called out to him. I found him seated at a table, his eyes red-rimmed, and his face lined and weary.

Feet apart, hands on my hips, I snorted. "You look terrible. What is it? Are you still troubled by confronting Erc?"

His hands scrubbed his face as he shook his head. "Not merely Erc," he muttered, "though he be a big part of it. No, I have been confronting my many failures. I prayed God would enlighten me, though he remains silent. Tell me, could what Erc said be true? Could I be wrong, did I misinterpret God's Will? Is this voyage folly?"

I nodded. "I see. So, that is why you haven't set a new sailing date."

An empty chair rested by the table beside him, and his eyes followed me as I strolled over and sat down. "Your god's will is your own affair. However, if you still ask if the Blessed Isles exist, I tell you most assuredly, yes they do. If you ask if it is possible to reach them, I honestly tell you, I don't know. But you will never know if you don't try."

He cocked an eyebrow. "That is true. You well know my reason to sail to the Isles, but tell me, why do you wish to voyage with me?"

"That is a matter between me and my gods." I hoped my smile would soften my words. "Your god is your affair, my gods are mine."

His face brightened a bit. "That was a sly answer, though one befitting you. You are right, of course. It was foolish of me to question the importance of the voyage." Leaning forward, hands clasped atop the table, he continued, "I want you to inspect the ship. Yes, I trusted Erc's abilities, though now I question everything about him. Make your measurements, and oh yes, complete your *calculations*, I believe you called them. Make certain our boat is seaworthy. Can you do that within the next few days?"

"Certainly. If I find anything amiss, I will bring it to your attention and we can discuss suitable remedies."

"Good." He nodded and then added with a grin, "We make an odd team, you and I, do we not?"

His jest was not lost upon me, though a larger truth filled my mind. "Would that Druids and priests had understood the importance of working together for the greater good long ago."

* * *

The days passed swiftly as I inspected every part of our curragh. Men of the village moved casks and bundles already stored aboard that I might view and measure each installed piece of it. Brendan was often at my side, asking questions as he paced about.

"The main beams at the bow make a poor fit," I observed as I pointed to their joining. Crooking a finger at a villager, I told him when he came near, "Go find Goban and bring him here."

Brendan leaned over my shoulder and peered at the joint. "Is it the gap between the two beams that concerns you? They appear pegged tight in place, so it seems a small thing."

"Not so small when we face into a raging sea, I'm thinking." I scratched my head as I considered the problem. "Replacing the beams will require another month's work, but perhaps bracing will serve to secure it. I'm hoping Goban can create a solution."

The villager soon returned with Goban in tow and I pointed to the joint. "Can you make an iron sheathe to strengthen this?"

"Can I make it, ye ask?" Goban grumbled. "Of course I can make such a simple thing." His eyes glinted. "The question is, can ye determine the proper angles, that it will fit as it should? If not, move out of me way and I will measure it for meself."

* * *

Eyes squinting in the firelight, I passed the needle and linen thread through the cloth to join the torn edges of my kirtle. It would be a rough repair, but serviceable.

"You should let the women do that," Laoidheach observed. "A woman would make a better job of it."

He sat behind me near the doorway, and I grunted a response over my shoulder as I continued my work.

"I see no reason why you wear the tattered thing," he continued. "You've been carrying about a splendid green Druid's robe, though never wear it. You should, you know. You earned the right and I would like to see you wearing it."

312

Yes, I had earned the right, but remained convinced I lost it after failing in my responsibilities to my King and the people of Rath Raithleann. It was a thing I would not discuss, even with my closest friend. I shrugged, keeping my eyes on my work. "There simply hasn't been a proper occasion to wear it. Perhaps I shall someday."

"No, my friend, it is a thing you should wear every day as befits your standing as a Druid. I wish to remind you—what? Augh!"

Glancing over my shoulder at my friend's latest antics, I was stunned to find him grappling with a black-robed figure. Even as I leaped to my feet, a hand flashed downwards, burying a knife in Laoidheach's chest.

Horrified, I shrieked, "No!"

Then I saw the face of the black-robed assailant—Erc! His features were gaunt, pinched, and he sneered, "The knife was meant for you. Next time, Druid, the next time you won't be so fortunate."

I rushed towards him, but he turned and sped through the door, his maniacal laughter ringing out into the night. Thoughts of the monk fled my mind as I dropped to my knees beside Laoidheach, who lay on the floor.

Wrapping an arm around his shoulder, I cradled him to me. His eyes opened and found mine. "So, my friend, how very strange. We saw this coming, did we not?" Eyes closing again he winced, and took a deep, ragged breath. "That day on the hill beside Aine's grave." He gasped again. "Remember?"

"Of course—"

"What was all that yellin'?" Goban stuck his head inside the door, and his eyes widened when he saw us. "What...?"

Tears streamed down my face. "Erc," I mumbled. "It was Erc."

Eyes fixed upon the knife hilt in Laoidheach's chest, he emitted a loud, unintelligible yowl. Hurrying to our side, the smith collapsed to the ground. "I'm goin' after the bastard, tonight, now—"

"No. You will not find him in the darkness. Stay with us." I wiped my eyes with the back of my hand. "Remain here, we...he..." A sob stifled my voice.

A small smile lit Laoidheach's wan face. "Soon I will stand beside my beloved wife." He looked to me. "So, you see, do not carry on so. Paradise awaits."

I clutched him to my breast, and nodded, unable to speak. My mind was swirling with grief mixed with the knowledge that my friend had taken the knife meant for my back.

Brendan stooped as he entered my hut, followed by a monk. "I thought I heard..." He stopped upon seeing the knife hilt and growing bloodstain on my friend's chest. "Ossian, who..." His hands scrubbed his face. "It was Erc, wasn't it?"

Bitterness against all Christians gripped me in that moment, though I held my tongue, and merely nodded.

Laoidheach whispered, "Promise me, my old friend; bury me alongside my beloved. It is much I ask, that I know, for you prepare to sail with the priest. If I ask too much—"

"No. No, of course it is not too much, and you have my vow I will do as you ask." At that moment, nothing else mattered; Brendan, the voyage, my promise to the Morrigan, nothing—only the request from my dying friend.

"I messed up again, didn't I?" He tried to chuckle but began choking on the blood filling his throat. At last he gasped, "I'm so very sorry that I can't go on the voyage with you." Again a smile touched his face. "Who will take care of you now, eh?"

Eyes dimming, though he was still smiling, he turned to Goban. "We've shared much together; good times and bad, my stalwart friend."

Tears streaming down his hard, leathery face, Goban nodded. "Aye. That we have, me lad, that we have."

Laying a trembling hand on Goban's arm, he whispered, "There is one last favor I request of you as well, though I fain not, fearing it too much to ask of a dear friend." He paused, gasping. "Remove the knife. Do it now, for my time passes swiftly and I would not die with Erc's filth within me."

Though I knew him as a man of strong heart, Goban wavered and his eyes found mine. At my nod, he knelt; his hand grasped the knife hilt. "Are you ready lad?" he muttered.

Laoidheach spoke not a word, but closed his eyes, and nodded, a gentle smile curling his pale lips. A long, final sigh escaped him as Goban withdrew the knife.

Silence gripped the room as I leaned forward with a moan, and clasped my dearest friend hard to my breast. Rocking back and forth with him in my arms, tears blinded my eyes, anguish my mind.

Thus I continued until behind me, Brendan intoned, "In Nominee Patris, et Filii, et Spiritūs Sancti, we ask you Heavenly Father to receive the soul of Laoidheach—"

Rage enslaved my heart and I spun about on my knees, spittle and venom spewing from my mouth, filling the air. "No! You did not have him while he lived, and by the Queen of Death herself, you shall not claim him now. He," I gasped, "my friend…died true to his gods…his soul belongs to them."

Brendan's clasped hands opened as he began to explain. "Ossian, at this time, surely you do not begrudge God's—"

"Damn you. Damn you and your blasphemous god." Hand trembling, accusing finger jabbing toward his heart. "You are responsible for this, Brendan. Erc was your man, and you knowingly harbored hatred in your midst. My friend's death rests with you."

Mouth open, Brendan stood there, eyes wide and unbelieving, speechless.

"You…you are not welcome here." My voice shook as I waved a dismissive hand. "G-Get out. Get out now. This is no place for," I paused, and then spat the word, "Christians!"

Brendan still hesitated, staring at me.

"Go!"

* * *

I wore the green robe in the morning. Stepping through my doorway into the predawn light, I saw Brendan near the shore, kneeling, hands clasped beneath his chin as he faced Trá Lí Bay.

My footsteps crunched upon gravel as I walked towards him, and he rose and turned about to face me. His eyes swept my robe, though he said nothing of it. Indeed, he said nothing at all, but merely stood there, waiting.

"Goban and I leave later this morning. You heard Laoidheach's dying request?"

"Aye, I heard him and know you must honor his appeal." His solemn eyes held me. "You wonder if I will wait here for you?"

I nodded.

"Despite all..." He shook his head as if to dispel what he intended to say. "You needn't worry. I will honor our agreement and shall not sail. This I promise you in God's name, I shall not sail until you return."

Gentle waves washed upon the shore, gulls dove, turned and cried against a gray sky as Brendan continued, "You were right in what you said. I knew narrow-minded hatred stood at my side and for too long chose to ignore it to my own ends. Brother Erc was my responsibility, so yes—Laoidheach's murder falls upon me. I have since prayed God's forgiveness, and yet for committing such a sin, well I know I must pay a heavy price." Eyes to the sky, he added, "In Your Name, Father."

Great weariness overcame me. Perhaps it was unfair not to forgive Brendan, but my heart and mind were still not prepared to do so. Still, I could understand him. "We are priests you and I. We hear our gods, try to obey their commands and bring their voices to the people. Though we do our best, often we will fail, for we are only men. How can we hope to interpret the will of a god? We make

316

mistakes, on occasion, grave ones. I admit to making critical errors, and yes, Erc was yours."

"Yes. Though we be only men, that does not excuse our mistakes. I should have sent Erc away months ago. If only I had I done so..." His face raised to the sky as he murmured, "For Laoidheach I will never forgive myself."

"All men carry burdens, they are a part of life." Arms crossing my chest, I turned to him with a cocked eyebrow. "I have my burdens. Laoidheach rests with you."

We stood together for a long while, facing the tranquil bay. A sigh escaped him. "Forgiveness does not dwell within your heart, does it?"

"No, not any more. Too much has happened. Too many have died. Memories are all that remain for me. They fill my heart, leaving no room for forgiveness."

"Then it is sorry for you, I am, for you are not a complete person. It is only through forgiveness as revealed to us through God's Own Grace that you may fully regain your humanity."

How could this priest possibly understand the turmoil stirring within me, born of never-ending sadness? My attention moved beyond the bay towards the distant sea, my voice husky with emotion. "Do not trouble yourself. I am human enough, Brendan. Oh yes, I am completely human, for only a human heart could harbor so much sorrow. That is not your concern, but rather a matter to be resolved in good time between me and *my* gods."

Chapter 31
To Old Friends

𝕴 looked back over my shoulder and raised my voice that Goban might hear above the cart's squealing wheels. "So, tell me. What did Brendan say when you told him of the two monks we held in the cave?"

Reins in hand, Goban sat slumped on the seat of the two-wheeled cart as it trundled north along the narrow trail towards Trá Lí and beyond. Dense thickets of gorse and heather crowded the trailside, obscuring the surrounding landscape except for the rugged mountains rising to meet the sky behind us.

He chuckled. "About as ye would expect, I think." Sitting up a bit straighter, a grin spread across his face. "At first he was furious that we had abducted his men. I'm thinkin' he's a good man too, for when I told him why and how we done it and that his men weren't hurt, he shook his head and laughed. It was a good joke on him, he said. Afore we left, he was sendin' out some men to fetch 'em back to the village."

Yes, I thought, *Brendan is a good man and I have no doubt he will stand by his promise to await our return before sailing*. Never would I have considered trusting the word of a Christian, but with Brendan, it was the man I trusted, not his faith.

Ever north we traveled. Laoidheach's body, wrapped in many layers of fine linen, lay stretched in the back of the cart. In the far distance and many days away rose a barren hill and, atop it, a single alder tree—in its shade, a lonely grave.

The faces of the people we met grew wary or sometimes angry at the sight of my emerald green robe. Only a few elderly folk approached me with reverence, addressing me as Wise One, asking for a blessing. I sighed, again realizing the Morrigan's words were true. Everything had changed, now nothing remained for me here on my native soil. My future, if I was to have one, lay across the sea to the west.

We followed familiar trails, those we traveled on our previous journey. It took us a week to come upon the rutted path leading to Saithne. Skirting that village of death, we turned towards the hill and our destination.

* * *

A smile touched my face as Laoidheach's laughter echoed in my memory. Though I grieved for my dearest friend, he would never leave me, not really. Always I would remember his face, his voice, the way he walked, the joy he brought to all about him.

Laoidheach was one with the gods now. Nothing remained that I might offer him, naught but a prayer that our gods favorably receive his soul, and that his afterlife would prove a blessed one.

The morning sun warmed me as I stood beneath it and gazed upwards, the spirit smoke of the sacral fire swirling about me. A cloud shaped, I thought, much like a lyre held my attention, and it was to that drifting cloud I offered my prayer.

"O mighty Lords of the Sidhe, purveyors of the everlasting, I speak to you of Laoidheach, born a spirit child of the wind and air, grandson of one of your own, the great god Belimawr. He was a man I knew and loved well, for we were as brothers he and I, men of two skins sharing a common heart.

"Find him worthy in your eyes, a man of music, poetry and gaiety who brought no harm to anyone for never harm dwelt within him. I beg you release my friend from the fearsome darkness of death and grant him entrance to paradise; allow him to dwell beside his beloved Aine at Tír na nÓg. Let him be known among the Golden Ones there as Laoidheach of the Silver Voice.

"O great Lords, I pray you look upon Laoidheach with kindness and hold him close to you forever. Permit him to continue to sing his songs of joy and praise always. These things you can do for my friend, a man who stood beside you in life, and who will honor you for all eternity. This is my prayer for him; these things I beg of you.

"Almighty gods of our fathers, we bow to your will."

* * *

A light wind entwined the flames of our fire as Goban and I sat beside the newly erected cairn covering Laoidheach's grave. The funeral ritual fulfilled, quiet we were, holding our own thoughts, thinking back, remembering.

It was Goban who broke the silence as he squatted beside me, his gnome-like muscular body contorted, tears streaking his twisted, grief-filled face. "Has he reached it? Has he arrived at Tír na nÓg? Has he found Aine? What do ye see, Ossian? Ye must tell me."

Cross-legged I sat, eyes closed, mind quiet. The vision came, the coalescence of a shimmering palette, and with it the words I spoke, though not my own, a gentle offering from Danu.

> Within a silent grove,
> She awaits him.
> Ancient Rowans towering,
> Verdant neath the sun's radiance.
>
> Welcoming arms outstretched,
> Graceful hands beckoning.
> Eyes aglow and tears-filled,
> As only a lover's should be.
>
> He is there, yes, he is there,
> Tall, straight and laughing.
> Striding forward to hold her,
> At Tír na nÓg.
>
> Together they cling,
> They kiss.
> Beneath the trees,
> Promise fulfilled.

Golden Ones now, the two,
Gift of enchantment joined.
As O so long ago,
The gods ordained.

Love everlasting,
Where time stands still.
As it must,
Within a silent grove.

Some thoughts a person must own for themselves, wrap tightly within them, treasure and lock away from curious minds and loose tongues. Such it must have been with Goban as he stood beside me, eyes closed, face turned to the sky. There he remained, unmindful of my presence until a sigh escaped him.

My eyes followed him as, head erect, shoulders square, he turned and strode towards our horses. I did not begrudge that Goban chose not to share his thoughts with me, for I held my own about Laoidheach and Aine and Tír na nÓg. And I locked them away.

* * *

A squalid, moldering hovel crouched beside the trail near the edge of a village and we arrived there with the dust of the road clogging our throats. A farmer leaning upon his hayfork who pointed the way told us the owner sold his red ale to travelers.

The cart we had abandoned atop the hill. Now Goban rode astride a horse and our return journey passed swiftly. My green robe, soiled during our travel north, was stowed in my bundle, so again I wore a kirtle and leggings. We stepped down from our horses, thoughts of cool ale filling our heads.

We were tying our reins to a bush, when a loud crash followed by the sound of breaking crockery erupted inside. Yelling ensued, the raised voices of arguing men.

Goban cocked an eyebrow, and smirked. "This sounds like a likely spot."

Two tall, burly lads emerged from the hut, a struggling man between them. They lifted him up, one grabbing the man's arms, the other his legs, and gave him a hefty backwards swing before pitching him a goodly distance through the air, where he landed on his face amid a cloud of dust with an, "Oomph."

Their victim raised himself on hands and knees, shook his head and then spun about, facing his huge adversaries. He lifted his face to the sky, howling like a wolf, and then leaped to his feet, dashing back into them, fists swinging.

I chuckled when I noticed the men were twin brothers who towered beside the door almost casually, lopsided grins on their faces. The man's blows bounced off them like hailstones thumping granite. Repeating their previous performance, they again lifted the man up, tossed him through the air and enjoyed a similar result.

This time the man lay still before finally turning onto his side. His hand went to his mouth, and a moment later he withdrew and inspected a tooth pinched between his thumb and forefinger. A disgusted sneer crossed his bearded, dust-covered face, as he cast the tooth aside and spat blood on the ground.

It was the first time I saw the man clearly, and laughter erupted from my throat upon recognizing him. "So Torcán, how goes your battle?"

He lifted his head and glared at me. "And who would you be to nose into another man's fight?" In that moment he knew me. "Ossian!" Staggering to his feet, he swayed and then lurched towards me.

Upon reaching my side, Torcán grabbed my arm with his left hand and began pounding my back with his right. "Ossian, my old friend. Oh, and what a fine day this turned out to be. I thought you dead."

Grunting beneath his repeated blows, I gasped, "If you don't stop beating upon me, I soon will be."

"Ah now, it's sorry I am." His broad grin gleamed within his dusty beard; his eyes alight with good humor. "It's just that I'm glad to see you. It's been, what, two years since we fought together?"

"Almost that, yes." I turned to introduce him to Goban. "This is—"

Torcán interrupted me as he stepped aside; feet spread, fists on his hips. "I am Torcán, son of Dubhgall, a warrior and sword for hire. I fought alongside Ossian and led our mounted warriors durin' a victorious battle against the Christians. Ah, what a fine fight that was."

Goban grunted and stared him up and down. "From the looks of ye, that was your last victory."

The warrior dusted his tattered clothing. "Oh, it's ashamed I am of my appearance. Times are hard for fightin' men." He frowned and winked. "A good war is what this land needs, I say; at least a small one to start coins a'flowin' again, eh?"

"I know ye now." Goban nodded. "Ye visited Tara a few years back, I think. I am Goban; ye come by me shop and purchased a sword from me."

"You're the man who...?" Recognition lit Torcán's eyes. "Aye, of course! Right you are, and a fine sword it was, for it served me well."

Eyebrow cocked, Goban asked, "It was? What became of it?"

"Ach, I told you times are hard." He pointed along the tree-lined trail towards the village. "A miserly shopkeeper has it now." Dropping his head and dragging a toe in the dust, Torcán muttered, "It's a sad thing for a warrior to admit, but I had to sell my sword so's to eat, you see."

"Come then," I said, slapping his shoulder. "We stopped for a bit of ale, but perhaps some stew as well if it is tasty enough."

We were walking towards the hovel's door when the brawny twins turned to face us, shoulder to shoulder. The one on the left shook his head. "There'll be none of that 'til we see a coin to pay for it all."

Torcán looked to me with a shrug. "These are good lads, but there's been a slight misunderstandin' between their father and me over payment for a mere few mugs of ale."

He turned back to the brothers. "Now, don't be shamin' me in front of my friends...there's the good lads. If you'll just go in and speak with your father—"

"We'll not be speaking with our father 'til we see a coin," the same brother replied.

"So tell me lads, were you raised on sheep's milk? Stand up to your father, I say. Tell him Torcán always pays his debts."

His face remaining unperturbed, the young man held out his hand, his thumb rubbing his fingertips. "Yer coin?"

I grabbed Torcán's shoulder as he took a quick step forward, fists clenched at his sides. "Wait. There needn't be another *misunderstanding* here." Removing a silver coin from the purse at my waist, I tossed it to the young man. "Take that to your father. It is more than sufficient to pay for the ale Torcán already drank plus everything we will require."

We trailed behind them as the twins, grinning as one, turned and entered the hovel. Surprisingly, the single room exceeded the impression offered from the outside. Six tables with benches arranged either side, and the aroma of fresh hay scattered upon the ground filled the air. Behind a short counter hung shelves lined with bottles and mugs. The gray-bearded man leaning on the counter and scowling at Torcán I assumed was the lads' father. He had much the same burly look about him, though he stood a good head shorter than his sons.

We settled around a table, mugs and ale bottles standing before us, and long it was we spoke of old times. Bottle after bottle arrived along with steaming bowls of lamb stew. Darkness fell, and candles grouped on the counter cast a dim glow within the room. Local men, farmers by the look of them, came and went, while ever-growing clusters of empty ale bottles filled our tabletop.

"And so," Torcán asked, "whatever became of your friend the bard, Laoidheach?"

"He's dead." I lowered my face, sipped my ale and then went on to tell Torcán about it. I spoke of my best friend.

When I finished, he wiped the makings of tears from his eyes with the back of his hand. "Ah now that's a sad thing, my friend, a sad thing. Laoidheach was a good man, I think." He shook his head. "We've all lost many good friends, eh? Dead, maimed, gone away somewhere..." He raised his mug. "To old friends, wherever they may be."

Lifting our mugs high, Goban and I echoed, "To old friends."

The night grew long, the ale flowed and the room emptied of all save the father and his twin sons. We paid them scant attention though the hulking brothers sat at the table beside us. Torcán was sharing a tale with us when the father strolled over with more bottles. "If it's more ye'll be wantin', I'll be needin' another coin from ye."

My hand went to my purse, but Torcán grumbled. "Another coin, you say? I doubt you've seen so much silver in the past year. Off with you, unless you're wantin' my fist in your eye."

"A likely thing that," the father sneered. "Do ye want more ale or don't ye?"

Torcán flushed and began to rise, but I laid a hand on his shoulder, pushed him down on the bench and gave the man a coin. "I don't begrudge a man a coin or two when he serves good ale. Keep the bottles coming, my man."

"You pay too much," Torcán muttered as the father walked away. "Now, what was it I was saying?"

Goban poured ale in his mug, and looked up. "Ye were tellin' us about the maid who received a cow for her services."

"Oh yes, as I was saying—"

A twin leaned over and interrupted, grinning at Torcán. "Ye'd best enjoy yer ale while yer wealthy friend is here. Ye'll be getting no more of it after he's gone."

Torcán ignored him and continued his story. "So, this maid says, 'It won't be—'"

"I'd be talkin' to ye, little man," the twin goaded him. "Ye'd best be a'heedin' me lessin' ye'd be wantin' more of what we already gave ye."

His face glowed, but Torcán continued. "She says, 'It won't be me who's—'"

The big man rose, stepped to our table and laid his hand on Torcán's shoulder. "I said ye'd best be a'hearin' me—"

It was trouble the brother offered, and he got it. Torcán slapped the hand away, leaped to his feet and threw a fist into the man's teeth.

The man staggered backwards and his brother and father rushed forward to grab Torcán. Goban hurried to his feet to side our friend.

"Men," I began, as I stood, thinking to avoid the foolishness. "I see no reason why—"

The father's fist crashed against Torcán's jaw, sending him reeling across the room. Goban kicked a twin on the shin and then turned away, ducking as a mighty swing passed over his head.

The father and other twin pursued Torcán, who dodged behind a table.

Crouching, his fists swirling before him, Goban danced about the big man confronting him—a horsefly circling a bull.

My small friend was over-matched, so fearing for his safety I hurried forward. "Now see here—"

The twin's roundabout punch caught me in my stomach, doubling me over. The following blow I didn't see coming, only lights bursting in my head when his fist connected with my chin.

Backwards I tumbled, coming to rest on the floor, gasping for breath as I found myself propped against the counter alongside Torcán, who it seemed had suffered a similar fate.

He turned to me and grinned. "Oh, a sportin' family they are, may the gods bless them." Scrambling to his feet, he whooped, "Here we go!"

A sporting family? I snorted. *They brawl for sport?*

It was pure idiocy, and I glanced about, concerned for Goban. I spotted him astraddle the fallen giant. How he toppled such a colossus I couldn't fathom, but Goban sat upon the man's chest, pummeling him with his fists.

From the corner of my eye, I saw Torcán exchanging punches with the father. My attention shifted to the other twin, who strode over to Goban, lifted him bodily in the air and heaved the small man across our former dinner table, where he disappeared amidst the clatter of breaking of bottles and shrill curses.

Idiotic or not, the fight was on, so I staggered to my feet, and rushed headlong towards the brother who had tossed Goban. He saw me coming as I ran towards him, stepped aside as I missed with a punch and then gave me a shove. Off-balance, I plunged over the table, landing atop Goban in a tangle of arms and legs.

"Get off me," my friend squawked.

This was my first brawl, and, lacking experience, I wasn't faring well. It occurred to me that perhaps I could outsmart the twins' brute force. Our heights were much the same, though I was no match for their muscular frames. Rather than rushing about, I would approach my adversaries with guile and deliberate determination.

The brother who pushed me was grinning as I grabbed the table edge and heaved myself erect. Filled with confidence, I advanced, circling about, my fists poised and moving in front of me, my muscles coiled to deliver a blow. Multi-colored lights flashed before my eyes as the man's fist seemed to come from nowhere to connect with my chin.

Down I went, rolling across the floor, once more coming to a hard stop with my shoulders resting against the counter. The room was spinning 'round; nearby were panting, grunting, an incoherent shout and the thuds of exchanged blows.

Someone crashed against the counter beside me, overturning the candles, and the room went dark. No doubt Goban and Torcán encountered trouble with the father and his giant sons. They needed my aid, so I shook my head, reached up to the countertop and pulled myself upright.

Lacking any sense of the positions of friends or foes, I groped my way through the darkness. A dimly seen shadow moved before and slightly below me, so I leaned closer, hoping for a better look.

"Yeow!" The irrepressible yelp escaped me when hard knuckles encountered my nose. Tears streamed from my eyes as I cupped my throbbing nose in my hand.

"Ossian?" It was Goban. "Was that ye, lad?"

I spun about, encountered a wood bench and sat down on it. Rocking back and forth while still cupping my nose, I almost gagged when blood trickled into my mouth. In that moment I became a casualty, lost to the fight.

Goban's hand grasped my shoulder. "Are ye hurt, lad?" he muttered. He might have said more, but another loud crash came from the vicinity of the counter followed by the sound of shuffling feet.

"What say ye, men?" the father's voice rang out in the darkness. "Have ye had enough?"

No response came. I was gasping through my open mouth, my nose clogged, streaming blood and on fire.

"What say ye?" the man called again.

"Aye, that's enough," Goban replied.

"Well then, we want to thank ye boys for a fine evenin's entertainment. Stay here and make yourselves comfortable for the night, ye've already paid for it. I'm quite the jolly host, wouldn't ye agree? We'll be happy to accommodate ye again tomorrow." The father and sons' laughter joined, and I heard the sound of backslapping as they stumbled through the door.

As for Torcán, he never uttered a sound.

* * *

Goban held my arm as he squatted before me, staring at my nose. "Oh, it's sorry I am, my friend. I thought it one of the brothers loomin' above me in the darkness, so I let me fist fly."

Pre-dawn light revealed the battle-scarred room in gray shadows. Seated on a bench, I glared at him past my swollen nose. "'I let me fist fly,'" I mocked. "Do you often let it fly away when you've no idea where it's going?"

"No, well, that is, I thought…" He cleared his throat. "So is your nose broke, do you think?"

I winced as I swiped at the dripping thing with a linen rag, and growled, "And just how would I be knowing that? All I'm certain of, it's swollen to twice its normal size."

Throbbing pain had allowed me no sleep throughout the night, though I had removed my blood-spattered kirtle, replacing it with another from my bundle. It was with a foul temper I glanced at Torcán, who still lay beside the counter, flat on his back and snoring.

"Look at him there." I pointed. "He sleeps like a gorged bear, while…ach." Glowering, I stood and started towards him. "We'll see about that."

Goban arrived alongside me, and chuckled as he stared down at Torcán. "Well, at least the man's not dead."

Arms crossing my chest, I stood over him and prodded his stomach with my toe. He smacked his lips, smiled and then resumed snoring. I prodded him again, with no intention of being gentle about it.

Torcán awoke with a snort, shook his head and then leaped to his feet, his balled fists outstretched before him.

Hands upraised, I backed away. "Whoa, warrior. The war's over."

Purple swelling surrounded his red eyes as he gawked at me. "It is?"

"Aye, so you can lower your fists."

He scrubbed his face with his hands, and then glanced sideways at me. "Did we win?"

Dabbing away blood oozing from my nose, I groaned. "I'm afraid not."

"Bah." A grin spread across his face as he winked at Goban and pointed to me. "Now there's a painful nose for you. The brothers can throw a punch, can't they?"

Goban grunted, and scurried behind me as the warrior continued. "Ah, but it was a brawny fight nonetheless, wasn't it?" On wobbling legs, he glanced around and reached across the counter for a bottle. "I say we celebrate it."

My stomach churned at the thought, and I waved a dismissive hand. "I had quite enough last night, thank you. Besides, Goban and I must be leaving soon and we'll not be traveling with muddled heads."

"Yes, and to Trá Lí, I recall you mentioned last night." Torcán took a long swig from the bottle, and then wiped his mouth on his sleeve. "And why would you be goin' to such a place? I've been there and little there is to it."

"To Trá Lí and a bit beyond," I nodded, "along the coast of the penninsula south of it. A man waits for us."

"Ah yes, I know the place." He scratched the tangled beard on his chin. "It was in the mountains there we fought a small battle, ten years ago it was. I remember the fight well because it was then poor Aimhirghin, son of Morann, got his head chopped. Did you know him?"

My attention was on Goban who was making a sly attempt to avoid my notice by busying himself straightening tables and benches. "No, I...no."

"Oh well, it doesn't matter then, does it?" Still rubbing his chin, he cocked an eyebrow. "It's a dangerous country the two of you will be travelin' through. Yes," he nodded, "I'd best be goin' with you, to protect you so to speak."

It was an appalling offer. "But, that's—"

"Oh, don't be thankin' me for it." He waved a casual hand. "I noticed the coins in your fat purse and a shopkeeper in the village here holds all my weapons, armor, baggage and such. In fact, he now owns my horse as well. So, you see. You can pay the man to retrieve my kit and horse and that will be thanks enough. Besides, if we run into trouble along the way, I wouldn't offer much protection for you lackin' Goban's fine sword in my hand, would I?"

It wasn't the need for protection from trouble that worried me. It was the likelihood of him provoking it. My doubts about Torcán wavered as memories of the battle at Lough Derg returned, where I knew him as a trustworthy ally and gallant fighter. I still owed him much gratitude, and the coins in my purse would serve no purpose at sea aboard Brendan's ship.

Before I could complete my thoughts, he grabbed my arm, pushing me towards the door. "Come on, my friend, we must hurry. It's but a short walk to the village and, if it's leavin' here we plan, we'd best be about it. If that shopkeeper isn't up and stirrin' yet, then by the gods, I will stir him."

Chapter 32
Warriors

To our east, gray clouds hung low, obscuring mountain peaks. White mist filled the high valleys. It required more than gusting wind and a spattering drizzle to dampen Torcán's spirits. Rain dripped from the end of his nose, soaked his red cape and beaded on his bronze armor.

He grinned. "Ah, and what a fine day it is to be a free man; all Eire lies before us." His hand swept the panoramic collage of green-hued fields spanning the rolling hills in our foreground. "Just look at it, lads, just look at it. A willin' man with a keen sword in his hand can do much, and yes, he can win much."

Goban slouched in his saddle; a soggy blanket drooped over his head. "Willin' I'll be to win a dry camp for the night."

Our horses plodded along the muddy, southerly track leading us back towards Trá Lí and the penninusla beyond. Goban received his wish, for we came upon a stacked-stone shepherd's hovel before nightfall. Finding it empty, we moved our gear inside and lit a fire.

Soon, Torcán was scrubbing his mouth with the back of his hand, before his teeth renewed their assault on a roasted goose leg. He looked up at me with a wink and grin.

"It's like old times, eh? Sittin' 'round a fire with friends while enjoyin' a good meal?"

I licked my fingers, and grinned back. "Yes, but without the need of facing a battle tomorrow."

"Ach." He waved the goose leg like a dissenting finger. "Battles is what grows hair on a man's chest."

He gnawed the leg again, then pitched the stripped bone through the open doorway. A contented sigh escaped him as he lay back, propped on his elbows.

"So, you meet a man beyond Trá Lí, you said. What're your plans then, if you don't mind me askin'?"

Many knew of Brendan's plans to sail, so there was no reason to withold my answer. "Goban and I will rejoin a priest named Brendan. We will sail with him on a voyage to the west to find **Tír na nÓg**."

"You join a Christian priest? To find Tír na nÓg?" He shook his head as if to clear his mind. "What manner of foolishness is that?"

"Think it foolish if you will." I shrugged. "Perhaps it is, but that is what we plan."

Again shaking his head, a frown formed on Torcán's face, but he remained silent.

As I leaned forward, my hand encountered Goban's simultaneously reaching for the last goose wing. I grinned. "Take it, please."

"No," the smith grinned in return. "It's yours. You paid the farmer, and a tightfisted rogue he is, so take it."

We were politely arguing, gesturing back and forth over possession of the wing, when Torcán muttered, "I want to go with you."

I dropped my hands into my lap, unsure I heard him correctly. "You want to go with us? But you just said the voyage is foolish."

"I said no such thing." He sat up, crossing his arms over his chest. "I said searchin' for Tír na nÓg is foolish, not the voyage."

"It's all the same."

"You think so?" Torcán stood, his finger pointed down at me. "No. They are not the same." Eyes alight, his aimed finger swung to the hovel's door. "What's out there across the western sea? That's what I ask. Who knows? Just think of the adventure of it."

He began pacing. "Perhaps there are new, undiscovered lands filled with treasure; sparklin' cities of gold teemin' with beautiful women draped with fabulous jewels—"

Goban waved the goose wing at me as an offering, and I shook my head, interrupting Torcán. "That is the making of dreams, and unlikely."

"Of course it is likely just a dream. Didn't I just say that very thing?" He hadn't, but I remained quiet as he continued. "Still, we don't know for certain, do we? No man knows what lies across the western sea. Maybe there are unknown lands and cities of gold. It's possible, isn't it?"

"Well, I suppose so, but—"

"And there you have it. Think of the adventure if such exist."

Goban snorted. "It's likely the only adventure ye'll find will be alongside us in the innards of a fish."

"Maybe so, but what of it?" Torcán chuckled. "You think to live forever my friend? At least I might end my days by providing a fish a fine dinner."

He again sat, and looked to me, crossing his arms. "Do you know how old I am?"

I tried to ignore the sound of Goban devouring the goose wing as I shook my head, and he continued. "Thirty-nine. That's old for a warrior and well you know it. My sword arm is strong as ever, but I'm losin' my quickness." He sighed. "It's lucky I've been all these years, and many fine years I've seen." His eyes grew bright as he leaned forward. "Think of it, Ossian—horns a'blowin', war drums throbbin', banners flyin', warriors screechin' and singin' their war songs. You've seen it yourself, and what man wouldn't want to be a part of all that?"

He sat quiet for a while, firelight flickering on his rugged face. "I lied today, you know. Winning riches as a warrior here in Eire is for young men. I missed my chance." He reached down, picked up a twig and stirred the coals. "In time, I'll come upon a likely lad who… Ah, but what of it?"

Thinking I understood him, I nodded. "And the voyage offers a chance, slight though it be, for riches and glory. Is that right?"

"Yes. Those are my thoughts, foolish as they are." He cocked an eyebrow. "Can I go?"

Rising, I stepped around the fire and took the hand of this sturdy, reliable man I had come to like very much. "Yes, though I must discuss it with Brendan. Your strength will be of value to us and you will take the place of Laoidheach."

I had gained a valuable ally for the voyage, but sighed at losing the goose wing.

* * *

We rode single-file along the trail with Torcán in the lead and Goban bringing up the rear. Heavy brush crowded the trailside, dense woodlands beyond. Each of us held our own thoughts, when Torcán stopped. I reined in my horse, puzzled.

He reached into a bag hanging beside his horse's withers and removed a gleaming brass helm trimmed in red leather, its peak crested with a gilded hawk in flight. It was a beautiful thing, the hawk itself a work of art.

He saw me admiring it and grinned, his voice low. "You're thinkin' it's worthy of a king, eh?" Seating the helm upon his head, he tightened the leather chinstrap. "In truth, it was made for a chieftain among the Dal Messin. Garbhán son of Fionn, his name was, but he— Well, I claimed it as a prize, seein' as that unlucky gentleman acquired a bad habit of holdin' his sword point too low."

Despite his many failings, Torcán was a bold man I found it easy to admire. My grin matched his as I glanced about. "Why did you stop? If we pick up our pace—"

His hand waved me to silence, and he winked, still keeping his voice muted. "Listen. What do you hear? Tell me, but do so quietly."

About me, the forest was silent, and though I listened intently, I shook my head and whispered, "What? I hear nothing."

"Exactly." He nodded. "Not a sound. No singing birds or scurrying woodland creatures and such it has been for a while. So I ask myself, why is that? We pass along the trail causing a disturbance, yes, but even further back among the trees there's none of the natural sounds of the forest."

Goban walked his horse forward, and muttered, "Right he is." He cocked an eyebrow at Torcán. "What're ye thinkin', then?"

"Perhaps it's nothin' at all," the warrior shrugged, "but then again, it's possible there be men out there." He dismounted, handing me his reins. "I'm goin' to see for myself. Do you wait here. If you hear my yell, come fast, for I'll be needin' you." He drew his sword, parted the brush and stepped from view.

I looked to Goban. "Bandits?"

The smith shrugged and stepped down from his horse. His eyes swept the trailside as he stood, feet spread wide, his hammer in his fist.

I had attached a leather strap to the Staff of Nuada, and wore it diagonally across my back. Drawing it over my head, I hopped to the ground. If danger loomed, the Staff offered no sign of it.

Clouds scudded past the sun, bringing a misting rain that contributed to the oppressive silence. Tension built in my shoulders and I rolled them about to ease it while my attention fastened to first one side of the trail, and then the other. Time passed, with it, the clouds and rain, replaced by a chill wind.

Goban shivered and snorted. "It's true what they say about Eire's weather. If ye don't like it, wait a wee bit, for it's sure to change, but not necessarily for the better."

Brush shook far up the trail and Torcán appeared. Brisk strides brought him to our side.

He brushed leaves from his cape, and then glanced back over his shoulder. "We've been followed for fair—six men, three on either side of the trail."

Bitterness rose in my throat. Only a short distance remained until we met Brendan and sailed. I nodded towards the underbrush. "They ride through that?"

"They're afoot. We've maintained a steady pace, but good men would have no trouble remaining abreast of us."

"They plan to rob us?"

Despite the cool wind, his face dripped sweat, and he reached to his horse for a flagon of water. "I don't think so." He gulped the water, and wiped his mouth with the back of his hand. "The men are warriors, not bandits, and two wear the yellow and black checked kirtles of the Corcu Duibne."

Goban kicked the trail, spattering mud on the nearby foliage. Then he looked to me and I nodded. "Tell him."

Puzzlement hovering in his eyes, Torcán asked, "Tell me what?"

In simple, clipped sentences, Goban told how the Corcu held him and Laoidheach as slaves. He went on to speak of how I arrived to free them by killing the two warriors.

Torcán's eyebrows knitted together and he pursed his lips. "It seems I keep company with criminals." Quiet laughter burst from his throat and he stepped forward to clap Goban's shoulder. "What of it? The Corcu pass their laws out of their asses, eh?"

He turned to me, eyes alight and grinning. "Come. Mount up. It's time we dispel their stench."

The trailside vegetation seemed to crowd upon us, and I did not share his enthusiasm. "Do you not fear ambush?"

"Nah." He leaped to the back of his horse, his cape swirling, and pointed forward. "They no longer follow us. Beyond the bend is a clearing. The six Corcu came together there and are awaitin' us. Ah now, you've got to admire an accommodatin' reception."

Mounting, we paused, looking to our weapons. Goban glanced about. "Can we ride around them?"

"No," Torcán growled. "There's no avoidin' 'em. We face them now, or risk them killin' us in our sleep. Now then, listen carefully." His eyes moved from Goban to me. "Those bastards came here for a killin' and nothin' less. They'll be wantin' to talk, to brag about what they plan for us. I intend to throw the fight right into their

338

teeth, unsettle them right off so to speak. Ride into them hard and do your best to scatter 'em. You'll know when. Are you with me?"

I bowed to his experience and judgment. The man was fearless, a poet's vision of the pure warrior—a poem Laiodheach never wrote. It appeared the fight was unavoidable, and if we were to survive, it would be due to his experience.

* * *

We trotted our horses into the clearing. The Corcu were there, standing six abreast. Torcán urged his horse towards the center of their line, and pulled back hard on his reins. His horse reared, hooves flailing the air in the faces of the Corcus.

"Stand aside!" he bellowed, his sword swirling above his head. "Move away, or by the gods, we will move you!"

The warriors shuffled in their rank and exchanged glances. A burly man in bronze armor, their leader I supposed, stepped forward. "You will—"

Torcán's sword slashed downward, a blur of flashing steel. The leader fell to his knees, a fountain of blood spurting from his neck.

Holding my sword low, I kicked my horse's ribs and guided him on a direct path towards the warrior standing at the far left of their line. He saw me coming and attempted to dodge to my left, but my horse's shoulder struck the man, spilling him to the ground.

Spinning about, I dashed towards the next man in line. At almost the last moment I realized he held a pike, directed at my chest. Reining hard right, I slapped the pike aside with my sword. Whirling my horse in a tight circle beside the warrior, I delivered a backhand slash. He shrieked as his severed hand fell to the ground.

The pikeman was finished, but my first foe was struggling to his feet, so I rode him down again. Reining my horse, I loomed over him.

He lay upon his back, fear gleaming in his eyes, palms outstretched towards me. "I yield."

Leaning down, my sword at his throat, I snarled, "Were you at Rath Raithleann?"

The man's eyes grew wider, and he shook his head.

"You're lying." I spat in his face. "I ask again, were you at Rath Raithleann?"

Eyes closed, he nodded, covering his face with his hands.

Rage took me as a memory returned: Ceara sprawled upon the ground beside her slain sons. I thrust the sword point deep.

Furious yelling drew my attention, and I glanced up to see Goban pursuing an enemy who darted into the heavy brush and disappeared. Of the six Corcu, only the pikeman and fleeing man remained alive. Torcán knelt beside a fallen warrior, inspecting the contents of the dead man's purse.

Bloodlust still pounded in my ears in the presence of my enemies, and I turned back to the wounded pikeman. Thinking to finish him, I leaped down from my horse. The man was kneeling, head down and sobbing as he attempted to staunch the blood flowing from his wrist. I raised my sword, but hesitated when he looked up. He was no man, but a mere boy, at best fourteen, too young to have taken an active role in the attack upon my village.

Tears streamed down the lad's face and he sniffed. But, he had courage too. "Go ahead," he said. "Strike if you will."

Boy or not, fury still held me. He was Corcu spawn, so I might have accommodated him, but by pausing, a measure of reason returned. These men knew we would pass this way and waited for us. How could they know such a thing?

"That man," Goban snorted, pointing towards the woods as he strode towards me, "fled like a frightened hare." He stopped beside me, staring at the wounded boy. "What of this one?"

"We shall see. Build a fire, will you?" Turning to my horse, I removed my bundle, and from it, rolled bandages and bags of medicinal herbs.

The boy's face was deathly white, his body trembling from agony and blood loss. I ripped a strip of bandage lengthwise and bound it tight above the stub of his arm. Blood still oozed from the wound, but the flow stopped.

"What's your name, son?"

"What matter it now?" he responded, face downcast, his voice weak and trembling. "I-I'm a dead man."

"Perhaps. Perhaps not. Now lie down." He did as I directed and I wrapped my blanket about him. "I shall do what I can for you. What's your name?"

His eyes searched mine. "Ross. I am called Ross."

"So Ross, tell me. The lot of you have been following, and waited here to attack us. Why?"

"Y-you know why." The lad's teeth were chattering. "We—we thought there was only the two of you. Had we known about him," he nodded towards Torcán, who was busy scavenging the contents of the Corcu's packs, "we w-would have brought more men."

Goban had the fire blazing, and I motioned for him to retrieve a fallen Corcu sword. I would use it to cauterize the ghastly wound. My attention returned to the boy.

"Yes, well that was your mistake, wasn't it? But how did you know to wait for us along this trail?"

The boy bit his lip, and shook his head.

"Ah, I see. You won't tell me." He seemed a simple lad, unschooled in the wiles of men. "So, it must have been magic. You learned of it from a great magician who—"

"No." The boy's eyes closed. "M-magic is Satan's tool and we have no use for such. A message c-came to us from," he gasped, "a monk who told us to w-watch this trail and wait. He said you would come."

I glanced at Goban, who nodded when I muttered, "Erc."

Turning to the boy for confirmation, I asked, "This monk, his name is Erc?"

The lad didn't respond, so I leaned forward, looked into his eyes...and sighed. He was beyond answering.

Chapter 33
The Odor of Wolfsbane

We passed through Trá Lí in the murky silence of early morning. Only a spotted dog standing near a cottage noted and yipped at our presence. Holding to the rock-strewn trail, we pressed on, following close upon the bay's shoreline, mountains clad in autumn foliage towering above our left shoulders. I grew ever more anxious as we neared our destination. Had Brendan waited?

We rounded a bend in the shoreline and a fisherman surrounded by his nets came into view. His boat drifting within the quiet waters near the shore, he lifted his face as we drew near.

"So friend," I called to him. "You've a fine morning to be upon the bay. You've found the fish?"

Gray locks strayed beyond his tattered woolen cap, and cool eyes peered at me from a weathered face. "Only a few small ones," came the typical reply of a wary fisherman who would protect his favored fishing spot. He scratched his grizzled chin, and then nodded. "I know you. I'm thinkin' ye be that Druid the father's been waiting for."

Relief flooded through me and I smiled. "Yes, I am that Druid. Brendan hasn't sailed, then?"

"No. He's not sailed, nor will he." The elderly man shook his head. "I fear father Brendan be dead."

I recoiled in my saddle as if struck by a physical blow. "But how...?"

"They say he grew suddenly ill just last night. Only yesterday I sees him walkin' the shore. As healthy as you and me, he was." The fisherman offered a knowing wink and tapped his temple with a forefinger. "An odd thing that, if ye asks me. This morning, monks gather before the good father's doorstep and even now the poor man may've breathed his last."

It was as if the fisherman's voice came from far away as his words and my thoughts cluttered my head. What was that last he said? Perhaps Brendan yet lived?

"You say there is a chance he is not dead?"

"Maybe." The fisherman shrugged. "I only know—"

I swung my horse to the trail and heard nothing more he said. Only a short ride would bring us to the village, and though the trail was too stony to gallop, we hurried as best we could.

We topped a rise and the clustered cottages came into view. As we drew near, I could see that at least some of the fisherman's words were true. Monks gathered before Brendan's doorstep.

The faces of kneeling monks turned to us as we reined-in and dismounted. One, a tall, skinny man, intercepted me as I strode towards Brendan's door.

He recognized me, as did most of Brendan's monks. "No, Ossian." He shook his head. "You may not enter."

If the priest was dead, I would see it for myself. I brushed him aside.

The cottage's interior was dark, its shutters closed, a single candle offering but a dim glow. A black-robed monk kneeling at Brendan's bedside rose like a shadow.

His solemn voice broke the stillness. "You are not welcome here. Father Brendan lies within the Hands of God."

Master Tóla taught the dangers of standing between a man and his god, especially for those of a differing faith. In that moment, it was not danger to myself that concerned me.

"He is dead?"

A long moment passed before the monk replied. "Soon. His soul slips from this life to the glorious next where he shall stand beside his Maker. Now go. Leave him in peace."

Stepping to Brendan's side, I lay my hand on his damp forehead. It felt hot to my touch and I bent down, placing my ear against his chest. He began mumbling, his words incomprehensible, yet still I could hear the slow, rhythmic pounding of his heart. His breath was in my face. I gasped and stood erect, taking a quick step back.

Much more had I learned from the Master. From his alchemy lessons, I knew the odor of wolfsbane. The priest should already be dead and it was unlikely I could save him.

The agitated monk began, "I asked you to go. Now, if you will—"

"Quiet, man," I rasped. "Brendan was poisoned. Quickly now—when did he last eat?"

"Poisoned?" His eyes grew wide as my words filled his mind. "But that's...no, that's not—"

"When did he last eat?"

"Last night. He ate dinner here alone." He gulped. "Are you certain?"

"His breath reeks of wolfsbane." I walked to a window and threw back the shutters. Light flooded the room, revealing Brendan's flushed face.

"Goban," I called through the open window. "Go among the village and bring peat charcoal. Be sure it's peat, now. When you return, pound it into fine powder. Do it quickly."

The monks were on their feet, some staring, others glaring at me. Ignoring them, I looked to Torcán. "Bring my bundle. Then I will need a flagon of wine." I thought a moment. "No. Two flagons."

The monk was regaining his senses. "Here now. What manner of pagan ritual do you plan? Father Brendan is in God's capable hands, and—"

My mind was filled with the urgency of the moment, but I needed the monk's aid. "Brother, I do not wish to offend you or your god. Father Brendan is the victim of foul murder." I sighed. "Too much time has passed since he was poisoned, so little I believe I can save him. Still, would you not have me at least try?"

The man frowned. "If you plan to invoke the aid of the old gods, then no."

Of course I planned to call upon the Lordly Ones, but I would respect both his faith and decision. "If that be your will, I shall not. However, there are treatments that might still help him."

"You think me a fool who does not understand the value of herbs? Brendan despises your gods as you do his. However, if there is a chance…" His face softened and he nodded. "Yes, of course. How can I help?"

Pails of water were brought that Brendan be cooled with wet cloths. I prepared potions using herbs hoarded in my bundle; foxglove to strengthen his heart, willow to lower his fever and finally the charcoal powder mixed with elder and wine to absorb the poison and cause the priest to expel it.

The monk, who I learned was called Brother Tobias, remained at my side throughout the day. He was quick to help when called upon, but many times I saw him standing, staring through the window.

He was standing thus late in the day when I asked, "You wonder who poisoned Brendan?"

Tobias turned, shoulders sagging, scrubbing his face with his hands. "No. I have no doubt who is answerable for it."

"And…?"

"Broth…the man Erc no doubt ordered it. Two of his friends remained among us." Stiff-faced, eyes glaring, he continued. "Brothers Mark and Jonas. It was Brother Jonas who delivered father Brendan's dinner last night. Neither man arrived for morning prayers or has been seen all day."

He closed his eyes. "May God forgive them all."

Erc. Yes, it had been in my thoughts that he was behind it as well. He wore hatred like a cloak. That he sought vengeance against Brendan came as no surprise. As for the two monks, I knew nothing of them.

Oil lamps burned and the night grew late before Brendan showed signs of improvement. His fever waned while his heart beat stronger. For the first time I began to hope we might save him. Tobias retired for the night, leaving me alone by Brendan's bedside.

* * *

"Allow him to die, Ossian."

Her soft voice whispering in my ear surprised and warmed me, though not her words. She arrived as a formless spirit, but I pictured her face in my mind and smiled.

I gazed down on the priest's flushed face. "I'm very sorry, My Queen. I cannot abandon Brendan when I might save him. Though I detest his religion, he is too good a man to die by foul murder."

"What do I care about murder? This man threatens Tír na nÓg." Her voice grew seductive. "You killed priests and monks in the past, or at least had them killed. He is your enemy. You owe him nothing. Let him die."

Though I might owe Brendan nothing, I owed much to the honorable Druidic customs instilled in me by my father and Master Tóla. "Allowing Brendan to die is the same as killing him by my own hand. I'm sorry, Morrigan, that I cannot do. You are Goddess of Death. You have the power to take him this instant."

"Yes. I have that power, but killing priests of opposing beliefs dwells within the provenance of men, not gods. The Christian god has killed no Druids, and I am not so foolish as to kill his priests."

My thoughts turned to the Lough Derg battlefield, and I chuckled. "No? Perhaps not, though you shit on them."

"Oh yes, that." Her low, friendly laughter surprised me, for it was a woman's laughter; not at all a thing I expected. "It served my purpose that day to spread disquiet among the Christian ranks. You think goddesses have no sense of humor?"

I leaned back, stretching my arms, feeling them tingle as their stiffness dissipated. "You, Morrigan, never cease to surprise me."

"Yes? You never cease to frustrate me, my Ossian. I ask this simple thing of you. Rise and walk away from Brendan's bedside. Do it. Leave this man's fate in the hands of his god."

Her words tore at my soul, rekindled memories of flaming skies, tempted me to do as she asked. Yet, even beyond my personal honor as a Druid, walking away was not so simple as she suggested. "I have no future beyond Brendan's boat. You know that. Have you not warned me more than once that remaining here in Eire would be foolish? I must go. Across the western sea lies whatever future the gods ordained for me."

There was wistfulness in her words. "Oh, Ossian. What you say is true, though I hate the thought of it. If only you could remain here that we might..."

I longed to know all she might add, but lacked the courage to ask it. Her voice firmed. "So, Brendan will sail, and you will be aboard his boat. What will you do if he actually arrives at Tír na nÓg?"

It was a question I had asked of myself many times. "If that be the case, long before he lands the Staff of Nuada shall destroy his boat and all aboard it."

"All, Ossian? Knowing your friends and you shall perish as well?"

My shoulders sagged under the wretched weight of an unforgiving burden. "I will fulfill my promise to the Lordly Ones to protect Tír na nÓg, so yes, Morrigan...all."

* * *

Brendan continued to improve with the coming of day. As I ministered to him, often my thoughts turned to the Morrigan. Was it possible she grew to care for me as a man? At times her words seemed to...ach. I flushed at my wishful imaginings and dared not speak them aloud even to myself. She was a queen among the Lordly Ones. The gods would rightly deem my thoughts impertinent vanities.

My eyelids began to droop before Tobias arrived. Brendan required a continuance of the same care, so I gave the monk detailed instructions before stumbling off to collapse in my crude hut. There I remained enjoying untroubled dreams until the sun was high.

Coban seemingly always maintained a pot of hot stew, so I stopped by for a bowl and a friendly word before returning to Brendan's bedside. There was little change and, since Tobias was willing, I took the opportunity to free myself, knowing at once where I would go.

The mountain loomed above me. It was there I met her last. I hurried along the narrow upward winding trail bordered by hedgerows of spiny, head-high gorse, hope pounding in my chest.

The clearing opened before me, and there the stone where we talked side by side. I hurried to the stone and sat upon it, swallowing back the hope that rose in my throat.

A breeze carried the salty aroma of the sea while a lark hiding within nearby shrubbery trilled to the early afternoon sun. A vast panorama spread before me: the craggy headland across the rippling bay, low gray clouds where the sky met the western sea.

There I remained, alone with my poor thoughts, surrounded by Mother Earth's splendor—and she came, so quietly as not to disturb the lark.

"You wait for me?" Her low voice hinted at a chuckle.

A flush crawled up my neck as I stood and bowed. "I...that is, yes, Morrigan. It seems you...yes, I waited for you." I kicked myself for acting like a boy caught with his finger in the honey jar.

Her violet eyes lingered on me then rose to rest upon the view. "It is lovely here. Not so very different from much of our island, but lovely just the same."

I stepped aside so that she might sit upon *our* stone. "Yes," I agreed as my hand swept the vista. "Has any land been so blessed by Mother Earth?"

"I think not." She settled upon the stone, slender hands smoothing her blue gown. "There are many lands from which to choose. Yet, why is it you think your gods arrived here and are so loath to leave it?"

Now her hand swept the horizon and a rainbow arced across the bay. She laughed and clapped her hands at her own creation.

It was an enchanting moment and I was bewitched by her. Such an astonishing thing—the volatile Goddess of War and Death behaving like a playful girl. Could it be that by assuming human form she became almost human? The question was beyond my understanding or caring, for my heart melted. Would that this remarkable time together might last forever.

Perhaps it truly was her magical presence that emboldened my silly tongue. "When I see you now, in this way, Morrigan, I fear my thoughts are not those of an adoring servant."

Her eyes twinkled within her flushed, upturned face. "You say so, little man? Have you forgotten who I am?"

"I know who you are, a queen among the mighty Sidhe. You are many things, but most important to me, you are the most delightful, beautiful woman I have ever seen."

She rose from the stone, her face cold. "This discussion serves no purpose. You have said quite enough."

A lump grew in my throat. Perhaps I had said too much, but words continued to fly from my mouth like wild geese. "Yes, I stand insignificant in your sight, but can no longer remain silent. Soon I leave Eire forever. We share this short time together and I muster all my courage to say that you have stolen my heart, Morrigan, as no woman ever has or will again."

She cocked an eyebrow; her harsh laughter rang in my ears. "You think to sway me with your pretty words, mortal? I confess I find you handsome. No man ever tempted me as you have. Yes," she nodded, "your Queen admits to being tempted. Does that surprise you?"

Chastened and feeling foolish, I bowed. "My Queen, I apologize for my impertinence. With your permission, I will return to the village. Brendan is improving and I must prepare for our departure."

Not waiting for a dismissal, I spun on my heels to hurry away.

"No. Wait."

Turning back, I stood before her, hands on hips.

"You are a terrible man and confuse me so." Tears filled her eyes. "Do you think I wish to see you sail away now, my lo...?" Her hands flew to her face, covering the flush on it. She turned from me, her arm outstretched as if to push me away. "Yes, you are right. Go. You must go now, for I am the Morrigan. It is not proper that you see me thus."

One quick stride and my arms were around her, spinning her about, my lips crushing hers. Slender arms encircled my neck as she melted against me. It was as though a thousand years passed as we remained so until her hands began pushing against my shoulders. She stepped away.

Taking my hand in hers, she led me along a faded path through dense foliage that opened into a secluded grove. Murmuring spring water swept past round, moss-covered stones. The air held the musty, moldering aroma of an ancient forest.

The Morrigan stopped and turned, offering a seductive glance as her gown fell to the woodland floor.

My robe followed though I spread it upon the leaves so that she could lie upon it. I joined her there where the heat of our passion rose and fell beneath the primeval trees.

Shadows crept along the ground as Belenos sailed across the sky. Quiet and happy we were as we laughed like excited children. Lying together tenderly following each lovemaking, we spoke of important things and small things without mention of a future together, for never was there hope for such a thing between us. There could be only the now, this moment, and I reveled in it.

While laughing at a silly comment of mine, she quieted and sat up, body rigid, face turned to the sky. She nodded as if replying to an unheard voice and looked to me, worry lining her lovely face.

"Lugh calls. I must go this instant to join all the Lordly Ones on an urgent matter. A very odd, evil presence has arrived here..." She shook her head, her puzzlement plain to see.

Nothing I cared about Lugh's problems just then. Disappointment filled me as I sat up while she stood and hurried to don her gown.

Stepping away she smiled and blew a kiss. "Do not be troubled, my dearest one. We shall meet again before you sail."

Amid a swirling, golden snowstorm she was gone.

* * *

"I've given thought to this fellow, Erc, everyone's talkin' about." Torcán sipped cider from his mug as he sat at the table in Brendan's cottage. "He killed your friend Laoidheach and later alerted the Corcu to your passage. He was behind poisonin' Brendan. No doubt, he lurks nearby and will try again to kill one or the both of you."

I shrugged as I placed a fresh damp cloth on the priest's brow. "Little chance he will have. We sail when Brendan is well enough."

"Ah, yes. But until then you are both at risk. The man's shown he's dangerous, and you must never allow your enemy to take the upper hand." He shook a knowing finger towards me and winked. "Unsettle him; make him counter you, that's the way."

Easing back in his chair with a sigh, he crossed his outstretched legs at his ankles. "I'm thinkin' to ask the aid of some likely lads who know the country and go search for Erc. If we find him, I'll kill him. If not, we'll put him on the run and upset any plans he might be makin'."

Torcán's words rang true. Given the chance, Erc would strike again. If it was possible to find him…yes, the warrior was experienced, relentless and the proper man for the task.

* * *

His helm glinting in the mid-morning sun, Torcán rode from the village, four mounted and armed local men trailing behind him. Woe be to Erc if he was found.

Late that afternoon, Brendan roused from his long sleep, and I had hot broth brought for him. Tobias's hand ladled it into Brendan's mouth, while I stood by gazing through the window.

Two riders appeared in the distance, approaching the village. Slowly they rode, and I was turning away from the view when it came to me that one of the horsemen was Torcán. Five men rode from the village, only two returned. Hairs prickled the back of my neck and a sense of foreboding swept over me as I darted through the door.

A crowd of villagers and monks gathered about the two riders as I hurried towards them. Goban jogged across the village center to join me and walk at my side.

Frowning, Torcán peered down at me from atop his horse as I stopped before him. Dust streaked his face and clothing. The rider beside him slumped, head hanging.

"We…" Torcán began and then hesitated. Face stiff, his haunted eyes swept the crowd. "Erc was waiting for us. He had two…creatures at his side. Three men are dead."

A moan rose about us; the shrieks of wailing women filled the air. I stepped forward, grasping Torcán's reins, desperate to capture his meaning.

In a soft voice, intended as comforting yet encouraging, I asked, "What happened, my friend? Think it through carefully and tell us."

His chin fell to his chest where it remained for a long moment. Sobbing came from within the crowd. When his face lifted, he gazed out over the gathering. "I am so very sorry—all of it was my fault. Had I but known..." He swallowed, eyes downcast. "We searched but a short while for Erc, but he made findin' him easy for us. He built a fire in the mountains and the smoke drew us to him. We found him standing at the entrance to a small valley. Beside him crouched two great crimson, cat-like beasts."

Gasps and muttering commenced among the villagers. Awestruck by Torcán's words, I waved my hand for silence that he might continue.

"Erc's cats came upon us like flashing, snarling red streaks. Almost as tall as our horses they were and they pulled the men down. Horrible it was to...." He shook his head as if to erase the scene from his mind.

"And the two of you fled," a voice called from the crowd.

"No." Torcán's eyes hardened as he found the speaker. "Three men were down when Erc called back his beasts. He permitted us to live."

Such a thing was impossible. Enormous crimson cats he described them? No such beasts existed.

A remembrance of flaming skies above Dún Ailinne returned and I shook my head. "It is unlike Erc to offer mercy. Why didn't he allow his beasts to kill you?"

"To deliver his message, I'm afraid." The warrior's lined, sad face fixed upon me. "He said you must come before him tomorrow night." He pointed to a high mountain. "You must go there and

354

meet him alone." He sighed. "If you do not follow his orders exactly, he vowed to come here and turn his cats loose on the village."

I took a step back as though his words slapped my face. To say I felt no fear would be a lie, for the thought of facing the fiend and his hideous beasts filled me with dread.

"If ye go," Goban muttered beside me, "I go with ye."

"No." Torcán leaned forward in his saddle. "Ossian must go alone."

"But that's a stupid demand," Goban growled. "Of course he shall do no such thing."

"Right you are, so Ossian mustn't go at all. Here's how I see it…"

My mind worked while they discussed it, and finally I raised my hand. "Enough. I will go."

Both began protesting at once but I waved them into silence. "Don't you see? I must go. If not, Erc will fulfill his promise and bring his creatures here. Villagers will be slain and I cannot permit it. No. Erc has named the time and place for our final meeting, and I will not disappoint him."

I forced a grin while holding back a shudder. "Have no fear. I have a plan to overcome Erc's cunning and monstrous beasts."

I didn't mention the many self-doubts whispering in my ear. One thing I knew, for in truth it was the only plan I had. I would face Erc wearing my emerald robe, Nuada's Staff firmly in my hand. My fate would rest in the hands of the gods.

Chapter 34
Erc's Lair

ittle sleep had visited me during the night and I rose to face a cold, gray dawn. Goban arrived and we shared hot cider and a cold crust, though little conversation.

Later, I pulled my robe close against a bitter wind and strode across the village center towards Brendan's cottage. Was the chill that ran down my spine a product of the wind or dread lingering within the background of my thoughts? I glanced towards the mountain holding Erc and his crimson beasts.

"May the gods protect me," I muttered and hurried along.

Arriving at the cottage, I shoved the door open to find Brendan robed and standing in the center of the room. Stooped, both hands clasping his staff, the priest swayed as his pale face turned towards me.

A smile twisted his face as his sunken eyes found mine. "So, Druid. I'm sorry I was unable to provide the welcome planned for your return."

Brother Tobias stood near, his face taut, and he gave me a quick glance. "I warned the father against rising, but... Father Brendan can sometimes be a stubborn man."

"Sometimes?" I snorted. "Father Brendan has the temperament of an obstinate horse and it appears its strength as well."

Brendan grumbled under his breath as he lowered himself into a chair. He attempted a genuine smile as he looked up at me, though trembling hands exposed his weakness. "I'm told I owe you my life." He shrugged, pursing his lips. "Until now, I never realized how difficult it would be to find words to thank a man for that, but I humbly thank you."

I nodded. "When first I saw you, there seemed little hope. Your gratitude rightly belongs to the man who taught me how to treat wolfsbane poisoning."

"Hmm. You cannot escape my appreciation. Brother Tobias told me it was you who discovered the poison and took charge of my care. Thank you, Ossian."

"Of course." I smiled, pointing to his bed. "Now then. You shouldn't be stirring about. Please lie down."

"In a moment." He waved a dismissive hand. "First, we must discuss your decision to confront Erc and..." His eyebrows knitted as his hands dropped into his lap. "Could your friend's report be true? Erc is sided by demonic red beasts? Don't you think it more likely the sight of seeing men falling somehow affected the man's mind? After all, men under duress—"

"No." My shoulders slumped. "Torcán is an experienced warrior. If he says the beasts exist, you can rely upon it."

"Impossible," Brendan muttered. "What has Erc done? What manner of evil could create such creatures?"

He reached to a box on the table before him and turned with an offering. "Take this. If the evil you face is as monstrous as we fear, it will aid you."

I reached forward to accept his gift, but jerked my hand away. He offered a crucifix.

"Thank you for your offer, but..." Brendan swayed in his chair. "Brother Tobias, help me walk the father to his bed."

Though the affects of the poison waned, the priest remained a sick man and he staggered between us until we laid him on his bed. Little could be done for him, so I turned to leave, but in so doing, felt something beneath my foot. The crucifix. It must have fallen from Brendan's hand. I picked it up and handed it towards the monk.

"No, Brother." Tobias stepped away, his hands behind his back. "My apologies, Wise One; habit you know." He shook his head and began again. "Please, take it. Evil awaits you on the mountain."

He took a step forward, laying a hand on my arm, pleading in his eyes. "I prayed for you last night. I prayed to God Himself that He would watch over you." He shook my arm as his tremulous smile grew. "I must tell you for it is a marvelous though terrible thing. God answered me. For the first time in my life He spoke to me. He told me you will face evil beyond imagining, something you must not attempt to face alone."

I was unsure of this monk and the words of his God, if such they were. "Yes, I know. Erc and his creatures are—"

"Not just them, Ossian, bad as they are." His eyes grew wide. "God revealed there is something more, some thing, some horrible, evil thing, though what it is He did not say. Call upon Him and—"

"I rely upon Eire's mighty gods. They will stand beside me as they have always stood beside me. They are enough. Besides, why do you care about the fate of a Druid?"

"I wish you no harm, Ossian."

I tried to pull away, but his grip on my arm tightened. "Make no mistake. Now, you must hear me because the thing you will face, whatever it is, threatens us all."

What was this evil *thing*, if such existed? The Morrigan's words returned. "A very odd, evil presence has arrived here..." Was there a connection to Tobias' warning?

The monk's words built upon my dread as he shook his head. "Don't you see? You will need God's help more than you or I or," he pointed to Brendan who lay quiet, "even the good father can hope to understand. God will help you." He was shaking my arm again. "Why would you reject His help? Take the crucifix, and call upon Him, I beg you."

The trinket brought back scenes highlighted by flames, and I thought to toss it away alongside the hated memories. Yet, the monk's pleading was well intended, and worthy of respect. The crucifix dropped into the pocket of my robe along with the thought to dispose of it later.

I strode to the door and glanced back over my shoulder. "Your god has a name?"

He nodded. "Jehovah."

* * *

"I'm still sayin' we should go with ye," Goban grumbled as he sat on my hovel's dirt floor, his hands busy with a leather cord. "Erc be a'waitin' and ye'll stand no chance against him and his cats."

My forced confidence did not reflect my true thoughts. "I've told you I have a plan to confront him."

Torcán snorted. "A lot of good it'll do to plan against those fiends." He laid out an armload of leather armor—helmet, greaves, wrist bracers, a mantle and gorget. "Wear these under your robe. A villager offered 'em up for you. He's tall; not so much as you, but they should fit you well enough."

"It's a kind offer, but you've seen Erc's cats. What benefit will leather armor serve against them?"

"Yes, I've seen his cats, though I wish I hadn't." He shook his finger at my nose. "The armor will serve you better wearin' it than leavin' it here, I say."

"It'll make ye all the tougher to chew, anyway." Goban grunted, rose and dropped the leather cord over my head. He had woven a protective shield knot, the edges of its four corners a never-ending path meant to confuse my enemies. "It's a small gift, I know, but some claim there is power in such things."

"It is a mighty gift." My fingers traced the edges of the knot as I nodded. "I thank you for it."

"Ossian, lad, don't be doin' this foolish thing. Stay here—"

He trembled beneath the hand I laid on his shoulder. "No, my dear friend, though I do not take pleasure in climbing the mountain. Neither do I welcome the thought of Erc and his beasts coming here

360

to this village or any other. Don't you see? I must submit to his terms by going alone. If I fail, you and Torcán will be needed to stand beside Brendan and the villagers. Regardless of his promise, it's possible the man will come here."

In the end, I agreed to wear the mantle, bracers and greaves beneath my robe, my sword belted to my waist. Despite the precautions, Nuada's Staff and the gods themselves would determine my fate.

* * *

My horse picked its way up the narrow mountain trail. Torcán had given instructions on the paths to follow and I held to them by starlight and my horse's senses. There was never doubt of my destination—a red glow at the head of a high valley served as a beacon to lead me on.

Chanting prayers to the night's silence, I paused on the mountainside and gazed ahead. What was the source of Erc's radiant signal? Likely a bonfire, but—

Clank.

My hand grasped my sword hilt as I wheeled in the saddle, alert to all the sounds of the night. I was not alone. What was back there? Hearing nothing further, I continued on, occasionally casting a backwards glance.

Boulders blocked the trail at the mouth of the valley. Just ahead, the flickering red glow rising into the darkness cast black shadows across the steep mountainside. I dismounted, and tied my horse to a bush.

My memory flashed back to the first time I laid eyes on Erc. Even then his face burned with hatred of me. This night's meeting had been long in coming, an inevitable event ordained by the gods. The circumstances were not such as I would have chosen, but there was no help for it.

The silver snake pommel rested in its pouch at my waist, and I placed it atop the Staff. After a final deep breath, wary steps carried me through the oppressive darkness, winding among boulders and leading to a level clearing.

Erc waited there, a robed silhouette standing before an open pit, the source of the red beacon that lit the night sky above us. The stench of molten metal filled the air, like the odor of hot iron on Goban's forge.

Beside the former monk crouched a great, crimson beast. Stories were told of lions that lived on the far side of the world. It was said they sported shaggy manes around their necks, and such was the case with Erc's creature. Yet, the face and eyes were not altogether feline. They were cat-like, yes, but contorted, almost human— almost, for in that moment it snarled, revealing long, gleaming fangs.

My eyes swept the boulder-strewn clearing. Torcán reported two such cats. Caution was the word as I strode forward to stand before Erc.

He stood arms folded over his chest, the red glow illuminating his hooded face. "So, Druid, your arrogance led you here as I knew it would. Yes, you believe yourself invincible, and have proven the fool I knew you to be."

"And before me I find the loathsome scum I expected. My mouth reeks with your foul presence." I spat on the ground. "You chose—"

The red glow revealed curled lips as he snarled, "Your insults—"

"You chose," I shouted him down, "to abandon the ways of men, to cower here on this mountain like a wolf at bay, to stand as a beast among beasts. What manner of evil have you conjured here?"

"Conjured?" He rubbed his hands together and laughed. "You are right. For years I thought it was God's words whispering in my ear, but no." Eagerness filled his voice and his chest swelled. "I now know the truth—my only truth, for I have heard and met the great Lord Sonneillon."

The name meant nothing to me. I waited, knowing in his fervor, and because in fact he was a vain, dull-witted man, Erc would reveal all.

"You don't recognize his name, do you?" He cackled. "No, only those of your trifling pagan spirits. But you know him, as all men know him, for he exists within us all. You know him, Druid, for he devours souls like the striped caterpillar consumes leaves. Sonneillon, mighty Lord of Hatred, and," he pointed into the fiery pit, "he dwells there."

The glowing chasm and crimson cat crouching at Erc's side provided ample evidence that his words were true. In his madness, the monk had called forth a demon.

The depths of his depravity sickened me. "You side a demon against your fellow men?"

"My fellow men? My—fellow—men?" Erc sneered. "I ask you. When have my fellow men stood beside me? For siding the *good*," he spat the word, "Brendan, I earned a beating for my trouble."

"Wait." He gestured to the beast beside him. "I was wrong." The crimson cat bared its fangs as he continued. "Permit me to introduce one who chose to stand with me: Brother Jonas. Behold the power of Sonneillon."

Jonas? He was one of the monks who poisoned Brendan. The other was Mark, and one cat had yet to appear. My heart sank, as the monk continued.

"You understand now, don't you, Druid? It was Sonneillon who suggested poisoning Brendan, and my friends Jonas and Mark who killed him."

From the beginning I held little hope of overcoming Erc and his creatures. If the demon could transform men into beasts, there remained no chance at all.

He was a vile man, and bitterness coated my tongue. "You would do such a thing to your brother monks who claim you as their friend? You would stand aside while your demon altered them into beasts?"

"Oh, they were quite willing. They understood they could better serve my purposes in their new forms." Erc grinned, rubbing his palms together. "They are magnificent, don't you think?"

"They are hideous; serving little purpose, the profane creations of a twisted mind."

"They serve little purpose? I remind you that as men they slew Brendan, and as cats, the puny villagers who came here to take me."

"Then you follow a simple-minded demon. Brendan lives."

Erc's finger jabbed towards me. "You lie."

"It's true." I shrugged. "Wolfsbane proves of little consequence in the presence of Druids. Even a novice could have cured Brendan." This last was not true, for Brendan should have died. Yet, a seed of doubt might erode Erc's confidence.

"If Brendan lives," he began to laugh, "I will return to the village, and then—" he bent over laughing. "Then Jonas and Mark shall devour him."

Madness consumed him; his chilling, maniacal laughter filled the night sky. More I wished to know, but he continued. "I have invited my Lord to join me tonight. He will arrive from the depths to find me rejoicing over your death."

"May the Lordly Ones destroy you all."

The Staff trembled a warning in my hand as Erc mocked, "Your gods are weak and I've grown tired of you. Prepare to die, Druid."

"Mark," he called, and stones rattled behind me.

Spinning about I muttered a prayer to the Morrigan, asking she receive me in death and hasten my journey to Tír na nÓg. The cat, Mark, loomed above me atop a boulder.

The beast was quick. It leaped and knocked me sprawling before I could bring the Staff to bear. Sharp claws slashed the front of my robe, failing to penetrate the leather mantle, but the Staff went spinning out of my hand and beyond reach.

The creature was past me in an instant, and I drew my sword. Sweat poured from my brow as I jumped to my feet. Why hadn't the cat killed me while I was down?

"He's playing with you," Erc laughed in response to my unspoken question.

Rumbling in its chest the great beast paced back and forth ten paces before me. My mouth grew parched and I licked my lips, watching its muscles tense.

"Now, Mark, kill him," Erc yelled, and the beast sprang forward.

I held the sword hilt in both hands, shoulder high, but the cat swerved as something swished past my ear, struck the beast's flank and fell to the ground with a clank—a hammer.

A glance over my shoulder revealed Goban and Torcán jogging forward. So, it was they who followed me up the mountain.

"Glory 'o, me boy 'o," Torcán shouted as he swirled his sword above his head.

Though they ignored my order to remain in the village, my heart swelled upon realizing that, should death find me this night, I would fall alongside stalwart men. Who could hope for more?

The cat's attention held on my friends, who separated, both men taunting it. The beast's head turned first to one, then the other, which offered me a moment to retrieve the fallen Staff.

I held the Staff waist-high, and the remembered lightning surged from the snake pommel. Mark, the cat, screamed as the force raked its flank. With a mighty leap, it landed upon a tall boulder, and spun about with a snarl.

Torcán shouted, "It's hurt, but—"

"Ossian! Behind you," Goban shrieked

Turning, I found the other cat, Jonas, streaking towards me. The Staff came to life, lightning snapped and crackled, striking the beast.

"Look out! Here he comes again," Torcán shouted behind me.

"Flank him," Goban cried.

I dared not turn around. For a moment, I thought Jonas would continue on as the lightning engulfed him, but the beast tumbled forward and thrashed out its evil existence amid a flaming inferno.

Goban's yell spun me about. "No, Torcán, no."

Never had I seen such a thing. The warrior sat astride the cat's pitching back. What was the man thinking?

How he managed to mount the beast I could not imagine. 'Round and 'round the creature whirled. Torcán's left hand clung to its mane, while his right swung his slashing sword.

The creature turned its head, snapping at Torcán's legs, then fell and rolled, but somehow the warrior clung tight. Dread filled me as the cat dashed behind a boulder, reappeared for an instant while it rounded the glowing pit at a dead run and disappeared into the darkness.

"After them," Goban shouted.

I took a step in pursuit, when behind me came, "Druid!"

Erc's challenge stopped me, and I turned to face him.

Holding forth a dagger, he raged, "You think you've defeated me? Meet me with a blade, you bastard, if you dare."

The man's taunt mattered not at all. Torcán's well-being held my thoughts, but something struck my back and clattered to the ground as I began to turn away—Erc's thrown dagger. I blessed the armor beneath my robe before fury took me, my hands longing to grasp the monk's throat.

Erc backed away to the edge of the pit as I approached him, his claw-like hands flexing at his sides.

"Come on, Druid," he hissed.

There was nothing more to say to the fiend, so I leaped forward, my hands grasping towards his throat.

Again, his maniacal laughter filled the night as he grabbed my robe and fell backwards over the rim of the pit. My own momentum served as my enemy, for I could not prevent him dragging me over the edge. Far, far below churned a lake of flaming molten metal. Horror clogged my chest as I fell towards my death.

Chapter 35
Where Evil Lurks

My mind lay frozen within an icy mist. Perhaps it was the certainty of my death or sheer terror that closed off all my thoughts as I plummeted into the glowing abyss. There were no last memories to carry with me into the afterlife; no muttered prayers or even a scream escaped my lips. I merely fell like a mute, mindless stone.

There was not even full awareness when her talons grasped me. Perhaps I knew her powerful, leathery wings pulled me back, away from the depths of the fiery chasm, though it seems more likely it wasn't until I later assumed that was the way of it.

Blood surged through my veins and air filled my lungs though my mind remained consumed by death. Her voice came from a great distance.

"Ossian. Can you hear me? Ossian. You are alive and, for the moment, safe. Look at me and hear my words."

Clarity of thought returned, bit by bit. She towered above me as I lay prone near the pit's rim. Wonder filled me, for she had arrived not as the Morrigan, but in the terrifying form I remembered from the abandoned cave of the Tuatha—Macha. My beloved came prepared to do battle.

"Have you recovered your sanity enough to speak?" Her impatience was evident as she glanced towards the abyss.

My husky reply revealed the state of my wits. "Hello."

"Hello? Hello, is it? Have you lost your mind?" Again she eyed the pit. "Stand and address me as a man should.

"Do it quickly, now," she urged as I hesitated, unsure of the sturdiness of my legs.

My legs wobbled, and I swayed to my feet, eyes blinking as my mind fought to return to the land of living men.

"Go. You mustn't remain here. Take your man, there," she pointed past me, "and leave this instant."

I glanced over my shoulder and discovered a wide-eyed Goban staring at us from behind a boulder.

Her urgency confused me, and I tried to make sense of it. "But why hurry away? Erc is dead and Torcán—"

"Sonneillon comes," Macha hissed.

She continued and I forced myself to concentrate on her words. "Even now, he scales the wall and will arrive any moment. Hurry. Go now, for you cannot stand against him."

At last my senses were returning. "No. I will not leave you here alone to face Erc's demon."

"Oh, my Ossian, sometimes you can be so..." She gestured towards the surrounding slopes. "I will not face Sonneillon alone."

Drumbeats commenced and echoed through the valley as my gods joined us—dozens of colorfully robed figures appeared high above me, surrounding the valley along the brush-covered mountainsides. They seemed almost dreamlike, though imaginings are not made of such solid stuff.

"Hurry. Save yourself," she pleaded, but it was too late.

A mighty hand appeared and grasped the edge of the pit, followed by a second. My eyes grew wide and I staggered backwards as a giant's head rose above the rim of the abyss. Coiled ram's horns framed a triangular face that gleamed like burnished copper.

Sonneillon's slanted eyes held on Macha as he heaved himself over the rim and stood nude before us. The monster was three times my height, and, like his face, his muscular frame gleamed like metal. Again I stepped back.

"Go, Ossian, run," Macha gasped. Her wings spread wide and she leaped skyward, swooping past the snarling demon's head.

Any energy I lost by falling into the pit instantly returned upon beholding the terrifying figure looming before me. Turning, I raced towards the rocks concealing Goban, slowing only long enough to retrieve Nuada's Staff along the way.

I nestled down beside my friend, and peered around the boulders, expecting to see what, I did not know.

The drums slowed and a bass voice called from the mountain. "Sonneillon! We the Lordly Ones will not tolerate your presence here. We demand you return to the depths from which you came."

The demon chortled, and called back. "Lugh! You and your followers have grown old and weak. You no longer hold sway over this land. The Christian god and his son, the Risen One, have replaced you. See before you a new and even greater power. The Lords of the Underworld have determined that we shall rule here. I command you to stand aside!"

"Very well then," Lugh's voice called back. "Here is my response to your command."

A lightning bolt streaked across the valley, striking the demon's chest. He staggered backwards under its impact, but if Lugh's lightning injured the giant in the least, I saw no sign of it.

"Puny pagan deities cannot harm the mighty Sonneillon." A fireball appeared in the demon's hand. "Take this for your trouble," and he hurled the flaming ball towards Lugh.

The cadence of the drums intensified, and my gods chanted as one. Their unified voices washed over me.

Fill ar ais le do ifreann...

Fill ar ais le do ifreann...

Fill ar ais le do ifreann...

Sonneillon laughed. "You demand I return to the Underworld? Ha. Even your combined powers are useless against me. Begone with you! I shall remain here and do as I please."

Never had I expected to see anyone or anything resist the Lordly Ones' singular will. Yet, it was obvious the demon remained altogether unaffected by them.

My mind swirled. The gods were said to be immortal, but were they? So much had changed across the land, as if the world had turned upside down. Now, I feared for their safety as they confronted Sonneillon. Some force, some power must exist to destroy the monster or at the very least drive him back to his lair.

"Ossian," Goban whispered. "This is no place for us. Come on. Let's try to find Torcán and get away from here."

I leaned upon the Staff and considered his urging. "Yes, by all means go. It is by far the wisest decision. As for myself, I cannot leave. My duty lies here. Druids are sworn to stand beside our gods to protect Eire."

"But, lad, ye can see for yourself the gods have no power over that thing. You're a Druid, sure, but in the end, a man. Ye can't hope to overcome that giant."

"Maybe, but don't give me up for dead quite yet."

"Ach," he sighed. "You'll be the death of us both for sure. You'll not be a'leavin' the gods and I'll not be a'leavin' you."

A smile touched my lips as I squeezed his shoulder. "Promise me that, should I fall, you will try to find Torcán and escape."

He dropped his face, then peeked up at me from beneath a cocked eyebrow and nodded.

I recognized his response for a ruse, so I pressed him. "Promise me you'll go."

"All right, all right, I promise." He pouted and gestured towards the demon. "Well, go on about getting yourself killed if you're going to. Oh…and it's been nice knowing you."

"Have faith my friend." I grinned, and again squeezed his shoulder.

Saying it wouldn't make it so, and the test of my own faith was yet to come. Power rested in Nuada's Staff held tight in my fist. It was with a mighty effort I swallowed my fear and strode forward to face Sonneillon.

The demon watched me approach and chuckled. "I take it you would be the Druid the monk Erc told me about. So, you killed him and his cats, did you? Such a pity. Heretic Christians often prove useful tools. As for you, you are like an insect in my sight and waste my time."

Nuada's Staff came alive in my hands. Lightning streaked from the pommel, raking the giant's chest and ribs. Horrified, I watched the Staff's energy deflecting from the demon's copper-like skin.

Hands on his hips, the giant snarled, "You would play games by tickling my ribs with your foolish toy? Very well, little man. Let us see how much you enjoy my game."

It was as though a wave of hot air struck me, bringing with it a sensation of utter hatred towards all men and all things. The Staff vibrated urgently in my hand and my mind calmed. Though it projected no damage on Sonneillon, at least Nuada's Staff served as a shield to protect me from his powers.

Behind me Goban shrieked, and I swung about to find him tensed, staring at me, hatred streaming from his eyes. The red glow within the valley illuminated his wild fury as, sword in hand, he rushed me and delivered a mighty blow.

My own blade swung upwards and sparks flew in a crash of steel. The Staff quivered in my hand, holding Sonneillon's hatred at bay, though I knew my friend was held victim by it. Little it mattered, for I barely avoided his next frenzied thrust towards my heart.

"Goban," I shouted over the throbbing of the drums. "It's me, Ossian."

Arms wide, muscles tensed, he gasped, "Yes, I know ye Druid, and I will carve your black heart from your chest."

There was naught I could do to dissuade him, for Sonneillon's power held him by his throat, as it would soon do all Eire if given

371

rein to do so. If I hoped to defeat the demon, my battle must begin here, against my friend.

Well I knew Goban's guile with a blade, for had he not taught me to use one? I retained my staff in my left hand while wielding my sword in my right. Perhaps it was the Staff's power that lent strength and finesse to my arm as I parried each thrust and slash.

In time, his great strength waned and his sword point dropped. Needing no further invitation, my sword swung down—the force of my strike spinning his blade from his fist.

Though Goban's power be spent, not so his mindless hatred as he cursed me. Wasting not a moment, I stepped forward and clouted him on his chin with the pommel of my sword. My friend dropped like a stone and lay unmoving.

Sonneillon's laughter joined the drumbeats in the canyon. Arms crossed over his chest, he taunted me. "So Druid. Do you think because you can best men you can defeat me as well?"

His enormous hand pointed to the hills surrounding us. "Not even your gods can do that. Look at them. See for yourself their contemptible efforts to overcome the great Lord Sonneillon."

The power of his presence struck me like a blow, and I took a step back as he hissed. "Join me, Druid. Erc spoke of you thinking to demean you in my sight, but in so doing revealed himself as weak and stupid. You, Ossian, possess strength, courage and wisdom. You are ambitious and will find me an eternal ally. Stand with me. Forget your powerless gods; crush your puny kings and the wretched masses beneath your heel. I offer you power and riches beyond your imaginings. Together we shall unite the Underworld's forces and govern this land."

Foulness filled my mouth. Though the demon's strength through hatred proved great, the deceit in his words was as transparent as spring water. He didn't need me. For him, I was merely a toy, a brief source of amusement. . .

"Think of it, Druid," he urged. "All you could ever need or desire can be yours. What is it you want? Take it!"

Another lightning bolt streaked across the canyon, striking Sonneillon's shoulder. He snarled and spun about, hurling a fireball though Lugh had already disappeared. The wildfire grew and crackled as smoke swirled along the mountainside.

To continue standing in the open appeared foolish, for I held no chance against him. Common sense dictated that I retreat while his attention was diverted. The same cluster of boulders still offered a refuge of sorts, but I took no more than three hurried steps towards them when I tripped and fell on my face.

Tink.

The crucifix. Brendan's forgotten gift fell from my pocket. I scooped it into my fist and darted towards the rocks.

Goban still lay where he fell, so I grabbed his arm and towed him behind me until I huddled behind the boulders. My friend lay still, uttering not a sound. I peeked around a stone, fearing the demon followed me.

His attention remained on the gods as a shower of golden arrows struck him, deflecting off his metal-like skin. Hands on hips, Sonneillon raised his face to the hills and laughed. Another wave of arrows arced towards him, causing no more effect than the first.

The crucifix warmed in my hand and it brewed a thought. Sonneillon was born of Christian beliefs and it might lie with Jehovah to destroy him. In that moment, Brendan's presence or even that of Brother Tobias would prove useful to call upon their god. As for speaking to him myself, I found the idea distasteful. No good had ever come of my encounters with him and his followers, and it seemed likely he would bear me no kindness.

The drums continued their thrumming as Macha appeared from the darkness and swooped 'round the giant's head while screeching her fury, her talons slashing at his eyes. Sonneillon shielded his face with his hands, swung a mighty fist towards her as she flew near and roared out his hatred when she soared skyward, barely avoiding his blow.

Enough of this. If Jehovah could help, though I knew nothing of him and cared less, I would attempt to speak with him.

"O Jehovah. I am Ossian, the Druid. Perhaps you know me as one who fought your followers many times, but now I call upon you to unite with the Lords of the Sidhe to defeat a common enemy. See Sonneillon, who would impose hatred across this land." I held high the tiny crucifix clasped between my thumb and forefinger. "Though no right I claim to ask it of you, I humbly beg you to strike him down."

There was no response from Jehovah, but little I expected one. Sonneillon remained by the pit's edge, laughing and hurling fireballs at my gods. If he gave me further thought, he showed no signs of it.

Another lightning bolt struck the monster while more arrows showered down upon him. If the Lordly Ones refused to give up the fight, I would swallow my pride and continue to call upon the Christian god.

"Look upon them, Jehovah. See the Lordly Ones. They battle a demon rooted in your mysteries, not theirs. You desire to rule Eire? If so, stand forth and prove yourself worthy by shielding it now, just as the Lordly Ones defended it for thousands of years."

It is ashamed he should be for standing aside while the Lordly Ones fight his battle for him. So I thought, as the drums pounded ever louder.

Macha swooped in again, talons wide, screeching her battle fury, slashing at his face.

Sonneillon's great hand reached out and captured her leg, pulling her down towards his grinning face. My heart leaped into my throat as her wings thrashed the air in her attempt to escape his powerful grasp.

Nuada's Staff had already proven useless, but I grabbed it and stood erect. With the Staff in one hand, I raised high the crucifix in the other, thinking to rush forward to her aid.

Before I took a step, lightning sizzled through the air, striking the demon's hip, turning him. A second bolt struck his back, staggering him forward to the very brink of the abyss. Relief flooded me as Sonneillon released Macha, his arms flailing the air to avoid pitching forward into the glowing chasm.

Enough! Enough! The gods risk all against this monster, and Jehovah must act! Their desperation led to my own, so I pleaded to the Christian god.

"What must I do to gain your aid? You demand my belief in you? Is that the bargain you require? If so, you have this Druid's promise to accept you. However, if you insist that I forsake my gods and worship you alone, I swear on the Staff of Nuada that I will never do, and will damn you with my last breath. I adore reason, not tyrants. Upon my honor, I will remain here and die beside the Lordly Ones before abandoning them."

Sonneillon snarled, his pointing finger sweeping the mountainsides. "You cannot harm me. Neither can you hold me here."

His derisive laugh blended with the pulsing of the drums. "Now, I shall leave this place and stride across the land where I will be joined by other Lords of the Underworld. We shall be invincible and I warn you to stand out of our way."

He must not be allowed to escape this place. My mind was frantic, devising and rejecting plans to hold him within the valley. Only one possible hope remained. The god of the Christians must act, so I offered my final plea.

"Jehovah. If I know you within my Druid's heart as the god of a great religion, will you not find room in yours to accept me for who I am? My faith is all I can offer, for, in the end, it is all I own. Will you stand with us? If you exist, I—"

The earth rumbled, and the ground pitched like waves at sea, tossing me from my feet. My fingers clawed the earth for a handhold, and exultation filled me at witnessing Jehovah's power.

The soil crumbled beneath Sonneillon's feet, and, arms flailing, he stumbled backwards towards the pit. The demon swayed, roared and fell from view over the rim.

I thought him gone, but his great hands re-appeared, clinging to the edge of the pit. The ground continued to roll beneath me, my attention holding to Sonneillon's struggle to pull himself up from the fiery abyss.

Lightning bolts sizzled through the air, once, twice, three times, blasting free the demon's desperate grip. Fiendish hatred struck me like a great ocean wave as he fell away, screeching his fury.

I continued lying flat, for it seemed Jehovah wasn't done with Sonneillon. The grating of stone against stone resumed, and the circular rim of the glowing pit began closing in upon itself. The fiery glow dimmed, then disappeared as the edges of the evil chasm ground together and sealed.

The thrumming of the drums died away. Wings fluttered overhead and the Lordly Ones' laughter chorused around me.

Lugh's voice thundered within the valley. "So, Ossian. You called upon the Christian god for aid. Your Lords of the Sidhe find your decision well met and thank you for it. Our many blessings upon you, Wise One."

Relief flooded me. I worried how my gods would accept my agreement with Jehovah, for of course they knew of it. I muttered blessings in return. They stood together to hold Sonneillon at bay until Jehovah arrived to shake the ground, though it was Lugh's lightning bolts that broke the demon's grip and returned him to his underworld. Ah, it seemed a fitting ending.

Only the crackling fires on the mountainside could be heard, for otherwise quiet filled the valley. My gods had departed—perhaps all save one.

"Jehovah, your humble servant thanks you for siding us to overcome a great demon. Yes, the Lord of Hatred was defeated this night, though I fear he is not vanquished and will return again and again throughout all the ages to come.

"We made a bargain and you now own a piece of my heart. It will take time for us to understand one another, eh?" I chuckled. "I pray we both have the patience for it."

A nearby groan brought me to my feet. Goban.

I stood away at a cautious distance lest vestiges of Sonneillon's hatred still dwelt within him.

My friend sat up and shook his head. His eyes swept the clearing, coming to rest on me.

"You're alive," he muttered. Goban rose to his knees and bowed. "No man who betrayed ye as I did deserves the honor to remain your friend. Still, I beg ye forgive me weakness in the face of the monster."

"Goban, my friend, I—"

"Never has anythin' defeated me so easily as that demon did. He possessed me mind, and I couldn't... Tell me, lad. Am I forgiven?"

"Aye." I grinned. "You're forgiven."

"Thank ye, Ossian, you see I..." He glanced around. "Where is that fiend, anyway?"

"Sonneillon's gone. The gods—"

"They killed him, eh? Hah. A good job that, I say."

He hung his head, then looked up, his eyes haunted. "Were they truly here? I mean, was it I lost me mind and only dreamed the gods joined us?"

I nodded. "They were here, but I wouldn't advise speaking of it when we return to the village."

"Yes, those villagers would think me crazy, wouldn't they?" He sighed. "Well, I can't say I'd blame 'em for it. In truth, it may be you and I are both crazy. Anyway, I'll keep me mouth shut right enough."

Whistling broke the silence; a lilting tune coming towards us.

"What do ye know?" Goban cackled. "That be Torcán, the dirty scoundrel."

The warrior rounded a boulder, stopped short upon seeing us and glanced around. "What happened to the glowing hole?"

"What hole?" Goban snorted.

"And the mountain's on fire."

"We know. Now tell us—what of the cat? It's dead?"

Admiration filled me as Torcán shrugged. "Would I be standing here talking to you if it wasn't? I owed it to the spirits of the poor village lads it killed to make an end to it. Ahem. You see, I—"

"Ach." Goban shook his finger at the warrior's nose. "You're a madman to go about ridin' a beastly cat. That's what ye are, a madman. Your story will wait 'til we reach the village. Ye can tell Ossian and me all about it over a mug."

"Ah," Torcán winked, "you've a keen wit about you, my friend, a keen wit indeed. You've a keg?"

"Of course, I've a keg."

I jerked a thumb over my shoulder. "And I've a full wine flask on my saddle."

"So," Torcán stepped forward and slapped my back, "is it any wonder they call you Druids 'Wise Ones?' Lead on, for I suffer a powerful thirst."

Their banter continued as we rode down the mountain; needful words to release lingering tension. Little I added to it, for I was thinking of my gods—and I had a new one to consider.

Chapter 36
Destiny's Winds

orrigan waited upon the ridge, her white gown ablaze within the setting sun. Her concerned frown greeted me as I limped into the small clearing.

"You're injured?"

"Just sore and bruised, is all." I grinned, leaning upon the Staff. "Then again, I wouldn't be here at all had you not saved my life last night."

"Nay, it was you who saved us all," she gasped, and rushed forward into my arms, our hearts pounding, lips joined. There we remained until her slender hands pushed me away.

Delight filled her face and she cocked her head as she stepped back and looked me up and down. "I hoped to find you wearing your splendid new robe."

"No. I discovered it upon wakening this morning. It was a surprising gift. I thank you, but it is a Master Druid's robe. I am unworthy and may not wear it."

"Your gods will decide your worth, Master Ossian."

"Master? But—"

"Quiet. Lugh himself bestowed the title upon you. Besides, the robe wasn't my gift. It was Brigid who wove it of the finest scarlet linen. With her own hands, she embroidered the golden serpent across the front. She brought it to you during the night." Her eyes twinkled. "The most beautiful of all the goddesses seems to admire you very much. Perhaps I must keep closer watch over you."

Laughter filled me as I thought back to the night Laoidheach spent with Brigid atop the fairy mound. "Very well." I chuckled. "I shall wear the robe with pride to honor my gods. Yes, at the proper time, I shall wear it."

She cocked her head and smiled. "Do you know who you are, my love? Do you realize what you've become?"

"Does it matter? I doubt any man can say he fully knows himself this side of Tír na nÓg. If I can say that I am the man who gained the Morrigan's love, it is enough. Regardless, it seems an odd question when I sail with Brendan in just a few more days."

"It is because of your sailing that we must talk, for there is much to tell you. The Lordly Ones are pleased with you, my love. Lugh also insisted I release you from your vow to sail with Brendan. You need not go. The decision rests with you."

"Then it is a simple decision. I pledged to you that I would go with Brendan to ensure he does not reach Tir na nÓg. Nothing has changed about that. And haven't you told me more than once I have no future here—that my destiny, whatever it may be, lies to the west? In truth, I am honored that Lugh chose to notice me, but I sail with Brendan."

"You are your father's son, and reflect the best of Master Tóla's teachings. Yes, destiny guides you, though little I thought the poor creature I discovered in the cave so long ago could come so far. Never would I have thought that, by your leaving, I would grieve so much."

Eagerness filled me. "Then sail with me. You can remain aboard in many forms, unnoticed—"

"No, my beloved. That I cannot do, though my heart yearns to follow you. Within the cave of the Tuatha I told you, my duty lies here. Souls must be reaped, and upon these shores I shall remain so long as a single Irishman remains loyal to the Sidhe."

It would be a hard thing to leave her, though I knew I must. "Promise me, then, to someday meet me at Tír na nÓg."

"Of course, my love. It is there beneath the magical Rowans we shall meet, though I feel it will be many years from today. There is something more, an important thing between us. We must...oh."

Arms widespread, she raised her face skyward, as if listening to an unheard voice. "There is fighting in the lands of the Airgialla. Warriors have fallen. I must go. Promise to meet me here on the eve of your sailing."

I nodded, and she disappeared within a glittering rainbow.

* * *

A pipe played somewhere, animating the dancers within the village center. Erc and his beastly cats were dead and word had quickly spread, sparking the celebration. Joy reigned within the small, festive gathering, but then again, it was a tiny village.

Beneath a cloudless sky, Brendan idled across the table from me, his flushed face little revealing the poisoning that should have killed him. Nevertheless, Tobias, ever the steadfast monk hovered over him, his worried eyes rarely leaving his beloved Father.

A smile lit the priest's face as the dancers swirled about. "There is joy and richness among our people, and I shall miss them during our voyage." He chuckled. "In my youth I was quite a dancer myself."

"Then by all means, join them." I chortled, sipping ale from my mug.

"Father Brendan will do no such shameful thing." Folding his arms over his chest, Tobias scowled. "A man of his status—"

"Please, Brother," Brendan interrupted. "Pride is sinful in the eyes of God. We are all equal in His eyes.

My apologies, father." Tobias nodded. "You are right, of course."

"Look," I pointed and grinned. "Torcán and Goban have an audience. They've spoken of their adventures several times already, and each time their stories grow with the telling."

Brendan chuckled and turned his attention to me. "We all stood out in the darkness and wondered about the fires on the mountain," he muttered, his elbow resting on the table. "You've said little during the past two days, but it must have been a terrible thing that, confronting Erc as you did."

His words washed past me as my foolish stomach rumbled in anticipation at the enticing aroma of broiling meat, fresh-baked breads and pastries. The ale must suffice while delicious aromas hovered in the air.

"It's been in my thoughts to say more to you about it, and I will," I admitted. "However, today is for relaxing and enjoying being alive. I'll say this, though. Your Christian mysteries contain malevolent spirits more fearsome than any that ever before threatened these shores. Had it not been for the intervention of Jehovah himself, I would not be sitting here with you this day."

"You called upon Him?" Tobias asked, his hands clasped beneath his chin.

"Aye. That I did."

"Glory be." His hand swept from his forehead to his chest as he made the sign of the cross. "God be praised."

"Yes, may His Name be praised, but one moment." Brendan frowned, waving a hand. "God and his son, Jesus Christ, bring love, kindness and understanding to the world. He offers everlasting life to those who follow Him. You imply there is evil in that?"

"Of course not. No doubt you are right in your high regard for Jehovah and his son."

A sip of ale cooled my throat, the sun beamed agreement with my temperament. I stretched forth my legs, lazing in the pleasantries of the afternoon.

"It is a beautiful day, Brendan, and here we sit chattering away like old women." The mug in my hand swept 'round the crowd. "Look about. The villagers enjoy themselves. No doubt they are smarter than the both of us."

Brendan cocked an eyebrow. "You avoided my question. Why?"

"And why not? Breathe deep the fresh air, my friend. Feel the sun's warmth on your face. It's a fine day to be alive, isn't it? What is past is past and we mustn't cast a cloud upon this perfect day. Ah, now look." I pointed. "Women are laying out the food."

A grin spread across my lips as I rose, offering the priest a hand. "Come. Up with you, lazy priest. My stomach offers its apologies, but insists I see to its needs right away."

* * *

Six days later, final preparations for the voyage were complete. On the eve of our sailing, my mind wandered as I took the trail above the village, anxious to fulfill my promise to the Morrigan.

During the past few days I shared with Brendan all that happened on the mountain. The importance of the arrival of the demon Sonneillon was not lost upon the priest. His comments about the Lordly Ones held my thoughts while I trekked up the narrow trail.

"I am overjoyed that you found God on the mountain," he told me. "A true miracle though it was, you were mistaken in thinking your pagan gods joined you there to confront the demon. It is understandable why you believe as you do. You learned only pagan beliefs during your youth and Druid's training. They are all you know.

"Listen to me and make no mistake, Ossian, for what I tell you is His Truth. There is One God, and He stood with you on the mountain long before you called upon Him. Consider this, for it explains what and who you encountered. The beings you saw were His emissaries—His angels, Saints, or perhaps both. I ask you: Is it only possible that the spirits your people have worshipped for generations are, in fact, God's representatives?"

What manner of foolishness was that? Though I listened politely, I knew my gods well. Hadn't I spoken with them many times? Did I not know and love the Morrigan? It seemed Jehovah held truths well beyond Brendan's simple beliefs. Then again, how could I know Jehovah's thoughts?

I chuckled as I remembered my father's words. "Do not place over much reliance in the Lordly Ones; they can be a capricious lot."

It seemed the Christian god moved in ways to suit his own purposes as well.

Regardless, little I knew of Jehovah, though no doubt his will would prove as enigmatic as those of the Lordly Ones. Such busied my mind as I wound along the narrow path among the gorse.

If gods can hold all men in their hearts, why can't men hold all gods in theirs? Perhaps that is a singular failing of men. Perhaps our hearts simply aren't large enough to contain more than one faith. What a pity. I fear it will prove a bane for humanity throughout all time.

* * *

"Tomorrow you sail and your time upon our lovely island will come to an end. Are you saddened by it?"

She lay beside me upon our bed of leaves, the place of our lovemaking. Her question broke the spell of my daydream, one where I spent eternity lying there in her arms.

"In a way, of course." I rolled over, facing her, my head propped in my hand as I stroked her hair. "Do you recall Socrates' words? 'Man's life is like a drop of dew on a leaf.' Think of it, Morrigan. Even though ephemeral, was not the dewdrop important to the leaf? Did it not for a brief, glittering moment combine with others of its kind to bring luster to the garden? Looking back, I made many mistakes and lost all here. Yet, it is as a dewdrop that I shall remember my life here."

"It is a lovely sentiment, but what of tomorrow's dew?"

"What of it? The future for this land is bright, I think, but my time will have passed. Other than you, no one will remain behind to long remember me."

"Oh, but that is not true." She sat upright and smiled down at me. "There will be one more. We must discuss our son."

"Our sun? Belenos?" I glanced up, feeling the warmth on my face. "What possible—?"

"No, you foolish man. Not Belenos." A breeze touched her hair as she chuckled. "I speak of our child, your son."

Baile of the Honeyed Speech fled my mouth, leaving me speechless.

"Have you swallowed your tongue? Have you nothing to say about becoming a father?"

A father? I was to become a father? The voice emanating from my throat was unfamiliar, like that of a croaking frog. "I...that is... How old will he be?"

"How old? When he is born?" She snorted. "Have you lost your wits?"

"Yes!" Leaping upright with a whoop, arms crossed over my chest, my feet dancing a jig, I twirled 'round and 'round.

Laughter crinkled her nose, the sound of it like that of tinkling bells. "Yes, but he must have a name. We must speak of that before you leave, you know."

A name? My head reeled, so I hurried to regain my seat beside her. I strove to calm myself, for naming a son was no small thing. The naming ritual would be required to ensure approval by the gods and good fortune for the child. It was a silly thought. A goddess sat beside me.

While my eager mind still searched for a name, she offered, "I think to call him Cáerthann, for it is beneath the Rowans we pledged to someday meet at Tír na nÓg." Then, Morrigan spoke the words of Ogma in little more than a whisper.

> Within the Grove stand the Peasant Trees,
> seven their numbers be,
> The Birch, a well-known song of love,
> The Alder, blesse'd healer's glove,
> The stately Rowan stands alone, evermore the diviner's tree.
>
> The noble Elm courageous,
> festooned with spearpoints of blood,
> Unbelove'd Hawthorn, alas,
> The Wild Cherry, a Fairy lass,
> The bending Willow stands firm within
>   mighty windstorms and flood.

Cáerthann. The name rolled around in my mind, a word some substituted for Rowan, and I nodded. "It is a fitting name. There is magic in the Rowan just as there is magic in a changeling child. Yes. I agree. Our son shall be called Cáerthann, son of Ossian, son of Ciann Mehigan, son of Gicrode."

A smile touched her lips as she laid her hand upon my arm. "Wherever you may be, know that your son shall take large steps across this land."

In that moment, my plans changed. "I will not go with Brendan. You have foreseen that if I sail with him, I shall never return. Now I have a choice. Lugh released me from my vow, so my first responsibility lies with our son now."

"No, my love. You must go. We have spoken of this before. Eire undergoes a time of sweeping change and nothing remains here for you. Your future lies to the west with Brendan."

"I am sick unto death of the sweeping change of which you speak, for it has stolen much from me. My entire family, friends, the future I hoped to enjoy are all gone now. Only you remain, and soon our son who I value above all things. I will not permit the damnable change upon this land to steal the two of you from me as well."

"You will not permit it?" Her eyes grew large. "Perhaps you have forgotten the Corcu Duibne? Oh my Ossian, why would you think to throw your life away when it would do our son no good? The Corcu have sworn vengeance against you and demand blood for blood. Their warriors number in the thousands and they won't stop coming until you are dead."

"Nonetheless, here I will remain."

"Do you think to benefit our son or your own stubborn self?"

Blood rushed to my face. Ah, sometimes she could be so annoying. "I think of holding my son in my arms. How can you ask me to turn my back upon him and sail away, never to return? What kind of father, what manner of man would not want to see his son grow tall beside him? Should I leave, Cáerthann would think his father a coward, and rightly so. No. I will stand before my enemies. My principles—"

She squeezed my arm, shaking it, her nails biting deep. "Who cares about your precious principles? Don't you understand they don't matter anymore? What matter principles while you lay dying with an arrow in your back? What's more, if the Corcu find Cáerthann with you, they will kill him as well. Stand up to the enemy like a man you say, but I say this: Our son deserves a chance for life. You will not kill him while you defend your principles."

"Morrigan, I understand your bitterness, but I would never endanger our son."

"Go then. You may find my words bitter, but you know I speak the truth. Have you forgotten your friends Goban and Torcán? It is because of you they pledged to sail with Brendan. Would you abandon them? Or would they choose to remain here and die at your side?"

Once more destiny's forces gathered 'round to form an inescapable trap. Yes, I was obligated to my friends as well. I could remain in Fire and die for no good purpose, or fulfill my vow to sail with Brendan, never to see my own son.

Knowing she was right, frustration welled within me upon realizing I had already lost my son. "In truth, I really never had a choice, did I?"

"No. I'm afraid not."

"Very well, I shall go." I stood, looking down at her. "However, in so doing I shall feel that my son is dead to me, and I dead to him before he is even born."

"No, my love. It is merely your sadness at this moment that makes you say such things. Wherever you go, I know you will think of our son often, wonder about him, hold hope in your heart for him. And Cáerthann shall grow to know and love you through me for I will tell him of his father, the wise and courageous Druid who earned the everlasting respect of his gods."

"You honor me, My Queen. Here, take this." I removed the serpent ring from my finger and handed it to her. "Tell our son it belonged to me, and my father before me and his father before him. It's a small inheritance, but give it to him when you see he has earned the right to wear it."

Tears misted her eyes as she took the ring, and nodded.

"I leave it to you to tell Cáerthann of his heritage. Let him learn the knowledge of the old ones and the mysteries of the Druids. At last, permit him to be his own man as he strides forward into Eire's future."

"You have my promise to do as you say. True. He must become his own man, but beneath the Lordly One's guidance and protection, of course, as will befit his position."

Was it the Lordly Ones' protection she intended, or the guardian wing of a doting mother? I knew her well, and chortled. My son must grow strong and wise if he hoped to stand free from the Morrigan.

She rose to stand before me and laid her hands on my shoulders. "Sail, my beloved, and may destiny's winds carry you towards a mighty future. Never look back, do not rue what you lost here, for the past is the victim of time. Always remember. Cáerthann shall serve as your legacy to this land. Your son will bring honor to your name. I am sure of it."

"Ah, Morrigan, at the point of death it will be your name on my lips."

She cupped my face in her hands. "And it will be your name I speak, my love, when we meet on the shore of Tír na nÓg."

* * *

My solitary prayers completed, swift steps carried me atop a large stone where I stood, my feet widespread, Nuada's Staff planted against the level surface. My scarlet master's robe billowed in the wind; the coiled serpent, emblazoned with heavy gold thread, glinting in the dawning sun.

On the beach below, Goban and Torcán stood to one side as villagers bustled about loading the last of the provisions. The curraugh's two white sails displaying their red Christian crosses stood stark against the rolling sea's blue horizon. Brendan was there along with his monks. One by one all stopped what they were doing to stare up to me.

Brendan's mouth was moving, his words borne away by the wind, but his waving hand urged me to join them. The time had come to sail, and with it, the fulfillment of the Morrigan's prophecy. Never again would I set foot on my homeland. Ah, but what mattered that?

Trusting in the wisdom of my gods to determine my fate, I stepped down from the stone on light feet, striding towards the beach. Though my face remained calm, my heart glowed.

There would be a son.

I would be remembered.

CPSIA information can be obtained at www.ICGtesting.com
Printed in the USA
LVOW12s1758140115

422812LV00008B/1236/P